The Dreamer, Her Angel, and the Stars

Linda S. North

Yellow Rose Books

Port Arthur, Texas

Copyright © 2011 by Linda S. North

All rights reserved. No part of this publication may be reproduced, transmitted in any form or by any means, electronic or mechanical, including photocopy, recording, or any information storage and retrieval system, without permission in writing from the publisher. The characters, incidents and dialogue herein are fictional and any resemblance to actual events or persons, living or dead, is purely coincidental.

ISBN 978-1-935053-45-3

First Printing 2011

9 8 7 6 5 4 3 2 1

Cover design by Donna Pawlowski

Published by:

Regal Crest Enterprises, LLC
4700 Highway 365, Suite A, PMB 210
Port Arthur, Texas 77642

Find us on the World Wide Web at
http://www.regalcrest.biz

Published in the United States of America

Acknowledgments

To Susan Thompson, Stacey Watts, and Ang, who were there at the beginning.

A special thanks to Lara Zielinsky for her assistance.

To Brenda Adcock for her eagle eyes, and to Lori L. Lake who has the patience of Job.

For Danny Gail, who is my port in the storm.

Chapter One

THE FORWARD MOMENTUM of the Harley's wheels kept the six-hundred-pound motorcycle from tipping over as it leaned at a forty-degree angle into the twisting curve. Ariel Thorsen straightened the Harley out of the bend and into the flat stretch of highway before squeezing the clutch and booting it up to fourth gear.

A glimpse in the rearview mirror showed company rapidly closing in behind her. She hoped the driver wouldn't follow right on her tail or attempt to pass on the narrow, twisting highway.

The next section of road extended for two miles, allowing her to kick the Harley into fifth gear. The increased speed brought some relief from the sweltering humidity of the early July afternoon. Usually, it was cooler along this high ridge east of Chattanooga. But erratic weather patterns, resulting from the greenhouse effect, were still in evidence some fifty years after a worldwide ban on all fossil fuels and other pollutants.

She had smoothly maneuvered the next curve and entered the straightway when suddenly the motorcycle's back tire deflated making it hard to control.

She froze for a nanosecond, but then managed to ease up on the throttle and keep the bike from skidding out of control. The Harley's electric turbo engine whined as it decelerated, allowing her to maneuver toward the edge of the highway where the guardrail hugged the mountain's rock face. She hoped the vehicle behind her wasn't traveling too fast around the curve. Even with the required electronic sensors it posed the threat of hitting her.

Tires squealed, and she tensed her body, squeezing shut her eyes as an eternity passed in a second, leaving only silence and the pounding of her heart. She opened her eyes, released a prolonged sigh of relief, and detected the sound of a door opening behind her.

Approaching footsteps stopped a couple of yards away, and a baritone voice asked, "Sir, do you need any help?"

After pushing down the kickstand, she slid off the Harley's seat and stood. She removed her black, full-faced helmet and pivoted to face a middle-aged man wearing a charcoal suit with a gray bow tie. From his appearance and the black limousine parked against the rail behind him, she surmised he was a chauffeur.

He gaped at her with surprise before doing a slow, appreciative sweep of her figure, then saying in a friendly manner,

"Miss, do you need any help?"

"Could you please help me move my motorcycle out of the way?"

He made a surveying sweep of the area, his gaze stopping on the wide, grassy shoulder across the highway, and said, "Across the road is a good place. I'll push it over for you."

"Thanks. I'll contact the Harley dealership to come out and pick it up."

Seeing no approaching traffic, she crossed the highway. The man followed pushing her Harley. He maneuvered the bike up on the grassy shoulder and engaged the kickstand down.

She placed her helmet on the bike's seat, knelt, and inspected the back tire, not seeing a puncture, but it was flat. One drawback to owning a vintage fifty-three-year-old Harley was that unlike modern tires, which didn't go flat, these could, and only Harley-Davidson dealers stocked them.

She stood and unzipped her black Tefla-hide jacket to allow in cooler air. From her waist bag, she withdrew her IMP — an Intel Micro Processor — and unfolded it, expanding it to twice its one-and-a-half-inch size to display a vid screen allowing two-way communication. She powered it on, held it a foot from her face, and said, "Contact Chattanooga Harley-Davidson's service department." The IMP made the requested connection.

While she was arranging to have the Harley picked up, the back window of the limousine slid down. A white-haired elderly man motioned the driver over.

As she was concluding her call, the driver returned. "Miss, I'm Danny Mitchell, Mr. O'Shay's chauffeur, and he'd like to know if you want a lift to Stellardyne's front gate where security can arrange for someone to pick you up."

The O'Shay name was one she recognized. The probability was high her benefactor was a relative of Kiernan O'Shay, the well-known driving force behind Stellardyne. "I'm Ariel Thorsen," she said. "I was on my way to Stellardyne with some important documents requiring my mother's signature that have to be posted before the close of business today. My mother works in the engineering department."

"I'm sure he won't mind taking you all the way to headquarters."

"Let me have a minute to get the documents, and I'll be ready."

Mr. Mitchell crossed the highway to speak to his employer. Ariel secured her helmet on the bike with the helmet lock and removed her siblings' school applications from her saddlebag. She realized now that she was very lucky she'd avoided a wipeout on the bike. She had been traveling over the maximum posted speed limit. She wouldn't have had to hurry if the post office droid hadn't delivered the applications to her neighbor, who'd returned from vacation earlier in the day. Ariel was grateful the neighbor brought the mail over as soon as she noticed the wrong address on the envelope.

Mr. Mitchell motioned her over to the limousine. Ariel crossed the highway, feeling both relieved and thankful for the ride.

THEODORE O'SHAY WATCHED with interest as the statuesque and curvaceous young woman crossed the highway toward the limo. Danny opened the door, and she slid into the seat across from Theodore. She graced him with a smile while the seatbelt automatically fastened around her. He held out his hand for a shake and introduced himself.

"I'm Ariel Thorsen." She took his hand in a firm but gentle grip.

Theodore placed his hand on top of the silver-knobbed cane resting between his knees. "What a mighty fine motorcycle you have. An antique, by the build of it."

"Yes, a 2045 Harley-Davidson Deluxe Glide. I won it in a Tennessee State Lottery drawing two years ago."

"What is it they say about a Harley? You're not living until you ride one?"

"Life begins when you get one."

"Ah, that's it." He paused. "Danny informs me your mother is an employee of Stellardyne and you want her to execute some documents."

"Yes, her name is Joanna Thorsen. She's a data processing supervisor in the engineering department."

"I'm the head of the legal department and will send a notary to her office as soon as we arrive at headquarters."

"Thank you. I appreciate your help."

"I'm glad to be of service." He leaned back in his seat and studied her discreetly for a moment. "Ariel. What an unusual and lovely name. An elemental spirit from Shakespeare's *Tempest*, I believe?"

"Yes, but my mother named me after Ariel the mermaid in her favorite childhood movie, *The Little Mermaid*, an old Walt Disney classic."

While Theodore preferred masculine attractiveness he wasn't immune to admiring beauty for its own sake. She wasn't in the same category as his niece, Kiernan, who, with her dark auburn hair, trim but shapely mouth, and oval face, was what he considered along the classical lines.

Still, her generous lips, expressive light blue eyes, slightly up-tilted nose, and high cheekbones fit together to fashion a very attractive face. Her smooth, light complexion was almost flawless except for the tiny dark mole above the corner of her upper lip. In an earlier age the fashionable of all classes–both male and female–considered such a mark stylish, applying artificial ones to their faces. Light blonde hair fell a good six inches past her shoulders, lending her an ethereal aspect as if she indeed were a spirit, or an angel. He'd wager heads turned in admiration when she strolled by.

"I don't recollect seeing it. My favorite old classic movie, or movies, was the old *Star Wars* saga. When I was a boy, I would imagine I was Luke Skywalker." Remembering that time, he let out a melancholic sigh. "It's a pity they don't produce movies like that anymore."

"They're my favorite movies, too. When I was growing up all the kids in my neighborhood would watch them on the EM and after the movie, we would pretend we were the various characters." The EM was the Entertainment Module, a combination of a three-dimensional live-feed video media projector, surround sound stereo, and video game center, usually round, about the size of a baseball.

Pursing his lips and tapping a finger on the top of his cane, he studied her for a second. "Let me guess — you were Princess Leia."

"I was Han Solo."

"Han Solo was a roguish fellow, I believe. You're not a rogue are you?" Theodore narrowed his eyes in an attempt to appear serious, but he couldn't keep one corner of his mouth from lifting up.

Amusement reflected in her eyes and voice. "I've never been accused of being a rogue. It was because Han Solo owned the *Millennium Falcon*."

Presenting his sweetest grandfatherly face, Theodore asked, "Do you mind me asking, my dear, are you in school, employed...?" Theodore always played on his age, which was ninety-one, and his polite and genteel way of conversing to obtain information. He found most people thought the elderly innocuous and were willing to be more open.

"Right now I'm on summer break from my job as a physics professor at Missionary Ridge Junior College."

"You have a doctorate in physics?"

"Yes, I do. I graduated almost a year ago from the Massachusetts Institute of Technology and started my professorship at Missionary Ridge soon after." Ariel's tone held a note of pride when mentioning her alma mater.

This information impressed Theodore. She possessed not only beauty, but also brains, which in his opinion were an attractive combination. "MIT is the number one school in the world for physics."

"Yes, it is."

"Tell me more about yourself. Do you live in Chattanooga?"

"In East Ridge. We still live in the house I grew up in."

"I take *we* to mean you and your mother, and…?"

"Yes, my mother and my brother and sister, Seth and Leigh. They're twins and celebrated their tenth birthday a few weeks ago."

"Your mother is a single parent?"

"My father died in a commuter helio-jet crash when I was seventeen, and I've stayed home to help in caring for my brother and sister."

"You helped your mother, as well as managed to attend college and obtain a PhD?"

"I was able to take my courses and participate in classes through the Internet Direct Link from my home."

"Still, there's a lot to be said for attending a university in the flesh, so to speak." Theodore winked. "Fraternity parties, football games, you know, the important curriculum a university offers."

"The university required all doctoral candidates attend the actual campus for laboratory classes. So, I spent two semesters on campus to complete my degree and to obtain my certification as a professor." Grinning devilishly, she added, "Don't worry. I did manage to squeeze in enough time for the important things, such as parties and football games."

"That's the old college spirit. Though, I wager your mother missed having you at home to help. It's rare to find a young adult willing to live at home and assist one's parents."

"The twins were seven when I attended campus, and my mother was able to afford an after school daycare program for them."

"But you're still living at home with your family. Your mother must be a good cook," Theodore teased.

"I enjoy living at home. And yes, my mother is an excellent cook. Cooking is one of her hobbies."

"I'll wager you're a good cook as well. No Pop-hots on your menu," he said, referring to the pre-cooked meals that heated within a matter of five to ten seconds after popping the box or lid. Theodore detested them and employed a chef to prepare his meals.

"I can whip up a few meals from scratch that can pass the taste test."

"I hope you have a beau who appreciates your cooking."

Her eyes reflected amusement, as did her voice. "I'm not sure whether the term *beau* applies, but I do have a girlfriend."

Intelligent, beautiful, and a lesbian, he thought, then asked, "Are there wedding bells in your future?"

"No, we've only been dating for a couple of months."

"I see." Tapping one finger on the cane knob, he fell silent to consider the information he'd gathered.

The limo slowed as they swung onto the road to Stellardyne. The guard on duty at the security post performed the required retina scan on Mr. Mitchell and Theodore. Ariel was introduced as a guest and her name and time of arrival were duly noted in the visitors log.

Theodore said, "We have arrived, my dear. Please allow me to escort you into the building and arrange for you to see your mother."

"Thank you for helping me. I hope I didn't inconvenience you."

"Oh no, not at all. I'm happy I could be of service."

Danny helped Theodore out of the seat before he gallantly offered his hand to Ariel, who accepted his assistance.

Theodore escorted her into the building and instructed the security guard on duty to provide Ariel a pass and to contact her mother.

He said, "It was a pleasure meeting you, my dear. May I provide transportation back to your home after you conclude your business with your mother?"

"That's very kind of you, but I'll borrow my mother's car and return for her when she gets off work."

"Perhaps we will meet again sometime."

"Yes. It was nice meeting you, Mr. O'Shay."

Giving her a parting nod, he entered the elevator reserved for those who worked on the top floor. As the elevator door slid shut, he caught another glimpse of the lovely young woman and rubbed his chin in thought.

In his office suite, Theodore's secretary greeted him brightly.

"Good day, Franklin. There's nothing pressing on the agenda, is there?"

"The only item on your calendar is the three o'clock meeting with Ms. O'Shay to go over environmental standards."

"I want you to send a notary to Joanna Thorsen's office in engineering's data department, pronto. Oh, check on my order at the Bartholomew Art Gallery. Kiernan—Ms. O'Shay's birthday is less than two weeks away, and I want my gift to arrive in time."

"I'll do that right away, sir."

Theodore entered his office, taking his seat behind the antique mahogany desk, and said, "Telecom on—contact Brady Cohen." He focused his attention on his ten-inch wafer-thin desktop telecom screen.

After a few beeps, the image of a balding middle-aged man flicked on the view screen. "Brady Cohen Detective Agency. Ah, Mr. O'Shay. It's been a while. What can I do for you?"

"Mr. Cohen, I have a special assignment for you."

"Yes?"

"I require you to do an in-depth investigation to include history, family, associates, hobbies, medical information, and the most current photographs. I'll pay you double your normal fee if you can complete it within a week."

Mr. Cohen seemed to pick up on the importance of this request as indicated by his sudden shrewd expression. "I understand. I'll jump right on it and work it 24/7. I'll need the name and any other information you have on the individual."

Theodore relaxed into his chair. "Her name is Ariel Thorsen."

Chapter Two

KIERNAN HANDED HER uncle a tumbler with its finger of brandy and watched him lean back into the sofa and take a sip, lifting his shaggy white eyebrows in approval. They had arrived ten minutes earlier at Kiernan's estate following her thirty-eighth birthday celebration hosted by Stellardyne's senior executives.

She settled into the overstuffed leather recliner across from him. "I love your birthday present." Her uncle had presented her with an oil painting of Deer Falls, which was located on the estate grounds. She studied the massive, natural stone fireplace where a painting of the Southern Appalachians in autumn now hung. "I'm going to hang it right above the mantel."

Surprise widened Theodore's eyes. "You mean you're going to remove the Jean Henriksen? It's been hanging over the mantel since Shanna built this place."

"It's about time for a change of scenery don't you think? I'll hang the Henriksen in my study." She took a sip of her brandy before asking, "How did you manage to sneak the artist up here and I knew nothing about it?"

"Security arranged all the details. The artist came up here on the days you were at the office."

With a gentle motion of her wrist, Kiernan swirled the tumbler she held, watching as the amber liquid formed a vortex. She took another sip of brandy, shutting her eyes, as the fatigue of the day caught up to her.

"Kiernan, don't fall asleep. There's something we need to discuss."

Startled, she opened her eyes, focusing them on her uncle. "This sounds like something serious."

"It is." Taking another sip of brandy, and placing the tumbler on the end table, he sent Kiernan a shrewd look. "You're thirty-eight years old and forty will be here before you know it."

"Uh oh, after my past five birthdays, I should know where you're heading with this. You're about to give me the traditional birthday speech."

Theodore guffawed. "I can give you the traditional birthday spanking instead."

"Let me think about which one I'd prefer."

"Kiernan, this is serious. You're not married, and you have no offspring. You're running out of time. You have two years to find a wife and produce an heir."

She pressed her lips together for a moment in exasperation. "I know, Uncle, but I haven't met anyone I'm willing to commit to...and certainly not marry. And those I've met, they're not exactly wife material, or mother material."

"What was wrong with Millicent Tyler? I talked to her father, Vincent Tyler, last Thursday, and he says Millicent is still upset that you broke up with her."

"Ha! Upset my ass. It's not even been a month and she's sunning herself on some beach in Italy with that pop diva — what's her name — Lady Killer, and I guarantee you she's shedding no tears. Millicent—"

Her Uncle's loud laugh interrupted her. After a few seconds, he wiped his eyes and said, "Kiernan, dear, it's Lady Keela, *not* Lady Killer."

"Close enough. Millicent isn't the brightest star in the heavens, and I want an intelligent daughter. I also want a wife who'll stay home and nurture her, not a wife who wants to flit from party to party leaving her in the care of a nanny." Kiernan recalled the three months she dated Millicent. The conversations revolved around Millicent repeating the latest gossip, what party they should attend, fashion, and where she could spend her parents' money. Why Kiernan put up with Millicent for three months, she didn't know. Even the sex became boring after a few weeks.

"That Conrad girl, what's her name, Joyce? She's intelligent, a law degree from Harvard, and is a senior partner at Bernhardt and Bernhardt. She could easily handle her case work from home."

Screwing up her mouth to show her distaste, Kiernan said, "I *do not* want to come home after a grueling day and listen to her discuss the latest tax laws over dinner."

"She's a family and marriage lawyer."

"That's even worse, since I certainly don't want to discuss who's divorcing whom and how they're trying their damnedest to screw each other over the settlement. Besides, she has a strong resemblance to last year's Kentucky Derby winner." Feeling a bit sheepish about this last remark, she hastily added, "Not that looks are that important."

"You could have fooled me. I've never seen you with a woman who wasn't considered attractive." He snapped his fingers. "I know. Kimberly Montgomery. She's now single."

"I never liked her for some reason, and she belongs to Millicent's little set of cliquey friends. In fact, almost every available woman I know runs with Millicent. If I didn't know any better, I would think Millicent was cloning herself." A cloud of frustration settled on her features. "God, why are all the available women in my social group so...so...you know what I'm saying?"

"I know exactly what you mean. Perhaps you should consider finding a nice woman from a different social class. See how well it's worked out for me and Jack?"

Kiernan swept a hand through the right side of her hair, flipping it off her shoulder, while considering her uncle's words. She liked her uncle's partner, Jack Spivik, and thought he was a good match. From a blue-collar background, even though he married into wealth, Jack continued to work. Stellardyne had hired him twenty-three years earlier to head the security department, and soon after, he caught Theodore's eye. Thirty years separated their ages, but things worked out, and they were devoted to each other. "Too bad Jack doesn't have a sister—one who likes women and is under the age of forty."

"There is a lot at stake here. With full control of Stellardyne, you can take the company in the direction you want to go. That won't happen unless you carry out Shanna's stipulations."

Kiernan's grandmother, Theodore's older sister, Shanna Kiernan O'Shay, built Crestview Estate some sixty years earlier on three thousand acres of mountaintop property skirting the Cherokee National Forest and Ocoee River.

Shanna O'Shay founded Stellardyne, which rapidly became the leading designer and manufacturer of the freighter and transport spacecraft that plied the solar system between Earth, the Martian colonies, and the mining colonies on Jupiter's moons.

It took a generous sip of brandy for Kiernan to quell the sudden twinge of anger toward her grandmother, who had died of a massive stroke seven years earlier at the age of 102. "God! What Grandmother was thinking when she made that idiotic stipulation in her will, I'll never know. It's so antiquated and reeks of arranged marriages. Not even royalty engages in that practice anymore." Frowning, she muttered, "Senile old harridan."

"Face it Kiernan, you were out of control, reckless. You caused her many sleepless nights. She thought if you settled down and had a family you'd learn responsibility."

Kiernan had to agree with her uncle's words. After her graduation from Harvard she led a reckless lifestyle, spending seven years racing flitters, the tiny, one-person space racers. She indulged in fast living, attending a different party almost every weekend in Asia, Europe, and all places in between, including the Martian colonies. Then there were various affairs, often involving the wives of diplomats, heads of states, and royalty. She was fortunate some irate husband or wife hadn't killed her or had her assassinated.

"Grandmother certainly didn't have room to pass judgment.

She was no saint by any stretch of the imagination. She never bothered to marry Grandfather Markos. I think she never forgave me for that affair with the Brazilian President's wife, and blames me because the Brazilian freighter deal fell through. She wanted revenge for that as well as not being able to control my life. Now she's reaching out from wherever she is—Hell most likely—to control it." She paused, before adding defensively, "And I'll have you know I'm responsible now. Stellardyne's profits have skyrocketed since I became president."

"Yes, and Shanna would be proud of you."

Kiernan suppressed her sardonic reply. She had hired the best lawyers to research contesting her grandmother's will, but that would open up the strong possibility the will could linger for years in the courts. If she wanted all of Stellardyne under her control, not just the forty-five percent she inherited, she had no choice but to adhere to the stipulation in her Grandmother's will to marry and produce an heir by her fortieth birthday.

"You know, I could go along with marrying and producing an heir, if I could do it all within a year and divorce. That I could probably endure. It's the part where I remain married for at least five years and reside with my spouse that I find detestable. Grandmother really knew how to twist the knife."

"Kiernan, she loved you. Besides the responsibility, I think she wanted you to find the same happiness Maureen found with Nicole. You were all she had left after they died."

"If you say so. If Mother Maureen had lived and taken over Stellardyne, we'd be well on our way to the stars by now." Sighing sadly, she recalled the day both her mothers, Maureen and Nicole, died en route to the Martian colonies to celebrate their fifteenth wedding anniversary. For no apparent reason, the shields failed on the spaceship, and a stray meteor tore through the engine room triggering a massive explosion. With Maureen's death, Kiernan was left at age thirteen the only heir to Stellardyne and to her grandmother's massive fortune.

Before her grandmother's death she held a position at Stellardyne overseeing two departments, and preparing to take over the reins. She admitted she performed only the basic requirements so she could spend most of her time playing.

All that changed when her grandmother died. Kiernan had the chance to make her dream come true to build light-speed spacecraft capable of reaching the stars, which was something Shanna was never interested in doing, owing to the unproven technology.

Forty-five percent control of the company wouldn't allow Kiernan to fulfill her dream. Ten of the stodgiest old men and women in the solar system held the other fifty-five percent in a trust. Except for Uncle Theodore, who was the only member of the trust backing her plans, they had no confidence in her vision.

After draining her tumbler, she said, "Well, Uncle, any suggestions of where I might acquire a wife. A suitable one?"

Theodore pursed his lips for a second, his eyes reflecting a sly gleam. "As a matter of fact, I may have the perfect candidate for you. She's beautiful, intelligent, articulate. Did I say beautiful?"

"Oh, no! In no way, shape or form do I want you to select a wife for me."

"Why, I have you know I've excellent taste!"

"I agree you do when it comes to fashion, furnishings, and handsome young men." She snorted dismissively. "But women are out of your field of expertise. No thanks. I'll pay a consultant who specializes in finding spouses, if that's what it takes."

"You mean a matchmaker? That's almost as antiquated as Shanna's stipulation."

"It's not that kind of matchmaker. These days a professional with a degree in psychology matches you up with a potential mate. God knows what kind of mate you would pick."

"O ye of little faith." He rose, reaching inside his coat, and handed over a four-by-six-inch digital notebook with a flourish. "Take your time going over this, my dear, and let me know Monday what you think. I'm wagering you'll find out I have excellent taste in women." He leaned over, kissed her cheek, and made his exit.

She popped up out of her chair and called after his retreating back, "Uncle, what kind of mischief are you up to? I'll do my own spouse picking without your interference, thank you kindly." He took a swat with his cane at one of the beetle-like vacuuming robots that didn't move out of his way fast enough. "Uncle, don't hit my bot!" Ignoring her, he continued on his way.

After settling back into her chair, she put the leg rest up for more comfort and flipped open the notebook thinking that her uncle's selection was probably some heifer that favored a drag queen or was so hideous she'd have to work longer hours so she wouldn't have to come home.

As soon as she activated the notebook, a three-dimensional image of a young woman appeared on the screen. Her heart stopped for a second, and she couldn't stop her mouth from dropping open or the feeling of delighted surprise. "Oh! My! God!"

KIERNAN WAS MARKING an area in an electronic departmental report when her secretary announced over the desk-com, "Ms. O'Shay, Mr. O'Shay is here to see you."

"Send him in, Kelly." She knew the reason for her uncle's visit this morning.

Schooling her features to placidity, she peered toward the door as her uncle entered with a jaunty saunter and a decidedly smug manner.

He stopped, threw her a satisfied smirk, lifted his brow, and drawled, "Well?"

Still maintaining her placid expression, she innocently asked, "Well, what?"

"You'll have to admit I do have excellent taste when it comes to selecting brides." He settled into the leather chair in front of Kiernan's desk, placing his cane between his knees.

"I'll admit in this instance you do possess excellent taste in women, and I was quite impressed with the information you presented me. She's intelligent, extremely so—summa cum laude from MIT and a PhD in physics. She's healthy, and, she's responsible."

Kiernan had been impressed that Ariel Thorsen took on the responsibility of helping her mother after her father's death. Not many young people would make that sacrifice, and in Kiernan's mind, it meant Ms. Thorsen would take her responsibilities seriously as a wife of someone of Kiernan's standing.

"And she's beautiful. I'm sure you didn't notice though." He pretended to flick a piece of lint from the arm of his jacket.

"Yes, and beautiful. Perhaps younger than I would like. You know, trophy wife."

"Trophy wife?" Theodore said amused, "I'd hardly call her that since you're only around thirteen years older than she is. And, if people got that impression..." He shrugged. "They'd be envious."

"Perhaps. But I'm buying her, so to speak." She said pointedly, "This must never leak out. The media would have a feeding frenzy."

"I can't see that happening. I won't say a word, not even to Jack."

"How did you find her? Was it through her mother?"

"I suppose in a roundabout way you could say that. She was on her way to Stellardyne when her motorcycle broke down, and I provided her a ride. She made quite an impression on me. And, you've read the information on her."

"I would like to meet her as soon as you can arrange it. But before I do, you and I need to discuss what the negotiation points will be so we can work up the prenuptial agreement."

"God, Kiernan, where is the romantic in you? You make this sound like nothing more than a business arrangement."

"It *is* nothing more than a business arrangement. I need a wife and someone to bear an heir. Romance has nothing to do with it. And romance, I'm sure, will play no part in this agreement. Another thing—I'm curious as to why she'd agree to this. I know money would be a motive to many people, but reading her background information, she has a career and earns a decent salary. She's not in debt, and she doesn't strike me as a material girl or a gold digger."

Theodore shifted uneasily in his seat, tapping his finger on the knob of his cane. "I...ah...haven't approached her with any of this."

"What? How did you gather the information on her? Including medical history for her and her family?" Suddenly, realization struck. Widening her eyes, she put her palms up in denial. "Oh no, Uncle, you paid someone to...to...do something illegal. There are laws on the book that could have you serving some serious jail time."

"Let me explain, my dear. I wanted to know your opinion before I approached her with the particulars. You know, have you scope her out."

Leveling a pointed stare at her uncle, her voice hardened. "Did you hire someone to obtain information on her and hack her medical files?"

"Yes. I can't see you agreeing to carry a child—"

"Ha! You're right about that."

"So, I wanted to know if there were any problems in that area and if her medical records and those of her family indicated any hereditary anomalies. She and her family are remarkably healthy, and their genetic profiles are free of any flags for genetic disorders." Confidence emerged on Theodore's face, and his tone of voice was now one of satisfaction. "The fusion of your DNA with hers will produce an exceptionally intelligent, and, I'm sure, beautiful daughter. I'm eagerly awaiting being a great-great uncle."

Kiernan didn't like her uncle's information-gathering methods. Hacking into a person's data guaranteed a mandatory prison sentence and a hefty fine. She leaned back in her chair, crossed her arms, and narrowed her eyes. "What aren't you telling me?"

"Nothing, I assure you."

His guileless manner triggered a warning alarm in Kiernan's mind. Pinning him with a piercing stare, she lowered her voice to a deadly register. "You're hiding something else. I would advise you to tell me what it is."

Theodore hesitated, and Kiernan saw him deliberately smooth his features before he nonchalantly said, "She has a girlfriend."

Anger flushed her cheeks, and she glared at her uncle.

He continued, "Nothing serious, I'm sure, since they've only dated around three months."

"Nothing serious? For all you know they're engaged and have their china and silverware patterns selected and invitations to their wedding printed."

"They don't even live together and see each other only two times a week, three at most. They're more friends than anything else, going out to dinner, taking in a movie—that kind of thing."

"You had her followed and spied on, didn't you?"

Theodore assumed a shocked expression, somehow managing to sound outraged. "Of course I did. You are, after all, one of the wealthiest and most powerful people in the solar system, the force behind the most lucrative and growing business in the world. You need to know whether she's hiding anything or engaging in any harmful or embarrassing activities that could reflect badly on you, or Stellardyne. With whom she associates, what she does on her free time—"

A soft sigh of disappointment escaped Kiernan. She realized this woman was probably out of reach. After all she'd read, along with the pictures she'd viewed, she was almost convinced Ariel Thorsen would make an excellent wife and meet all expectations. Kiernan stood, pushing her chair back. At the side bar she poured a shot of brandy, all the while keeping her back to her uncle.

"Kiernan, don't worry. I'll arrange things, and you'll meet her soon. Things will work out."

She spun to confront him, her voice oozing sarcasm. "Sure, things will work out. What if she's not interested? You have another one lined up? Am I going to wake up one morning and hear all the news channels broadcasting, 'Coming up next is our exclusive story on Kiernan O'Shay. Money won't buy her love'?"

"You know that's not going to happen. Why, you're the most wanted woman on the availability list. When she hears what you're preparing to offer, she will agree to marry you. Who wouldn't?"

"And I suppose you've devised a *feasible* plan, Uncle?"

"I have and I believe it's feasible, very feasible. Joanna Thorsen, her mother, is an intelligent woman with an impeccable work ethic and has had two promotions since being in our employ. I think it's time we promote her to a junior executive position, one she deserves. As a celebration and a getting to know you by the powers that be, you will take her and her family out to dinner. This will present you the opportunity to meet Ariel Thorsen and decide whether or not she fits your criteria."

"I have introductory dinners with senior executives, not junior executives."

"My dear, you'll be setting a new precedent. When someone promotes to a junior executive position, you'll take them to dinner and meet the family."

Kiernan rubbed the bridge of her nose while thinking over what her uncle proposed. Why entertain this idea? She found the woman appealing, and from all accounts she thought Ariel Thorsen would make the ideal wife to fill the stipulations in her grandmother's will. Did she have any other prospects? She couldn't think of any.

"Very well," Kiernan said. "Do it. Now, you've worn out your welcome, and I've reports to go over."

After Theodore exited, Kiernan returned to her desk, opened her desk drawer, and withdrew an electronic notebook. She clicked it on, a flicker of excitement appearing as she viewed the image of Ariel Thorsen. She certainly wouldn't mind sitting across the dinner table from her for the next five years.

Chapter Three

TWO TOW-HEADED ten year olds greeted Ariel as she opened the front door and entered the foyer of her home. Excitement was evident in their voices, their barely contained energy, and in the brightness of their light blue eyes.

Seth wiggled like a happy puppy. "Mom got promoted, and she's celebrating by taking us out to eat."

"Yeah, and I vote we go to the Pizza Palace," Leigh said.

"And I vote we go to the Bamboo Garden." Her brother challenged with a pugnacious stare.

Ariel hung her helmet on the hat peg over the foyer console table and her jacket on the coat rack, before directing her attention back to the twins. "And I vote we let Mom decide, since it's her celebration. Where is she anyway?"

"Getting ready," the twins said in unison.

Ariel glanced from one to the other. "Okay, what do you two know about this promotion?"

Shrugging, Seth said, "The only thing I know is Mom said she got a promotion to junior executioner."

Leigh fixed a disparaging stare on him. "Nanobrain, that's a junior executive position."

Ariel laughed. "I think I like junior executioner better. Off with their heads!" This sent the two youngsters into a fit of giggles.

"Off with whose heads?" Joanna asked as she came into the living room.

Ariel regarded her mother with affection. "I hear congratulations are in order for your promotion to the position of junior executioner. I'm proud of you, Mom." She hugged her mother and placed a kiss on top of her honey blonde head.

"Thank you, sweetheart. The senior exec in charge of my department called me into her office and informed me that Milton Adams was promoted to senior executive, so I'm filling his old position. I get a twenty-five percent pay increase, so the food and drinks are on me tonight." She paused briefly. "Oh, on Friday night, Ms. O'Shay is picking up the tab."

This surprised Ariel. "You mean Ms. O'Shay, as in the O'Shays of Stellardyne?"

"The one and only, Ms. Kiernan O'Shay, President of Stellardyne, is treating all of us to dinner Friday night at Le Pierre's in celebration of my promotion."

"Mom," Leigh whined, "that's the night of Michelle's slumber party." She wrinkled her nose in disgust. "That place serves you dead snails to eat."

Hearing his sister remark on the menu at Le Pierre's, Seth scrunched up his face in distaste. "Yucky! Dead snails! Nasty! I'll retch-up. Mom, you promised I could go to the movies with Larry Jacobs and Joel Stanley."

Joanna sighed. "Oh, all right. I'll find a nice way of making excuses for you two. You would probably embarrass me anyway. And it's escargot, not dead snails."

Leigh lolled her head to one side. "Mom, that's just a fancy French word for dead snails."

Chuckling, Ariel crossed her heart. "I promise I'll be on my best behavior, but I'm not eating dead snails."

"I'm sure they'll have other things on the menu. Is everyone ready to go out and celebrate?"

"Mom, let's go to the Pizza Palace," Leigh said.

Seth glared at his sister. "We went there the last time. It's my turn to pick."

"Kids, since it is my celebration, I'm picking Salty Dog's. For those who don't want to go, there are always peanut butter and jelly sandwiches." This was effective in stopping further bickering about where to eat.

Ariel shot her siblings a smirk before saying to her mother, "I can't answer for those two, but Salty Dog's beats peanut butter and jelly sandwiches any day. Besides, you're treating."

Chapter Four

"GEEZ, MOM, DO we tip these guys?" Ariel viewed the three valets as she pulled up and stopped in front of the entrance to the Chattanooga Grand Hilton.

"I'll take care of it," her mother replied. The valet opened the passenger door and assisted her out of the car.

Ariel exited the car and handed the electronic ignition key card to a young man who adroitly slid into the driver's seat and drove off toward the parking garage. Joining her mother on the walk in front of the imposing glass double doors, Ariel tilted her head and said, "Shall we?"

"We're a few minutes early, so let's find the restroom and," Joanna said in a faux-haughty tone, "avail ourselves of their accommodations."

Ariel gallantly motioned with her hands toward the doors. "After you, my lady."

A uniformed door attendant opened the doors and greeted them. "Welcome to the Chattanooga Grand Hilton."

Ariel glanced around the grandiose lobby with its gold and dark red décor. "Geez, it's absolutely royal in here." Gazing up, she saw an immense, bowl-shaped chandelier and thought she could easily fit her car into it with room to spare. The Chattanooga Grand Hilton, constructed in 2019 and touted as the premier hotel in the Southeastern region of the United States, was the location of Le Pierre's, a five-star French restaurant with a staff of five world-class chefs. Ariel was certain a person probably couldn't buy a bottle of water for less than fifty dollars. She couldn't even imagine how much the dinner would cost—not that the price would matter to Ms. O'Shay.

They made their way through the wide expanse of lobby, past the opening to the restaurant, and down a wide hall until they came to their destination. Ariel opened the door for her mother and followed her into the lounge. The room's decor consisted of an elegant sofa in wine-and-gold brocade, two matching chairs, and a floor-length mirror on one wall.

"I'll wait out here," Ariel said as she inspected her reflection in the mirror, checking her appearance, and making sure the black raw silk jacket she wore over a red blouse fell in place for the proper fit. Next, she checked the matching black trousers, and glanced down at her new, black pumps to see whether she had scuffed them.

Her mother said she wanted to impress Stellardyne's president, and one way to accomplish this was by wearing quality clothes, which also meant expensive clothes. Ariel was never fashion conscious, and shopping for clothes wasn't her favorite pastime, but for her mother she made the sacrifice and accompanied her to one of the better class malls. Her mother insisted on paying for Ariel's outfit and shoes.

She saw her mother's reflection in the mirror. Joanna stopped behind her and said, "You're beautiful, sweetheart."

Ariel turned away from the mirror, checking her mother's blue long-sleeve dress. "Thanks, Mom, so are you."

"Thank you." Joanna's dark blue eyes sparkled with excitement. "Are you ready to meet one of the richest and most famous people in the known universe?"

Ariel assumed an expression of mock enthusiasm. "Geez, you think she'll autograph my arm?"

ARRIVING AT LE PIERRE'S a few minutes early for dinner, Kiernan surveyed the private dining room she'd reserved, checking to see that the orders she'd given a week earlier were followed. The maitre d' seated her at a table with an immaculate white tablecloth, three place settings, and a centerpiece of delicate pink and lavender miniature orchids.

For the past two weeks, Kiernan had been anticipating this day and wanted everything to be perfect. She took particular care in selecting her outfit for this occasion, picking a forest green pantsuit that enhanced her eyes. The cut lent her the appearance of being taller than her petite five feet five inches.

Movement at the entrance caught her attention. The maitre d' escorted in two women. At once, her eyes riveted on the elegant figure of the beautiful young woman with pale-gold hair. Kiernan promptly stood in greeting, feeling her face beaming. The two women stopped a few feet from the table, and Kiernan forced her attention on her main guest, Joanna Thorsen. She did notice Joanna was a lovely woman, but not possessing the same beauty as her daughter.

She held out her hand and introduced herself. "I'm Kiernan O'Shay."

Joanna took the offered hand and shook it. "I'm Joanna Thorsen, and this is my daughter, Ariel."

Kiernan gazed up into the loveliest blue eyes she thought she had ever seen. They appeared almost lavender in the subdued light. Ariel was far more beautiful than in her photographs. Ariel's warm hand was in hers for a shake and all Kiernan could manage to say was, "Hello."

"It's a pleasure to meet you, Ms. O'Shay." The soft alto voice with its slight Southern accent was easy on the ears.

Kiernan said, "The pleasure is mine."

ARIEL TOOK ANOTHER bite of her appetizer, a crabmeat-stuffed mushroom, while listening to the conversation between her mother and Ms. O'Shay. She tried to study her host discreetly, without appearing rude. The first word she'd use to describe the head of Stellardyne was vibrant. Her compact, wiry form was a dynamo of barely contained energy, showing in the way she moved and carried herself, as well as reflecting in her smoky voice. Her eyes, set off by olive skin and in a shade of light green with a dark line circling the outside of the irises, were what Ariel thought her best feature. She could easily imagine those eyes belonging to an enigmatic creature from some mythical forest. She found herself the focus of those eyes on more than one occasion. Their intensity seemed to see right through her, bringing a glow of embarrassment to her cheeks that she attempted to disguise by directing her attention to what she was eating.

Those eyes centered on her again, seeming to smolder with an inner light that brightened the green and stopped Ariel's breathing for a second. The heat of a blush flooded her face, but she couldn't drop her gaze from those eyes.

"Ms. Thorsen," Kiernan said, "I think I heard somewhere you're a physics professor."

"Yes, at Missionary Ridge Junior College," Ariel said, promptly regaining her poise.

"That seems like a fascinating profession."

"I'm not sure how fascinating it is, Ms. O'Shay, but it is interesting."

"Please, call me Kiernan." She faced Joanna. "And you also, Ms. Thorsen. It's Kiernan when we're in a social setting like this." She winked. "We'll reserve Ms. O'Shay for the office and in business settings."

"I'm Joanna."

Green eyes, still smoldering, fixed once again on Ariel, and Ariel's body reacted with a rush of heat. "I'm Ariel."

"Your name is lovely and suits you well."

"Thank you." Ariel glanced at her mother. "I've my mother to thank for the name. She could have chosen Gertrude or Matilda."

Both Kiernan and Joanna laughed.

Joanna said, "I named her after Ariel the mermaid from

Disney's movie *The Little Mermaid*."

"That's an old classic I remember seeing when a child." Kiernan returned her attention to Ariel. "Is that one of your favorite movies?"

"I like the movie, but my favorites are the old classic *Star Wars* trilogy."

Kiernan said, "You know, they're over a hundred years old and still remain at the top of the list of most favorite movies of all time — mine included."

"They're your uncle's favorite movies as well."

"Oh, that's right. You've met Uncle Theodore. I seem to recall him saying he assisted you when you had problems with your motorcycle."

"Yes, he did. He was very pleasant and charming."

"He's one of the remaining few of the generation still maintaining the old school southern charm."

"I agree," Ariel said and changed the subject to a topic that interested her. "Ms. O'Sh — Kiernan, I would like to know your opinion of Dr. Hakira's experiments with matter-antimatter that he's conducting at the Tokyo Science Institute. Has Stellardyne an interest in developing light-speed engines utilizing his research?"

"Oh my, you are up on all the current research. Of course Stellardyne has an interest."

"Has Stellardyne a plan for developing such an engine?"

With a touch of humor, Kiernan said, "Now, Ariel, I can't comment on our ongoing research. For security reasons."

"Theoretically speaking, how soon do you think a ship will have the capability to travel at light-speed utilizing the research Dr. Hakira has to date?"

"Speaking theoretically, of course, there's a good possibility of that occurring within the next four to five years."

"Wow. That's a relatively short period. What concept of spaceship design do you envision? I —"

"Oh, no," Joanna said, "don't start her on that subject, or you'll be here all night. Creating spaceship designs is one of Ariel's hobbies"

Kiernan regarded Ariel. "Oh? Why aren't you working for Stellardyne?"

"My mother is exaggerating. I sometimes assemble plastic models of spaceships."

Joanna glanced at her daughter with affection before saying to Kiernan, "Ariel also built spaceships in the back yard when growing up."

Kiernan said to Ariel, "You mean model rockets with solid fuel propulsion engines?"

"No. I pretended I was a space adventurer and built my own ships out of cardboard boxes and plywood. They never left the ground, except in my imagination."

Kiernan's expression and voice were soft. "That's where all the great accomplishments originate—in the imagination, and dreams. As a child I imagined I'd one day fly a spaceship to different planets. I had a lot of adventures on the imaginary spaceships I drew."

"Have spaceship. Will travel," Ariel said. "That was my motto as I zoomed about saving the universe." She felt her cheeks heat up and hoped Kiernan wouldn't think that trite.

Kiernan's laugh was low. "That's an excellent motto for a swashbuckling space hero."

That low sound caressed the back of Ariel's neck, sending a pleasant shiver down her spine. "I thought so. I've read articles on your spaceship, *Celeste*, and I was wondering whether you would answer some questions about her?"

CELESTE WAS ONE topic Kiernan could talk about all night. It thrilled her that Ariel was intently listening to her accounting of the ship's specifications. Apparently Ariel had done her homework. She asked intelligent questions pertaining to *Celeste's* hydrogen fusion thrust engines and the state-of-the-art force field shielding system.

Hunger drove Kiernan to pause and take a bite of her food before resuming the conversation. She glanced at Joanna, seeing amused indulgence. Kiernan knew she wasn't being a good host to her employee, but she couldn't refrain from taking this opportunity to have Ariel's undivided attention.

Ariel said, "Kiernan, I understand some of your ideas went into *Celeste's* design."

"That's right. When Grandmother informed me she was building her, I rushed to my drawing board. A month earlier, I'd earned my bachelor's in aerospace design from Embry-Riddle and wanted to prove myself. Of course, as far as my grandmother was concerned, my business degree from Harvard mattered most. She indulged me, but as it happened my ideas impressed her enough that she instructed her engineers to incorporate them into the design. Some of my design concepts were not feasible, so *Celeste's* hull and interior are only thirty-seven percent my creation."

"Thirty-seven percent is a considerable amount. From the pictures I've seen, she's a beautiful ship."

"Oh, she is, and I would love to give you a tour of her," Kiernan said with pride and barely controlled eagerness.

"I would love to see her." The excitement in Ariel's reply also reflected in her eyes.

The prospect of showing *Celeste* to Ariel drew out a current of excitement in Kiernan, but before she could invite her for a tour, the beep of an IMP interrupted the conversation.

Joanna reached in her purse, retrieved her IMP, and answered it while Kiernan and Ariel sat silently. After a moment she said, "I'll be over right away to pick him up." Joanna dropped the IMP back in her bag. "That was the mother of my son's friend. He has a stomachache. I apologize—"

Waving the apology aside, Kiernan said, "I completely understand. It was a pleasure meeting you, Joanna." The three women rose.

Kiernan took a last appreciative view of Ariel and bestowed her most winsome smile. "And you as well, Ariel. I'm certain we'll meet again."

KIERNAN TOOK A stroll around the garden, enjoying the profusion of colorful flowers her gardeners had planted. Surrounded by all this beauty, she recalled dinner from the night before, or to be more precise, she recalled the blonde-haired angel who had captivated her attention so much that she had not even been aware of what she was eating.

During dinner, she had to force herself to focus on the supposed guest of honor, Joanna Thorsen, but like a compass needle, her attention would swing, and once again point north to Ariel.

Her instincts screamed that Ariel was the one to fill the role of her wife and the mother of her child. She possessed all the qualities Kiernan would want in a spouse: intelligence, the ability to converse on a number of subjects that interested both of them, and she was well spoken, well mannered, and exceedingly beautiful with a natural grace. Even her blushes were charming. She'd feel proud to introduce Ariel as her wife to both her social set and to the dignitaries and heads of state she often entertained as the president of Stellardyne. She held no doubt Ariel could carry her own in any social situation.

She was sure Ariel would make an excellent mother. After all, she had experience helping her mother with the care of her two younger siblings.

Ariel Thorsen was worth the price Kiernan was willing to invest in obtaining her goals.

There remained the problem of Ariel's girlfriend. It was in Kiernan's favor the relationship appeared to be more of a friendship, considering they didn't live together and saw each other only on the weekends. Besides, she was Kiernan Deirdre O'Shay, one of the most powerful and wealthy people in the solar system. Many thought her attractive, accomplished, and brilliant. What red-blooded lesbian wouldn't think she was a catch?

Her instincts told her she couldn't come out and ask Ariel to marry her. No, that approach wouldn't work. So she contemplated doing something she wouldn't do in a million lifetimes were it any other woman — romance Ariel, aggressively and relentlessly. She'd find time to see her three or four times a week, take her to the best restaurants, fly to Moscow for the upcoming ballet opening, and shower her with attention.

Suddenly, she realized what she was considering and couldn't quite believe she was thinking it. Romance? This was a business deal. Had she lost her mind? Then again, persuasion, flattery, wining and dining were sometimes exactly what it took to close a deal. Romance could fall into the same category. And if 'acting' the romantic could help Kiernan acquire Stellardyne — why not?

She hurried back up the walk toward the house to launch the wheels in motion.

Chapter Five

GLIMPSING HER WRISTWATCH, Ariel knew she had plenty of time to stop by Chattanooga Harley, have the shop check the back fender rattle that started a couple of weeks after she picked her bike up, and arrive at Mysha's apartment by two o'clock. The doorbell rang as she reached to take her black Tefla-hide jacket off the coat rack. At the door, she peered out the peephole, spying a woman holding a flower arrangement. She opened the door, and the delivery woman held out the arrangement. "I have a delivery for Ariel Thorsen."

Right away, Ariel knew they were from Mysha. She beamed when the delivery woman handed over the arrangement, but was embarrassed when the woman winked while witnessing her obvious pleasure. After thanking the woman, Ariel took the flowers to the kitchen and placed them on the table. This was the first time Mysha sent her flowers and the sweetness of the gesture touched her.

She studied the arrangement, noticing the assortment of various kinds of pink and cream lilies, miniature pink rose buds, lilac asters, and others she couldn't name, all placed in a pink, metallic vase. She could tell they were expensive. And the fact that a living person delivered them, not a droid, let her know they were from an upscale flower shop. She hoped Mysha hadn't spent too much.

As she reached for the envelope from First Bloom Florist, her mother entered the kitchen, stopping in surprise when she saw the arrangement. "From Mysha? It's not your birthday, so what's the occasion? You must have done something special to please her." Joanna waggled her eyebrows.

"Mom!" Ariel tried to sound indignant, but failed miserably, her beaming face betraying her.

"Aren't you going to open the card? I want to know what it says."

By the flatness and size of the envelope, Ariel knew it was an old-fashioned handwritten one and not a card containing a recording of the sender's voice and three-dimensional picture or video. Clutching it to her chest, she sighed in a theatrical fashion. "It's private, it's mine, and I'll not share."

"All right, be that way." Joanna stuck her tongue out before gazing back to the flowers. A moment later, she glanced up at her daughter and asked with concern, "What's wrong?"

Ariel handed the card over.

Ariel, please join me for dinner Friday night aboard Celeste. Have spaceship. Will travel.
Kiernan.

Below the signature was a telecom number for her office at Stellardyne.

Joanna peered back up at her daughter. "It appears you made an impression if Ms. O'Shay's sent an invitation to go aboard *Celeste*."

A surge of excitement raced through Ariel at the thought of seeing the spaceship followed by disappointment. "That's the night Mysha and I are planning to see the documentary film on the discovery of Atlantis. I'll call Ms. O'Shay Monday and tell her thanks for the invitation, but I have other plans."

"You would love to go though, wouldn't you?"

For a few seconds, Ariel was silent. She gnawed her bottom lip while weighing her answer. Suddenly, she had a vivid recollection from the night before of green eyes that on more than one occasion had seemed to drink her in and a low smoky laugh that sent delicious shivers down her back. "Yes, I would. But I'm not sure what the intent behind those is." She motioned with her head to the flowers. "And the invitation to dinner makes it almost sound like a date. If she'd called instead and said, 'Let's do lunch aboard *Celeste*, so I can show you around,' and didn't send flowers—what do you think?"

"If she had sent you red roses I would be concerned about her motives. It's probably innocent. You know, she comes from an entirely different social class. Sending flowers may be the way they do things when sending an invitation for occasions such as this. She did enjoy talking to you, and she did say she'd love for you to see her ship."

"And I said I'd love to see her ship, but I'll have to think on it some more. Either way, I'll call her Monday." An unpleasant thought occurred. "You don't think she'd take it out on you if I refused?"

Joanna drew her head back in surprise. "Of course not! I've heard she's very professional in her business dealings. If you accept her invitation and she thinks it's a date, you can always tell her you have a girlfriend."

"You're right." She leaned over to plant a kiss on her mother's cheek, and then headed toward the front door, calling behind her, "Later!"

ARIEL WAS HALFWAY between wakefulness and falling asleep when the warmth pressed against her left side stretched like a cat and purred, "Hmmm, babe, I'm famished. All that *exercise* has me needing nourishment. How about ordering a pizza?"

Ariel yawned and shifted to gaze at her lover. Mysha shifted onto her knees with her hands pushing against the small of her arched back, shoulders back, and pert breasts thrust forward in an attempt to stretch a kink from her spine.

Admiring the enticing display her dark-skinned lover provided, Ariel reached up and tweaked a dusky nipple. "Make it one with green pepper and mushroom topping."

Mysha playfully slapped her lover's hand away. "Let's make it half green pepper and mushroom topping, and the other half sausage."

"Okay, you call while I take a shower."

Ariel moved to leave the bed only to have Mysha pull her back and slide a leg across her hips, preventing her from going anywhere. Mysha moved partially over her and gave a brief sniff. "Hmmm, you smell good to me. All sexy like you've been making love and you're ready for more."

"Amazing, I say, simply amazing. You should be a detective. You have a knack for *sniffing* out the clues."

Mysha nipped Ariel's nose. In an upper class British accent she said, "Elementary, my dear Watson." She gazed with liquid brown eyes down into Ariel's.

Ariel caught one of Mysha's black curls and twirled it around her finger, thinking how cute her dimples were. Mysha was as dark as Ariel was light. At five feet ten inches, she was a half inch taller than Ariel. She said she inherited her height from her Watusi ancestors. Ariel inherited her height from her Viking ancestors. Ariel was aware that they often drew admiring looks from both males and females when they were out together. It didn't make her as uncomfortable when those same stares were directed at her when she was alone. She knew others saw her as attractive. But to her, the outward appearance was superficial. Her parents had instilled in her that outward beauty was fleeting—inward beauty was what counted.

She'd met Mysha five months earlier when arranging for the local Harley Owners Group, or H.O.G, to sponsor a fundraiser for the Special Olympics. Mysha served on the board of the Special Olympics of Chattanooga. Her full-time profession was as an area supervisor for Tennessee's Social Services Department. Ariel volunteered to represent her local H.O.G chapter and help coordinate the event.

The two women worked well together. Ariel was attracted to Mysha's dedication and her sense of humor. Mysha exuded warmth and friendliness, and had a way of talking and listening that made Ariel feel special.

After the event, Mysha asked her to go to a movie, and, later, out to dinner. Two months of being friends rapidly escalated into more and they became lovers. In fact, Mysha was Ariel's first relationship that included sex.

Ariel's parents were open on the subject of sex and had expected her to experiment, but they imparted to her that sex should be with someone you respected and who respected you. She hadn't met anyone who she was interested in seriously, and until now wasn't inclined to take any relationship to a physical level. She wanted to wait until she found that special person she could connect with on an emotional level first, and share the physical as an expression of her feelings.

She felt this person was Mysha. Ariel had been the one to initiate their first sexual encounter. She wasn't yet in love with Mysha, and Mysha hadn't come out and expressed those sentiments, but she did have feelings for Mysha of warmth and caring. She was sure Mysha felt the same way. They wanted to take things slow and not rush into any commitments.

Mysha kissed her and Ariel heard her lover's stomach roil. "Order the pizza before you fade before my eyes."

Mysha rolled off her and reached for the IMP on the bedside table. Ariel slipped out of bed and entered the bathroom, ordering the computer to activate the shower to setting three, and moved underneath the warm spray of water, enjoying the relaxing way it soothed her body.

A short time later, the shower curtain opened, and Mysha slid behind her. She ran her hands up Ariel's sides. "The pizza will be here in about forty-five minutes, but they always say that and it's at least an hour." Mysha breathed in Ariel's ear. "Want me to wash your back?"

The hot air in her ear made a delicious shiver rush down Ariel's spine. "Hmmm, yes."

Warm, soapy hands slid up Ariel's rib cage to cup breasts, squeezing softly, drawing from her a throaty rumble of pleasure. The sensation of wet breasts pressing into her from behind sent a jolt of arousal to her groin. Leaning her head to one side, Ariel felt nibbles along the side of her neck, sending tingles down her back.

Mysha's fingers pulled Ariel's tender nipples and drew out a deep rumble from her throat. Mysha continued kissing and nuzzling Ariel's neck before delicately tugging an earlobe with her teeth. The feel of her lover's hand sliding down the front of Ariel's slick torso, followed by fingers gliding through the rough thatch of hair to her entrance, elicited a sharp intake of air, and she leaned her head back onto Mysha's shoulder.

A growl sounded next to her ear. "Want more, baby girl?" The rich timbre of Mysha's voice tickled, creating a gaggle of goose bumps that skittled down Ariel's neck, arms, and back.

"Yes. More."

"Have you been a good girl?" Mysha lightly rubbed her fingertips over the swollen knot at the apex of Ariel's crease.

"Yes." Ariel leaned farther back against Mysha, widening her stance, rolling her pelvis, and pushing her center against the teasing fingers.

Mysha removed her hand from Ariel's breasts to encircle her arm around the trim waist, pulling Ariel tightly against her so she wouldn't fall. A nip of Mysha's teeth on Ariel's earlobe caused a low drone to escape her throat as Mysha swiped her tongue in her lover's ear and sexily purred, "That's not what I hear. I hear you've been a bad girl. A very bad girl."

Ariel moaned, her undulations becoming stronger and more forceful, but Mysha kept the same slow rhythm, continuing to lightly stroke as she said, "Do you know what happens to bad girls?"

Ariel bit her bottom lip, mewling as the stroking of Mysha's fingers teased her to a heightened state of arousal. But the touch wasn't enough. She needed it hard and fast. "Please, harder."

"No, no. Bad girls aren't rewarded. Bad girls are punished. Now, Ariel, are you a bad girl?"

"Yes, ohh, yes, please, ahh." Ariel took in gulps of air. Her hips strained toward Mysha's hand for a firmer touch, but Mysha would only tease with her fingers.

"Yes, you are, but you'll be a good girl for me won't you?"

"Ye...Yes."

"And do what I tell you to do, won't you?"

"Ahhh...yes."

Mysha applied a firmer pressure, rapidly stroking her fingers over Ariel's clit, her fingertips barely sliding in and out the opening. Ariel thrust frantically against her hand.

"Now, babe, give it to me," Mysha commanded.

Ariel threw her pelvis forward, suddenly freezing, grinding out a raspy sound from deep within her throat. Mysha did not slow her movements or decrease the pressure until Ariel relaxed. Mysha gentled her touch. "I have you."

Bones melted, and if not for Mysha holding her up, Ariel would slide to the bottom of the tub. After a few moments, she gained enough strength to twist in Mysha's arms, and say seductively, "Want me to wash your back?"

"MERCY, I CAN'T possibly eat another bite or I'll burst wide open." Mysha flopped down on her pillow, and loosened the drawstring of her sweatpants.

"Uh, me too." Ariel flipped the remainder of her pizza crust into the open box on the floor and leaned against the headboard. Stretching the front of her light blue shirt out to see the tomato stain, she said with disgust, "Geez, it never fails, I'm always spilling something on my favorite shirt."

"It'll come out in the wash." Mysha placed her hand on Ariel's bare knee, stroking it up her leg to her panties, and back down to the knee. "What did you have to eat last night at that fancy-dancy restaurant you went to?"

"Crabmeat-stuffed mushrooms, shrimp in garlic sauce with a side of rice pilaf, and a garden salad."

"Sounds good, but was the food worth the five-star rating?"

"It was good, but not as good as Salty Dog's." Salty Dog's was Ariel's favorite seafood restaurant with prices one could afford, and the food was delicious and plentiful.

"Hmmm, bet it was three hundred bucks a plate, and you got four itty-bitty shrimp the size of my little toe arranged in some kind of artistic pattern."

"Eat there often?"

"Not in this lifetime. I heard most of those places skimp on the grub, but gouge you on the green."

"It was eight itty-bitty shrimp the size of my pinkie arranged in an artistic pattern. And the highlight of the meal was the brandy pecan pie I had for dessert with a cup of real Brazilian coffee." For decades, coffee had been a rare and expensive commodity due to a fungus brought about by the greenhouse effect that devastated the plants. Recently, new fungus- and heat-resistant strains of plants had been introduced, but it would take years for the coffee plantations to be established enough to impact the availability and price.

"Oh, sounds scrumptious...and expensive. That one cup of coffee probably cost more than the meal." Mysha scooted up next to Ariel, leaning her back against the headboard. "Tell me what this Ms. High and Mighty O'Shay paragon is like in person?"

"She seemed very nice and not at all the bitch the media describes."

"Is she as sexy in person as she is in her pictures and on EM?"

"Oh, yeah, is she ever. The media pics and vids don't do her justice. She's a mega supreme babe for sure—OUCH! Why did you do that?" Ariel glowered accusingly at Mysha.

"A simple *yes* or *no* will do. I don't want to hear about you drooling over her."

Ariel rubbed the pinch mark on her upper leg. "I didn't drool over her. We talked."

"Yeah? What kind of things did the two of you talk about?"

"Mostly about her spaceship and theories on light-speed travel. She's very intelligent and knows a lot on the subject. Did you know she has a degree from Embry-Riddle in aerospace design, as well as a business degree from Harvard?"

"Not only a Momma Mega Bucks, and a babe, but a real Einstein, eh?"

"I was surprised she was so smart. I mean, about anything other than business. Hmm, she invited me to have dinner with her on *Celeste* and give me a tour."

"You mean her spaceship? You're kidding. That's the most famous spaceship, space yacht, whatever, there is. When are you going?"

"I'm not going."

Mysha leaned back, assessing her. "Why not?"

"It's for Friday night, and that's the night we're going to see the opening of the Atlantis documentary."

"Hey, babe, we can go to that another night. There are people out there who would sell the patent rights to their DNA to go on a tour of *Celeste*." Mysha's eyes took on a mischievous glint. "Besides, I want to know all about her zero gravity orgy room."

"What?"

"You know? Her little romper room, where she has the orgies."

This was news to Ariel. For some reason, Ms. O'Shay didn't strike her as someone who was into that sort of thing. From what Ariel knew, she tended to be private in her personal life, not granting interviews. Plus, the worldwide business community and most of the governing bodies on Earth and off-world held her in respect. Then again, Ariel had heard Ms. O'Shay had been wild in her younger days before she took over Stellardyne. Casting Mysha a dark glower, Ariel said, "Where the hell did you hear that?"

"Damn, babe, you need to watch some news on the EM instead of those boring science programs. Everyone has heard about it. The *Enquirer* channel always has a scoop about it, and who's been free-floating with her."

"Mysha, you can't believe what you see or hear on the tabloid channels. They fabricate those stories from their lurid imaginations."

"Hey, you know the old saying, where there's smoke. But don't ask her to show you the room. She may want to demonstrate it for you, and I don't want to have to bust her nose for coming on to my girl." Mysha leaned over to kiss her on the cheek.

Ariel still was undecided, but inclined to accept the invitation.

She needed more convincing. "You think I should go, huh?"

"You would be a fool not to. And when you're back, you can call me and describe the interior of her ship. She won't allow anyone to take pictures."

Mysha's endorsement convinced Ariel to accept the invitation. A sly expression crept its way onto her face. "I'll check to see whether they have a gift shop onboard and buy you a postcard of her zero gravity orgy room. Maybe she'll autograph it. 'To Mysha, if you're ever in the neighborhood, float on in.'"

Mysha grabbed her pillow and whipped it against her. Ariel screeched and snatched her own pillow up to flail Mysha. Soon, things escalated into a wrestling match with Ariel managing to get the upper hand. Straddling Mysha's waist, she held her wrists to the bed, swiped her tongue over Mysha's lips, and said seductively, "You've been a naughty girl, Mysha. Do I need to discipline you?"

Mysha wiggled in anticipation and said in a purr, "Umm, I think you do."

Chapter Six

KIERNAN WAS PERUSING the specifications *Celeste's* chief technician, Dwayne Campbell, sent on the scheduled overhaul that would put the ship out of commission for the next twelve weeks.

Kelly announced over the desk-com, "Ms. O'Shay, there is a call for you from a Ms. Ariel Thorsen."

She had been expecting this call ever since she sent her invitation to Ariel on Saturday. Her heartbeat raced and she inhaled deeply. "Put her through, Kelly." She hastily patted her hair and stared expectantly at the telecom screen. The Stellardyne logo faded into the smiling image of the caller, and Kiernan said, "Hello, Ariel. How are you?"

"I'm doing well, Ms. O'Shay."

"Please, call me Kiernan."

Ariel smiled. "I called to tell you I accept your kind invitation to dinner, and I'm looking forward to seeing *Celeste*." Ariel dropped her gaze briefly before returning it to Kiernan, her cheeks showing a tinge of pink and her voice sounding shy. "And thank you for the lovely flowers."

Ariel's shyness imparted a vulnerable and innocent air, halting Kiernan's heartbeat for a second. "I'm glad you like the flowers, and I'm more than happy to give you a tour of *Celeste* and have your company at dinner. I'll pick you up at your home at five o'clock on Friday."

"Is there anything I need to bring?"

"No, just yourself. If you have a tendency for motion sickness, you may want to take something before we embark on the shuttle, since the ride can be rough until we leave the atmosphere."

"I'm not prone to motion sickness. Again, thank you. I'll let you go back to your work."

Wanting to stretch out the conversation, Kiernan said, "I'll have you home by...say...two a.m.? I'm sure you'll want some time after dinner to view Earth for a while. There may even be a tropical storm or some other interesting phenomena going on."

With her eyes bright and voice sounding a note of excitement, Ariel said, "That sounds wonderful. I can't wait."

Ariel's eagerness caused a surge of energy in Kiernan, but she knew she had stretched out the conversation as long as she could. Reluctantly she said, "I'll be seeing you soon."

"Yes, Friday night. Bye." Ariel's image dissolved and the

Stellardyne logo reappeared.

Barking out a laugh of both pleasure and triumph, Kiernan pushed her chair back from the desk, twirling it around twice. She glanced at the clock on her desk and realized she was late for a staff meeting, which was a first for her. She had never been late to a meeting since she became president of Stellardyne. But Ariel Thorsen was worth being late for.

A HURRIED RAP sounded on her bedroom door, followed by Leigh rushing in, excitement in her voice. "Ariel, she's here, hurry up, gosh you ought to see that car. It's as long as our house and it's one of those new floating ones!"

Ariel stopped brushing her hair. "You need to wait until I invite you in after you knock, Leigh, and not barge into my room."

"Err...sorry, but she's here, so hurry up."

Ariel walked to the window and stared out. A white limo was parked at the curb in front of the house, sitting on squat struts instead of wheels. She had pictured in her mind Ms. O'Shay arriving behind the wheel of some sporty Mercedes, or something similar, and as expensive. This limo far surpassed any little sporty model in both price and technology. Only a few of these aero-autos were on the market, and at a price that only the extremely wealthy could afford.

Ariel recalled watching a science program last year on the engineering and technology that went into constructing them. The vehicles hovered some three feet above the road surface utilizing the same technology for shielding spaceships from debris. This required reducing the force field greatly in size to repel a solid surface beneath it. Minute fluctuations in different areas of the shield enabled the driver to maneuver the vehicle in any direction. These vehicles were touted as the future replacement for wheeled vehicles, though she was doubtful that they would ever be inexpensive enough for her to afford one.

A group of neighborhood kids stood in the yard gawking at the limo, and she was sure many of her neighbors were peeking out the windows wondering who was in it and why it was in front of her house. On second thought, they probably already knew since the twins had more than likely bragged to their friends about Ariel's invitation, and the friends told their parents.

She sidled over to the full-length mirror on her closet door, checking the appearance of her peach-colored linen slacks with the matching jacket over an ivory pullover blouse. She didn't notice any problems.

"Hurry up, or she'll drive away without you," Leigh said impatiently.

"All right, calm down." Ariel was anything but calm herself. She felt the sensation of soap bubbles floating in her stomach every time she thought about going into space, seeing Earth from orbit, and taking a grand tour of *Celeste*.

She hung her tan clutch bag, the color matching her flat-heeled shoes, over her shoulder by its chain, followed Leigh down the hallway, and entered the living room as the doorbell rang. Her mother opened the door to a husky dark-skinned man in a gray suit. He touched the bill of his black cap and in a deep bass voice said, "I'm David Washington, Ms. O'Shay's driver. I'm here for Ms. Ariel Thorsen."

Joanna moved aside, motioning toward Ariel. "She's right here."

"I'm ready," Ariel said. She leaned over and kissed her mother's cheek.

Joanna whispered against her ear, "Have a good time. And don't forget to mind your manners."

"Yes, Mom." The twins gaped in awe at Mr. Washington. She snapped her fingers toward them and said, "I'll see you two in the morning."

Seth said, "I'm staying up 'til you're back so I can hear all about the ship!"

"I'm staying up, too!" Leigh added.

Joanna looked askance at the two. "We'll see."

Ariel accompanied Mr. Washington toward the car. He rapidly strode ahead, saying, "Coming through," to open a way through the gaggle of neighborhood children gawking at the limo.

He assisted her into the seat right behind the driver's side and across from Kiernan O'Shay. Her host gave her a friendly smile, quickly sliding her gaze over Ariel before saying in a throaty drawl, "Hello, you look very nice."

"Thank you. So do you," Ariel said with a hint of shyness, feeling underdressed when she saw the sleeveless, dark rose dress made of some kind of silky material her host wore. She also noticed the strand of pearls around her neck, with a pearl in each earlobe.

Ariel ran her gaze down in a discreet way to the bodice of the dress, cut in a dip and showing the beginnings of the swell of nicely shaped breasts. She thought she had better focus on Ms. O'Shay's face before her inspection became a blatant stare. But before she could do so, Ms. O'Shay crossed her right leg over her left, drawing Ariel's attention to them. The dress stopped a couple of inches above the knee and Ariel noted dark sheer hose with tiny dark dots on them and a pair of black high heels.

Ogling the legs, she thought she sure wouldn't mind seeing them in a bathing suit. Realizing what she was doing, she promptly brought her eyes up to Ms. O'Shay's face, seeing bright eyes watching her with what appeared to be amusement. The sudden rush of heat in her cheeks made Ariel blush all the more. Trying to cover her embarrassment, she said, "Your limo is wonderful, and beautiful. I wouldn't know we were moving if I didn't see the scenery pass."

"Thank you. If you would like something to drink, there's a foldout bar in the middle of the seat." Kiernan inclined her head toward the back of the seat next to Ariel.

"No thank you, Ms. O'Shay."

"Please, call me Kiernan."

"Kiernan."

"That's better. Tell me more about yourself. I know you have an interest in spaceships, ride a motorcycle, and you're a physics professor. Tell me what you like about teaching physics."

Ariel described the classes she taught, her students, and colleagues, while Kiernan listened. Soon, the topic slid into the different theories of faster than light-speed travel as well as discussions of the various theories of dark matter and anti-matter. Once again, Ariel was impressed by Kiernan's knowledge of these subjects and before she knew it, they arrived at the O'Shay Earth-Side Space Port.

Ariel gazed in awe at the gigantic transport shuttles parked along the different runways, some in the process of having engines, parts, and equipment loaded for use on the O'Shay Orbiting Docks for the construction of new freighters and transports.

The limo slowed, heading down a runway in the direction of a lone, white arrowhead-shaped shuttle waiting on the farthest runway with its green running lights burning to indicate it was preparing for takeoff.

Glancing at Kiernan, Ariel saw her host's attention not focused on the view outside the window, but on her. Kiernan's eyes smoldered, bringing heat to Ariel's face. She gave her host a slight smile before returning her attention to the view out the limo's window.

KIERNAN WATCHED ARIEL stare wide-eyed out the window as the shuttle rapidly ascended through cloud cover and saw her stiffen slightly as the mild g-forces pushed her back against the seat.

The shuttle shook from mild turbulence, and Ariel dug her fingers nervously into the armrest with apprehension painting her features. Kiernan closed her hand over Ariel's and squeezed in reassurance.

Soon, the shuttle broke through the cloud ceiling and hurtled rapidly upward, the white and gray carpet of clouds below them, the horizon shading to midnight blue eternity.

The shuttle continued to climb and one could see the horizon curve downward, giving Earth the appearance of an upside down bowl of blue and green. Gone were the smog and haze that had hung over the heavily industrialized parts of Earth during the first half of the century before the Clean Earth Act was enforced. Now Earth's features were sharply distinct and identifiable.

"Beautiful, isn't it?" Kiernan squeezed Ariel's hand once more, and suddenly her body weighed nothing. She would have floated from her seat if not for the seatbelt.

Hearing a gasp of surprise from Ariel, Kiernan riveted her gaze on her guest, thinking she had never seen anyone so beguiling as this woman, whose lips parted in amazement, her eyes bright, and her hair floating in strands of gossamer gold about her face. She appeared angelic, and Kiernan couldn't help but to reach out, feeling the softness of a strand of hair slide like silk through her fingers. Watching the strands splay and separate into a wide splash of gold, her heart skipped a beat.

Ariel's expression was one of wonder. "It feels as if I'm dreaming or falling asleep—the weightlessness, that is. Has the interior of *Celeste* ever been in zero gravity for an extended period of time?" Ariel watched her right hand slowly bob in front of her.

"Yes. When she's going through a maintenance routine, the rotation of the gyro-grav system is shut down for some time for certain diagnostics to be performed, so no gravity."

"I read the gyro-grav's rotations power a dynamo that charges a series of batteries with enough energy to keep it going for twelve hours, as well as maintaining the lighting and air supply if the engines shut down."

"One of grandmother's innovations. The story is that she got the idea when she saw a field of wind turbines in the Midwest. Stellardyne was the first to develop and use the dynamo system."

Ariel returned her attention once again out the window. "Is the silver line in the distance one of the solar arrays?"

Kiernan said, "That's the North American array, which supplies power to Canada, the USA, and Mexico. I'll point out the other arrays to you when we're aboard *Celeste*."

Gazing overhead, Kiernan said, "Look up."

Ariel's eyes filled with awe at the vision of the white, six-sided cylindrical spaceship suspended against a backdrop of stars. "Oh, she's magnificent."

"She is, isn't she?" Kiernan said with pride, leaning partly over Ariel to get a better view out the window, which put her close enough to inhale her scent and feel the brush of a strand of floating hair across her face. A strong current of arousal flooded her and she hastily resumed her seat, feeling weak. Now, she knew a marriage to Ariel would have to include the physical aspect. She was confident Ariel would agree to this. Ariel probably found her attractive, if her inspection of her assets in the limo was an indicator. Besides, Ariel was young and healthy and probably had a normal sexual appetite. Kiernan didn't think the other woman would be averse to including sex in the arrangement.

As the shuttle zoomed toward *Celeste*, Ariel said in awe, "Wow. She's bigger than I expected. It was hard to tell when we were so far away."

"She's twenty meters higher, or longer, than the Washington Monument."

"You told me her dimensions and I researched them later, but—"

"Yes. I know. It's often hard to judge size by numbers. Sometimes you need something to compare."

"I read the crew numbers twenty."

"Yes, when she's going to Mars or beyond. Tonight I have five crew on duty who reside aboard her carrying out maintenance and some engineering routines. *Celeste's* chief technician, who is also First Mate, is one of those who resides aboard. The Captain, pilots, and other crew aren't currently needed since *Celeste* is in a fixed orbit around Earth. I'll have my chef aboard for tonight and wait staff as well."

Celeste loomed larger and larger the closer the shuttle approached, allowing them a view of docking areas, portholes, and airlocks. *Celeste's* bow was tapered, and the ship's body widened toward the aft where her engines were located, reminding one of a milky quartz crystal spar.

The gleaming white hull appeared to close in on them until it seemed to be nothing but an expanse of white wall with blinking blue lights at the open shuttle bay door through which the shuttle entered. They landed in an area outlined in blue lights.

"There is no air in the landing bay, so an umbilical will attach to the shuttle's aft door, and we'll exit through that." Kiernan let her gaze play over Ariel's features, focusing for a moment on the kissable dark dot at the upper left corner of her mouth, before moving on and seeing the tousled blonde hair, finding it quite alluring and very suggestive of having made love.

Apparently, Ariel noticed Kiernan's scrutiny of her hair, because her cheeks pinked, and she ran her fingers through her locks, saying self-consciously, "I must look a mess."

Running her fingers through her own disarrayed hair, Kiernan said, "All a part of space travel and nothing a comb can't fix. When we disembark, I'll take you to my quarters to freshen up before the tour."

A two-note chime sounded and a female voice over the shuttle's intercom announced, "Ms. O'Shay, you may disembark."

Kiernan unfastened her seatbelt and moved to the aisle, waiting for Ariel. "Are you ready?"

"Yes." Ariel's excitement lit up her eyes, quickening Kiernan's pulse.

She took Ariel by the hand, leading her out of the shuttle and through the umbilical. The feel of Ariel's warm hand in hers sent tingles through her body.

They reached the end of the umbilical and entered into the ship's corridor where a medium-built man with sandy hair and dressed in a blue jumpsuit greeted them. "Welcome aboard, Ms. O'Shay."

"Dwayne, it's good to see you. How do you like your new duties?"

"Oh, I'm loving them, Ms. O'Shay."

"Good. I would like to introduce you to my guest, Ariel Thorsen." To Ariel she said, "This is Dwayne Campbell. He was one of the technicians for my flitter, *Solar Flair*, back in my racing days. After I hung up my helmet, I assigned him as one of the foremen on our orbiting docks in charge of testing finished freighters. I recently assigned him as chief technician and First Mate of *Celeste*."

"Nice to meet you, Ms. Thorsen. I hope you enjoy your time on *Celeste*."

"I'm sure I will. It's nice to meet you, too."

Kiernan gave him a brief nod before leading Ariel down the corridor to her quarters.

While watching them go, a speculative gleam appeared in Campbell's eyes.

THE DOOR TO Kiernan's quarters slid open and Ariel followed her host into a foyer leading into the living area. The sight before her was jaw dropping. This wasn't some cramped set of quarters — not even a roomy set of quarters — but appeared to be the equivalent of an entire townhouse, judging by the size of the living area. Right away, she focused on the floor-to-ceiling window with its breathtaking view of Earth.

Next to her Kiernan said, "Breathe, Ariel."

Ariel pulled her gaze away from the window. "I never imagined..."

"It's magnificent, but it will still be here after the tour, and I'll let you stay as long as you want."

Ariel said sheepishly, "I'm eager to take that tour, too."

"Why don't we start here in my private quarters?"

The living area was spacious, containing a modern design sofa, two love seats, and three comfortable armchairs. Watercolors and oils hung on the walls picturing the planets and other cosmic wonders. Contemporary sculptures were scattered strategically about the area.

Next was the formal dining room with its gleaming modern steel and glass table that could easily seat twelve guests. The dining room also had a floor-to-ceiling window. A compact table in front of the window had two place settings, suggesting this is where they would dine.

Going back into the living area through another door, they entered a recreation room with an EM on the coffee table, and in one corner, a bar. The window in this room also stretched from floor-to-ceiling. From here, they walked through another set of doors leading to a spacious bedroom. A queen-sized bed sat in front of a view window.

They exited the bedroom back into the recreation room. Kiernan led her through a set of doors into a vast bedroom dominated by a window extending to cover a portion of the ceiling and curving over the king-sized bed beneath it.

Ariel was impressed. "Wow, this gives a new meaning to sleeping under the stars."

A door in the bedroom led to an office with a state of the art computer and communications system. Their last stop was the bathroom with its sunken tub and overhead skylight so one could contemplate the heavens while bathing.

Kiernan glanced at Ariel's hair. "I'll leave you here so you can powder your nose."

THE VIEW OUT the port window in Kiernan's dining room was spectacular. The continent of Africa lay half in shadow and half in light.

Ariel was full of questions when Kiernan took her on the tour, showing her engineering, the waste disposal facility, hydroponics, bridge, gym, and the gyro-grav system. The observatory room particularly impressed Ariel, with its electronic telescopes, and three-dimensional display of the solar system with the planets matching their current rotations and orbits around the sun.

Kiernan had dismissed her wait staff after dinner, and it was only the two of them in her quarters now. The lights were on low so the full effect of Earth-glow was visible. Ariel stared raptly at the view outside the window while Kiernan was content to sit across this intimate table, sipping her coffee and watching how the Earth-glow cast an ethereal light about Ariel's features and made them appear even more angelic.

Ariel rotated her chair around to face Kiernan across the table. "I'm sorry. I'm being a poor guest."

"Don't apologize. I understand completely. I was the same way when I took my first space trip."

"Oh, how old were you?"

"It was on my tenth birthday and one of my presents was to spend a few days on a newly constructed Stellardyne freighter before her maiden voyage to Io."

"I know you've said you've been to Jupiter, but have you ever thought about going beyond, to Saturn?"

"It would take close to a year for a round trip, and I couldn't be away from Stellardyne that long."

"A year is a long time, but it would be interesting to see the rings of Saturn."

"I agree. Perhaps one day I'll take that trip." Kiernan waited a few moments before saying, "I have tickets to the Moscow Ballet for next Friday. Travel would be on my personal strato-jet. We'd have plenty of time to take in the ballet and go out to dinner. It's only a four-hour trip, so we wouldn't have to stay overnight in Moscow."

"I appreciate the offer, but I have other plans."

"Tell me what nights are convenient for you. I won't have a problem acquiring tickets."

A stiffening of Ariel's features let Kiernan know this wasn't going to go her way. Ariel's voice also possessed a taut quality. "I'm not sure of your—if you're asking me out on a date, I need to tell you I'm involved with someone, and I'm not interested in dating anyone else."

"How involved?"

Ariel's eyes widened, her features now stony. "We're dating only each other."

"Are the two of you considering marriage?"

Ariel's tone was frosty. "Excuse me, I don't mean to sound rude, but that's none of your business."

"Do you love her?"

"I'm not interested in going out with you."

Kiernan thought she had no choice but to present her proposition to Ariel now. She would have preferred to wait, but Ariel's reaction indicated she would be reluctant to see her again. "I have a proposal for you—a business proposition and I want you to hear me out."

"A proposal? What—"

"Let's go out to the living room where we'll be more comfortable, and I'll explain."

Ariel hesitated before tipping her head once in consent. Kiernan led her into the living room, waiting while Ariel took a seat at one end of the sofa, before she took a seat beside her.

After taking a moment to organize her thoughts, Kiernan said, "What I'm going to tell you must remain between the two of us. I trust you to keep this confidential. Will you agree?"

"That would depend on what it is, Ms. O'Shay."

"Let's say, it's nothing unlawful, I'm not confessing to some crime. But this is something that would cause me a great deal of embarrassment if it got out."

Ariel's expression was unsure before she said, "I agree. Whatever you tell me will remain confidential."

"Thank you. Now, where do I begin? Stellardyne, and the direction it is going in, is very important to me, and to the world. I want to develop light-speed spaceships capable of taking us out of our solar system and to the stars. I can do this if I can have complete control of Stellardyne. At present, I have only forty-five percent control—the rest is in a trust. However, those controlling the trust don't agree with my plans. They have no vision. I'm sure you can appreciate why I need to have all of Stellardyne's resources at my disposal. With your help, I'll be able to do this."

"My help? I don't understand."

"When my grandmother died, she left specifications in her will providing me full control of Stellardyne if certain conditions were met. Those conditions are that I marry and produce an heir by my fortieth birthday, which is less than two years away. That's why I need you to marry me and bear my child."

The expression on Ariel's face was one of disbelief. "This is... You can't be serious, I—"

"I'm very serious. I realize this particular stipulation in my grandmother's will is preposterous, but there's nothing I can do to change it. Believe me, I tried. Getting Stellardyne, all of it, is the most important step to achieving my dream. I'm prepared to make it worth your while."

Ariel sprang from the sofa, gaping at Kiernan as if she were crazy. "No. I'm not interested. I would like to go home now."

Kiernan quickly stood and faced her. "Please, hear me out before you decide."

"No. I don't want to marry you, or anything else. Please, I want to go home."

Anger flared that Kiernan swiftly smothered. She wasn't in the habit of having anyone tell her *no*. She had to make Ariel see reason, even if it meant playing hardball. "I'll take you home, once you hear me out. Now sit, and let me finish."

"I don't want to hear it. Take me home."

Kiernan kept her voice calm, but authoritative. "Not until you hear my proposal. I'm prepared to keep you here as long as it takes. And make no mistake, I'll do it, too."

"Wha...You...You're kidnapping me!"

"No, I'm not kidnapping you. You can go as soon as you hear what I have to say."

Glaring at Kiernan, Ariel resumed her seat on the sofa, sitting stiffly on the edge.

Taking a seat beside Ariel, but not close enough to invade her space, Kiernan said, "This will be a business agreement. One that can financially benefit not only you, but also your whole family."

Ariel stared at her with open mouth, eyes wide, before her color heightened, and her features reflected her outrage.

Holding up her hand to forestall Ariel from saying anything, Kiernan said, "When we divorce, we'll have joint custody of the child, and I'll provide you with your own home, and a yearly income of fifty million dollars for the rest of your life. We can work out arrangements for where the child will reside, and holidays, that kind of thing."

"I'm *not* interested in anything you have to say or offer—"

"I'll provide your family an income of twenty million dollars a year. Your brother and sister will be able to attend the best colleges, and your mother will have a wonderful retirement without having to worry about the future."

"The answer is still *no*!"

"Why, Ariel? Any other woman would jump at this chance."

"I'm not any other woman. My family doesn't need your money and I have a girlfriend."

"Do you love this woman you're dating? Have the two of you even discussed marriage or a long-term commitment? Can she give you what I can give you?"

Kiernan received a flinty stare. "What part of 'none-of-your-business' don't you comprehend? I don't know you, and I certainly don't love you. Now, take me home!"

From her statement, Kiernan knew Ariel was a romantic at heart. Softening her expression and voice, she said, "I find myself attracted to you, very much so, and if we marry, we could work on making the marriage more—much more than business."

Ariel shut her eyes and let out what sounded like a frustrated sigh before opening them. "I don't know how your social class does things—but where I come from you fall in love before you marry. I could never love a person who thinks I can be bought, that love can be bought." With a forceful stare into Kiernan's eyes and her voice holding a hint of disgust, Ariel said, "And I would never have a child with that person."

"Make no mistake—I'm not buying your love. This will be a marriage in name only—business, if that's the way you want it."

"No!"

Kiernan wondered what argument she could use to convince Ariel. Then it came to her. "Let me put it to you this way—would you deny humankind the chance to go to the stars?"

Ariel stared at her, appearing confounded by the question. "Ms. O'Shay, you have plenty of time to find a woman who is willing to marry you and bear you a child. It shouldn't be that hard. But that woman isn't me."

"That woman is you. You have the qualities I'm searching for in a wife and in the mother of my child. No other woman will do."

Ariel shook her head. "I'm truly sorry, Ms. O'Shay. I would like to go home now."

Studying Ariel, she sighed in frustration, but managed to keep it out of her voice. "I'll take you home, but I want you to think about my proposal for a few days. I'll contact you on Wednesday at seven p.m. for your answer."

"And may I ask—will my refusal cost my mother her position at Stellardyne?"

Kiernan flinched, feelings hurt. She was irritated Ariel would ask such a thing and blurted out, "Of course not! Give me some credit here. This has nothing to do with your mother or her position. Now, I'll arrange for us to go."

For the first time in her life, Kiernan was losing. But she would use any means to keep Stellardyne, and her dream, from slipping out of her hands.

Chapter Seven

THE DOOR CREAKED open slowly, and Ariel heard her mother say in a hushed voice, "Kids, let your sister sleep."

She opened her eyes and stared at the ceiling, her thoughts quickly shifting to last night and the wonderful time she was having, until...

On the shuttle trip home, she was sullen and had refused to engage in conversation with Ms. O'Shay. Her host got the message Ariel wanted nothing to do with her and moved to another seat somewhere behind her.

When in the limo, she gazed out the window at the passing nighttime scenery to avoid conversation. Ms. O'Shay was silent, but the few times Ariel glanced at her, the woman stared intently at her in an indeterminate way. To be honest, Ariel didn't want to know what was going on behind those green eyes that glittered black in the limo's dark interior.

When the limo stopped in front of her house, she didn't wait for Mr. Washington to open the limo door before she opened it herself and ran up the walkway without a backward glance. She knew she was rude in not telling Ms. O'Shay thank you, but she didn't want to interact with her.

The twins had long since gone to bed when she opened the front door. Only her mother was up. Not wanting to explain all that had happened, she truthfully told her mother she was tired and would talk to her in the morning.

Now morning had arrived. She stumbled out of bed, took a shower, dressed in her blue sweats, and headed to the kitchen, almost tripping on the vacuuming bot rolling its way down the hall. No one seemed to be home. A note on the refrigerator door read that her mother had taken the kids to Skateland to drop them off for a neighbor child's birthday party.

She opened a container of Pop-hot cinnamon oatmeal and put it on the table then placed a glass into the drink dispenser on the refrigerator door, which promptly asked, "Selection please."

"Orange juice." After her glass filled, she took it to the kitchen table and slumped in to her seat. She glanced at the clock and saw it was 10:15.

As she was finishing breakfast, she heard a noise at the kitchen door. Her mother entered the room.

"Good morning, sleepyhead," Joanna said, and kissed the top

of her head.

"Morning, Mom," Ariel mumbled.

Joanna took a seat across from her. "Why so bright and chipper this morning?"

A discontented sigh seeped through Ariel's nose. "It was awful, Mom. Well, not all of it."

"What happened?"

"She thought it was a date and tried to ask me out, even when I told her I wasn't interested. She wouldn't take *no*—" The ringing of the doorbell interrupted her. "I'll tell you the rest when you get back."

Joanna's face reflected puzzlement before going to answer the door. She returned a couple of minutes later with an arrangement of two dozen red roses.

Ariel stared at them with distaste. She shut her eyes, letting her head loll to one side, and made choking sounds.

"I take it these aren't from Mysha." Joanna placed the arrangement on the kitchen table in front of Ariel.

After seeing the attached card with the First Bloom Florist logo, Ariel pushed the roses away. "Throw them in the garbage."

"Aren't you going to read the card and see for sure who sent them?"

"I don't need to read it to know."

"Maybe she's sending them to apologize for her behavior."

"Mom, they're red roses, if you get my meaning."

Joanna reached a finger out and stroked one of the blood red petals. "I see they are. Now, tell me what happened."

"She wanted me to go to the Moscow Ballet with her so I told her I had a girlfriend. Oh, Mom, it was terrible. She wouldn't take no for an answer, and even had the nerve to ask me whether I loved Mysha. I told her it was none of her business." Ariel couldn't reveal too much since she'd promised she wouldn't say anything about the proposal.

"Sweetheart, she'll have to give up if you show her no interest." Indicating the roses with a tilt of her head, she added, "I bet that's the last you hear from her. Other than Ms. O'Shay, how was the tour of *Celeste*?"

"It was the most marvelous thing I've ever experienced. *Celeste* is really beautiful. You should see Earth from space—incredible."

"The kids will want to hear all about it."

"I'll be over at Mysha's tonight, but I'll tell all of you about it tomorrow at dinner."

"Are you going to tell Mysha what happened?"

"Yes. She'll want to know about the ship, and I'll tell her everything." She wouldn't mention the proposal, of course. "Mysha will go bust her nose."

Joanna said dryly, "Not that I approve of those methods, but maybe it would teach Ms. O'Shay a lesson that 'no' and 'I'm dating someone' are to be taken seriously."

Ariel didn't know why, but she had a gut feeling not even a broken nose would teach Kiernan O'Shay that lesson.

THE VIEW OUTSIDE Kiernan's bedroom window was a dismal one of the nearby mountains appearing to her as ominous black giants against the gray smudge of dawn. They served as a fitting backdrop to her dark thoughts. Ariel refused her offer — refused her. Perhaps by Wednesday, she would change her mind. But Kiernan had a sinking feeling Ariel's mind was made up, and it wouldn't be what Kiernan wanted.

She went to her sitting room and over to the desk to check for any messages on her telecom. There were three. Two were from friends, and one was from her uncle. She decided to listen to her uncle's message first.

Her uncle's image filled the screen. His voice was cheery, too cheery for Kiernan. "Hello, my dear. I know you're out having a wonderful time tonight with that charming young lady, and I'm sure she's having a wonderful time as well. Please call your old uncle in the morning and share all the details. All the details, that is, that wouldn't shock your old uncle. I'll be home all day tomorrow and hope to hear from you soon."

Frowning, she muttered, "What is there to tell, Uncle Theodore?"

"I'M GOING TO bust her nose!" Mysha declared angrily.

Ariel had arrived at Mysha's ten minutes earlier, and, after an earth-shattering kiss hello, she sat with Mysha on the sofa and told her about the night before and today's roses. She had to bite her tongue to keep from telling Mysha the part concerning the business proposition. She now regretted giving her word that she would keep it confidential. Keeping this information from Mysha, and her mother, made her feel dishonest. But, what purpose would it serve to tell them? It would upset her mother and make Mysha even angrier.

"Yeah, I knew you would say that," Ariel said dryly. She knew Mysha would never do any such thing because she was really a softy at heart.

"She had better not send you flowers or try asking you out again."

"I made it clear I wasn't interested, and I'm already taken." Bestowing a sweet smile on her lover, she added, "You're my girl. The only one I want."

Mysha took her in her arms, kissing her with a big smack on the lips. "Babe, you're my one-and-only. Ms. Mommy Warbucks O'Shay better stay away from my girl or she'll need a plastic surgeon—make that a whole team of plastic surgeons to fix her nose." She placed a brief kiss on Ariel's nose. "You know, I can't take you to Moscow for the ballet, but I can show you a good time in Beijing."

"Oh, sweetie, you know I would love to go with you, but it wouldn't be right for me to take off from my job, not with this semester starting soon, and especially since I was off for the summer."

Mysha had accepted an invitation to attend the National Society of Social Work Professionals' yearly workshop and conference scheduled next month in Beijing. She was leading a workshop as well as receiving an award for her published research on outreach to rural populations. The conference was all expenses paid for two weeks, and she could invite a guest.

"Come on, take a week, or a weekend."

"Mysha. You know I can't."

"Yeah, well, I'll miss you terribly."

"But think of all the sweet things we'll do when you get home to make up for what you missed while away."

Mysha's eyes seemed to spark. "Oh, yeah. Two weeks' worth of pent up frustration to work through. Sweet indeed. Speaking of something sweet—you want to go out and get an ice cream cone?"

Ariel said in a seductive tone, "You want something sweet? I'll give you something sweet." She proceeded to kiss Mysha thoroughly, making her forget all about going out for ice cream for the better part of the day.

THE DISPLAY ON the kitchen clock flicked to 6:58 p.m., speeding Ariel's heart rate with anxiety at the impending telecom call. She tried to ignore the two dozen red roses on the kitchen table that arrived that morning, and were the latest in a string of deliveries every morning since Saturday. She wanted to toss them in the garbage, but her sister wanted them for her bedroom. Ariel agreed she could have them, but she made sure she removed the cards and tore them to pieces before handing the roses over. She never read any of the cards because she didn't want to know what Kiernan had written, thinking it would upset her. Glancing at the clock, she saw the time was now 6:59. Earlier, she informed her mother she was expecting an important telecom call and wanted privacy, so she would take it in the kitchen instead of the living room. She clicked off the view screen, not wanting to see Kiernan, or have Kiernan see her.

The telecom trilled, shooting a surge of anxiety through her. She wiped her damp palms on her jeans and said, "Telecom, on." Her voice shaky from nerves, she answered, "Hello."

"Ariel, this is Kiernan."

"The answer is no. Please don't send any more flowers—don't contact me again." She promptly disconnected the call and ordered, "Telecom, block last number from caller."

Feeling her stomach flutter with nerves, she took a deep breath to calm herself, almost gagging as the scent of roses assailed her nose. Hurriedly snatching the arrangement off the kitchen table, she rushed out to the back porch, opened the garbage can, tossed the roses in, and slammed the lid with a finality she hoped would shut out this whole incident for good.

NOT EVEN TWO analgesic tablets and the cup of coffee Kiernan was drinking were eliminating her headache. She shouldn't have come into work today. That would be a first for her. Since she'd taken over as Stellardyne's president, she had never taken a sick day. She hadn't managed to fall asleep until the early hours of the morning. Her thoughts played out scenarios to convince Ariel to change her mind. She thought of everything from paying her girlfriend to leave her, talking her mother into interceding, and kidnapping and brainwashing her. She had a hunch the first two wouldn't work. The last one was one of those crazy ideas one would never act on, similar to imagining what you would like to do to your bitter enemy, if you could get away with it.

Kelly's voice came over the desk-com, "Ms. O'Shay—"

Kiernan flinched and snapped, "I thought I told you I didn't want to be disturbed."

The desk-com remained silent and Kiernan leaned back in her chair, massaging her temples. Suddenly her office door opened, and Theodore walked in.

She glared at him and snarled, "I'm not in the mood."

He took a seat in the burgundy armchair in front of her desk and studied her. "I take it she said no."

"I don't want to discuss it. Now, if that's all, I have a headache, and I'm not in the mood for chitchat."

"My dear, if it will help, perhaps I should talk to her."

"Ha! Oh, yes, that would work. What could you possibly say to persuade her to change her mind?"

"Ask her what she wants and give it to her."

"She doesn't want me—that's for damn sure. Nor fifty million a year and her family set up for life." She took a sip of coffee before saying, "You know what I think? I think she's crazy. Any other woman would jump at the chance." But of course, Ariel wasn't any other woman. She was 'the' woman, and Kiernan couldn't have her.

"Kiernan, she may change her mind in a week or two when she thinks it over. Don't lose hope."

She shot him a glare. "Lose hope? I'll probably lose more than hope. I'll lose Stellardyne, too."

"As you said before, there are others who would jump at the chance."

"But they wouldn't be her, and I don't like to settle for second choice. I hate to be rude..."

He stood to leave. "Things will be better in a week or two. You'll see. And we'll find a candidate—several candidates who will make you forget her."

"Whatever," Kiernan said dismissively, taking another sip of her coffee, as he exited her office.

Chapter Eight

THEODORE WATCHED AS his husband took another bite of steak and chewed heartily, clearly enjoying it. Jack was what one would term a meat-and-potatoes man. He detested quiche, sushi, and foods with names he couldn't pronounce.

Of course, he indulged Jack by having his chef prepare all of his favorite dishes, which included barbecue ribs, fried chicken, pork chops, meat loaf, and fried catfish. Despite his hearty appetite, Jack maintained a trim and muscular figure.

"Jack. I have a favor to ask," Theodore said.

After swallowing his food and taking a swig of sweet iced tea, Jack said, "Ask away."

"I have a fraternity brother, John Woodard—you've met him. He contacted me recently and asked if I could find a position for his niece. She was working in security for ConCorp, which as you know, is on the verge of filing for Chapter 7 bankruptcy. Her position was cut—"

"I don't need another person. Besides, ConCorp is our main competitor, and I would hesitate to hire anyone that had any connection with their security office...in any capacity—not after their involvement in that corporate espionage scandal with Lunaway. Wasn't it John who represented them in court?"

"I don't think you have anything to worry about. John's involvement with ConCorp is through. ConCorp is all but finished. Besides, there's a good chance Stellardyne will expand in the next two years. You'll need the extra personnel—experienced personnel."

This caught Jack's attention. "What do you mean expand?"

"Let's say Kiernan has plans that have a good chance of being implemented." Theodore wasn't at liberty to disclose the stipulations in Shanna's will.

"Travel at the speed of light. If man were supposed to go that fast, God would have made us sunbeams. Kiernan doesn't have the backing from her trustees to take us in that direction." Jack went back to eating.

"Very well. Forgive me for trying to do an old friend a favor—and you a favor as well," Theodore said, and sighed in disappointment.

Jack stopped his fork half way to his mouth. "I'll need her full name and social security number to do a background check."

"Her name is Sherry Woodard — and you won't have to do all the work. I'll check her background. How about I contact her and have her report to you next Monday?"

"I'll have to clean up one of the spare offices and set her up a computer, but I guess that'll work out."

"Thank you, dear heart. I'm sure you won't regret hiring her."

SHERRY WOODARD SAVED her most recent security report, locked her computer, exited her office, and knocked on the office door of her supervisor, Jack Spivik.

"Come in."

She entered the office and stared across the desk at her boss of two weeks. In a serious tone she said, "Mr. Spivik, we have a breach in security. Someone downloaded the specifications for the enhanced hydrogen drive engines."

This information had Jack sitting up straight in his chair, unease on his features. "What do you have?"

"I finished running a check on the computers in engineering—"

"I thought engineering was Miller's assignment."

"It is, but I finished my assignment early and told him I needed something to do. I volunteered to take engineering."

"What did you discover?"

"The computer used was for a data processor in engineering with no authorization to access the hydrogen drive engine research. It took some work, but further investigation showed another computer accessed this computer for the specific purpose of throwing us off the trail. Two other computers were used, but I managed a trace to the original."

"Who's been downloading who shouldn't?"

"Computer number forty-two registered to a Joanna Thorsen."

Jack accessed his computer to research the name. "Ah, ha. Here we go. She recently received a promotion to a junior executive position in engineering data processing four weeks ago. Access the records for her e-mail and telecom calls for the past four weeks — make it six weeks. I want you to intercept any e-mail she sends to recipients outside of Stellardyne, and block any attempt to download information to a micro-disc. Ferret out every nook and cranny her computer has for accounts, passwords, whatever."

"That might take up to a week since passwords and codes are not easy to decipher."

"Work overtime if needed and I'll pay you a bonus."

"Are you thinking what I'm thinking?"

"She's selling the information to a competitor is what I'm thinking."

"Corporate espionage."

"Great work, Sherry."

"Thanks, Mr. Spivik. I hope we're not too late. It would be a shame if con—competitors got their hands on the plans."

Jack nodded, while the bitter taste of bile flooded his mouth. He would have Theodore fill Kiernan in on the details—he wasn't up to taking a one-way trip to Neptune.

Chapter Nine

IT WAS EERILY quiet when Ariel walked in the front door—too quiet for a Friday night. The EM wasn't on and no sounds of two rambunctious siblings wreaking havoc. She hung up her jacket and helmet before listening for sounds of her mother moving about the house. She knew her mother was home because her car was in the driveway. All was silent. "Mom?"

The squeak of a door opening down the hallway caught Ariel's attention and a few seconds later her mother appeared with a stricken face, her eyes red and face splotched.

A chilling fear gripped Ariel. "Mom, what is it...Seth...Leigh—"

"No, they're fine. They're over with their friends."

Ariel sighed with relief, but something was clearly wrong, she placed her hands on her mother's shoulders, studying her closely, and asked concernedly, "Something's wrong. What is it?"

Joanna sighed deeply, her voice weary. "Let's sit down so I can tell you."

Ariel followed her over to the sofa, sitting beside her, and regarded her with worry, before asking anxiously, "Mom...what happened?"

Joanna inhaled, her visage stark and voice shaky. "I'm accused of corporate espionage."

Ariel gasped in disbelief. "What!"

"Someone downloaded the specifications for Stellardyne's new engines into my computer, and they think I've done it."

"That's crazy! Why would they think that?"

"My computer was used, as well as my passwords. That makes me guilty since I'm the only one who has my passwords."

"This is some kind of mistake. Someone else has to know them."

"Apparently so, but they don't believe it. I can't understand why anyone would do that, would download the specifications to my computer."

Shaking her head in disbelief, Ariel couldn't think of a reason either, and then it dawned. "This is Kiernan O'Shay's doing, to get back at me! That bitch!" Seeing her mom's befuddled face, Ariel said, "Because I turned her down."

Joanna shook her head in disbelief. "I can't believe she would do this because you turned her down for a date. That's ludicrous."

"No, Mom, there's more to it than a date."

"What do you mean? She didn't come on to you, did she?"

"No, it was nothing like that...unless you put a proposal of marriage in that category."

Joanna's mouth dropped open in shock. "What? You mean she wants you to...marry her?"

Ariel explained and when she finished, Joanna said, "I can't believe it. I mean...I can't believe she would do this to me to get back at you. And this...inheritance thing...sounds like something out of the pages of a Regency romance." Joanna shook her head. "There must be insanity running in that family."

"Ole Granny O'Shay was sure insane. And you know what they say about apples not falling far from the tree." Frowning, Ariel said, "I'm going to call that bitch up and tell her I'll go to the news media with this."

"Don't do that, sweetheart. I don't want this mess in the media. I've agreed to a polygraph examination on Wednesday, and the results should be back the next day. I've already placed a call to a lawyer who handles these kinds of cases. I have nothing to hide and the test will prove I'm innocent."

"Still, I'm going to call and confront her."

"Ariel, don't. For my sake, please don't."

Hearing her mother's plea and seeing the beseeching request in her eyes, Ariel conceded with a sigh. "Oh, all right. But I'm going with you when you take the polygraph."

"I'll be fine. You don't have to take off work. My lawyer will accompany me."

"No. I want to be there."

Joanna leaned over and kissed her daughter's cheek. "Sweetheart, I love you, and I don't know what I would do without you."

"I love you too, Mom. Things will be okay. You'll see."

"DAMN, BABE. THAT'S crazy. Why would she frame your mother to get back at you for not going on a date with her? I bet she has a dozen babes lined up who are panting to go out with her and has already forgotten about you."

A pang of guilt stabbed Ariel for telling Mysha this version of the story, but at the same time anger. "God, Mysha! You think my mom's a thief!" Hurriedly, she left the sofa and paced, debating whether she should tell Mysha the real circumstances.

She decided against it, for a number of reasons, one was if word ever got out, Ms. O'Shay might blame her, and things could get worse. She did trust Mysha, but sometimes things had a way of slipping out, and she didn't want to involve Mysha in this situation if Ms. O'Shay ever found out she'd informed her. Another was she didn't want to upset Mysha before her trip to China.

She had called Mysha the night before and begged off their usual Friday night together because her mother was upset, and Ariel wanted to be there for her. She'd promised Mysha she would fill her in today on what happened, and later, drive her to the airport for her scheduled flight to China that night.

Mysha put an arm around her shoulder, led her back to the sofa, and sat beside her. "Calm down. I don't believe your mother is a thief. But this doesn't make sense. So O'Shay has a reputation for being a bitch—but hell—I've never heard she would do something like that over something so petty. If you cheated her in a business deal, maybe. Yes, I think your mother was framed, but I'd bet it was someone other than O'Shay. Maybe someone was jealous she got the promotion, thinking it should have been theirs, and did this."

Ariel didn't believe that was the case. Her mother would have mentioned any conflict or sour grapes over her promotion. Joanna's fellow workers held her in high regard and liked her. She told Ariel they were in agreement she was best suited for the position.

She didn't want to discuss the subject anymore and get into a possible argument with Mysha before she left for her conference. "Maybe you're right. And the polygraph Mom's taking Wednesday will prove she's innocent."

Mysha drew her in for a hug. "I'm sure it will, babe. In a few days, this will all seem like a bad dream. And if it will make you feel better I can still bust her nose for you."

"You're bad," Ariel said as she snuggled against Mysha's neck.

"That rich bitch might well find out how bad." Mysha rubbed Ariel's shoulders in a comforting circle. "You're all tense. Let's go to the bedroom and I'll massage your back."

Ariel kissed Mysha's neck. "I know where your massages lead."

"Babe, you can count on it."

THEODORE WATCHED AS the trio of Joanna Thorsen, Ariel Thorsen, and Joanna's lawyer, Ian Broxton, exited the conference room where the polygraph tests were conducted. He nodded in greeting, but the two Thorsens ignored him.

Ian Broxton held out his hand for a shake. "Theodore, how are you?" They both belonged to the Rotary Club and attended the Chattanooga Lawyers Association meetings.

"I'm fine, Ian. How are Theresa and the kids?"

"They're doing well. Amber's a freshman at Tennessee State,

and Keith's a junior at Brentmore Academy."

"Little Amber is in college? My, how time flies. The last time I saw her she was still in braces."

"She still is. They should come off soon."

Theodore changed the subject. "Benton and Greene said they would send us the results of the test tomorrow before noon. I'll send you a copy of the findings. You should receive them tomorrow around two."

"I appreciate that, Theodore. I'll arrange a meeting with my client for four and go over the results with her."

From the corner of his eye, Theodore saw Jack and Evelyn McCall, the technician from Benton and Greene, exiting the anteroom. "I better let you go. I need to consult with Jack."

"I'll be seeing you soon," Ian said, and then hurried down the hall toward the elevator where his client and her daughter were waiting for him.

Theodore clutched his cane tightly in his hand and tried to catch up. "Jack. Hold up a second."

Jack heard him and spun around to face him. Ms. McCall also stopped, shifting the briefcase-sized instrument container she carried from her left hand to her right.

Theodore caught up to them. "Jack, I'll need you to send the polygraph report to me as soon as it's delivered. I'll need to make a copy and rush it to Ian Broxton tomorrow. I'll go over the results and consult with Kiernan — better me than you."

"No problem," Jack said in a relieved tone. "Better yet...have the report sent to Mr. O'Shay as soon as it's ready."

Ms. McCall answered, "I'll do that."

Theodore's thoughts were on Kiernan. "Such a tragedy — for everyone — if she's guilty."

AFTER LEANING BACK into the armchair in Ian Broxton's office, Ariel's attention strayed to the right wall, only vaguely interested in a set of prints depicting a foxhunt scene from the 1800's. She next glanced with disinterest at the diplomas and the glass front bookcase with its numerous volumes of law books. Her mother occupied the chair next to her.

The door opened, and Ian Broxton entered. "Sorry to keep you waiting, Ms. Thorsen." He placed an electronic notebook on his desk as he took his seat. He flipped open the notebook, activated it, and lifted his eyes to Joanna. "I have the results of the test and have gone over them." His features sobered. "Ms. Thorsen, the results aren't good. They indicate you weren't truthful."

Both Joanna and Ariel sucked in their breath. Joanna grabbed her daughter's hand in hers, clutching it tightly.

Ariel blurted out angrily, "This is some kind of mistake!"

"I told the truth," Joanna protested. "How can the test show otherwise?"

"Ms. Thorsen—"

"This is Kiernan O'Shay's doing!" Ariel almost shouted. "She's behind—"

"Ariel!" Joanna put her hand on her daughter's arm, forestalling her from continuing. "Let Mr. Broxton finish."

He regarded Joanna gravely. "Ms. Thorsen, as you're aware, Benton and Greene have developed an almost foolproof method of determining whether a person is truthful or not. The Greene polygraph has been proven over the years to be 99.7 percent accurate—"

Ariel interrupted and said with disgust, "Ms. O'Shay bribed them. She—"

Joanna softly squeezed her daughter's hand. "Ariel, please, let him finish."

Ian regarded Ariel with curiosity, before asking, "What possible motive would Ms. O'Shay have in doing that, Ms. Thorsen?"

Ariel stared him straight in the eyes. "I refused her offer of marriage."

Her statement appeared to stun him. He recovered, scrutinized Ariel, and demanded, "Please explain that statement, Ms. Thorsen."

Ariel proceeded to do just that.

"WELL, MY DEAR, what is it you want to do?" Theodore asked from his chair in front of Kiernan's desk.

Kiernan closed her eyes, rubbing the lids with her right thumb and forefinger. "I can't believe she did this. She recently received a promotion and is making a good salary—at least twenty-five percent more than her prior salary. What possible motive would she have?"

"Good old-fashioned greed is my guess. I've been a lawyer for almost seventy years, and I can tell you even those with the greatest material wealth are often those who aren't satisfied and want more. Her new position provided an excellent opportunity for gain. She would have gotten away with it if only a routine security check had been performed. Jack's new hire discovered it. Sometimes it takes a different set of eyes to catch things that would normally seem innocuous."

"Still, I'm a good judge of character and Joanna Thorsen did not strike me as a dishonest person. My instincts are rarely wrong. Are you sure—"

"Kiernan. Be reasonable. You're letting your... expectations...concerning Ariel Thorsen cloud your judgment. All the evidence points to her guilt. Her computer contained information that had no business being there, and she has no plausible explanation. Benton and Greene are the best in the business, and their results are accepted by almost every judicial system in the world as evidence."

Kiernan ran a hand through her hair and shifted uneasily in her chair, reluctantly thinking her uncle might be right concerning her judgment—at least in this matter. She wanted to believe Joanna Thorsen was innocent. But her first priority was to the company. "She could have done some serious damage to Stellardyne if she passed our new engine specifications on to any of our competitors. Are you positive she didn't get this information to any of them?"

"Jack isn't one hundred percent sure, but it appears she didn't, as the specifications were never attached to an e-mail, and the computer doesn't record it ever being copied to a micro-disc. I hate to say this—take my advice and make an example of her. If you don't, others will attempt the same thing. This will also send a strong message to whomever she was prepared to sell this to that you're serious and won't tolerate this sort of thing."

"If she's found guilty how much time will she serve?"

"She has a clean background and it appears she never sold the information. However, the intent was there, and the law does treat this as attempted theft. Six months is the minimum and a fine of one hundred thousand dollars. I think the judge will be lenient and sentence her to less time and a reduced fine. We can always make that recommendation."

Kiernan said, "Press charges. As you say, it will send a message."

"I'll take care of everything, my dear. It might take a few days to write the report and go through the process."

"Very well," she mumbled, her thoughts running to one thing now. Ariel would hold her to blame, and she would never stand a chance of changing her mind on accepting the proposal.

Chapter Ten

ARIEL PULLED UP another quiz on her computer to grade. She almost hadn't come in to work today, but her mother said she would be fine and for her to go. A soft knock on her office door alerted her to a visitor, maybe a student or colleague. "Computer, save." She looked to the door and said, "Come in."

She was surprised when Theodore O'Shay walked through the door and said, "Dr. Thorsen, might I have a minute of your time?"

Ariel was puzzled as to why he was here. This had to have something to do with her mother. She motioned to the chair by her desk. "I have class in twenty minutes."

"This shouldn't take long." He seated himself, placed his cane across his lap, and gazed at her with somber eyes. "I'm here to talk about your mother."

Ariel let out a harrumph and said, "Somehow, that doesn't surprise me. Unless you're here to tell me this whole thing is a farce, I'm not interested in hearing what you have to say."

"I'm afraid it's anything but a farce. Things aren't good for your mother. Kiernan plans on pressing charges—"

"She's innocent and you know it," Ariel said indignantly. "This is all some sort of revenge for—" She fell silent, wondering how much he knew about Kiernan's proposal, and debating whether she should tell him.

Theodore took away that decision. "For your refusing Kiernan's proposal. She would never do anything like that."

"Apparently she has. I'm prepared to testify in court to that fact."

"Dr. Thorsen—may I call you Ariel?" She gave him a barely perceptible nod. "That would prove nothing. She offered you a business proposal and you rejected it. Did she once threaten you with retaliation if you refused her proposal?"

Mr. Broxton, her mother's attorney, had asked her the same question. "That's the only explanation. My mother never sold information or intended to sell information."

"Ariel, let's face facts. Your mother had the specifications for our newest engine design in a hidden account on her computer. Only she had the password, and she has no explanation for why or how the specifications were on her computer."

"She was framed!"

"Her polygraph test showed she wasn't being truthful. You

know the reputation of Benton and Greene. They're the best and most reliable in their field, and their testing is virtually foolproof."

"But I bet they're not bribe proof!"

"Be reasonable—"

"Reasonable? Reasonable is that this is all a sham—lies. My mother is innocent!" She glowered at Theodore. "If that's all, you may leave. I'll show you out." She stood and opened the door, waiting for Theodore to exit.

Theodore swiveled in his chair. "I'm here to help. There is a way to get your mother out of this situation. Ariel, please take your seat and listen to what I have to say."

Ariel hesitated before smacking the door shut and returning to her chair. "Go on."

"I assure you, Kiernan has no idea I'm here talking to you, and I would appreciate it if you would keep this confidential."

Ariel wanted to roll her eyes. Here was another O'Shay with a confidence they wanted her to keep. She let out a sigh. "Yes."

"Whatever you may believe, Kiernan did not frame your mother. She would never do that."

She rolled her eyes and said sarcastically, "Oh no, of course not."

"Kiernan did discuss with me that you rejected her offer. She was quite taken with you, and it was a big disappointment for her when you refused her proposal. What I'm about to tell you...I don't know whether Kiernan will go along with it or not, but it is worth a try for your mother's sake and that of your siblings." He regarded Ariel closely before continuing. "If you were to take Kiernan up on her offer—"

"That is out of the question!"

"Hear me out, my dear."

Ariel studied him before saying, "Continue."

"Your mother can fight this charge and possibly win, but it would ruin her. What kind of future would she have? Decent employment prospects would be hard to find. It could take months for this to go to court. And what toll would that take on her, and your siblings? Then there are the court and legal fees—"

"I'll help her—"

"Yes, you will. But will you be able to support your family, and pay off her legal debts?"

"I'll take out a loan if I have to."

"My dear, be realistic. Do you have enough of a credit history, or work history, to secure a loan for what could well be a legal fee of well over a hundred thousand dollars?"

Ariel's eyes widened with shock. "I...I'll find a way."

"I know you want to do whatever you can for your mother and family. No price should be too great. Accept Kiernan's offer on the condition she doesn't press charges. Her offer is generous and your family won't have to worry about their future. I think she would accept. She needs you, Ariel, as you need her." He stood and headed to the door, stopped, and regarded her before saying, "Thank you for your time, Dr. Thorsen."

Ariel barely knew he had departed. Her heart beat in thuds that were almost painful, her breathing shallow and fast. Panicking, she didn't know which way to go. Never had she found herself in the position of making such a tough decision.

The only *tough* decision she'd ever had to make was which college to attend. All the prestigious universities with top physics programs offered her full scholarships. Of course, it hadn't been that tough. She wanted to attend the best one, and the best was MIT.

It was easy to be in a relationship with Mysha because she didn't push her into making a decision on further commitment.

It was easy to accept a professorship at Missionary Ridge Junior College rather than the more prestigious ones offered her at MIT or Cal Tech. The professorship at Missionary Ridge allowed her to stay at home with her family and help her mom.

Besides, with her family she had a familiar routine, and her mother took care of those mundane little things Ariel found tediously dull like keeping track of bills and shopping, with Ariel contributing money, doing some chores, and watching the twins if her mother was delayed or had some errand.

Her mother had encouraged her to take one of the more prestigious positions, telling her she could cope with the twins, her house, and job with no problem. But Ariel used the excuse the Missionary Ridge position wouldn't have the pressures of a major university and would afford her the opportunity to see whether teaching was what she preferred, instead of going into research. If she found she liked teaching, she could always accept a professorship at one of the more prestigious universities.

Now she had a decision to make—a difficult decision. She could let her mother go to trial and accept the consequences, offering what support she could. Or she could consider taking up Ms. O'Shay's offer if it meant her mother would be safe. Logic dictated one decision would be the path of least resistance to help her family. But it would by no means be the easy choice for herself and her future.

Throwing her head back, she pressed her hands to her face before ordering, "Telecom on. Contact Brice Stafford, audio only."

"Brice Stafford," her teaching assistant said.

"This is Ariel, I have an emergency."

KIERNAN WAS SKIMMING over the latest online issue of *The Wall Street Journal* when Kelly announced over the desk-com, "Ms. O'Shay."

"Yes, Kelly?"

"Security at the front desk states that a Ms. Ariel Thorsen got past the guard at the front gate and is now here demanding to speak with you. They want to know whether they should call the police—"

"Of course not. Have security send her to my office right away," Kiernan crisply ordered.

"Yes, ma'am."

Kiernan knew Ariel was here to plead her mother's case. If she were in Ariel's shoes, she would do the same. She wanted to see Ariel, but not under these circumstances.

Not a day passed she didn't think about Ariel and what she could have done to convince her to accept her proposal. In a way, she was angry with Ariel and thought her a fool. She could provide her and her family a secure future. She admitted part of her anger was because Ariel had dealt a blow to her ego by refusing her offer. But the greater part of her anger was due to Ariel making it difficult for Kiernan to obtain what she wanted.

"Ms. O'Shay...Hey, you can't...come back..." Kelly's voice said over the desk-com.

The office door opened forcefully and Ariel strode in with an irate Kelly following close behind.

"Ms. O'Shay, I —" Kelly protested.

"It's all right, Kelly, you may go," Kiernan said, and stood behind her desk to face her visitor.

Kelly shot Ariel a glare before exiting the office.

Kiernan surveyed Ariel, noticing her black jacket, blue jeans, and a pair of black Tefla-hide boots. Her hair was in a ponytail, leaving no doubt she had ridden her motorcycle over. With a stiff stance, she glared at Kiernan with outright hostility.

"Have a seat so we can talk." Kiernan motioned with her hand toward the armchair in front of her desk.

Ariel ignored Kiernan's request, her voice strident and accusing. "This is your way of getting back at me for not accepting your proposal, isn't it?"

Feeling a rush of anger, Kiernan replied with irritation. "I resent that remark. I would never do anything like that. That's not me. Not me at all."

"So you say. You expect me to believe that?"

"Yes, because it's the truth," Kiernan said emphatically, annoyance still evident in her tone.

"No, it's not."

Kiernan let go of her anger with a sigh. She knew nothing she could say would convince Ariel otherwise. "She failed the polygraph test."

"I don't care. My mother isn't a liar or a thief. She didn't need the money. How do you explain that?" Ariel followed her words with a challenging stare.

"I'm sorry. I know you believe her and I respect your loyalty. But, I can't let her get away with this. If I do that, others will attempt it. Corporate espionage is a crime. She could have damaged this company. I'm sure, seeing as she has no criminal record, or even a speeding ticket, the judge will be lenient. Perhaps a few months in jail—"

"I'll do it," Ariel said quietly.

"Do what?"

"Marry you and have your child, *if* you don't press charges against my mother."

Kiernan couldn't believe what she was hearing. This is what she wanted. But did she want Ariel like this—coming to her under these circumstances? Ariel would always believe Kiernan set this up and she'd resent her. But Kiernan would have Stellardyne and the resources she needed.

Kiernan tapped a button on her desk-com. "Kelly, cancel my three o'clock meeting with quality control, and get Mr. O'Shay in my office, pronto."

"Very well, ma'am."

Kiernan saw Ariel was pale and had placed her right hand on the back of the chair for support. "Have a seat, Ariel, before you drop." She went to her bar. "Can I get you anything to drink?"

Ariel ignored the offer. "Does your proposal still stand?"

Kiernan finished pouring her drink and took a sip of brandy before leaving the glass on the bar. Turning to Ariel, she searched her eyes. "Yes, my proposal still stands. Fifty million a year to you, and twenty million for your family. There are, of course, a few more things I would like to include in the agreement."

"What things?" Ariel asked suspiciously.

"If you take a seat I'll tell you."

Ariel slipped into the chair and perched on the edge. Kiernan walked to the front of her desk and leaned back against it, facing her. "I want you to take the name O'Shay. Our child will also carry the name O'Shay."

Ariel nodded in agreement though her frown conveyed her distaste.

"You're going to be my wife. And you'll have obligations as my wife. One obligation is that you must maintain a certain decorum, and you'll have specific duties. I expect you to accompany me to any social function I attend, be it related to business or otherwise. There'll be times I entertain at home and at those times you'll be expected to be by my side and act as a gracious host.

"This includes you showing me respect in public. I don't expect you to fawn over me, but I would like for you to at least pretend you hold some regard for me."

Ariel closed her eyes, her posture sagging slightly, and let out a resigned sigh. "All right."

"There is another matter. You will tender your resignation from your teaching position effective immediately."

Ariel's eyes popped open, and she straightened up. "I can't do that! I'm under contract until June."

"All you have to do is tender your resignation and tell them it is family related, and you must resign at once. If they give you a hard time, I'll deal with them."

"Please enlighten me as to the reason for your...command...before I do that."

"I want you to have time to adjust to your new status and duties as my wife—and after our child is born, you'll have enough duties taking care of her to occupy your time. My grandmother's will states I'm to stay in the marriage for at least five years, and we will reside together throughout the duration of our marriage. I expect you to agree to this, and reside in my home, Crestview."

Ariel put her head in her hands and shook it in apparent disbelief.

"Oh, since I am required to have an heir within the next two years, you will agree to be impregnated with an ovum, which contains both of our DNA, within one year after we're married."

Kiernan heard the shuddering breath Ariel took before she said, "Yes."

"I'll have those things put in the contract. However, this won't go into the contract, but will be part of an oral agreement between us. You will have no further contact with Mysha Leavill."

Ariel stared at her in disbelief. "You can't do that. She has a right to know!"

"She has no rights! Not where you're concerned." For some reason, Ariel's statement infuriated her. She took a moment to calm herself and continued, "You may contact her by telecom and tell her you're breaking it off with her, but you will not see her, and you—"

"God damn you to hell, Kiernan O'Shay!" Tears rolled down Ariel's cheeks. She wiped them away with her hand.

"Ariel—"

Kiernan started to say more, only to have Kelly interrupt her by announcing over the desk-com, "Ms. O'Shay, Mr. O'Shay is here to see you."

"Tell him to wait a few minutes. I'll tell you when he can come in."

"Yes, ma'am."

Kiernan walked to the other side of her desk, opened a drawer, and withdrew a box of tissues. She handed the box over to Ariel, waiting while she dried her tears.

When she saw Ariel was composed, she said, "Did you tell anyone of my proposal and the reasons for it?"

"I only told my mother," Ariel glared pointedly at Kiernan "after your false accusations."

Kiernan didn't let her irritation show at that last remark. "Was there anyone else?"

"Ian Broxton, my mother's attorney."

Ian Broxton was reputed to be honest and wouldn't reveal what was an attorney/client confidence. "Caution your mother if she tells anyone the reasons behind my proposal it won't only embarrass me, but you as well. I don't want people thinking you're a gold digger, or that I bought you. I'll create a story of how we met and fell in love, and you'll go along with it."

"My mother will know why I'm marrying you. That you're a vindictive bitch!"

"I may be a bitch, but I'm not vindictive, at least not where you're concerned. This is about me getting Stellardyne. I know these are unusual circumstances. And as such, I don't want to make a big social event out of this. As I'm sure, you don't either. We will have a private ceremony at Crestview, attended by immediate family, and my household staff. I'll arrange it for the Saturday following this one." Kiernan wanted it soon so Ariel wouldn't change her mind.

"But...that's only eight days away."

"That shouldn't present a problem, unless you have something more pressing to do," Kiernan said in a tone of voice that said she knew Ariel had no plans, pressing or otherwise.

Ariel exhaled. "I guess that day is as good as any."

"I want you to come out to Crestview tomorrow morning and get acquainted with your new home and the staff. I'll come by your place at nine to pick you up."

Ariel glared at Kiernan, her voice indignant. "Crestview will never be my home."

"That might be how you feel. However, it'll be where you will reside for the foreseeable future. I'll also talk with your mother when I come out to pick you up."

"Don't expect a warm welcome."

Not commenting, Kiernan leaned over her desk to push a button on the desk-com. "Kelly, send in Mr. O'Shay."

"Yes, ma'am."

Kiernan returned her attention to Ariel, not saying anything further, but noticing she was still upset.

The door opened and Theodore entered. "Kiernan, what's...Ms. Thorsen?"

"Ms. Thorsen—Ariel—has agreed to marry me, and we need the prenuptial agreement drawn up as soon as possible. I need you to clear your calendar today so I can get with you and go over some of the details."

"I can arrange to have it done, but what's the rush?"

"The wedding is going to be held a week from tomorrow in a private ceremony at Crestview."

Brief surprise passed over Theodore's face. "I'll be able to have it done by next Tuesday for you and Ms. Thorsen to go over."

"Very well. We won't be pressing charges against Joanna Thorsen."

"I'll take care of it," Theodore said.

Kiernan said to Ariel, "I'll arrange for David to take you home. I don't want you on your motorcycle—not while you're upset."

"I'm perfectly capable."

"You don't need to be taking your bike out on the road—"

"Dammit! Don't tell me what I need, or don't need! I'm riding it home!"

Noticing Ariel's flushed face and frown, Kiernan decided not to press the point and make Ariel more upset.

Ariel stood. "If that's all?"

"Uncle Theodore, please give us a few minutes alone."

Theodore exited the room, closing the door quietly behind him.

Kiernan walked up to Ariel, searching her face and eyes, before softly saying, "Ariel, we can make this work. We can make this into what a marriage should be. I'm willing to try."

Ariel lurched back, disbelief on her features. She met Kiernan's eyes with a glacial glare and said contemptuously, "Get this straight, Ms. O'Shay, I hate you, and that's not going to happen. Not in a million years." She pivoted and stomped out of Kiernan's office.

Kiernan watched her go, thinking the five years the will was consigning her to could very well feel like a million years—especially if Ariel held on to her resentment. Then she remembered that old adage "Time changes everything." She would have to wait and see whether it would apply to this marriage.

"WHAT? YOU CAN'T be serious!" Joanna was beyond shock, feeling she had entered some surreal world.

"I'm very serious," Ariel replied. "I've agreed—"

"No! You're not marrying her. I forbid it!" Joanna sprang from her chair to gape at her daughter, who sat on the edge of the sofa.

"I've agreed. If I go back on my word, there's no telling what she'll do."

"I don't care, you're not doing it!"

Ariel stood, placing both hands on her mother's shoulders. "It's my choice, and the only choice."

Joanna broke out of the grasp, agitation in her movements. "No, Ariel, it's not. I won't allow you to do this—not for my sake."

"It's not only for your sake. Think of the twins. Ms. O'Shay was prepared to press charges against you. If you go to prison—what then?"

"That's a chance I'm willing to take."

"No, Mom. You can't take that chance. Sit down. I want to tell you some details of what I discussed with her."

"I'll not hear them."

"Please, Mom, listen, that's all I'm asking."

Silence stretched for a good ten seconds until Joanna sighed and said, "Fine, but I'm not changing my mind about this. And what about Mysha?"

Ariel's eyes ghosted over with pain. "I'll handle things with Mysha. But for now, listen, and please don't say anything until I finish."

Joanna took a seat on the sofa, and Ariel sat beside her to fill her in on the main details of the agreement. Joanna bit the inside of her mouth to keep from commenting. Finally, Ariel finished and searched her mother's eyes as if hoping for some understanding.

An oppressive sadness pushed Joanna near to tears. "Sweetheart, what you're doing is sacrificing yourself, and the child you'll have, and you know it. I don't care if she gives us a billion dollars a year, it's not worth it, and I won't accept her money." She put her hands on either side of Ariel's head and searched her eyes. "Sweetheart, please don't do this. We'll fight her."

"We can't take that chance. Think of the twins and how you being imprisoned would affect them. I have to tell you truthfully, Mom, I'd have a hard time taking care of them without you."

"It's worth a try."

"No, it's not. I'll not risk it and neither should you. Even if you're found innocent, you'll still have a reputation in shambles, and people will know the details. It'll be all over the news. You won't be able to get a decent job, and this could jeopardize Seth and

Leigh's chances of attending the best colleges. Your trial could stretch out for months, even over a year, and the legal cost would be exorbitant. I can't allow this to happen. Not when there's a way out."

"Sweetheart, marrying her will ruin your life."

"It's my decision and nothing you can say will change it now."

Joanna searched her daughter's eyes. Ariel had a decidedly stubborn streak. Once she made up her mind, you stood little chance of changing it. Oh, she would listen to whatever advice Joanna offered, and often she saw the logic in the advice and might choose another course of action, but hearing her daughter now, Joanna knew Ariel was set on this course. Nothing she said would change it—not on this, maybe the most important decision Ariel would ever make in her life. Not only the most important, but also one that had far more serious consequences for now, and the future. Joanna couldn't protect Ariel from the consequences she would reap, only offer advice her daughter might or might not follow. "I want you to contact Ian Broxton before you sign any agreement."

"I'll do that."

Joanna started weeping, drawing her daughter into a close embrace.

Ariel's own tears fell as well, but there was one thing about which she was certain: no sacrifice was too great for her family.

JOANNA RETIRED EARLY from exhaustion and grief, leaving the twins in Ariel's care when they got in from school. Ariel told them their mother didn't feel well and to let her rest. She didn't feel like cooking dinner, so she let them decide which Pop-hot to eat. When they retired to their respective rooms to do their homework, she went to her own room.

She reached for her IMP on the nightstand by her bed and checked to see whether there were any calls. One message was from Mysha. She'd called Mysha early yesterday morning to update her on the polygraph test. Mysha was sympathetic and supportive, even volunteering to fly home right away after the awards ceremony on Friday night and not wait until Sunday. Ariel informed her not to do it, that at this point nothing could be done.

With shaking hands, she ordered the IMP, "Play message."

Mysha's image appeared on the screen. "Hello, babe. I miss you and I hope your mom is doing well. I know this is tough on you, and I wish I were there to help. I'll be home a week from Sunday to help out any way I can. I know Beijing time is fourteen hours ahead of you, but don't hesitate to call at anytime. I'll try calling you Monday at seven in the morning, your time, before you leave for work.

"The workshop is going great and almost everyone here has read my paper and thinks it's wonderful. Well, I had better go. Give my best to your mom. See you Sunday. Bye bye."

Ariel dropped the IMP on her bed and smothered sobs into her pillow to keep the twins and her mother from hearing. How was she going to break the news to Mysha that she was marrying Kiernan O'Shay? Oh, God, why now? she thought. This is one of the most important times in Mysha's life — receiving recognition for her work — and how could Ariel ruin it for her? She would have to explain when Mysha got back. Ariel didn't care what Kiernan O'Shay wanted. Mysha deserved to know why.

Her thoughts shifted to Kiernan, rage engulfing her, and she screamed into her pillow, her words muffled, but the anguish behind them was understandable: "I hate you! I hate you!"

Chapter Eleven

THE BLUE SEPTEMBER sky promised a good day. The sunlight had that certain slant giving everything a golden sheen portending the change of the season from summer to fall. Kiernan exited her silver BMW, smoothed down her chocolate brown jacket over her camel pullover blouse and straightened the waist of her chocolate brown trousers. She surveyed the modest residence of her fiancée and saw a slight movement of a curtain in the living room window.

On the stoop she reached out to push the doorbell, but before her finger touched the button, the front door opened. Joanna Thorsen stared at her with disdain.

"Ms. Thorsen, may I come in?"

Joanna moved aside, allowing Kiernan to enter. She said nothing, and Kiernan glanced around before directing her attention to Joanna expectantly. "Is Ariel here?"

"Yes, she's in her room. I understand you want to talk to me," Joanna stated in a chilling voice. "I also have some things I want to say to you...in private." Joanna led her into the living room. "Have a seat, Ms. O'Shay, it doesn't matter which one."

Kiernan sat at one end of the sofa and Joanna sat in a recliner at an angle, facing Kiernan. They stared at one another for a few uncomfortable seconds before Kiernan said, "Ms. Thorsen, I can imagine how you feel. Your—"

"Don't dare presume to imagine how I feel," Joanna said in a voice shaking with rage, her face livid. "You have no idea how I feel. You've destroyed this family—destroyed my daughter's happiness. For what? For your own selfish ends, that's what. I hope I live to see the day you pay for this!"

Kiernan locked her eyes on Joanna's. It was all she could do to keep a straight face. The unmitigated gall of this woman to pretend she was the wounded party, when she brought this on her family by stealing from Stellardyne. She knew whatever she said had little chance of being well received, so she decided to get right to the point. "Ariel and I made an agreement. I didn't force her into doing this—"

"Yes, Ariel informed me she approached you. But I think you falsely accused me knowing my daughter would do this. Had she not gone to you first, you would have sought her out and made the offer not to prosecute me if she entered into this agreement."

Kiernan couldn't believe what she was hearing and had to fight back her anger. "I'll not discuss this anymore. What I have come to say is the reasons for this marriage—both my reasons and the reason Ariel accepted—must be kept within the family. It could cause problems down the road if those reasons were ever made known, with not only me, but with you, as well as with Ariel, our child, and your family."

"Rest assured, Ms. O'Shay, I'm aware of that and have no intention of disclosing the reasons."

"Thank you."

"Another thing—I don't want your filthy money. My daughter isn't for sale."

"I never intended it like that—"

"I don't care how it was intended. I don't want it. Give it to a charity."

Kiernan kept her expression stoic, but inside she was seething, thinking Ms. Thorsen should get an Academy Award for her act. She wouldn't refuse the money. "I'll leave that up to you to do. Please, tell Ariel I'm ready to go."

Without saying a word, Joanna rose from the chair and left the living room.

Kiernan let out a frustrated sigh, and mumbled, "Ha! That sure went well."

Hearing a rustling sound, Kiernan glanced up to see Ariel walk partway into the living room, stop, and regard her with wintry eyes. Kiernan stood and surveyed her, taking in Ariel's pink, button-down long-sleeve dress shirt, tucked into a pair of dark red dress slacks with its thin black belt encircling her waist. "You look very nice."

Ariel ignored the comment, her voice bland. "I'm ready."

Kiernan walked to the door and Ariel followed. Joanna didn't make an appearance.

Once they got into the car, Kiernan ordered, "Ignition on. Destination, Crestview Estates."

THEY RODE IN silence for a few blocks. Ariel studied the interior of the car, noticing the wood inserts on the dash and the light gray seats. She stealthily moved her right hand down to the side of the seat, feeling it. She bet it was real leather and not Teflahide or any other of the faux stuff. Expensive cars never impressed her. She felt a glimmer of amusement when she thought if Kiernan had ridden up on a Harley Road King, she might have been impressed.

The silence was broken when Kiernan said, "I didn't see your brother and sister. I'm eager to meet them."

"They spent the night with their friends."

"I'm assuming you've told them you're getting married."

"Yes, last night. They weren't informed of the reason why, and were instructed to keep quiet about the...wedding, until after the ceremony."

"How did they take it?"

"They were surprised." Both had asked her why she wasn't marrying Mysha. She told them she and Mysha were now only friends and she wanted to marry Kiernan. It made her even angrier with Kiernan that she had to lie. Much to her chagrin, the twins thought it was "Mega Supreme" as they were sure she could persuade Kiernan to take them on a tour of *Celeste*.

Kiernan said, "I have my chef preparing something for lunch I'm sure you'll like." She glanced at Ariel. "How do grilled chicken breasts on homemade sourdough rolls and a garden salad sound?"

"Okay, I guess," Ariel said in a disinterested voice.

An awkward silence ensued. Ariel watched the scenery out the passenger window.

A few minutes later Kiernan said, "I arranged a trip for us to the Caribbean after the wedding."

Ariel remained silent, continuing to stare at the view out the window while thinking, oh yeah, this is just peachy. A honeymoon. I hope she doesn't expect anything. *That's* not going to happen.

"Have you ever been to the Caribbean?"

Ariel shot her a sideway glance, keeping her answer flat. "No."

"I think you'll like it. We'll fly down on my strato-jet two days after the wedding and stay for a week. I own a villa in Saint Thomas where we'll stay. I also have a yacht I keep there. The Virgin Islands are beautiful — white sandy beaches, snorkeling, even fishing if you want."

Ariel returned her attention to the passing scenery, pointedly avoiding any comment, and thinking she needed to plan ways to keep from interacting with Kiernan while on this...trip. Maybe she would take a selection of e-books to read, and say she didn't feel well.

They drove on in silence, Ariel's thoughts on Mysha, who had called right at seven o'clock that morning. The beep of the IMP woke Ariel from a sound sleep, which she had slipped into around three a.m. after an exhausting bout of disturbing dreams.

It was dark in her room, so Mysha couldn't see her very well on her IMP's vid screen, but she was able to hear the exhaustion and strain in Ariel's voice and asked whether she was okay. Ariel explained that the stress of the accusations against her mother, and not knowing what would happen, was getting to her. They talked a few minutes more — or rather, Mysha talked while Ariel listened. Mysha was excited about the upcoming awards ceremony and had written a speech. The event was being video recorded. Mysha would obtain a copy and show Ariel after arriving home. After the call, Ariel was wound too tight to return to sleep, so she reluctantly got up to start her day.

Ariel heard Kiernan say, "Computer. Request music. Selection two." Right away, a song from a popular musical began to play over the car's stereo system.

After traveling a few miles, they merged into I-75 and proceeded north until exiting onto US 64/74 east, passing through Cleveland. A couple of miles past Ocoee, they exited onto a road skirting the Ocoee River, continuing for a few more miles until veering onto a one lane road leading up a mountain.

Kiernan ordered, "Computer, music off." The music stopped. "We're almost there." A pause and Kiernan said, "Ariel, you'll be meeting my staff, and I would appreciate it if you would show me some consideration and not be so distant."

Ariel asked sharply, "What exactly do you want me to do…Ms. O'Shay?"

Kiernan glanced at her with a frown, impatience in her tone. "Can you at least act cordial? And please call me Kiernan. I'm your fiancée."

Ariel had a sudden impulse to give Kiernan a derisive laugh. Controlling it, she assumed a lackadaisical expression and voice. "I'll make an effort to do so…Kiernan."

"Thank you," Kiernan replied brusquely, waiting a few seconds before adding, "I know this marriage is far from ideal for both of us, but it's necessary if I'm to reach my goals. Telecom on. Voice only. Crestview."

Ariel ignored her, but inside she was seething. Kiernan O'Shay was a selfish bitch. Nothing and no one mattered except her goals and dreams. She didn't care who she hurt to achieve her ambitions.

After three chimes, a voice over the telecom said, "Crestview, Mrs. Belfort speaking."

"Mrs. Belfort, we should be there in five minutes."

"Yes, ma'am. I'll inform the staff of your arrival."

Ahead lay a guard station and by it a gate across the road. Kiernan said, "This is the main entrance. There are three unpaved roads, trails actually, leading up to the estate. The roads surrounding the property are patrolled day and night, so if you ever go out for a stroll outside the main estate grounds in the evening, please notify the guard station. I wouldn't want you accidentally stun-gunned."

"Thanks for the warning."

"Oh, we do have the occasional bear wander onto the grounds. They'll leave you alone if you leave them alone. If you walk after dark, it would be a good idea to carry pepper gas and an IMP with you, just in case."

Ariel considered this for a moment. "I don't think I'll be taking any midnight strolls."

Kiernan stopped the car in front of the gate. A guard in a tan suit exited the station as Kiernan ordered the computer to lower her window.

He scanned her eyes with a retina identification device. "Ms. O'Shay, I see you have a guest. Do you wish her registered?"

"Yes, Troy, I do. This is my fiancée, Ariel Thorsen."

"Congratulations." He glanced over to the passenger side. "Ms. Thorsen, stay where you are and I'll walk around to you and do the scan."

"Computer, lower passenger window." Kiernan said to Ariel, "A precaution. Everyone I know who comes here regularly, or works here, has a retina scan, including me. This prevents impostors."

Ariel could well understand someone like Kiernan taking these precautions, especially in light of the kidnapping of the prime minister of France's two children in 2086, when an impostor had plastic surgery done to resemble the children's aunt, entered the prime minister's residence, and abducted them. They were never seen again after a ransom was paid. No one knew their fate.

Troy arrived at the passenger window, holding out the retina scanner in front of Ariel's eyes. "Fix your eyes on the red light," he said, "and don't blink."

Ariel did as instructed, and after a few seconds, Troy removed the device and said, "All scanned and on record. Have a nice day."

Troy swiftly trotted back to the station and opened the electronic gate. Kiernan drove through, and after going some three hundred yards, she steered in between two gray and tan natural stone posts on either side of a one lane paved road. Spanning the posts at the top was a wrought iron arch with an elaborate design worked into it consisting of the words *Crestview 2037*.

The house was hidden from view by the row of old hemlock trees lining the road. A few hundred yards down, the road made a sweeping curve, providing Ariel a good view of the grandeur of Crestview. She had researched and seen pictures online, but they didn't do the house justice. The house was crafted from native stone and Alabama steel forged especially for the house in an antique Birmingham mill. The sun glinted off the tinted picture windows dominating the edifice. The deeply pitched roof with wide overhanging eaves reminded her of pictures she had seen of

Swiss chalets.

Kiernan swung the car around the circular drive and parked it at the end of a flagstone walk. A wide set of steps led up to a broad veranda with stone railings.

Waiting for them was Mr. Washington, Kiernan's chauffeur, and a young red-haired man. Both were dressed in outfits consisting of a gray coats, white shirts, pale pink ties, and gray pants. The young man opened Ariel's door and held out his hand. She took his hand and he assisted her out of the car. Mr. Washington opened Kiernan's door and helped her out. She joined Ariel on the flagstone walk and introduced her, "Ariel, you've already met David Washington. He's the senior chauffeur and manager of the garage."

His deep voice conveyed warmth. "Welcome to Crestview, Ms. Thorsen."

"Thank you, Mr. Washington."

Next, Kiernan introduced her to the lanky redhead. "This is Michael McLeod. He's the junior chauffeur and David's assistant. He will be your chauffeur."

"Welcome, Ms. Thorsen," he said shyly.

"Thank you, Mr. McLeod." Ariel wanted to say, thanks but no thanks, I can drive myself, but now wasn't the time to argue the point.

"Call me Michael, ma'am."

"Michael," she acknowledged, smiling when he flushed beet red. She thought she could certainly relate to how he was feeling, as she too was cursed with the blush genes.

David said, "I'll show you in, Ms. O'Shay. The staff is in the dining room waiting to meet Ms. Thorsen."

"Very well, lead the way."

They walked up the wide steps, onto the stone veranda, and up to a set of tan double doors. David opened the doors and moved aside, allowing Kiernan and Ariel to enter before he and Michael followed.

Ariel trailed Kiernan into the foyer, hearing their footsteps resound on the polished, light gray stone floor. Kiernan ambled around the foyer wall and into an open and airy living room with golden oak floors. Right away, Ariel saw floor-to-ceiling windows that provided a breathtaking view of the Cherokee National Forest and mountains. She took in the massive fireplace with its light gray stone front and noted how it reached to the ceiling. Over the mantel of golden oak was an oil painting that from the distance appeared to be a waterfall. There were two dark blue overstuffed recliners she was sure were real leather, a love seat, and a sofa, done in matching and complementary fabrics of blue, pale blue, ivory, and gold stripes. Various carpets lay scattered about on the oak floor. A grandfather clock made of golden oak and burnished gold-toned metal stood against one wall.

Kiernan led Ariel into a dining room where five people were gathered in front of a table. Kiernan introduced her to a solidly built middle-aged woman dressed in a white long sleeve shirt and black skirt. Her gray hair was gathered into a bun. "Ariel, this is Mrs. Marla Belfort. She's my steward and runs my household."

"Welcome, Ms. Thorsen. We all welcome you to Crestview," Mrs. Belfort said graciously.

"Thank you."

"This is Faye Lloyd," Kiernan said. "She's in charge of maintaining and programming the housekeeping robots, as well as troubleshooting any computer problems." Faye was a stout, middle-aged woman with faded red hair and a moon face.

Faye gave a friendly nod.

"This is Dora Valdez. She's Ms. Lloyd's assistant." Kiernan introduced a young, petite, caramel-skinned woman with dark hair and dark flashing eyes.

Dora smiled shyly and Ariel returned her smile.

Kiernan next introduced a man who appeared to be in his early thirties. "Ricardo Leon is my chef. I've had people try to steal him away from me, he's that good."

Ricardo was of medium height and build. He wore his black hair cropped against his scalp, and his blue eyes were very noticeable in his tanned features. "And the reason I don't leave is that Ms. O'Shay has liked everything I've prepared and has never once complained." He winked and added, "And she pays very well."

Kiernan laughed. "Ricardo, you're worth what I pay." She turned her attention to the handsome, slender dark-skinned man standing next to her chef, introducing him. "This is Robert Jones. He's Ricardo's assistant."

"Hello, Ms. Thorsen." His voice was a rich tenor.

Ariel said, "Hello to you too."

Kiernan said to her steward, "Mrs. Belfort, I believe a toast is in order."

"Yes, ma'am, a toast is definitely called for," Mrs. Belfort said. She indicated a bottle of champagne sitting in a silver ice bucket on the table. A number of crystal flutes were lined up in front. David and Michael had joined the group, and she addressed David. "Mr. Washington, please assist me."

David took the bottle out of the ice bucket, and Ariel saw it was Dom Perignon. She drank very little alcohol, but knew the price for a bottle was astronomically expensive. David worked the cork off with a loud pop, and the bottle emitted a faint fog of gas, but the contents did not foam out. He filled the glasses, and Mrs. Belfort handed the first to Ariel, one to Kiernan, and distributed the rest of the glasses to the staff.

Mrs. Belfort made the toast. "This is indeed a happy time for us here at Crestview. We welcome you, Ms. Thorsen, and eagerly anticipate having you here as the wife of our employer, Ms. O'Shay. We wish you and Ms. O'Shay all the happiness this life has to offer."

All drank the toasts, but Ariel took only a sip of her drink.

Kiernan's eyes twinkled. "I would like to propose a toast. David, let's have a refill."

David filled everyone's glass, and Kiernan gazed at Ariel, saying solemnly, "I am indeed a fortunate woman to have you come into my life. I look forward to our life together as a married couple."

The staff called out, "Hear, hear" and downed their drinks. It was all Ariel could do to take a sip. She pasted on a smile and tried to inflect some warmth into her tone. "Thank you, Kiernan." She couldn't force herself to say the same.

"THE WEST WING houses the staff, laundry room, storage areas, and the air and heating facility. But first, I'll show you what's downstairs in the east wing, and then we'll go upstairs."

Ariel followed Kiernan down a wide hall with various nature prints decorating the wall. Kiernan stopped at a door on the left and opened it, moving aside to let Ariel enter first. "This is the library. I have many first editions and you're welcome to read them, but there are special procedures you have to use in reading some of the more fragile books. Mrs. Belfort will tell you what they are." Ariel noticed the orderly shelves of books and the enclosed bookcases probably containing the more rare editions.

She was next shown Kiernan's study, and from there they went to a recreation room complete with a pool table, EM, antique pinball machines, and a state-of-the-art interactive game room allowing one to feel as if they could step into the game and interact with the three-dimensional characters.

Kiernan opened another door. "This room is yours to use for an office or anyway you see fit." The room contained a beautiful pecan wood desk with a polished surface holding a computer and telecom system. A matching bookcase stood against one wall.

From there they walked to the far end of the hall to see a spacious gym area complete with all the latest exercise equipment and a sauna room.

The tour of the downstairs completed, Kiernan led her upstairs and showed her four spacious guestrooms.

Ariel followed her down the hall to another door which Kiernan opened. "This will be your suite of rooms. Come on in and I'll show you where everything is located." She entered into what was apparently a sitting room with a moderate-size fireplace. Light blue trim accented cream walls hung with various nature prints. A blue and cream sofa sat to one side of the fireplace. In front of the sofa was a coffee table of rich, tan wood that matched the end tables on each side of the sofa. An EM sat upon it. Across from the coffee table, a light blue recliner angled toward the fireplace. Against one wall was a half-moon console table with a wall mirror over it, and a door set to the left. On the opposite side were a bar and a desk with a computer and telecom.

"You're free to change the décor and purchase whatever you want in the furniture line," Kiernan said.

"No. It's very lovely."

"Thank you. I chose the theme and the furniture."

She led Ariel through another door. Ariel had never seen such a big bedroom except in magazine pictures.

It was light and airy due to the view window on one wall. A queen-size bed with a headboard made from light-colored wood had been positioned close by the window. A patchwork quilt, in various colors, covered the bed. One corner of the room held a love seat upholstered in various shades of blue velvet. Against one wall sat a chest of drawers and a dresser in a color matching the headboard.

Kiernan opened a door in one corner of the room. "This is your dressing room and closet." Ariel walked in and saw a vanity on the wall with a lighted mirror. On one side of the wall a full-length mirror was mounted. This room led to a walk-in closet with hangers and shelves on each side, as well as a shoe rack. The closet alone was almost as big as her bedroom at home. Ariel knew she could never fill a closet this size.

They toured the spacious bathroom next and Ariel was impressed with the floor of sky blue marble swirled with lighter and darker colors of blue. An enormous sunken tub backdropped by a full-length window with a view of the mountains caught Ariel's attention. "Ah...no one can see in, can they?"

"Not at all. The windows have a special tint allowing you to see out, but they're impossible to see through from outdoors. If you don't want a view of the outside, you can darken them. Computer, darken window."

Ariel watched the window gradually darken. "Is the computer system active throughout the house?"

"Yes, but don't worry, there are no hidden vid or audio devices to spy on you. I have the computer programmed to do ordinary things like turn lights and appliances off and on. It also controls the EM, which has emitters in every room, even in here so you can watch your favorite shows while relaxing in a hot tub or listen to your favorite music. EM on. Video on." A 3-D image appeared high on the wall, over the tub. "EM off. There is a separate intercom system on the night stand by your bed in case you need to contact Mrs. Belfort."

They walked back out into the bedroom, and Ariel followed Kiernan over to the one remaining door. Kiernan opened the door and moved back to allow Ariel to peer in. "This is the nursery. Most of the furnishings are mine from when I was a baby, so we'll need to refurnish it with more modern items...when the time comes."

Ariel swallowed hard, feeling her stomach flutter nervously. She didn't comment and noticed Kiernan was watching her.

Kiernan must have seen her unease, because she closed the door behind her and headed back out into the sitting room. She opened another door next to the console table and Ariel followed her into a sitting room very similar to the one she was to have, except the colors were muted blues and grays.

"This is my suite. The main entrance is next to yours out in the hall." Kiernan led her into the bedroom. Seeing the bed with its slender cherry wood pillars at each corner caused Ariel some embarrassment at being in such a personal place. The other furniture in the room matched the bed. "This bedroom suite is a family heirloom and dates from the beginning of the twentieth century."

Kiernan had provided a commentary on every room they entered, much as she did on *Celeste*. Ariel couldn't imagine living in a house this grandiose, and she seriously doubted she would ever feel Crestview was home.

THE MELLOW CHIMING of the grandfather clock downstairs in the living room marked the midday hour.

Kiernan said, "I hope you're as hungry as I am."

"Yes, I am," Ariel admitted, surprised that during such a stressful day she could even think of something as mundane as food.

"We'll take lunch in the garden room."

Once downstairs, Kiernan led Ariel through the dining room and into a light and airy room. A table sitting in front of a window provided a lovely view of the garden. Robert stood waiting by the table and pulled the chairs out for them to take their seats. Kiernan settled back into her chair, noticing Ariel observing the garden where two squat garden bots were attending to the profusion of various fall flowers.

Robert waited a few seconds, before saying, "Ms. Thorsen, Ricardo has prepared seasoned chicken breast on a sourdough roll. To accompany this, there is a garden salad, and for dessert, homemade apple pie. May I inquire as to the condiments you would like on your sandwich and the dressing for your salad?"

"Mayonnaise, please. For the salad, I'd like oil and vinegar."

"Our selections of beverages are hot tea, iced sweet tea, white wine, various colas, or coffee."

"Do you have milk?"

"Yes, ma'am, we do. Skim milk and whole milk."

Ariel appeared confused before asking, "You mean...dairy milk? From cows?"

"Yes, ma'am, from cows."

"I'll have a glass of whole dairy milk, please," she said, sounding a tad eager and wearing a pleased expression.

Kiernan smiled indulgently when she heard Ariel's order. By Ariel's pleased manner, she could tell dairy milk wasn't on the menu at the Thorsen residence. It was a rare commodity these days, and expensive, most people able only to afford the soymilk substitute.

The bovine species nearly went extinct with the spread of a devastating virus in the late 2020's. It wasn't until the early 2050's that an effective anti-viral was discovered. Dairy and beef cattle herds were rebuilt, so to speak, from frozen bovine embryos, semen, and ovum, but a few more decades would pass before the dairy and beef herds reached the numbers where real dairy products and beef would be plentiful and affordable enough for the average citizens of the world to include in their weekly diet.

Robert asked, "Ma'am, what will you have with your sandwich and salad?"

"I'll have mayonnaise on my sandwich, Caesar dressing for the salad, and a glass of sweet tea."

He departed, and Ariel returned her attention to the garden while Kiernan studied her bride-to-be, thinking she would like to see Ariel sitting at this table everyday taking lunch with her. Of course, that would happen only on the weekends and holidays when she was home from the office.

On many days, Kiernan took her breakfast in her suite, and she let her thoughts wander to imagining Ariel joining her. An image unexpectedly flashed in her mind of Ariel in a blue silk robe sitting across from her at the table in her sitting room. This brought to mind another image of waking up in the morning with Ariel sleeping next to her in bed. Robert interrupted those thoughts by bringing in their lunch and placing it before them.

As they ate, Kiernan relayed to Ariel the history of Crestview, then covered the story of her grandmother's life and the founding of Stellardyne. Kiernan could tell Ariel was intrigued to learn Shanna O'Shay started out manufacturing her unique design for atomic thrust engines for the military and branched out into spaceship manufacturing sixty years ago.

Ariel even managed to ask questions without sounding surly. Kiernan thought that at least they had two things in common: an interest in spaceships and theories on light-speed travel. Perhaps these common interests were enough to create a friendship, if nothing else.

ARIEL HAD TO admit the lunch was delicious. The apple pie she was finishing up was to die for, as was the glass of real milk. Kiernan had informed her the apples were from Crestview's own apple orchard that had existed on the property before Crestview's construction. The orchard had originally been part of a holding from around the mid-twentieth century.

Ariel was finishing her milk when Kiernan said, "I've made arrangements with Christiana Sinclair to have you fitted for an outfit for the wedding, as well as other clothing you'll require for our trip. I'll pick you up Monday morning at eight."

The latest fashions never interested Ariel, but she did know Christiana Sinclair was the owner of Christiana's, located in Atlanta, which was one of the most exclusive and expensive dress boutiques in the South.

Ariel asked uncertainly, "You mean...a wedding dress?" She found herself envisioning something traditional in white. She should show up for the wedding in a pair of ratty jeans and her black biker jacket. She didn't much like the idea of a wedding dress or of Kiernan helping her pick out clothes and paying for them. This seemed too familiar to her.

"Not your traditional wedding dress, but a nice dress or pantsuit. I also need to select an outfit. Jack is taking pictures of the occasion, and we'll want a memento."

An awkward silence followed, lasting almost a minute, before Kiernan brought up another subject. "There is something of importance we need to discuss. After we're married, you'll need to be careful where you go and how you conduct yourself in public. Believe me, when the paparazzi find out you're my wife, they'll be searching for you, following you. I'm going to have Jack talk to you concerning measures you can take that will discourage them."

"About the paparazzi...my family, I don't want them hounded."

"I'll have Jack inform your mother about the paparazzi and how to discourage them. He, of course, will assist her in doing this. The media won't approach only your family, but also your neighbors and coworkers to fish for stories and information. In a few weeks, this will be yesterday's news, and your family won't be bothered...as much."

"That's certainly not very reassuring."

"Unfortunately, that's one of the disadvantages of being who I am and who you will be as my wife. You'll have celebrity status now. Your name will be in the gossip columns, on the news, and in the tabloids. Some of what you'll see in the media will be fabrications and can be hurtful, so you'll need to learn to have a tough skin and ignore it."

"I don't care what they say about me as long as it doesn't hurt my family, and they leave them alone."

"I want you to know—I'll protect you, and your family, to my fullest capability."

"How will you do that?"

"If things become out of hand, I'll throw a few libel suits in their laps. And if that doesn't work, I'll buy out any tabloid, news network, or newspaper, and fire everyone involved. And I'll make damn sure all those involved will only find employment bussing tables."

A cold determination glinted in Kiernan's eyes leaving Ariel no doubt that Kiernan would do as she said.

Chapter Twelve

"K.D., DO YOU want to tell me who that delicious morsel is and where you've been hiding her?" Christiana asked as she took the seat next to Kiernan and regarded her smugly. They were in a private viewing room at Christiana's boutique for customers like Kiernan who wished to remain out of sight of any other customers.

Kiernan watched Ariel disappear into the dressing room with one of Christiana's shop assistants. Narrowing her eyes, she pinned Christiana with a measuring stare and said, "She's not what you're thinking." She and Christiana had been friends since rooming together at Foxcroft Preparatory School. Kiernan had fronted the capital to help her open her boutique.

"Oh? You call to arrange a private showing room, inform me you're bringing someone who you refused to identify, and everything she wants is to go on your account. So, enlighten me as to who I'm supposed to think she is," Christiana said suggestively, and then gave Kiernan a leering wink.

"Christy, we've been friends for a long time. What I'm going to tell you must remain between us. At least until Sunday morning and then you can broadcast it throughout the entire solar system."

"K.D., hello, this is Christy. When have I ever betrayed a confidence of yours?"

"Not even to Clifton." Clifton Melton was Christiana's husband and the mayor of Atlanta.

"I could tell Clifton the moon fell into the Atlantic Ocean, and all he would say is 'that's wonderful dear.'" Christiana smirked and added, "So, let me have the juice—every last drop."

Kiernan felt a certain amount of pride. "That, my dear, is my fiancée."

Christiana's mouth fell open, her eyes popping wide. She stared at Kiernan in bewildered shock, as if she couldn't believe what she was hearing.

"Aren't you going to say anything? The cat got your tongue?" Kiernan leaned over and waved her hand in front of Christiana's eyes.

Christiana blinked a few times before exclaiming, "You're pulling my leg! I don't believe it!"

"Believe it, because it's true. We're getting married in a private ceremony, family only, on Saturday morning. Ariel Thorsen will soon be Ariel Thorsen O'Shay."

A slightly dazed expression remained on Christiana's face. "K.D., when did all this happen?"

"Recently, and that's all you're getting from me. Aren't you going to do the best wishes thing and tell me how lucky I am?"

Christiana hugged Kiernan. "This is wonderful, still unbelievable, but wonderful. I'm happy for you. She's beautiful. Who is she?"

Kiernan knew what Christiana was asking. She wanted to know whether Ariel held any social standing anywhere in the world. "She's a wonderful person who's loyal to her family, unselfish, not shallow, and has integrity." Kiernan leveled a serious look at Christiana that relayed a message, as did her words when she declared, "She's an O'Shay."

HEATHER, THE WILLOWY blonde boutique assistant, surveyed Ariel appraisingly. "That's an excellent choice for you. The blue makes your eyes appear a shade darker and goes very well with your hair color and complexion. It is also flattering to your figure."

Heather's gaze strayed to Ariel's breasts, giving them a brief but appreciative inspection. Ariel wanted to roll her eyes. It never failed. Every time she went out in public, her generous and well-shaped breasts drew attention from both males and females. She owned a t-shirt a friend made for her, emblazoned across the front with *My IQ is 178,* and she wore it a few times until she realized it only directed more attention to her breasts.

Heather rotated Ariel by her shoulders to face the floor length mirror so she could get a view of her appearance. Ariel admitted the royal blue dress was very becoming with its slim skirt reaching to her ankles and slit on the sides to three inches above the knees. The sleeveless bodice crisscrossed in the front and circled around her neck, which left it backless. It definitely wasn't a wedding dress, but Ariel really didn't care what she wore. Kiernan was buying it so she would let her decide.

Heather handed her a pair of matching shoes with three-inch heels. Ariel slipped them on and walked around the room a few times to get the feel. She stopped in front of Heather and said, "Let's get this show on the road."

"You mean let's strut your stuff out on the catwalk."

Ariel snickered at the comment and followed Heather through the dressing room curtain and out into the viewing area. Kiernan was in conversation with a dark-haired woman.

Kiernan peered up, her eyes widening. "Oh, yes. You're absolutely..." Words seemed to fail her for a few moments. "That dress is gorgeous. Turn around and let me see the back."

Ariel did so, feeling self-conscious, but relieved her blushes never extended to her back.

Kiernan said, "Walk around some."

Ariel had the sudden urge to do what she termed the 'butch stomp' she sometimes affected when she was decked out in her full biker regalia of black Tefla-hide jacket, black Tefla-hide pants, and black boots. Refraining, she instead did a sedate amble in a circle.

"Christy, add it to the purchase order," Kiernan said. "Now, bring out some outfits appropriate for the event we discussed earlier, and have Ariel try them on. Then we'll see what you have in casual clothes. Ariel, come over here and let me introduce you to Christy. She'll help you select anything you want."

Letting a sigh of exasperation escape through her nose, Ariel knew it was going to be a long day.

ARIEL GAZED OUT the limo's window at the nineteenth and early twentieth century buildings of Atlanta's older downtown district. She thought about how they reflected a charm not seen in the modern malls. It was close to noon when they finished selecting and ordering clothes. Christiana invited them to go to a new Indian restaurant but Kiernan declined, saying she had one more stop to make and, afterward, she and Ariel would lunch at a bistro she knew.

The limo pulled up in front of a quaint brownstone building with two green and white awnings stretched over two picture windows on each side of the glass door. Ariel read the sign above the door, painted with gold lettering: *Barnett Jewelers*.

"I made arrangements with Mr. Barnett for a private showing of wedding rings," Kiernan stated and glanced at Ariel as if to gauge her reaction.

Ariel fought to maintain a neutral façade. Wedding rings had never crossed her mind.

Kiernan went on to say, "Barnett's has been the O'Shay family jeweler for close to eighty years. They are honest and discreet. I informed Mr. Barnett of our upcoming nuptials, and he will keep it confidential."

David escorted them to the door and opened it. As soon as they entered, an elderly man dressed in a black business suit greeted them affably. "Ms. O'Shay, welcome."

"Thank you, Mr. Barnett." Kiernan glanced at Ariel with pride. "Let me present my fiancée, Ms. Ariel Thorsen. Ariel, this is Donald Barnett. Donald's father was jeweler to my grandmother."

"It is a pleasure to meet you, Ms. Thorsen." He took her hand in his and gave it a gentle shake.

"Nice meeting you, Mr. Barnett."

He said, "Now, if you two will follow me, I'll take you to a room so you'll have privacy for viewing."

They followed him into a back room and took seats at a counter. Mr. Barnett reached under the counter, brought out a tray covered with a black velvet cloth, and set it before Kiernan. He lifted up the cover to reveal an assortment of diamond engagement rings, their facets catching the lights and reflecting an array of sparkling rainbow colors. Ariel did a double take at the size of some of the diamonds.

No way would she wear an engagement ring. She kept her features and her voice smooth. "Kiernan, I...at this time, could we please forgo a diamond ring?"

Inspecting Ariel closely, and thinning her lips slightly, Kiernan said, "It's customary to have an engagement ring."

Ariel could tell this didn't please Kiernan, but it was important to her. An engagement ring symbolized, at least in her mind, a promise of a loving and committed future together—not an agreement amounting to little more than a business arrangement. "I know. But..."

Kiernan's lips tightened for a second but she relaxed and said, "If that's what you want. However, we will return at a later date and make a selection. Donald, please show us your selection of wedding bands."

Again, he reached under the counter and arranged a tray filled with wedding bands before them. Kiernan selected rings to inspect and had Ariel try on a few, but nothing seemed to satisfy Kiernan. Ariel tried to be cooperative, more because the sooner they made their selection the faster she could get back home. She indicated the ones she liked by placing them to one side.

Glancing up, Ariel saw Mr. Barnett studying her closely, but dispassionately. Once more, he brought out a tray, placing it on the counter top. Ariel watched as he selected a ring from the tray, positioned it on a black velvet pad, and put the pad before her.

Ariel picked up the ring, studying it carefully. She noticed its molded and engraved garland of pale pink gold roses around the circumference and the thin, yellow-gold roping edging the band. She thought it was beautiful.

Kiernan said, "May I see it?" Ariel handed her the ring, and Kiernan took Ariel's left hand and slipped it on her finger. It fit perfectly. Holding Ariel's hand, she inspected the ring, and said softly, "I think it is lovely on you."

Ariel didn't reply, feeling uneasy, but somehow she managed to maintain a calm appearance and didn't snatch her hand away, though part of her wanted to.

Kiernan removed the ring, trying it on her own finger, but it fit loosely. She studied it before handing it to Mr. Barnett, and inquiring in a business like tone, "How many of these rings have you made and sold?"

"This is from a new mold I fabricated recently and the only one made."

"I want you to make a ring like this in my size, and then I want you to destroy the mold."

He appeared ready to protest when Kiernan said, "I'll pay you twice what you would charge if I came to you with a custom request."

"I can have your ring ready and deliver both rings to you on Thursday."

"Fine. Do it." Kiernan said to Ariel, "This way the rings will be unique and no one else will have ones like them."

Ariel was curious as to the reasons this would be important to Kiernan. She could understand if two people were truly in love why they might want this since the rings would symbolize the uniqueness of their love and would be theirs alone. "And this matters to you, why?"

Kiernan fixed her eyes on Ariel. "I always like having things no one else has—that belong only to me."

Ariel had the disconcerted feeling that Kiernan wasn't only referring to things, but to her as well.

Chapter Thirteen

RAIN FELL IN a soft but steady rhythm outside the window of Kiernan's study where she had retired after dinner to examine the prenuptial agreement drawn up by her uncle. She wanted everything in order before sending a copy to Ariel in the morning.

She picked up her cup of coffee, bringing it to her lips, and froze in disbelief. "What the hell! Telecom on. Contact Theodore O'Shay."

She focused on the telecom screen, and after a couple of beeps, Jack answered. "Kiernan, how are you doing?"

Smoothing her features, Kiernan replied with false cheerfulness, "I'm doing fine, Jack."

"I bet you're all excited about the wedding. She's a beautiful girl."

"Oh, I agree, she's very beautiful. I need to speak to Uncle Theodore."

"Hold on, I'll get him for you."

After a couple of minutes, her uncle's image appeared on the screen. "Kiernan," he said in a jovial voice, "what can I do for you, dear?"

"Is Jack still there? Or anyone who can overhear our conversation?"

"It's only us. What's this about?"

"Stipulation number nineteen!" she spat out angrily.

Puzzlement crossed his features, then understanding. "Ah, the conjugal stipulation. I can increase the number of visits—"

"What the hell do you think you're doing?" Kiernan snapped, clinching her jaw tight. "I never said I wanted anything like that in the agreement."

"It's common to include this stipulation into agreements that are more of a business arrangement, such as this one."

"I don't care. I want it out!"

"Are you sure you want me to remove it? Marriage in itself does grant the persons the rights to a conjugal relationship. The only thing this stipulation does is put a number on the times per week that—"

"God damn it! It's...it's... Take it the hell out and don't argue." She wasn't about to have any stipulation granting her the power to request that Ariel engage in sex with her up to two times a week. No, she most certainly wouldn't make demands of that nature. She was sure it would distress Ariel and make Kiernan appear truly feudal, expecting sex as part of goods purchased.

"I have a copy on my computer and will correct it now. You should receive it tonight. I'll send Ariel her copy tomorrow by a certified carrier," Theodore said.

"Do that, and if I find anything else I'll let you know," she said gruffly and terminated the call. She took a gulp of coffee while thinking she certainly wouldn't object to a sexual relationship with Ariel. But with Ariel resenting her, *that* wasn't going to happen anytime soon. She was confident that once Ariel saw she wasn't a beast, things would change.

She wondered whether her uncle and Jack had such an agreement. That thought brought to mind images of her uncle and Jack doing things she tried not to imagine, prompting her to leave her chair hastily in search of some Irish Cream to put in her coffee.

A SHARP RAP sounded on Ariel's closed bedroom door, and Seth called out, "Ariel, you have a package you need to sign for."

Ariel had been waiting all day for the prenuptial agreement to arrive and wanted a chance to read it before taking it to her attorney, Joyce Conrad. Her mother's attorney, Ian Broxton, put Ariel in touch with Ms. Conrad, who agreed to take Ariel as her client. With the wedding only three days away, Ms. Conrad promised to go over the agreement immediately and discuss it with Ariel tomorrow. The clock on her dresser showed the time as 4:20 p.m. This left her with no time to read over the agreement before she could get it to her lawyer by the close of business.

With effort, she pushed herself out of bed feeling her head throb and throat ache from the cold she'd come down with after a sudden rainstorm surprised her while riding her Harley the day before. She tied the cord at the waist of her sweatpants, slipped into her house shoes, and not bothering about her hair, hurried out of her room. The front door was already open, allowing her a view of the young male carrier. She signed for the delivery and was shutting the door when her mother came out of the kitchen and saw the package in her hands.

"I take it that's the prenuptial agreement?" Joanna said with distaste.

Ariel opened the package, took out the folder, and leafed through the legal-size documents. "That's what it is. I'm going to run this over to Ms. Conrad before her office closes. She'll call me tomorrow when she has a chance to review it, and I'll go to her office to discuss it with her."

"You don't want to read it tonight and take it to her office in the morning?"

"I told Ms. Conrad I would have it to her today. Besides, with this cold and the medications I'm taking for it, I doubt I'd be able to comprehend what I'm reading anyway."

"Why don't you go and rest, and I'll run it over to her office for you."

"Are you sure?"

"You don't need to be out running around in this weather, and I have to go to the Produce Co-op anyway, so it won't be a problem."

"Thanks, Mom." The only thing she wanted to do was to crawl back in bed and pull the covers over her head. Not only because of the misery of her cold, but also because of the misery she suffered with the approach of her so-called wedding and how it would change her life.

Chapter Fourteen

JOYCE CONRAD SAT across the conference table from her client, Ariel Thorsen, as she explained the prenuptial agreement. Joyce knew Kiernan O'Shay from the various social gatherings and functions they attended in common, and they moved in the same social circle.

When Ian Broxton called her and said the daughter of a client needed to have a prenuptial agreement evaluated immediately, she had declined because her calendar was full. When he said it was the fiancée of Kiernan O'Shay, she agreed to take Ms. Thorsen as her client.

She wondered how Kiernan had kept her involvement with Ms. Thorsen out of the media glare, when in the past if she so much as talked to a woman the media automatically linked them romantically. She also wondered who this beautiful woman was who had managed to take Kiernan off the top of the most eligible list for at least the next five years, or indefinitely, if both parties agreed to stay in the marriage past the specified time.

The previous night she took time to search every social registry in the world, not finding her client's name in any of them. Finally, she ran a data search on the name of Ariel Lynn Thorsen, discovering some interesting matches. Ms. Thorsen was a physics professor at a local college and had graduated with the highest honor from MIT. The fact was Ariel Thorsen was nobody. No, that wasn't true any longer. Ariel Thorsen was definitely somebody now. But she remained a mystery.

Mystery seemed the operative word surrounding the marriage. She suspected from all the evidence that it was a sudden decision on Kiernan's part as the ordinary practice for prenuptial agreements was to sign them well in advance of the actual marriage and not a couple of days before the event.

Her assessment of the prenuptial agreement the previous night revealed that the marriage was more along the lines of a business arrangement. Apparently the primary reason was Kiernan wished for an heir. Joyce guessed she'd chosen Ms. Thorsen due to her intelligence and, perhaps secondarily, her physical appearance.

But why marry? Kiernan could always go to one of the private fertility specialists and specify what she wanted. She could well afford the exorbitant price for genetic material from a donor with superior intelligence, health, and, attractiveness. She could even have a surrogate carry the fetus to term.

There was more to this whole situation, she was sure. She had tried to engage Ms. Thorsen in a friendly discussion on how she and Kiernan had met and how long they had known each other, but only received vague responses letting her know her client did not wish to discuss the subject. Joyce had realized that she must stick to explaining the agreement, making sure the stipulations were in her client's best interests.

"The next stipulation, number nineteen, is usually standard in these types of contracts." Ms. Thorsen read over her copy of the contract. After a few seconds of reading, her client suddenly blinked, sucking in her breath and coughing violently. Joyce hurriedly left the table and exited the room, returning with a cup of water she handed to her.

Ariel gulped down the water, which finally stopped her coughing. She focused once more on the contract. After a few seconds, she peered up at Joyce, a note of bewilderment in her tone. "Please explain stipulation number nineteen."

"A marriage in and of itself entitles the couple to certain rights. These rights can include the enjoyment of companionship and the benefits of living in the same residence together. It also refers to the privilege of engaging in sexual relations with their spouse. What this stipulation does is state your spouse can request conjugal privileges up to two times a week."

Ms. Thorsen asked hesitantly, "What you're saying is...if my spouse requests...I have intimate relations with her...I would be required to do so?"

Studying her client closely, Joyce noticed a certain amount of uneasiness. "Essentially, yes. Is there a problem with this, Ms. Thorsen?" She, for one, would have no problems carrying out that stipulation. Kiernan was one of the hottest women she knew. That didn't mean her client thought so, and the more she talked to Ms. Thorsen, the more she saw this wasn't the proverbial blushing bride. Ariel Thorsen was less than enthusiastic.

Ms. Thorsen closed her eyes, and Joyce could tell she was under duress. Her client opened her eyes and said, "I've never heard of such a thing."

"Granted, it does seem to take the romance out of marriage. This stipulation is common in a prenuptial agreement that's more of a business arrangement and is usually discussed between the parties before being included in the contract. Ms. O'Shay did not discuss this with you?"

"No," her client said quietly.

"If you wish it changed, I can contact Mr. O'Shay today, and if Ms. O'Shay is in agreement, we can have this amended before the wedding."

"No. Leave it like it is," Ms. Thorsen said with a sigh.

Hesitating, Joyce debated whether she should question her client further, but somehow she knew she would not be forthcoming. "There are a couple more points to go over, and we're finished."

Joyce covered the rest of the agreement with her client, noticing a strain about her features. Finally, they reached the end.

"That about does it, Ms. Thorsen. I'll meet you tomorrow in Mr. O'Shay's office at three."

Ms. Thorsen said wanly, "Yes, thank you."

ARIEL OPENED THE door of her electric mini coupe and slid into the driver's seat, closed the door, and slumped against the steering wheel, her mind going over stipulation number nineteen. She couldn't believe Kiernan would put that in the agreement. Surely she must know Ariel hated her.

When Ms. Conrad asked her if she had a problem with the stipulation, it was all she could do to keep from screaming of course she had a problem with it. She hated Kiernan's guts. But Kiernan was calling the shots. She couldn't tell Kiernan she wouldn't marry her unless she agreed to remove the stipulation. She didn't know how she would fulfill her obligation. And what was she going to tell Mom? She would provide general answers and never mention the stipulation.

A wave of nausea washed over her, followed by a headache. All she wanted to do was go home, crawl in bed, and sleep—for the next hundred years.

"AH. HERE SHE is now," Kiernan heard her uncle say as she rushed through the door and into her uncle's office. He was standing by a moderate-sized rectangular table at the far side of the room. The mountains were in prominent display outside the window behind him. Seated at one side of the table were Ariel and her attorney, Joyce Conrad.

"Sorry, I'm late," Kiernan said in a rushed voice. "Business call."

Joyce rose from her seat and held out her hand for a shake. Kiernan took it in a firm grip. "Joyce, is everything going well?" Kiernan wanted to get right to the point and forgo social formalities.

"No problems."

Kiernan let go of Joyce's hand and noticed Ariel's scowl and the dullness about her features. "Ariel, how are you?"

Ariel shot her a cutting glance and curtly replied, "Okay."

Theodore took his seat. "Well then. Let's get this on the way."

Kiernan walked to the other side of the table, taking a seat beside her uncle, and across from Ariel.

"Ms. Conrad, you and your client have had a chance to go over the prenuptial agreement?" Theodore asked.

"Yes, we have."

"Are there any points you and Ms. Thorsen wish to discuss?"

Raising her eyebrows slightly in question, Joyce studied her client and asked, "Ms. Thorsen, do you have any points, or questions, you wish addressed? Now is the time to voice any concerns."

"No!" Ariel barked out emphatically, her cheeks and neck reddening with what was surely anger.

Joyce appeared taken aback by her client's outburst. She regarded her closely before directing her attention back to Mr. O'Shay. "We are in agreement with the stipulations."

He addressed his niece. "Kiernan, is there anything you want to address or add?"

"No. I'm satisfied with the terms," Kiernan stated while keeping her gaze on Ariel. Since she first entered the office, Ariel had avoided her and displayed a snarly attitude, making her feel greatly annoyed. She wondered whether Ariel divulged to Joyce the circumstances of why she was entering into this marriage. Not that Joyce would break a client's confidentiality and tell others, but it grated on Kiernan to think Joyce would know Ariel wasn't enamored of her and felt forced into this marriage.

"That leaves us with the signing to do." Theodore reached over and pushed a button on a com-unit. "Franklin, we're ready for you and Ms. Farleigh to come in now."

After the two witnesses entered, all parties signed the document, and Theodore dismissed Franklin and Ms. Farleigh. Rubbing his hands together, he said, "Now, let's all have a celebratory drink."

Kiernan saw Ariel roll her eyes before slowly standing. She hastily went around the table to Ariel, whispering loud enough for only her to hear, "Stay here a moment." Kiernan said to the others, "You two go on. I want to speak to Ariel."

Theodore and Joyce left, and when they were out of earshot, Kiernan took Ariel by the elbow, pivoted her to face the window, and said in a stern and low voice, "I don't know what your problem is, but it stops here. The agreement is signed, and we'll be married tomorrow."

Ariel's face shaded pink and she clipped her words. "That's

true, but I don't have to like it."

"No, you don't. However, I would appreciate it if you would show me some consideration. You're embarrassing me in front of a peer, and that I *will not* tolerate."

"I'll endeavor to do my best," Ariel said frostily.

"I have no doubt your best in anything always succeeds." Kiernan took Ariel's hand. "Let's join the others, shall we?"

Ariel dipped her head in assent, and Kiernan led her over to the other two, noticing Ariel managed to produce a smile, but her eyes were icy.

Chapter Fifteen

A SOFT TAPPING sound roused Ariel from sleep, and she opened her eyes to the light before she instantly closed them against a stabbing lance of pain through her temples.

"Ariel, it's time to get up," her mother called from the other side of the door.

"All right, I'm up," she ground out hoarsely from a sore throat, making herself sit up. Pain pounded behind her hot, gritty eyes.

She forced herself to her feet, slipped on her housecoat and made her way to the bathroom. She caught her reflection in the mirror over the sink, startled at the fevered brightness of her eyes and the little dark smudges beneath them. She opened the medicine cabinet, pulled out the box of disposable thermometer tabs, removed one, and placed it against her forehead. After a faint beep, she removed the tab and read 101. Her sore throat almost prevented her from swallowing the analgesic tablet for her headache and a cold tablet to alleviate her symptoms. Feeling as bad as she did, she took another cold tablet in hopes of faster relief. Not that it would do that much good, as she had been doubling the dosage lately with very little effect.

After a hot shower, she dressed in her housecoat and made her way to the kitchen where everyone was seated around the kitchen table. Seth and Leigh were enjoying a breakfast of pancakes.

Her mother put down the English muffin she was eating, and Ariel saw her assessing her condition. Finally, Joanna said, "I see you got about as much sleep as I did."

"Sleep? Who needs it? I sure don't."

"I made a pot of the real stuff this morning. That should wake you up."

Ariel almost asked what the special occasion was, but bit her lip, thinking her mom probably prepared the expensive commodity in an attempt to add some cheer to what was, to date, bound to be one of the lowest points in her life. A clean cup was on the counter by the vintage coffee pot. She picked it up and filled it, sloshing some over the side of the cup.

She grabbed an absorbent towelette from the dispenser and sopped up the spill. Seth was singing, "Ariel and Kiernan sitting in a tree, K-I-S-S-I-N-G."

Leigh joined in. "First comes love, then comes marriage, here comes Ariel with a baby carriage."

"Shut up!" Ariel snarled and whirled around, glaring at them.

The twins stared at her in shock with their mouths hanging open.

"That's enough you two," Joanna ordered. "Go get ready."

"But Mom, I haven't finished eating," Leigh protested.

"Then go out in the dining room and finish."

"Mom," Leigh whined.

"Don't argue, do it. Now!"

Both kids exited, and Ariel seated herself at the table across from her mother. "I'm sorry." A creepy shiver crawled down her back thinking about the last few words to the song. "That's not the image I need right now."

"Sweetheart, you don't have to do this—"

"Mom, please don't harp. I'm doing it."

After an uneasy silence, Joanna said, "Don't you want to eat something? I have some pancake batter left and can make you a stack."

"No thanks. I'm not hungry."

After Ariel finished her coffee, she got a glass of orange juice and took her seat at the table, noticing her mother scrutinizing her hair.

Joanna said, "I'm thinking a French braid would go really nice with your dress. I can do it for you."

So what if her hair was a squirrel's nest. Ariel didn't care, but apparently her mother did. She said unenthusiastically, "That'll be fine, Mom."

"I'll make your face up, too."

Ariel rarely used cosmetics. "That bad?"

"You do look tired. How's the cold?"

"Not good. I'm taking medication, but it doesn't seem to be working as fast as it should."

"Uh oh. I hope you're not getting the flu. You did have your flu vaccine this year, didn't you?"

"Yes." Ariel took a sip of juice and stared off into space.

"Mysha called last night."

Ariel jerked her attention back to her mother.

"She said she has been leaving messages for you on your IMP and wanted to know whether it was working. She wanted to tell you she managed to get an earlier flight out of Beijing and will arrive home around six tomorrow morning. She wanted to know if that would be a good time for you to pick her up."

On Thursday, Ariel had tried calling Mysha but couldn't reach her, so she left a message on her IMP that things were the same. It disgusted her that she lied. Deliberately, she had not read any of the messages from Mysha after that call as it would be too painful.

"What did you tell her?"

"The truth—that you've had a bad cold for the past few days and went to bed early. I told her you wouldn't be able to pick her up at the airport. She's going to take a taxi and call you later."

For a moment, silence, until Ariel let out a shuddering sob. Joanna left her seat and knelt by her daughter, holding her close, her own tears falling.

"YOU ARE LOVELY, my dear." Theodore's eyes twinkled as he checked Kiernan over. She was dressed in a rich cream jacquard outfit with gold embroidered flowers that fell a couple of inches below the knees. Over it she wore a matching cropped jacket with a Mandarin collar and slim dolman sleeves with side slits.

"Thank you, Uncle." Kiernan glanced around the living room, making sure everything was in order. A dozen floral arrangements of cream and pink roses adorned the room. Two arrangements sat in front of the fireplace, spaced far enough apart for the ceremony to take place between them.

"I think I'll go over and talk to Judge Baker and Jack," Theodore said. He kissed her cheek, leaving her to her thoughts.

She glanced at the grandfather clock and saw it was a quarter after ten. The ceremony was due to start at eleven. Earlier, she'd sent David out in one of the limos to pick up her bride and future in-laws. Thinking about Ariel as her bride made her stomach feel as if it contained a tiny fish swimming around.

Judge Margaret Baker, who had been a friend of both her mothers, would perform the ceremony.

Jack hurriedly came up to her. "David called. They're coming up the drive now."

Kiernan's nervousness increased until a school of fish was now swimming in her stomach. "Jack, go out and escort them in. I'll alert the staff they're here."

"Kiernan, dear, do you need my help?" Theodore called from where he was conversing with Judge Baker.

Kiernan hurried over. "Uncle, please tell the staff they're here."

"I'll do that."

He left to carry out Kiernan's orders, leaving her with Judge Baker, who put her hand on Kiernan's shoulder and gently squeezed. "Relax, Kiernan."

"That's easy for you to say. You're only doing the marrying, not getting married."

"I've been on the receiving end twice. You'll survive it."

"If you say so." Kiernan crossed her arms in front of her chest, nervously rocking on her heels. After a few seconds, she asked, "Margaret, did Uncle Theodore give you the rings?"

Judge Baker reached into the pocket of her blue dress jacket and drew them out. "Here and accounted for."

She held them out in her palm. Kiernan noticed one with a red string tied around it, and she asked curiously, "What's with the red string?"

"Theodore did that so I wouldn't get them mixed up and hand you the wrong one. Yours has the string."

"That's a good idea." Kiernan went back to rocking her body back and forth on her heels.

Kiernan saw Judge Baker focus her attention past her and say, "I do believe your bride has arrived."

Kiernan whirled and caught her breath when she saw Jack escorting Ariel and her family toward her. She had eyes only for Ariel. True, she was with Ariel when they selected their outfits for the wedding, but seeing her bride in her home walking toward her in that amazing dress was awe-inspiring.

Ariel wore a cream satin gown with a fitted sweetheart bodice. The sleeves were between the elbow and shoulder and slightly puffed. It had a sweeping full-length bias skirt and matching belt sewn into the dress. Delicate embroidery of gold metallic thread in a curving vine design covered the dress. The ensemble complemented the outfit Kiernan wore. Kiernan's gaze traveled down the length of Ariel and back up to her hair. Ariel's French braid went well with the dress.

Kiernan met Ariel, grasping both of her hands, with her voice full of emotion. "You're very beautiful."

Ariel's expression was wooden and her voice stilted. "Thank you...Kiernan. You look very nice."

"Thank you. Let me introduce you to Judge Baker. She'll be officiating." Kiernan let go of Ariel's right hand but kept hold of her left hand. "But first, there are two members of your family I haven't met." She looked toward Joanna and the twins. "Hello, Joanna. You look lovely." Joanna was wearing a pale peach dress with an over layer of ivory lace.

Inclining her head, Joanna replied coolly, "As do you...Ms. O'Shay."

"Thank you," Kiernan replied warmly, ignoring Joanna's cold tone.

Ariel tugged her hand from Kiernan's grasp before introducing her brother. "This is my brother, Seth." Seth wore a gray suit with darker charcoal pinstripes over a pink shirt and a burgundy tie.

Kiernan stuck out her hand and he took it in his.

"How do you do, Ms. O'Shay?"

"I'm fine. Please call me Kiernan. We're family now."

He said shyly, "Kiernan."

"That's better." She peered at the gawky young girl who, despite her gangly appearance, Kiernan knew would grow into a beauty like her sister.

"This is my sister, Leigh," Ariel said.

"My, don't you look nice," Kiernan said while shaking her hand. Leigh was dressed in a light blue pantsuit. The jacket was similar to a tuxedo with a slim collar in a silky light gray.

Leigh blushed. "Thank you." Kiernan thought blushing must be a hereditary factor in the Thorsen family.

Kiernan took the group over to Judge Baker and introduced Joanna and the twins. Next, she introduced the twins to Jack and her uncle.

Her last introduction was to Judge Baker. "Ariel, this is Judge Margaret Baker. Margaret, this is Ariel, my bride to be," Kiernan said with pride.

Judge Baker took Ariel's hand. "It's a pleasure, my dear. Kiernan is a fortunate woman."

Ariel politely replied, "Thank you, Judge Baker."

"Please, call me Margaret."

Kiernan said, "It might be a good idea to take your family up to your suite and show them where the facilities are before the ceremony."

Ariel said to her mother, "I'll show you my rooms and where the bathroom is located."

Joanna gathered the twins, and all three followed Ariel up the stairs. Jack and Theodore left to check on a few things, leaving Kiernan and Judge Baker alone.

Judge Baker said, "She's quite lovely. You didn't tell me much when you called to ask me to perform the ceremony, except mentioning something about you meeting her through her mother. And you were evasive on how long you've known her."

Kiernan took a few seconds before saying, "Margaret, this is strictly a business arrangement." She debated briefly on saying more, deciding she would go ahead, knowing Margaret would keep it confidential. "Grandmother's will requires I marry and produce an heir before I'm forty if I'm to have complete control of Stellardyne. Ariel meets the requirements I want in a wife and in the mother of my child."

Surprise flashed across Judge Baker's features. She recovered and said, "Shanna always had a bizarre sense of humor. But this is really—"

"Warped. I could almost believe she got the idea from the plot of a B-grade Bollywood made-for-EM melodrama."

Judge Baker added, "Or a soap opera. Why would she write something like that into her will?"

"To control me. She couldn't do it while she lived, so she's doing it from the grave. I should go dig her up and hammer a stake through her heart."

Judge Baker laughed briefly. "Shanna always controlled Maureen's life until she married Nicole. But Nicole wouldn't stand for it."

"I have no choice, if I want Stellardyne."

"I'm sorry, Kiernan," Judge Baker said sincerely. "There is the matter of the marriage vows. I suppose you don't want to go the route of 'til death do us part and eternal love."

"Given the circumstances..."

"I have the vow for you. Actually, I've used it quite often. Business marriages seem to be the vogue these days."

"Thanks, Margaret."

ARIEL TOOK HER turn in the bathroom after activating the EM in her sitting room for the twins. When she exited the bathroom, she saw her mother sitting on the edge of the bed.

Joanna stood. "How are you feeling—healthwise that is?"

"I feel drained, and my headache is back. I found some pain capsules and cold tablets in the medicine cabinet and took those."

Joanna placed her hand on Ariel's forehead. "You feel feverish. You need to take care of yourself."

An irritated sigh escaped Ariel. "Yes, Mom, I will."

"Someone brought in your suitcase from the limo. I'll help you unpack your things, and this weekend I'll pack the rest of your clothes, so you can pick them up after your honeymoon."

Ariel wanted to shout it wasn't a honeymoon, though technically of course it was. And with stipulation number nineteen—she didn't want to think about it. "Okay, Mom." Ariel placed the suitcase on the bed, opened it, and handed Joanna a couple of pairs of jeans and four shirts. There wasn't much Ariel needed to bring, since Kiernan had bought her over a dozen outfits for casual wear and a few formal outfits for their...trip.

"Where do you want these?" Joanna asked.

"Go through the door over there and you'll find a dressing room leading to a walk-in closet. You can hang them up in there."

Ariel took her undergarments and pajamas over to the double dresser. She placed the bundle on the dresser top and opened one of the top drawers, only to discover it filled. On seeing the neatly folded panties and briefs, she did a double take. She picked up one pair of ice blue bikini briefs and checked to find them her size. She wasn't sure of Kiernan's size, but she judged her hips to be smaller than her own. A silky black pair caught her eye, and she checked, finding that they would also fit her. Both anger and apprehension seized her. Apparently, Kiernan had bought her undergarments—some very suggestive undergarments. Was Kiernan expecting to see her in them? Ariel chastised herself for acting like a Nanobrain. Of course Kiernan would want to check out the merchandise. After all, there was stipulation number nineteen.

She opened the second drawer and discovered bras in various pastels, as well as in red and one with black lace. This was too intimate, and despite her slight fever, her cheeks flushed warmer. She checked the sizes, and sure enough... She wondered how Kiernan knew her size and suddenly remembered going into the 3-D measuring booth for a scan of her body at Christiana's.

She hesitated before opening another drawer, but when she pulled it out, she found pajamas and other nightwear, some of which was suggestive reds and blacks. She didn't bother to inspect the sizes and slammed the drawer shut as her mother came out of the dressing room.

"I thought you told me you bought only a few items for your trip. There's almost a third of the closet filled with dresses, pantsuits, coats, you name it..."

Ariel walked past her mother and into her closet. The clothing filling up a third of the space was equal to at least four of her closets at home. Coats were in one section, pantsuits and dresses, both formal and informal, in another, as well as a section for casual wear. A check of the shoe rack showed more than a dozen pairs of assorted footwear. A variety of bags and purses hung above the shoe rack.

Her mother said from behind her, "I took the liberty to check the labels in the clothes. The ones having size labels will fit you. Some don't have size labels but have fancy nametags sewn inside with your name on them. I can tell you all are exclusive, and they sure don't come from Sears. I can't begin to guess how Ms. O'Shay did this in only a few days."

Ariel said nothing. She studied a pair of jeans, running a finger over the seams, instantly knowing the tailoring was to her measurements. Then in a matter-of-fact voice, she said, "She's Kiernan O'Shay, Mom. What she wants done is done. And when she wants it done, it's done. Who is to deny her anything?"

"REPEAT AFTER ME," Judge Baker instructed in an oratorical tone. "I, Kiernan Deirdre O'Shay, in the presence of those gathered here, take you, Ariel, to be my wife."

Voice solemn and gazing with earnest purpose into Ariel's eyes, Kiernan repeated the vows and went on. "I pledge to stand by you, not only in times of joy, but also in times of need."

Ariel glanced away from Kiernan's gaze. Kiernan squeezed her hand, obviously wanting Ariel's attention on her, but Ariel didn't want to give it.

Kiernan said, "I pledge to be faithful to you, and I will hold you in respect and honor the person you are."

Judge Baker handed Kiernan a ring. "Now place the ring on her finger."

Ariel glanced up, and Kiernan took Ariel's left hand to slip the ring on her finger.

"This ring is a symbol of my pledge to you." Kiernan's voice slightly wavered with a rush of unexpected emotion.

Ariel's eyes darted nervously away.

Judge Baker regarded Ariel, her voice reassuring. "Repeat after me, I, Ariel Lynn Thorsen, in the presence of those gathered here, take you, Kiernan, to be my wife."

A faint tremor ran through Ariel's body. Swallowing hard, she repeated the words, her voice trembling, and made the pledge to stand by Kiernan, not only in times of joy, but also in times of need. Lastly, she said, "I pledge to be faithful to you, and I will hold you in respect and honor the person you are." Tears now threatened to overflow.

Judge Baker handed over the ring. Ariel's hands shook, so Kiernan gently took the hand holding the ring and guided her.

The judge prompted Ariel with the final promise. Her throat constricted, and Ariel could barely speak. "Th...this...ring is a symbol...of my pledge to you."

"I now pronounce you married." Judge Baker gazed on the couple with pleasure and said, "You may now kiss."

KIERNAN GENTLY PLACED her hands on Ariel's shoulders, rising up slightly on her toes, and leaned in to give her a kiss. Ariel twisted her head away so that Kiernan ended up placing a kiss on her cheek instead. Ariel did not reciprocate, and Kiernan took Ariel's left hand back in hers, holding it gently but firmly.

The staff applauded and soon dispersed to help in preparing the dining room for the buffet.

"Kiernan, you and Ariel turn this way, so I can get another picture," Jack said while holding out a state of the art 3-D digital camera.

Kiernan glanced at Ariel and saw the tears on her cheeks. She turned to Jack, "Perhaps later."

Kiernan let go of Ariel's hand, watching as a teary-eyed Joanna made her way to her daughter and hugged her tight. She was dismayed to see mother and daughter weeping, feeling at a loss as to what she should do or say. Both Theodore and Jack offered their congratulations. She accepted them, excused herself, and went over to Judge Baker.

"Thank you, Margaret."

"I wish you and Ariel the best." Judge Baker pulled Kiernan in for a hug, whispering in her ear, "Something tells me this will end up being much more than a business arrangement."

Kiernan let a wistful sigh escape. "We'll see."

SETH MOVED OVER to Leigh and asked, "Why are Mom and Ariel crying? I thought you were supposed to be happy at weddings."

Leigh put her hands on her hips and said, "Nanobrain, mothers do that all the time when their children get married."

"Where'd you hear that? And why's Ariel doing it?"

Apparently overhearing their conversation, Theodore walked up to them. "Why, mothers have been crying at weddings since Adam and Eve. Are you two hungry?"

"I'll say," Seth said.

"How about let's sneak into the dining room and see what Kiernan's chef has prepared. I hear he has all kinds of goodies laid out."

"Yes," Seth enthused and shot his fist into the air.

"You're always hungry," Leigh said with mock disgust and wrinkled her nose. "Mom needs to check you for worms."

Theodore said to Seth, "Well, partner, lets you and I do some grub rustling."

"I'd better go along to make sure Seth doesn't eat too much and retches-up," Leigh said.

Kiernan and Judge Baker, overhearing the conversation between Theodore and the twins, laughed.

Judge Baker said, "They're around three years younger than my grandson, Tony. Only a few weeks ago his main interests were music and food. Now it's music, food, and members of the opposite sex."

"Just think, there are two of them who will be going through that stage at the same time. I'd hate to be in Joanna's shoes."

"You wait. Your time will come, and you'll be in those shoes."

Kiernan shook her head, a slight smile on her face. "That's a while down the road yet. Let's get everyone together and have lunch before Uncle Theodore and the twins eat it all."

Kiernan walked over to Ariel and Joanna. "I have a buffet in the dining room, so why don't we get a bite to eat."

Ariel said, "I'm not hungry. I'm going to go upstairs for a while."

Joanna admonished her daughter. "Sweetheart, you didn't eat anything this morning. You need to eat something."

Scrutinizing her bride closely, Kiernan noticed Ariel's pallid cheeks and weary appearance. In a tone sounding like an order instead of a request, she said, "Come with me. You need to eat, Ariel."

She took Ariel by the elbow and urged her forward. Balking, Ariel pulled her elbow out of Kiernan's grasp, her eyes scathing.

Unsettled by Ariel's reaction, Kiernan leaned back. "Ariel?"

Ariel shut her eyes briefly and then opened them, her expression and voice stilted. "Lead the way."

Kiernan thought the strain of the day was catching up with Ariel, and food and rest would be what she needed.

ARIEL FLOPPED BACK onto her bed, too tired to remove her dress or unbraid her hair. Her mother and siblings had departed twenty minutes earlier, right after the buffet. Somehow she managed to keep from leaving with her family. She wanted so much to go back to the comfort of her room at home.

"May I come in?"

Ariel jumped, startled by Kiernan's voice. She quickly stood, apprehension flooding her.

Kiernan, dressed in a pair of jeans and a knit pullover blue turtleneck sweater, said, "I have a wedding present for you, but I think you need to change into something more comfortable before I give it to you."

An uncomfortable feeling settled on Ariel, thinking Kiernan would stay and watch her undress. Then she remembered the dressing room. "I'll go and do that now."

Kiernan must have sensed her unease because she studied Ariel, her mouth tightening. "I'll wait in the sitting room."

Ariel removed her dress and went into her closet. She ignored the new clothes Kiernan bought her, selecting a pair of her faded jeans and a white Henley shirt, and quickly dressed. She slipped on her casual, black sport shoes, pulling the Velcro tabs to tighten them.

She found Kiernan in the recliner in the sitting room. Kiernan stood, and Ariel saw her gaze slide over her, no doubt wondering why she wasn't wearing some of the clothes she had purchased.

"I see you're ready. Let's go," Kiernan said.

Ariel followed Kiernan to the outdoor veranda.

Kiernan drew out her IMP from her front jeans pocket and spoke into it. "Michael, we're ready."

The sound of a deep, rumbling roar reached Ariel's ears. She spun toward the sound and saw a vintage, red hardtop convertible rapidly pull up and stop. Michael exited out of the driver's side.

"It's yours, a wedding gift from me. It's a 2017 Ferrari, with the original hybrid alcohol injection and electric engine." Kiernan's expression was expectant.

Ariel didn't know what to say as she surveyed the sleek lines of the sports car.

Kiernan said, "If you don't like it, I can have it exchanged for something else."

"No. It's...beautiful. Thank you."

"Let's go check it out. You can take me for a ride." Ariel heard a flirtatious quality to Kiernan's voice at this last part. They walked down to the car, and Kiernan opened the door for her. "Sit in it, why don't you, and get the feel."

Ariel slipped in the driver's seat, her body fitting comfortably in the plush, black leather bucket seat. She noticed the old-fashioned dashboard with its dials and gauges. This car lacked the safety features of today's cars. Undoubtedly, Kiernan did her homework, discovering when Ariel won her Harley she was required to take a special class to obtain a license permitting her to operate it and other vintage vehicles.

The price of the Ferrari exceeded the amount Ariel could earn working for ten years as a professor. The permits required to operate a vehicle having an exhaust system, no matter how clean the fuel, were expensive and difficult to obtain, taking months and sometimes up to a year. Then again, Kiernan O'Shay wasn't one to be denied anything she wanted, whenever she wanted it. Ariel's stomach lurched at what she thought Kiernan expected as payment, her mind touching on stipulation number nineteen.

Kiernan peered down at her from the open door. "Do you want to take her for a spin? I have all the special permits in case we get stopped by the highway patrol." She whispered conspiratorially, "I have a radar detection device installed, so you can rev her up."

Ariel blinked in surprise. Federal laws in the States prevented private ownership of electronic radar detection devices.

Kiernan must have seen her surprise and concern. "Don't worry, you can easily disable it. Besides, it's a special sensor Stellardyne developed similar to the ones on our ships used to detect transmissions. Of course, this one is the size of a pinhead with limited range. It's almost impossible to find in a search and will allow you plenty of warning to slow down before there is a trooper within a mile. So what say we see what she's got?"

"Some other time. I...I'm tired right now." She added in a stilted voice, "I thank you for the gift...it's very nice."

Kiernan seemed disappointed, which reflected in her voice. "I'll have Michael park it in the garage. Perhaps we can take that ride after we return from St. Thomas."

Ariel said with little enthusiasm, "Yes. I'll drive it then."

"I'll walk you back up to your suite so you can rest. I'll come back at six and take you down to dinner."

Kiernan held out her hand to assist her from the car. Ariel took her hand but stumbled when exiting the driver's seat and fell against Kiernan, who folded her in a tight hug. "Are you all right?"

Warm breath wafted across Ariel's neck. The softness of breasts pressing close sent a delicious shiver rippling down her spine. Confused by her reaction, she pulled away and mumbled, "Yes."

For an instant, she locked eyes with Kiernan's, which seemed to see her every thought. Quickly, she turned away, but not before seeing those eyes widen and brighten with what appeared to be desire. Heat flushed Ariel's face from both embarrassment and something she refused to name. Then a torrent of ice water filled her veins when remembering she had signed the contract and agreed to every stipulation in it—including number nineteen.

"HOW'S THE SALMON?" Kiernan asked.

Ariel's cold and fatigue squelched her appetite, and she replied in a barely audible voice reflecting her weariness, "It's good. I'm not very hungry." She took a bite on her fork, but didn't bring it up to her mouth.

"It's been a long and demanding day for both of us. Don't eat it if you don't feel like it."

They returned to their meal, Ariel picking at hers.

They finished eating and Robert removed the plates and brought in dessert. Ariel stared in puzzlement when she saw what was in the crystal dessert glass placed before her.

Kiernan said, "One of my favorites, vanilla tapioca pudding. If you don't want it, I happen to know there's a fresh cheese cake in the kitchen."

"No. This is all right."

Ariel had never had tapioca pudding and didn't recognize what the tiny opaque spheres in the pudding were. They reminded her of the frog eggs she used to see when she was a kid and rode her bicycle to the pond in her neighborhood to catch tadpoles. Taking a dab on her spoon, she tasted it, finding it pleasant, but couldn't get past the image of frog eggs. Suddenly nauseous, she hastily reached for her glass of water and took a gulp to wash the dessert down.

Kiernan apparently noticed Ariel wasn't enjoying the dessert and, motioning Robert over from his station at the sideboard, said, "Bring Ariel a piece of the cheesecake, and a glass of milk."

"I'm sorry," Ariel said in a weary voice. She couldn't remember a cold ever making her feel this ill and fatigued before.

"Don't be sorry. There is no rule saying you have to eat everything on your plate, or that you like everything that is served."

Robert brought out the milk and cheesecake, placing it in front of Ariel, and removed the tapioca.

After taking a bite, she put her fork down and wearily closed her eyes, wishing she could go up to her suite and lie down.

Kiernan said, "You're tired, and I think it's time for you to retire. I'll take you upstairs."

A jolt of apprehension seized Ariel. She opened her eyes, and the weariness and illness magnified her fear. She closed her eyes again, feeling wretched. She couldn't do this. If Kiernan touched her...

Ariel heard Kiernan say, "Robert, you may go," and then the sound of a chair moving back. She opened her eyes as Kiernan knelt by her chair, inquiring in a gentle and concerned voice, "What is it? What's wrong?"

Ariel didn't know what to say. She couldn't meet Kiernan's eyes and tell her she couldn't have sex. Too much was still at stake. She looked down at her clasped hands, too tired to think and cope—and she was getting a headache as well. The recent events, and her illness, had sapped her spirit and strength. She swallowed hard, feeling her neck muscles move, and said almost in a whisper, "I can't do it."

She took a tremulous breath, suddenly feeling Kiernan's hand under her chin, forcing her head up. Ariel wouldn't meet Kiernan's gaze, hearing her ask in a puzzled voice, "Can't do what?"

Ariel peered at her from lowered lashes, and said in a quavering voice, "I can't be...with you. I—"

"Be with?" Kiernan narrowed her eyes. Ariel saw the confusion in them. Suddenly Kiernan blinked, and surprise, then hurt, flashed across her features. She uttered, "Oh." Then she softly said, "Ariel, that's not going to happen. Rest assured you'll be in your own bed tonight, and I'll be in mine." She stood up, reaching out her hand for Ariel to take. "Now, this day has been wearing for us both. We both need our sleep."

Ariel furtively glanced at the hand, declining to take it, since she didn't want to touch Kiernan. She stood, and Kiernan dropped her hand before saying, "Let's go."

Upstairs, Ariel opened the door to her suite and Kiernan followed her in, shutting the door behind her. She regarded Ariel and said, "If you need anything, push the green button on the intercom pad and Mrs. Belfort will answer. She keeps her pocket com-call with her."

Ariel looked down at the floor. After an awkward silence, Kiernan said, "Good night. I'll see you in the morning. Breakfast is at nine in the garden room." She crossed Ariel's sitting room and exited through the door leading to her suite.

Ariel watched her go, too tired and sick to feel relief, or much of anything at all.

Chapter Sixteen

TAKING HER BREAKFAST at nine the next morning in the garden room, Kiernan stared across the table at the empty place setting across from her. She wondered when Ariel would make an appearance. She planned to show her the estate grounds this morning before they packed and prepared for their St. Thomas trip.

An impatient glance at her wristwatch showed 9:30 and still no sign of Ariel. She informed Mrs. Belfort to tell her when her wife left her suite. In the meantime, she went to her study to read the online wedding announcement her uncle had submitted the night before to all the media agencies. She wryly noticed the news made headlines on the majority of outlets, but was dismayed seeing the major networks camped outside the Thorsen residence, providing live coverage and speculating about her bride. Ariel wasn't going to like that.

At ten o'clock, Kiernan became concerned as to why Ariel hadn't made an appearance. She knew yesterday's event was wearing, but they'd retired to bed early. Perhaps Ariel was avoiding her by delaying leaving her suite.

She remembered Ariel's behavior at dinner the previous night when she thought Kiernan was expecting her to consummate their marriage. It hurt to think Ariel expected her to act the part of some medieval lord making demands of that nature on his unwilling bride.

She went up to Ariel's suite, knocked lightly on the door, and, receiving no answer, opened the door and entered into stillness. No signs or sounds indicated Ariel was up, so she quietly walked through the open bedroom door into semi-darkness. The window was darkened to almost maximum, shutting out the morning light. On tiptoe, she went up to the bed. Ariel lay on her side breathing erratically, as if disturbed by an unpleasant dream. Kiernan noticed a folded washcloth on the pillow by Ariel's head. Her first thought was that Ariel must have had a headache or fever during the night and wet the washcloth to put on her brow for relief. She became concerned, and pushed Ariel's hair back from her forehead to place her palm there to discover Ariel indeed had a fever, a high one.

She hurried to the bathroom, searched the medicine cabinet and found a digital thermometer tab. She took it back to Ariel, ordering the computer to turn the bedside lamp on low. She placed the digital tab on Ariel's forehead, waiting until she heard the beep, and took it off to read. She reached over to the bedside table and pressed the green call button on the intercom system to summon Mrs. Belfort.

A few seconds later, Mrs. Belfort said over the intercom, "Mrs. Belfort here. Do you need anything?"

"Please Call Dr. Carla Mendelson immediately. Tell her Ariel has a temperature of one hundred and four degrees, and if she can't get here right away to send another doctor. After you do that, bring me a pitcher of water and a glass."

"Right away, ma'am."

Sitting on the edge of the bed, Kiernan gently placed her hand on Ariel's arm, giving it a light shake. "Ariel." When she didn't respond, Kiernan raised her voice. "Ariel, wake up." Hearing a faint whimper, Kiernan tried again to rouse her. "Ariel, can you hear me?"

Wetting dry lips with her tongue, Ariel tried to speak, managing only a croak. "Water." A racking cough seized her.

Kiernan helped her up into a sitting position, lightly patting her back. "It's on the way. Are you in pain?" Kiernan watched as Ariel noisily swallowed before barely rasping out, "Head..."

Kiernan picked up the washcloth, which was only slightly damp and took it to the bathroom to rinse under cold water. After wringing most of the water out, she folded it over twice and returned to Ariel. Seeing her closed eyes, she touched her arm to get her attention, and Ariel sat up shakily.

"I've called the doctor to come out as soon as possible. Why don't you lie back down?" Ariel slid back down onto the pillow, and Kiernan placed the wet washcloth on her forehead. After a few minutes, she removed the washcloth, and replaced it with her palm. She still felt the heat. Kiernan was apprehensive, wondering whether Ariel had a virus or the flu. There were so many flu viruses going around it was hard to keep up with the vaccines. Despite all the advances in medical technology, there was no way to eliminate viruses that continued to mutate into new strains. Fortunately, science was now able to develop a vaccine and contain any new outbreaks of flu, but was that what Ariel was sick from? Kiernan had no way of knowing.

Mrs. Belfort entered with a tray carrying a pitcher of water and a glass. She set the tray on the bedside table and said, "Dr. Mendelson is on her way."

Kiernan assisted Ariel into sitting up, and took the glass of water Mrs. Belfort handed her, holding it to Ariel's lips as she took a sip.

Mrs. Belfort said, "I'm going downstairs to wait for Dr. Mendelson. If there's anything else you need, call me."

"Yes, I will." Kiernan sat on the edge of the bed. She took Ariel's hand in hers in an effort to convey her concern and care.

THE VOICES WERE soft and low. One Ariel knew, the other she did not. Someone lightly touched her arm, and the voice she did not know said softly, "Ariel, I'm Dr. Mendelson. I'm going to listen to your heart and lungs, take a sample of your blood, and find out why you're ill." Ariel opened her eyes and focused on the woman whose voice was kind. A kindly face fit the voice. Her dark hair was shot through with silver, and she possessed gentle, soft brown eyes. She noticed a strange instrument split at one end, each end placed in the Doctor's ears with a tail ending in a flat disc. Her mind struggled to name it, fuzzily remembering it was an instrument used many years ago by the medical profession to listen to a person's heart and lungs. It hurt to think, and she shut her eyes against the pain in her head. The covers gently slid from her chest. Ariel felt movement at the top of her nightshirt and a point of pressure above her left breast. "Take in a slow, deep breath, and let it out slowly."

Drawing breath through her mouth caused her to cough. Ariel struggled to sit up as the sensation of drowning seized her. A pair of arms encircled her shoulders assisting her up. After the coughing spasm subsided, the same arms assisted her back against the pillow and hands extended her right arm before a sharp point of cold pressed into the bend. She was conscious of the brief pain, but she couldn't respond to it.

Tired, she was so tired. It hurt when she breathed, when she swallowed, and her head throbbed with pain. Tiredness closed around her like a gray fog, and she floated in the realm between awareness and oblivion where time no longer existed.

DR. MENDELSON REMOVED the vial of blood from the tubular hemo-extractor, inserting it in the compact rectangular analyzer she held in her left hand. After a few seconds, the device beeped, and she read the results on the display screen before saying to Kiernan, "She has viral pneumonia."

"What! How could she have pneumonia and not show some symptoms yesterday?" Apprehension clutched her heart for a few beats.

"Analyses also show the common cold virus and an excessive amount of Bendyltrisuptyril in her system, which is a common ingredient in cold remedies. It would mask the pneumonia symptoms, but has side affects if you ingest over the required dosage. She shouldn't have contracted pneumonia unless she wasn't taking care of herself, eating right, sleeping, resting—"

"She did appear overly tired yesterday. I thought it was due to the stress of the wedding."

"Stress could well be a factor in compromising her immune system. Take it from me—I remember how stressful a wedding can be. Right after I said 'I do,' I dropped from exhaustion."

"You said side effects from the medication?"

"Too much can result in headache, nausea, diarrhea, tinnitus, or hives. Other side effects are euphoria, agitation, apprehension, and in some case studies paranoia. Side effects promptly disappear when ceasing the medication."

Kiernan thought about Ariel's behavior last night at dinner and her fear that Kiernan would make demands. She said nothing though, not wanting to share that with the doctor.

Dr. Mendelson reached into her bag and brought out a dermal infuser and a box of medication. She took a silver vial from the box and inserted it into the infuser. "I'm going to give her medication to prevent any bacterial infection and help with the viral infection. I'll also give her something to ease her fever and pain." She administered the dosages into Ariel's arm. "The analysis also shows she has some dehydration as well as low electrolytes and blood sugar. I'll order an IV drip and arrange right away for a nurse to come out and tend to that. It might be a good idea to have the nurse stay a few days and monitor her, also to assist in her care, and I'll leave instructions with the nurse as to diet and medications."

"Why use an IV drip? Can't you give her an infusion?"

"She needs a slow, but steady supply of medications and nutrients. An IV is the best method."

"How long will it take her to recover from this?" Kiernan asked with concern.

"She'll need plenty of bed rest for the next three or four days, and after that, she needs to take it easy for the next two weeks and not do anything taxing or strenuous. I'll call the nurse. She should be out within the next three hours."

Kiernan stroked Ariel's forehead still feeling the heat. She noticed the dryness of her skin.

Standing beside Kiernan, Dr. Mendelson gazed down at Ariel, and said in a quiet voice, "You know, despite her illness I can see how lovely she is. Her pictures are all over the news media today."

"Yes, I know," Kiernan said dryly.

"I hear all sorts of gossip from my patients, but not a word of this. One day you're supposedly involved with...someone...and all of a sudden, you're married to someone else. I must say, this took me totally by surprise."

"It took me by surprise, too." Kiernan realized that Ariel had taken her by surprise.

"I'm sure there is more to the story. But I have the feeling you're not going to tell me. I'll come by tomorrow to check on her."

"I'll call Mrs. Belfort to come up to escort you out."

"No need. I know my way. Kiernan, best wishes to you both and a bright future."

"Thanks, Carla." Resting her gaze on Ariel, Kiernan wondered what their future would be like if their marriage were not a business arrangement. Would it be bright and happy?

THE SOUND OF muffled footsteps alerted Kiernan that someone was entering the bedroom. She peered up from the chair at the head of the bed where she was watching over her sleeping wife. In a hushed voice, Mrs. Belfort said, "Ma'am, Ms. Robinson, the nurse Dr. Mendelson called, is here."

"Please, send her in. Oh, and do the necessary cancellations for the St. Thomas trip."

"I'll take care of that right away, ma'am.

Mrs. Belfort exited the room and a few seconds later an attractive dark skinned woman in a white medical uniform walked in carrying a bulky blue bag slung over one shoulder. In a low voice she said, "I'm Stephanie Robinson, Ariel Thorsen's nurse. Dr. Mendelson filled me in on the patient's condition."

"I'm Kiernan O'Shay, Ariel's wife."

"I hear congratulations are in order. I'm sorry this happened at such an important and happy time for you both." Stephanie's dark eyes reflected her sincerity.

"Thank you. My only concern now is for Ariel's health."

"Yes, of course, that's why I'm here." Stephanie put down the bag she was carrying and picked up Ariel's hand to monitor her pulse. After a minute, she set Ariel's hand back on the bed. "I'm going to set up the IV."

Stephanie retrieved her bag, set it on the end of the bed, and opened it to remove a portable stand that she unfolded and placed on the floor at the head of the bed. Next, she took out an IV bag and a sealed, sterile package containing the necessary tubing and needle. "This has a glucose solution, as well as fortified nutrients, and medication to help her relax." She hung up the bag on the stand and attached the tubing and needle. "I'm going to wake her and tell her what I'm doing. I don't want her alarmed and dislodging the needle."

Kiernan cringed when imagining a needle penetrating Ariel's

skin. "A needle? God, that's so outdated and barbaric. Why not hook an infuser to the bag and place it on her arm?"

"Infusers are for dermal use, and not for veins. The nutrients and medication will need to go through the veins, and needles are still the most effective way to administer them."

"We can fly to the outer edges of the solar system, but can't find the cure for the common cold, most viruses, and we still use primitive medical instruments."

Stephanie responded with an amused voice, not loud enough to wake her patient. "We did find the cure for diabetes, M.S, Alzheimer's, most cancers, and a host of other diseases. We use precision computer programs to do laser surgery on the brain and spine. I wouldn't call that primitive."

"I suppose," Kiernan said grudgingly.

Stephanie touched Ariel gently on the shoulder. "Ariel, wake up."

Ariel opened unfocused eyes, suddenly surprised. "Mysha," she mumbled.

Upon hearing Ariel say the name of her former girlfriend, Kiernan stiffened. She crossed her arms over her chest and tried to quell her disappointment. But she couldn't expect Ariel to forget Mysha. Ariel hadn't ended the relationship because she wanted to. She ended it because Kiernan forced her to.

"I'm Stephanie, your nurse. I'm here to assist you during your illness. Dr. Mendelson has ordered an IV for you. You're going to feel a prick on your arm where I insert the needle."

Stephanie retrieved a sterile-wipe from her bag, using it to clean the bend in Ariel's left arm. She tied a rubber tubing tourniquet right below the bend, found a suitable vein, inserted the needle, and made Ariel flinch. Stephanie taped the needle and part of the tubing to Ariel's arm to keep it from coming loose. She asked Ariel in a gentle voice, "Do you need me to get anything or do anything for you?"

"No," Ariel said, her voice weak.

"You let me know if you do. I'll be right here."

"Yes, okay." Ariel shifted her position slightly and closed her eyes.

Stephanie glanced at her wristwatch and watched Ariel's respiration for a minute before checking her wristwatch once more. To Kiernan she said in a subdued voice, "The main thing is for her to have plenty of rest and liquids. Tonight, we need her eating something light, such as clear broths, Jell-O, and clear liquids. She's to have no dairy products until her fever abates. I can remove the IV tomorrow night, if she eats and drinks enough." She withdrew a digital notebook from the pocket of her smock and handed it to

Kiernan. "Here's a menu she needs to follow for the next couple of days."

"I'll take it to my chef and instruct him to follow what's on here." An idea occurred to Kiernan. "When can she have visitors?"

"I would wait at least a couple of days. Not because of contagion, but visitors do tend to overexcite a patient. Of course, having a loved one participate in her care is also important and helps in the recovery."

Gazing tenderly at Ariel, Kiernan said, "I'll be here for her and help anyway I can."

THE NEXT AFTERNOON, Stephanie gave Ariel a sponge bath and helped her dress in a clean, pink flannel nightgown she found in the dresser drawer. Ariel knew it was one Kiernan had purchased for her, but didn't mind, as wearing something fresh and clean felt wonderful. Most of yesterday and this morning, Ariel spent sleeping, only vaguely aware a doctor had visited. Kiernan visited a few times to see how she was doing and asking if she needed anything. Seeing as Ariel wasn't in the mood for company, she stayed only a few minutes each time.

Mrs. Belfort entered the bedroom carrying a tray with Ariel's dinner and placed it on the rolling bedside tray by the bed. "Ricardo prepared you some of his 'fix you up' chicken noodle soup. He swears it will fix what ails you."

Stephanie moved to Ariel's side. "Here, let me help you sit up." Stephanie moved an arm around her and assisted her to an upright position while Mrs. Belfort leaned the pillows against the headboard, so Stephanie could gently make Ariel more comfortable.

Mrs. Belfort kindly said, "If there is anything else you want, please don't hesitate to have Stephanie buzz me. I'll get you whatever you need."

"Thank you," Ariel said, as Mrs. Belfort patted her arm before leaving.

Ariel took a spoon, her hand quavering slightly, and scooped a spoonful of the soup, dribbling some on the front of her gown. Stephanie gently removed the spoon from Ariel's hand, and said, "Here, let me do that for you."

Dismayed by her clumsiness, Ariel said, "I'm sorry."

"Oh, honey, there's nothing to be sorry for." Stephanie fed Ariel the soup, waiting patiently while Ariel consumed the spoonful before offering her more. The soup tasted delicious, and despite her illness, Ariel did feel hungry.

Kiernan entered and stood on the opposite side of the bed from

Stephanie. She asked warmly, "How are you doing?"

Ariel was silent, hoping to discourage Kiernan from staying. Stephanie said, "If Ariel eats enough I'll remove her IV tonight."

"That sounds like a good deal." Kiernan examined the contents of the bowl. "Chicken noodle soup? It looks good." She sniffed with exaggeration. "Mmm, and smells delicious. I hope Ricardo has more—I may want a bowl myself." Gazing over at Ariel, she asked, "Does it taste as good as it looks and smells?"

Ariel nodded. After another spoonful, she said, "No more."

"Would you like some apple juice?" Stephanie asked.

"Yes, please."

Stephanie reached for the glass of apple juice only to find Kiernan holding it. Kiernan said, "Why don't you take a break, Stephanie. I'll let you know when you can come back."

After Stephanie left for dinner and a break, Kiernan held the glass with the straw up to Ariel's mouth, watching as she drank. Ariel drained the glass, and Kiernan placed it back on the tray. "Would you like some Jell-O?"

Ariel didn't want Kiernan feeding her. She could try feeding herself, but Kiernan would probably make a fuss over her if she spilled any, and she didn't want Kiernan that close and touching her. She did want the Jell-O, though. "Yes," Ariel said in an almost inaudible voice.

Kiernan brought a spoonful up to her mouth, watching as she ate. Ariel ate three more spoonfuls until finally she had enough, twisted her head away, and sighed tiredly. Kiernan rolled the bedside tray away from the bed, took the napkin off Ariel's lap, and gently wiped her mouth. She assisted Ariel in lying down and drew the covers over her. Brushing her hand soothingly over Ariel's forehead, she asked, "Is there anything I can get for you?"

"I'm okay." Ariel wished Kiernan would leave her in peace.

"If there is, you let me know."

Ariel didn't reply. Feeling tired and drained, she let her eyelids close. She watched through half-closed eyelids as Kiernan sat in the chair by her bed, watching her as if she were some sick child. Ariel didn't like feeling helpless in front of Kiernan. As she drifted into sleep, someone tucked the covers around her shoulders, and softly stroked her forehead. Finally, the tread of light footsteps faded from her hearing along with consciousness as she slipped into sleep.

ARIEL'S NIGHT WAS peaceful, leaving her feeling more rested and stronger the next morning, but still fatigued. She ate a light breakfast of coffee and wheat toast with a light spreading of grape jelly. Stephanie had removed her IV the previous night, for which she was grateful. Ariel refused to use the bedpan that morning, and Stephanie ensured she didn't topple over in a slow walk to the bathroom.

Stephanie left for breakfast leaving Ariel at loose ends. She wished she hadn't forgotten to bring her IMP so she could check the messages. Then again, she wasn't up to hearing the calls Mysha probably left. She decided to watch the EM. "EM video on. Scroll at three-second intervals." The EM projected the 3-D images onto the far wall. She leaned against the headboard, watching the EM scroll through the channels, which mostly featured info-commercials, game shows, or outdoor adventures. The EM scrolled past a news channel, startling Ariel when she thought she heard her name. "EM — back two channels." She stared in shock at a picture of herself.

"...*mystery surrounding Kiernan O'Shay's marriage to Ariel Thorsen. What we know is Ms. Thorsen is a native of Tennessee, born and raised in East Ridge, right outside of Chattanooga, and is the daughter of...*"

In horrid fascination, she watched as portions of her life were there for the world to see. There were pictures of her in grammar school, high school, and in college, ones with friends and neighbors, and even pictures of her mother and father, as well as Seth and Leigh. Suddenly faint with shock, she didn't hear Kiernan come in, and jumped when she said, "It'll die down after a while."

A wave of nausea and dizziness hit her, and she heaved, but didn't vomit. Kiernan pressed the call button and said, "Mrs. Belfort, tell Nurse Robinson to come up here right away — Ariel is nauseous." Placing her arms around Ariel, Kiernan said, "EM off." She leaned Ariel against the headboard and stroked her hair back from her forehead. "I'm sorry this has upset you. Believe me when I say you'll get used to this, and learn to ignore it."

Ariel couldn't hold back her tears. She was hoping her family would escape publicity and scrutiny by the media. She should have known this would happen. Anything involving Kiernan O'Shay was news worthy. "My family...they...they...don't deserve this."

"No, they don't. As I told you before, I'll do everything within my power to protect you and them."

Ariel pulled away from Kiernan's arms, glaring at her accusingly, and harshly said, "I'll hold you responsible if anything happens to them."

"I'll accept that responsibility," Kiernan responded sincerely.

The sensation of the room tilting made her heave once again. This time she vomited into the clean bedpan Kiernan snatched from the floor by the bed, and held for her. When she finished, Kiernan helped her lie back on the pillows. Stephanie arrived and administered an infusion for nausea, which also served to calm her and make her drowsy. Kiernan left her bedside, returning with a wet washcloth, and carefully cleaned her face. Ariel watched Kiernan as she did this, seeing an expression of tenderness, her eyes soft and caring. This was the last thing she saw as she drifted into sleep.

ARIEL WASN'T AS upset after she woke around lunchtime. She didn't have much of an appetite and had declined to eat until Stephanie threatened her by saying if she didn't eat, she would hook her back up to the IV.

She managed to eat enough to satisfy Stephanie, spending the rest of the day in bed, listening to music, and trying to take her mind off the news story.

In the evening, she finished dinner, and was dozing off when Kiernan came in with a book in her hands, and said to Stephanie, "I'll stay with Ariel, while you take a break, and have dinner."

"Thank you," Stephanie said, before exiting the room.

Kiernan walked around to the other side of the bed, took the chair, and pulled it close to the bed to where Ariel could see her. "I would like to share my favorite story with you. I guarantee it will make you feel better and get well faster. At least it did for me. My mothers would read it to me when I wasn't feeling well. Shall I read it to you?"

Ariel almost declined, but she was curious, and something in Kiernan's voice made her forget for the moment her animosity. "Yes."

Kiernan appeared pleased. "It's *The Little Prince*, by Antoine de Saint-Exupery. Have you ever read it?"

"No."

"It was written over one hundred and fifty years ago. I think you'll like it. It's the story of a Prince who has adventures visiting different planets."

Kiernan read, the sound of her voice soothing. Ariel closed her eyes, drifting between wakefulness and sleep, where the story painted wonderful pictures in her mind, and she lived the adventures of the Little Prince.

"What is essential is invisible to the eye. It is only with the heart that you can see rightly," Kiernan read.

Ariel found these words a key to a door. She used the key to crack the door open. The light within that shone through the crack was barely a sliver of brightness. In this sliver of light was Kiernan's voice, soft and soothing, not only to her ears, but also to her heart. Her hate for Kiernan was slipping from her. But what would replace it?

Kiernan finished the story and closed the book. For a while, she watched Ariel sleep. She reminded her of a sleeping angel. Silently, she rose from her chair and gently tucked the covers around Ariel's shoulder. On impulse, she leaned over to leave a soft kiss on the pale brow, and walked quietly from the room.

Not asleep yet, Ariel felt the caress of lips against her forehead. The caress slipped into the crack in the door and entered the light. The door shut, and Ariel lost the key as sleep claimed her.

THE NEXT MORNING, Ariel said goodbye to Stephanie. She was now strong enough to bathe and dress without assistance, though still feeling drained of energy. During breakfast, Kiernan dropped by for a visit, but soon left, apparently sensing Ariel wasn't in the mood to talk.

Before lunch, Ariel showered and washed her hair, feeling a whole lot better. She decided she wanted to dress today, go out to her sitting room, get online, download some music, and maybe search for some interesting novels to download into her e-book. At this time, her checking account contained enough funds to cover her purchases. Much to her irritation, her money would soon run out and she would need to use funds from the account Kiernan set up for her.

She walked into her closet, reached for a pair of her well-worn jeans, and stopped as her hand stroked the pair of tailored jeans next to them. Why not? she thought. She'd eventually have to wear them. After removing the jeans from the hanger and draping them over her arm, she surveyed the casual blouses and knit pullovers, selecting a pink pullover blouse. Carefully scrutinizing the various pairs of shoes in the shoe rack, she decided on a navy pair of slip-on canvas shoes.

Back in her bedroom she opened the sock drawer and found a pink pair of crew socks. Next, she opened the underwear drawer and hesitated. The intimacy of Kiernan picking out these items brought a nervous flutter to her stomach, reminding her of a certain stipulation in the agreement. She chose a pair of panties and a bra she'd brought with her. After dressing, she checked her appearance in the mirror, admiring how the tailored jeans made her legs appear longer. As she walked out into the sitting room, there was a knock at the main door.

"Come in."

The door opened, and two excited tow-headed ten year olds descended on her. "Ariel!" They both hugged her and giggled excitedly. She held them close, looking up at the door as her mother entered. "Mom," Ariel said with delight.

Joanna closed the distance and swept her into her arms, after a moment separating only enough to touch her palm to Ariel's forehead. "Should you be out of bed, sweetheart?"

"I'm feeling better. Besides, bed is boring."

"We've come to visit and have lunch with you," Leigh said excitedly.

A rustling sound at the door caught Ariel's attention. She peered up to see Kiernan standing in the doorway with a strange expression on her face. Kiernan backed out of the door and shut it, leaving before Ariel could say a word.

KIERNAN GAZED ACROSS the dinner table at Ariel, who was paying more attention to her dessert than the conversation Kiernan was trying to engage her in. The wedding had been ten days ago and despite Kiernan's repeated invitations, this was the first time since the wedding night that Ariel dined in the dining room instead of taking meals in her suite. Tonight, Kiernan had practically ordered Ariel to dine with her, telling her that since she was feeling better, she expected to see Ariel at the dinner table every night. Ariel fixed a 'balky' stare on her, not saying anything. Kiernan hadn't thought she would show for dinner and was both surprised and pleased when she showed up on time and took her seat.

Kiernan had also suggested for the past few days that she take breakfast with her, but Ariel slept in, missing breakfast, and after she was up she would go to the kitchen, have a bowl of cereal, toast, coffee, and juice. Ricardo kept Kiernan advised about what Ariel ate during the day and informed Kiernan he had offered to fix her an omelet or something else, but Ariel always declined.

Lunch was the same story. Kiernan would invite Ariel but she refused, taking lunch in her suite instead. Much to Kiernan's chagrin, Ariel stayed mostly in her suite, and the times Kiernan paid her a visit, she was reading or online. Kiernan kept trying to strike up conversations, but Ariel made only cursory comments and avoided her, but Kiernan wasn't going to give up.

Rain was falling, and the forecast was for rain all day so Kiernan couldn't show Ariel the grounds and take her up to Deer Falls and the old apple orchard as she planned. If it was good weather the next day, she would insist Ariel go with her.

Kiernan wasn't used to anyone ignoring her, and she found Ariel's disinterest galling. Over dinner she tried initiating a conversation by picking a topic she knew Ariel would like, discussing String Theory, but Ariel showed no interest—or feigned no interest was more like it. Kiernan had one more ploy to use.

"Ariel." This got her wife's attention. "I want you to come to my study with me, see some of my designs for a prototype light-speed ship, and give me your opinion."

Ariel's attention seemed to perk up. For a moment, she hesitated. "Okay."

"If you're finished, let's go."

Kiernan led Ariel down the hall and into her study where she went over to a table holding a few folders and pushed them to one end. She stepped over to a wide cabinet with thin drawers, opened one, and withdrew thick papers she brought back to the table to spread out. "This is one prototype I've drawn up, and it's probably the one I'll go with...or something similar."

Ariel studied the plans and asked questions, which Kiernan answered while pointing out various features. Ariel imparted her opinions while Kiernan listened and made notes in a digital notebook.

Impressed with Ariel's insight and knowledge of engineering, Kiernan said, "You would make a great aerospace engineer. You know, you can work for me when the project initiates in another couple of years."

"It's very interesting, but I'm not trained as an engineer."

"You probably already have a lot of the basic courses and could easily get into a degree program at Embry-Riddle, or at your alma mater."

"Are you serious?"

"Of course I am. You can attend most of the courses online and probably complete your degree before our baby is born. And work from home after she's born."

Ariel appeared distressed by Kiernan's comment and looked down at the floor.

Kiernan felt like a moron reminding Ariel of her 'main duty.' She gathered up the blueprints to put back in the drawer. "I think that's enough for one evening. You're still recovering and need your rest."

AS KIERNAN PUT the blueprints away, Ariel inspected the study. Her gaze was drawn to a bookshelf with various trophies on it. She walked over to investigate, discovering they were racing trophies Kiernan had won. There were photographs of Kiernan standing triumphantly beside her racing flitter, *Solar Flair*. Next to the trophies was a model of *Celeste*.

While stroking a fingertip over the sleek lines and admiring the workmanship, she heard Kiernan say from behind her, "You can pick it up if you want." Kiernan came up beside her as Ariel picked up the model and held it at different angles to study it.

"One of the engineering team made it," Kiernan said, "when *Celeste* was still on the drawing board, and gave it to Grandmother."

"It's beautiful and must have taken considerable time and effort to construct. Is it a kit bash or made from scratch?"

"Kit bash?"

"It means to use components from other kits to create new models."

"I really don't know. Didn't you say you put together model spaceships, as well as made ones from plywood and cardboard?"

"Yes, I told you that when we first met at the restaurant."

"You did. That's right. I remember everything about that night."

A tide of heat surged through Ariel when hearing Kiernan's words and seeing the warmth in her eyes. She hastily focused on the model of *Celeste*. "I do have some spaceships I constructed from kit bashing. Some are really wild ones that could never actually be built." Shifting her attention from the model to Kiernan, she added, "They were ships I dreamed I would explore the galaxy in and save the universe."

"Have spaceship. Will travel?"

Ariel couldn't help but chuckle. "Exactly. You said that had been your dream too, when a child." Holding up the model ship, she said, "And see, your dream did come true. You have a spaceship."

"Yes, I do. But I would like to see yours, if you don't mind sharing."

Ariel couldn't tell whether Kiernan was serious. A brief study of her face showed what Ariel believed was expectation. "I'll get them and bring them back here — next time I go home."

Hurt flashed across Kiernan's features when Ariel mentioned home. But she hastily said, "I would like that." Then Kiernan gently asked, "Do you have other dreams?"

This question surprised Ariel. She wondered why Kiernan would care about any other dreams but her own. Ariel saw her expectant expression and decided she would believe it was genuine. "When I was in high school I wanted to be an astronomer." Shrugging, she added, "But when Dad died I concentrated on physics instead."

"Why?"

"I wanted to stay home and help Mom with the twins. There were no positions for astronomers close to home." Seeing the soft gaze regarding her, she asked shyly, "Wh—What dreams do you have?"

"Build spaceships capable of light-speed to take us out of the solar system, and to the stars."

Of course, Ariel knew this. Kiernan needed her, needed a wife to help put that dream in action. And an heir. There was a good chance Kiernan could never realize her dream unless she got control of the company. Ariel could well be the catalyst that shaped the future. That sent humankind to the stars. But at what price? What sacrifice? The price of a child? What price would future generations pay if Kiernan couldn't build her dream? Ariel didn't know.

Ariel swallowed and quietly said, "I'm sure that dream will come true."

"I hope it will," was the soft reply.

Chapter Seventeen

THE NEXT MORNING Kiernan entered the kitchen to find Ariel at the table eating a stack of pancakes. Seated with her was Ricardo, who was busy entering information into an e-notepad.

Ariel peered up briefly, flicking a smile, and resumed eating.

"Those pancakes smell good," Kiernan said accusingly to Ricardo. "Why didn't I have them for breakfast this morning?" It pleased her to know Ariel allowed Ricardo to prepare her breakfast and wasn't eating cold cereal.

Ricardo squinted up at Kiernan and lifted his brow. "Because it's Sunday, and you always have ham, eggs, and grits on Sunday."

"Perhaps I'll change the menu to pancakes every other Sunday." At the coffee pot she poured herself a cup.

"I'll make note of that. Ariel, are you sure there isn't anything I can put on the list? No favorite snacks or food?"

"Hmmm, I think I would like trail mix and yogurt raisins. Oh, and dried apple rings."

Ricardo said, "The dried apple rings we can do ourselves. The Jonathans are ripe, and I can send Robert up to the orchard to pick a basket full."

Kiernan took the seat next to Ariel. "I'm taking Ariel up to the waterfall and orchard as soon as she finishes breakfast, and we can pick some for you."

"I'll find you a basket." Ricardo left the table.

Ariel finished her last bite of pancakes and took her plate and empty milk glass over to the dishwasher. Kiernan inspected Ariel's jeans and short-sleeved red shirt. "It's pretty cool this morning, so you might want to put on something with long sleeves over your shirt." Kiernan wore a pair of jeans, and a green plaid flannel shirt.

"I'll do that and be right down."

"Go through the backdoor here at the kitchen and wait for me while I get one of the electric carts to take us up the mountain." Kiernan would normally walk the half-mile up to the orchard and falls, but Ariel was still recovering from her illness and didn't need to exert herself.

Ariel left to dress and Kiernan exited and headed to the equipment shed. She found the electric cart she wanted and drove it up toward the back porch. Ariel exited, dressed in a long-sleeve blue denim shirt and carrying a yellow apple basket. Stopping the cart in front of her, Kiernan said with a jaunty air, "Hop in."

Ariel put the basket behind the seat and slipped into the cart beside Kiernan.

On the ride up the mountain they passed a few wooded areas and clearings. At one point, they drove through a shallow creek that crossed the road, and Kiernan told Ariel the name was Washboard Creek. "At one time, some of the original settlers used it to wash clothes. Four families originally settled on this mountain in the early nineteenth century: the McPhersons, the Porters, the Bearfoots, and the Daniels."

She directed Ariel's attention to the left, pointing out a low stone fence in front of an apple orchard. They rode past the opening in the fence. "Apples later. I want to take you up to the falls first."

The road wound and curved, going upward, making more twists. When Kiernan pulled off the road she stopped at a path leading to a knoll and said, "The falls are only two hundred yards away, but we'll have to walk from here."

Kiernan guided Ariel down a well-worn footpath leading into a hollow and back up. A faint rushing noise sounded in the distance. The closer they walked to the falls the more distinct the sound became until it was a soft roar. They climbed up an incline in the path and stopped. Thirty yards away was the twin waterfalls, called Deer Falls. The fall closest to them was some twenty feet wide and the other only slightly smaller. From a height of forty feet, the water spilled into a pool below. The spray caught the morning sun, forming a rainbow halfway down. Where the water hit the pool a fine mist floated, unimpeded by sunbeams at this time of the morning.

The sound of the falls was loud enough to muffle voices so Kiernan gently took Ariel by an elbow and led her over to a broad, flat rock shelf. She helped her up on it and they inched over to the edge, which overhung a clear pool that appeared to be seven or eight feet deep. Kiernan leaned into Ariel and said close to her ear so her voice was heard over the falls, "This is a great place to swim in the summer. Farther down the stream is a good place to catch trout."

Ariel nodded in understanding. They watched the falls for a few minutes more until Kiernan took Ariel's hand. "Let's go pick apples."

Ariel didn't remove her hand from Kiernan's as they walked back to the cart. Coupled with their interaction the previous night in her study, Kiernan couldn't help but feel some satisfaction. Ariel seemed to be feeling more comfortable around her.

Kiernan drove the cart back the way they came and wheeled through the opening in the stone fence, drove to the middle of the orchard, and stopped. The twenty trees sported low branches gnarled from age, but they were loaded with a lot of reddish apples as well as some still green with only a blush of red.

"The Jonathans are ripe now. The Romes won't be ready for another couple of weeks." Kiernan took the basket from behind the seat and walked through the ankle-length grass to the nearest tree. The limbs were low enough for her to examine the fruit. She picked a few, and Ariel assisted her until they filled the basket.

Near a tree trunk, Kiernan set down the basket and picked out an apple. She leaned against the rough, brown trunk, wiped the apple clean on her shirt, and took a bite, gazing at Ariel as she chewed. She twisted the apple in her hand until the side not bitten was visible and held it up to Ariel's mouth. Full lips touched the rose skin of the fruit, and the flash of white teeth crunched through the ivory flesh. Kiernan inhaled and held her breath, and liquid heat flooded her veins. Ariel's eyes were half-lidded, and her face fused with pleasure as she chewed. There was a bit of fruit on her mouth, and Kiernan couldn't help but reach up to remove it, brushing her fingertips against the soft, full lips. Her fingers strayed and gently caressed the dark spot above the left corner, feeling a slight bump. She longed to touch that spot with her tongue and kiss those lips, opening them for her to enter and claim Ariel as her own.

"Ariel." The name came unbidden, caressing her tongue and throat as it escaped. She wasn't sure she spoke it aloud until Ariel ceased chewing, her eyes nervously darting away from Kiernan.

There was a moment of stillness backdropped by the high trilling of insects in the grass, and the faint rub of leaves in the trees.

A sudden rush of icy anxiety raced through Kiernan's veins. She realized that openly showing her desire disquieted Ariel. "I think that's enough for this morning. Let's head on back." Ariel wouldn't meet her eyes.

The ride down the mountain was one of silence. Ariel sat next to her as if frozen in ice, her eyes distant and cold.

THE WISPY PULLS of cottony mist evaporated in the morning sun as Ariel ambled through the entrance of the worn, gray stone orchard fence. She glimpsed the glistening rainbow diamonds of dew strung along the strands of a spider's web bridging a blackberry bramble and the edge of the stone fence wall. She walked toward the heart of the orchard, where the old monarchs grew with their gnarled limbs heavy with fruit. Kiernan leaned against the rough bark of the oldest of them. Her eyes were deep green pools full of mystery and secrets. Her smile was one of welcome and promises.

Kiernan said nothing but held a red apple in her hand, as an offering to her. No words were spoken and no sound was heard except the early chorus of distant birds welcoming the morning sun.

Halting in front of the silent figure, Ariel took Kiernan's wrist in her hand, feeling the throb of pulse where she pressed her thumb. Bringing the hand with the apple up against her mouth, she flicked her tongue against the fruit's tender skin before slowly sinking her teeth into the crisp, ripe flesh, tearing a chunk free and chewing. The sweet flavor of apple flooded her mouth. She closed her eyes, still holding the hand offering her the fruit.

The feel of warm fingers caressed a piece of apple from her mouth, and she opened her eyes. The face before her was rapt with desire, eyes smoldering, lips partly open to say, "Ariel."

The sound of her name flooded her senses, tilting her world on its axis, pulling her into a new orbit around those eyes and mouth. She fell from orbit and descended, placing her lips against the inviting softness, demanding entrance with a tentative touch of the tip of her tongue. Entrance was granted, and she trembled from the taste and feel, liquid heat coursing to her center, bringing forth a rumble from deep within her chest.

She surrendered herself to the moment and to the feeling, pulling the hand she held, now free of the apple, to the waistband of her pants, pushing it between the rough denim and warm flesh to that place aching for a firm touch. The nimble fingers found that aching place, the touch of them firm and hot as she arched into them, seeking sweet release.

The first wave broke and shook her body. Her eyes flew open. She saw the grayness of the early morning and the darker shapes of objects in her room. She stroked her fingers rapidly against her aching need and broke beneath yet another surge, her cry of release almost breathless.

She removed her wet fingers from her vagina and rolled onto her side, feeling confused by her dream and wondering if she were a betrayer. Her subconscious didn't lie. She was attracted to Kiernan in a visceral way. A pang of anxiety struck when she realized as much as she could crush this attraction during her waking hours, she couldn't when asleep. She must always remember what Kiernan had done and not let this physical attraction trick her into emotional feelings. Believing Kiernan was anything different from what she was — a conniving and vindictive bitch — would only cause trouble. She had better keep her distance. Then maybe the...attraction...would go away.

Chapter Eighteen

ARIEL SAT NEXT to the chauffeur, Michael, while he drove Crestview Estate's big, dually four-wheel drive pickup truck to take her to visit her mother. Michael had offered up one of Kiernan's two limousines, but Ariel didn't want to take the chance of drawing the attention of any of the media lurking around. Fortunately, for the last two weeks, the media had been leaving her family alone, partly because her mother's neighbors would call the police and complain the media vehicles were blocking the parking places in front of their homes and driveways. A few neighbors took it on themselves to block in any media vehicles with their own vehicles, making it impossible for them to leave without seeking out the neighbors responsible and getting an earful. The previous week, the neighborhood association received permission from the city to declare the curbs in front of residences as private parking areas. The police enforced this by ticketing and towing away any unauthorized vehicles. Ariel had a suspicion Kiernan was behind this effort because the city was so willing to cooperate.

She called her mother the night before, telling her she was coming over to pick up her motorcycle and IMP, visit for a while, and then go riding. Her family had visited three times during her recuperation from her illness—the last time was a week ago. She had been calling her mother and siblings every other night to say hello. She tried to keep the conversations brief as her mother had a tendency to ask personal questions about how she was getting along with Kiernan. Ariel always answered with a vague reply, usually saying 'okay,' and hurriedly changed the subject to how the twins were doing in school or asked about the latest neighborhood gossip.

There was another person she missed. Mysha. She'd deliberately put off contacting Mysha, partly due to her illness rendering her unable to cope with something so potentially upsetting. She didn't know whether she could have dealt with the drama, and trauma, of facing Mysha and telling her the reason for what she had done. She was stronger now, and offering Mysha an explanation was important, and she couldn't put it off any longer. She wasn't looking forward to Mysha's reaction, expecting the worst. She couldn't blame Mysha if she refused to see her.

Michael pulled the truck into the driveway. Ariel got out. "Thanks, Michael."

"Anytime you need to go anywhere let me know."

Ariel hurried up the steps, palmed the keypad lock, and opened the door with a loud and excited, "I'm home!"

"I see you are." Joanna said affectionately. She hugged her, and keeping her arms around Ariel, she leaned back, examining her closely. "You're looking good. You're not overdoing it, are you? You know you have to take it easy and not ride your motorcycle all over creation."

"Yes, Mom. I don't think it will kill me to go riding and get some fresh air." She took a seat on the living room couch.

Her mother asked, "Can I get you something to drink?"

"No, I'm okay. You don't have to wait on me. I know where the kitchen is."

Joanna said sheepishly, "Yes, I suppose you do." She hesitated before asking, "How are things...really?"

"Okay, I guess. It's kind of boring with nothing to do except read or go online." She paused. "I'm thinking about taking classes for an aerospace engineering degree."

"Oh?"

"Kiernan said she'll have the project on her light-speed ship up and running in two years and wants to hire me as a design engineer."

"How do you feel about doing that kind of work?"

"I think it'll be interesting, and I would enjoy it. Of course, I can probably go back to teaching physics after the baby..." Ariel couldn't bring herself to finish the sentence.

For a few seconds her mother didn't say anything. Ariel saw sadness flash across her face before she said, "You always did have a thing for spaceships. Do you mind me asking how you and Kiernan are getting along?"

"Now that she's back at work I don't see much of her." Of course, that was Ariel's doing. Ever since that day in the orchard she wanted to distance herself from Kiernan, fearing Kiernan would seek her out for sex, and, she might not be averse to complying. She no longer wanted to talk about Kiernan, so changed the subject. "Didn't you tell me the other night Seth and Leigh are due for their first report cards?"

"They should be out this Friday. I've received good feedback from their teachers, so I'm expecting good report cards. They should be home at three today and would love to see you."

"I'd love to see them too, but I want to go riding before dark." She was silent for a moment while contemplating how to broach a subject she knew was awkward. Taking a deep breath, she said, "Mom, I know you're out searching for a job. I want to help until you find one. In fact, if you don't want to go back to work—"

"No, Ariel. I'll not accept money from you."

"Why not? I always helped with the bills before."

"When you were living here."

"Please, Mom. I know you won't touch the money Kiernan gave you. But this is my money, and it's more than I could spend in ten life times. I want you to have some of it."

"Money Kiernan gave you?"

"Yes. Why not use it," Ariel said in a bitter tone. "I have no job, and I'll be earning it soon enough."

"Sweetheart, I'm—"

"I'll put some funds in my checking account at the County Employee's Credit Union. Don't forget, your name is also on the account, and if ever you need it, please use it. You don't even have to get my permission."

"I still have funds in savings. And I also have my application in at four places for a full-time position, so maybe I'll find a job soon."

"Just in case—okay?"

"I'll think about it."

Ariel knew she'd said about as much as she could on the subject and went on to something else. "Anything of interest happen lately?"

For a few seconds, Joanna was silent. "Mysha called me two days ago."

Ariel stopped breathing for a moment. "Why didn't you tell me?"

"I didn't want to do it over the phone. I wanted to tell you in person."

"What did she say? What happened?"

"She wanted to know why you married Kiernan."

"Go on."

"I told her you had your reasons, and I wasn't at liberty to divulge them. She asked me for the number at Crestview. I refused, of course. She then said for you to contact her and tell her why. She said you owed her an explanation."

Ariel said with an ache in her voice, "I'm so sorry I put you in that position."

"No, Ariel. It wasn't you who put me in that position."

ARIEL TUCKED THE bottom of her favorite black Harley-Davidson t-shirt into her well-worn riding jeans. Wearing this shirt with its flaming skull below the Harley logo always made her feel dangerous and slightly sinister. She sat on the edge of her bed, pulled on her black riding boots, and then stood up and stomped her feet a few times to get them to settle into the boots.

She surveyed her old room. Everything was as she left it, even the stuffed gray bulldog wearing a black jacket and black motorcycle cap sitting on her dresser top. She picked it up, feeling her heart lurch. Mysha gave it to her on the first night they made love. She opened the top drawer of her dresser, put the bulldog in, and closed the drawer.

Sitting back down on her bed, she reached over to her bedside table for her IMP. There were seventeen calls from Mysha. She couldn't bring herself to listen to them now.

Today would only be half a workday for Mysha, and she should be home. She clicked the activate button, her voice shaky. "Contact Mysha Leavill." Anxiety made her palms sweat, and she wiped them on her jeans.

After two beeps Mysha answered, "Ariel." Mysha's face on the screen seemed surprised.

"Mysha, I'm coming over."

"When?"

"Now."

"I'll be here." Mysha cut the connection.

Ariel waited a few seconds for her heartbeat to slow before hurrying down the hall to the kitchen. Her mother was cleaning out the refrigerator. "Mom, I'm going riding."

Joanna pulled her head out of the fridge and kissed her daughter's cheek. "Don't overdo it, and call me."

"I will. I'll be over next week and pick up my car." She went into the living room, removed her black jacket from the coat rack, and put it on. She took her helmet from its peg on the wall, opened the front door, and said on her way out, "Later."

THE WHITISH PATCHES of bark on the bare sycamores in front of Mysha's apartment made them appear as skeletal sentinels silhouetted against the gray October sky. They reminded Ariel of the bleak, surreal landscape she would expect to see in an old black and white noir film. Sometimes she wondered whether she had stepped into such a movie, forced to remain until the desolate and forlorn ending.

She parked her Harley by the curb and put her mind on automatic to enable her to walk up to Mysha's door. Before her finger touched the doorbell, the door swung open, and Mysha filled the doorway, her face cold and austere. Both remained silent, staring at the other. The dark and accusing look in Mysha's eyes cut Ariel to the marrow. She was flooded with shame and guilt.

Mysha moved aside and motioned with her head for Ariel to

enter through the door into what was once a place of warmth, caring, sharing, and, yes, the discovery of passion. Contemplating briefly the walls and furnishings, she expected to hear some echo of those things, but there was only silence, pregnant with reproach at her betrayal.

She focused once more on Mysha, seeing in her eyes the soft brown of a wounded doe.

"Why?" Mysha asked in a voice laden with sorrow. She clicked the door shut and leaned against it.

"It was the only way to save my mother from going to prison for corporate espionage."

"I don't believe you."

"It's the truth. I did it for my family."

"You know, I couldn't believe what I was hearing in the media. It didn't make sense for you to marry O'Shay after meeting her just twice. Why would O'Shay want to marry someone she met on only two occasions? No way. She's from a totally different world from us. She moves among the rich and famous and can have her pick of any available woman who moves in her circle. Why you?"

Ariel was at a loss as to what to say. "I...I can give you only my reasons...as I told you—"

"To save your mother. You want me to believe Kiernan O'Shay came to you and said, 'If you marry me, I won't prosecute your mother'?"

Ariel swallowed the sudden lump in her throat. "No. I went to her and offered to marry her if she didn't prosecute my mother."

"*What?* That has to be the craziest thing I've ever heard! What gave you the idea she would accept?" Mysha shook her head in denial.

"I can't give you her reasons for accepting."

Mysha placed her hands on her hips and searched Ariel's face derisively.

"It's the truth, Mysha. I'm not lying."

Mysha's laugh was mirthless. "Yeah, right. She might make a deal to fuck you for a while. But marry you? You're not rich or famous—what's in it for her?"

"Please, try to understand—" Tears threatened to flow and Ariel fought to keep her composure.

"No! You knew I would help. You should have waited until I got home and let me find a way to help you and your mother out of this situation."

"I was afraid my mother might be arrested right away and this would hit the media. I couldn't let that happen. Please understand."

"I understand perfectly! I was falling in love with you. I'm glad I found out what you really are before it was too late."

"Mysha, honestly, I care for you—"

"Honestly? Be honest, Ariel, how many times did you meet on the weeknights with her?"

"What are you saying?"

"What I'm saying is this story you've concocted about not being interested in O'Shay when she asked you for a date is just that, a story. You may have refused at first, but later changed your mind and started seeing her—"

"That's not true! I would never do anything like that!"

"Before long, you were involved with her. Maybe your mother did get caught stealing secrets...or was framed. But I bet that's all beside the point. You already had O'Shay hooked on your sweet and innocent act and probably hooked on something else as well." She gave Ariel's body a salacious once-over. "Probably got her in bed and sweet talked her into dropping charges while you were fucking her brains out and also fucked a marriage proposal out of her—"

"Damn you, Mysha! I can't believe you think I'm like that. You don't know me at all."

During the strained silence, Ariel's eyes ached with unshed tears. She understood Mysha being hurt and lashing out, but for Mysha to think she was a lying, manipulative bitch—

"You're right, Ariel. I really don't know you at all." Mysha sneeringly asked, "How much do you charge her to fuck you?"

Ariel barely kept from completely breaking down in tears. In a trembling voice, she said, "Mysha, I'm sorry. That's all I know to say."

"You've said enough. Get out!"

Mysha threw open the door, and Ariel quickly exited into the bleakness. The slamming of the door felt like a blow to her heart.

Ariel mounted her bike, wiped the tears from her eyes, and pulled on her helmet, yanking the straps tight. She would ride into the mountains today and give herself to the road, letting her bike take her away from the pain, and away from herself for a while.

Chapter Nineteen

"HOW WAS YOUR day, ma'am?" Mrs. Belfort asked as she took Kiernan's coat.

"It went well," was her automatic reply, even though she was exhausted from a hellacious day at the office negotiating with representatives of the Chinese Government who wanted to dissect every point in a contract for delivery of freighters. "Anything I need to know?"

"Michael drove Miss Ariel over to her mother's at nine this morning so she could pick up her motorcycle. Miss Ariel has not returned."

Kiernan hesitated before saying, "When she's back, tell her I want to see her right away. I'm going to my suite to shower, and then I'll be in my study."

"Yes, ma'am, I will."

Kiernan headed up the stairs for her shower and fresh clothes. If Ariel wasn't home by the time she changed clothes, she would call Joanna Thorsen to find out what was keeping her.

After she showered, she put on a dark green, cowl-neck sweater, and a pair of brown slacks. She glanced at the clock on her bedside table and saw it was only twenty minutes until dinner was served.

Dinner was the only time she'd been with Ariel in the last week. Kiernan had tried to entice her into going out to dinner one night, watching a movie at home, or going for a drive. But Ariel complained she was still tired from her sickness, which Kiernan knew was an excuse to avoid being in her company.

She had believed Ariel was actually opening up to her until that day in the orchard. Kiernan gave a mental cringe when she recalled what happened. Ever since that day, her desire for Ariel was right beneath the surface, erupting forth at the most inopportune times, like on the elevator at work when a pretty blonde woman got on, reminding her of Ariel. Or the scent and taste of the apple she ate for a snack one day, reminding her of how enticingly sexual Ariel had been when she took a bite of the apple Kiernan offered.

These memories, and her desire, were making it hard for her to concentrate on her work. Now she was having erotic dreams about Ariel that woke her in the early hours of the morning and prevented her from falling back to sleep unless she pleasured herself. But that method didn't always work, often leaving her frustrated and lonely, wishing the object of her dreams was sharing her bed. But the way things were going with Ariel, that wasn't going to happen.

She hastened downstairs to her study, sat at her desk and ordered, "Telecom on, contact Joanna Thorsen."

After three beeps Joanna answered, "Hello. Oh. Ms. O'Shay, what can I do for you?"

The vid-screen wasn't set on transmit at the Thorsen residence, so she couldn't see Joanna's face. But Joanna could apparently see her, so she kept her countenance neutral in light of Joanna's frosty tone.

This was always an awkward moment for her, because she was never sure how to address Ariel's mother. Joanna was always formal with her, letting her disdain of Kiernan show in referring to her as Ms. O'Shay.

"Ms. Thorsen, is Ariel there?"

There was a pause. "No. She left here at one."

"Did she say where she was going?"

"Only that she was going out on her motorcycle."

Kiernan couldn't help but let the uneasiness enter her voice. "Does she usually ride for this long, and when it's dark?"

The screen flicked on and Kiernan saw Joanna's face. "A few times she has ridden too far and didn't make it home until a few minutes after sundown. I'm sure that's the reason. It's been a while since she's had a chance to ride, and the time has probably gotten away from her."

"Do you think I should contact the Sheriff's department?"

"No. They would contact you if she were in an accident. She'll show up. She doesn't make it a habit of staying out late."

Kiernan hadn't informed Ariel she needed to have her driver's license changed to her married name, or have her new address and telecom number entered into the system. If she were in an accident, they would contact Joanna. "If you hear anything, please call me immediately."

Joanna hesitated and then kindly said, "I will. Call it a mother's intuition, but she's fine."

"Then I'll trust your intuition. Thank you, Joanna."

"You're welcome, Kiernan. Bye."

There was a knock at the door and Kiernan thought, *Ariel.* "Enter." Disappointment filled her when she saw it was Mrs. Belfort.

"Ma'am, dinner is ready."

"I'm not hungry. I'll go to the kitchen and get something later."

"Yes, ma'am. I'll tell Ricardo to keep it warm for you."

"Thank you."

Mrs. Belfort departed, and Kiernan's thoughts sped right away to Ariel. Kiernan wasn't thrilled Ariel rode motorcycles. They didn't call them suicide machines for nothing. She'd hoped that giving Ariel the Ferrari would get her attention on something safer, but Ariel had never taken the car out, not once. Kiernan had to have Michael take it for a spin a couple of times a week to keep it in running order.

She leaned back into her chair, worry nagging her, as well as a bit of anger that Ariel hadn't called to let her know she was all right. Perhaps she was visiting a friend. A thought entered her head, and her stomach contracted. No, she thought. She wouldn't... Not after Kiernan ordered her not to do it. Her memory replayed as much as she remembered about ordering Ariel not to have any contact with Mysha Leavill. She couldn't recall Ariel ever saying she would do as she requested.

A wave of rage rushed through her. She was with Mysha!

THE TEMPERATURE TOOK a drastic dip after sunset, pushing Ariel toward Crestview. It was hard for her to think of Crestview as home. She doubted she would ever think of it that way. Home was a refuge from the punches and knocks received while living life, and where one felt surrounded by love and caring. Definitely not the way she would describe Kiernan's residence.

She swung onto the road to Crestview and stopped at the gate, lifting her visor. The guard on duty, Henry, hastened over and shone the retina scanner into her eyes. Satisfied, he went back to the security station, opened the gate, and motioned her through. She continued up the road in second gear, then gently tapped the back brake before swinging her Harley into Crestview's drive, her headlight sweeping across the trunks of the trees lining the drive. Their black shadows closed in and shortened the closer the light came to them. A glance at the lighted face of the chronometer on the fork cap showed 6:50. Dinner was over, but there were always leftovers. She could prepare a plate and take it to her suite to eat.

She wondered whether Kiernan would say anything about why she was getting back so late. She had ridden up to Lookout Mountain, enjoying the freedom of riding, and she managed to lose herself for a while from the trauma of meeting with Mysha. She forcefully pushed her encounter with Mysha out of her thoughts, knowing she would weep if she didn't.

Gearing down to first, she pulled in the circular drive and parked her Harley to the side. She would ask Kiernan if she could have a space in the garage for her bike. This shouldn't present a problem, since the garage was big enough to hold at least a dozen cars. She had counted seven vehicles, including the Ferrari wedding gift.

She removed her helmet and pulled off her gloves with her teeth, dropping them into the helmet. She ran her fingers through her hair, bounded up the steps, and palmed the keypad. She was on her way to the stairs to go up to her suite when Mrs. Belfort appeared. "Miss Ariel. Ms. O'Shay said for you to see her as soon as you returned. She's in her study."

"Thank you."

She was turning to go down the hall to Kiernan's study when Mrs. Belfort said, "I'll take your jacket and helmet, and put them in your suite."

After handing Mrs. Belfort her helmet, she unzipped and removed her jacket, handing that to her.

Mrs. Belfort sniffed disapprovingly when seeing her black Harley t-shirt.

Ariel said, "What? You don't like it? Is it the flaming skull?"

"That's hardly suitable for a pretty young lady such as yourself. Makes you look like one of those...Brazen Hussies."

Ariel found it interesting that the prim Mrs. Belfort would know of the notorious all female motorcycle gang headquartered in Chicago. "Afraid I don't qualify as a Brazen Hussy. I don't have any tattoos...yet."

"Oh, that would not go over well with the Missus."

"Maybe I should get one then. You think Kiernan would like a flaming skull tattoo on my left back shoulder?"

Mrs. Belfort laughed in amusement and then shook her head. "What do *you* think? You better not keep her waiting."

Ariel made her way down the hall and knocked on the study door. Kiernan called out, "Enter."

Kiernan sat behind her desk staring angrily. Uh oh, Ariel thought. This didn't look good.

KIERNAN WATCHED ARIEL enter and stand casually in front of the desk. She pushed her chair back and raked Ariel up and down pointedly, stopping her scrutiny briefly on her chest, noticing with distaste the t-shirt she wore. She leaned back in her chair. "Well?" Kiernan asked, drawing the word out.

Ariel shrugged, assuming a nonchalant air. "Well...what?"

The impudence of this reply sent a rush of annoyance through Kiernan. She pushed up from the chair, sending it back, and stalked up to Ariel, "Don't you dare play games with me. You know perfectly well 'what.' I called your mother to see whether you were still visiting. She told me you left at one. Where were you for the last six hours?"

"I took a ride up to Lookout Mountain and stopped at some of the scenic overlooks."

"Where else did you go?"

Ariel's posture tensed, her gaze defiant. "That's none of your damn business!"

Kiernan ground her back teeth together and felt the pressure build in her forehead and temples. "Everything you do is my business. You remember that."

Ariel lolled her head to one side, directing her gaze upward as if this were all nonsense and boring.

This impertinent display grated, spurring Kiernan to push up closer, now in Ariel's personal space. She struggled to maintain her cool and her voice came out dangerously quiet. "You were with her...weren't you?"

"Her?" Ariel asked innocently, but her expression bordered on insolence.

"Don't you dare pretend with me!" Kiernan wanted to slap her.

"Yes, I dropped by to visit Mysha." Ariel's tone was matter-of-fact, but her posture tensed.

"After I told you not to see her ever again?"

"We had some things we needed to discuss."

Kiernan pushed up closer, now only a few inches away from Ariel. "Discuss? While you were in bed with her?"

Ariel's mouth shot open in shock. Taking a step back, she gave Kiernan an incredulous stare. "This is fucking unbelievable! Nothing like that happened!"

"Did you really go up to Lookout Mountain, or were you with her all the time, cheating? Cheating on me!" Kiernan's anger accelerated to the boiling point.

Ariel's eyes widened. "You're wrong. I didn't cheat on you, and nothing happened. We talked. That's all."

"Do you take me for a fool?"

"Yes! If you believe I did anything but talk then you're a fool!"

"Am I now? You admit you were with her."

"I wasn't even there ten minutes. I had to see her, to tell her...I had to put closure to our past. That's all."

One image seared through Kiernan's thoughts: Ariel and Mysha making love and Ariel giving to Mysha what should rightfully be hers as Ariel's wife. She grabbed Ariel by the upper arms, pushed her face close to Ariel's, and shouted, "You're lying! Never lie to me!"

"Take your hands off me!" She slapped Kiernan's hands from her arms, shoving her away. "Don't you ever again put your hands on me like that, or accuse me of lying. I'm not a liar...like some people I know." She accompanied this last part with an accusing glare.

Kiernan gulped in shock, appalled at how she'd let the argument escalate. Still, she couldn't help the jealousy and anger she felt because Ariel had disregarded her orders and seen Mysha.

Stepping back, she took a deep breath and scrutinized Ariel's expression and body language. Kiernan had to trust her own gut feeling which was that Ariel was being truthful. Ariel wasn't proficient in hiding her emotions or in subterfuge. "I'll accept that you're telling me the truth then. Did you reveal the reasons to...Ms. Leavill...for this marriage?"

"Only *my* reasons—that I did it for my family. Don't worry. I didn't tell her your reasons."

"Did the possibility ever cross your mind the media might have been following and taking pictures of you entering and leaving Ms. Leavill's apartment?"

Ariel's eyes widened, then she recovered and returned to her regular guarded expression. "No one followed me."

"Are you sure?"

Ariel's eyes darted away with nervous uncertainty.

Kiernan continued, "You have to be careful where you go and who you're seen with. I want a list of all the places you intend to frequent and of all the people you intend to visit. I want you to keep me informed when you're planning to leave the house and grounds, where you're going, and how long you'll be gone. And you're not to see Mysha Leavill again. Do I make myself clear?"

Ariel's face flamed dark red, twisting into a mask of disdain. "Who the hell do you think you are!"

"And I don't want to see you wear that shirt again. It makes you look...trampy."

"What the..." Ariel angrily stretched out the front of her shirt. "Oh? Is it the skull? Tough ta-ta. I like it. I'm even getting a tattoo that matches it. What right do you have to tell me who I can see and what I can wear?"

"I have every right! I'm your wife, and I'm Kiernan O'Shay. You're an O'Shay now, and it's your responsibility to act the part. Until you learn to do that, I'm making decisions on where you can go and who you can see. You need to watch what you wear when you're out in public. And there will be no tattoos. I'll not let you dress like trash. For your own protection and the protection of my good name and that of Stellardyne I can't have you—"

"Oh, no! If you're under the impression you can treat me like one of your subordinates at Stellardyne, then you're delusional! We may be married, but this isn't the Nineteenth Century, and I'm not your obedient little wife! I'm outta here. I need some fresh air." Ariel brushed past Kiernan and stalked toward the door.

Kiernan knew she had lost control of the situation and was now desperate to find a way to change it to her advantage. She decided to risk a ploy. Everything could blow up in her face if this didn't work. But she was a gambler at heart and risks were what kept her ahead of the game. She schooled her features into a mask of cold hardness, one she used when dealing with stubborn business associates, and firmed her voice to that of authority. "The marriage is off. I'll see my lawyer and have the marriage annulled. That shouldn't be hard to do since the marriage hasn't been consummated. The contract will then be void. I'll have my lawyer file charges against your mother with the District Attorney."

Ariel froze in place and spun to face Kiernan. "You bitch!" She stood there indecisively, and Kiernan watched a myriad of emotions flicker by before Ariel said, "Fine. I'll do it—provide you with a list, tell you where I'm going. I swear I'll never have contact with Mysha again. But you have to promise to leave my mother out of it."

Ariel's eyes and face had somehow become desperate and stricken. Seeing that and hearing her plea, Kiernan experienced a moment of regret for her threat. But her anger quickly smothered the moment of compassion. "Very well. You need to remember the consequences of your actions before you go traipsing off to visit old girlfriends." Kiernan watched Ariel's expression change to one of relief, before adding, "I have business to attend. You may go."

Ariel left quickly, slamming the door behind her so hard that Kiernan jumped. She turned her back and walked to her desk feeling a pounding headache coming on. She sank down into her padded chair and the anger seeped out of her gradually leaving her feeling weak and light-headed. She had wanted to end the conflict and prevail while she was ahead of the game, to let Ariel know she was serious when it came to her good name and Stellardyne. But it suddenly became clear to Kiernan that this wasn't a game she was playing at all. Ariel would end up hating her.

She let out a sigh. Maybe she had nothing to lose after all because it was pretty clear that Ariel already hated her.

ARIEL MUTTERED UNDER her breath, "Bitch" as she exited the room and slammed the door.

Anger filled her, and there was a sick feeling in the pit of her stomach for allowing Kiernan to intimidate her on where she could go, and whom she could visit. Suddenly needing fresh air, she tramped down the hall, through the recreation room, and out the paned glass doors to the rear veranda, then down the steps to the garden.

Not caring the temperature was well into the low forties; she followed the garden path lit by the faint luminescence of the nightlights set low along the flagstone edges. Her steps carried her to an ancient oak tree where she sat on the cold, stone bench underneath the low branches with their fall leaves clattering together like dry bones in the whisper of the night breeze.

She growled in frustration. Kiernan had her trapped. She could use her threat of an annulment, and prosecution of her mother, anytime she wanted Ariel to do something. But, what could she do to stop Kiernan?

Ariel couldn't shut off her racing thoughts. She stared into the darkness, feeling near to tears when thinking about her meeting with Mysha. Then her thoughts replayed her encounter with Kiernan, making her both angry and fearful.

Mysha was now the past, over and done. But Kiernan's threats of annulling the marriage and prosecuting her mother were immediate, and at any time, Kiernan could use those threats to control her. Ariel wouldn't put it past her to do that, considering she already had.

Really, what choice did she have? There was only one thing she could do, and do now while her anger at Kiernan bolstered her courage. She would worry about the consequences later.

KIERNAN EXITED THE bathroom, padded across the bedroom floor to her bed, and slipped between the covers, feeling the Egyptian cotton slide silkily across her naked body. She pulled the top covers up to her waist and sank into the puffy goose down pillow. "Computer, lights off." She closed her eyes and sighed with exhaustion, her mind racing in circles, rewinding and replaying what happened earlier when she confronted Ariel.

A lingering anger nagged her. Not only at Ariel for disregarding her wishes and seeing Mysha, but also with herself for allowing another emotion to control her actions: jealousy, an emotion almost foreign to her. She couldn't remember when she last experienced it. That others were jealous of her she knew; jealous of her power, her wealth, her appearance, and a host of other things.

She knew Ariel probably still loved or harbored strong feelings for Mysha. After all, no woman could be expected to shut off those feelings in a few weeks. Kiernan couldn't expect Ariel to feel the same deep emotions about her in such a short time of knowing each other. Did she want Ariel to? Could she feel the same about her? Too tired to analyze what her answer might be, she twisted onto her right side, fluffing her pillow to get more comfortable, when the sound of someone entering her bedroom made her freeze. "Computer, bedside lamp on."

Shock and astonishment held her frozen as she watched Ariel glide sensually to the side of her bed. Sitting more upright and pulling the covers up over her bare breasts, she asked, "What are you doing here?"

"Do you want me to leave?" Ariel's voice and eyes held a seductive quality, her mouth slightly parted. She slowly let the tip of her tongue touch her top lip.

Before Kiernan could gather her wits and say anything, Ariel opened her robe, letting it fall from her shoulders to slip down her arms and thighs and pool around her feet.

Kiernan gasped as she beheld the absolute perfection of the female body displayed before her. The golden light from the bedside table spilled across full, firm breasts with coral nipples and down the torso tapering to a trim waist that flared to shapely hips supported by long, beautiful legs. Seeing the patch of blonde hair at the juncture of the thighs, Kiernan swallowed. Desire punched her hard in the gut and reverberated in her groin.

Kiernan wet her lips. "Oh my God." No. This wasn't right. Right? Wrong? In a voice hoarse with arousal, Kiernan asked, "Why are you doing this?"

"Don't you want me, Kiernan?" Ariel slid onto the bed, reached out and swiftly took her in her arms to kiss her passionately.

Kiernan couldn't catch her breath. She tried pushing away, but the sheet slid down her body. Ariel stroked a hand across her breasts and massaged the palm over an already stiff and sensitive nipple.

All reservations vanquished, Kiernan pulsed with desire. Ariel's touch was liquid fire racing out of control through her body. She pulled Ariel tightly against her, rolling them over until she was on top, and touched her tongue to that dark dot at the corner of Ariel's mouth that so tantalized her. Moving her mouth to those soft lips and opening them with her tongue, she plundered the sweetness within. Languidly, she moved against Ariel, feeling her breasts press against the bountiful firmness of those beneath her.

Breaking the kiss, she pushed herself up and straddled Ariel's hips. Her hands hungered to touch Ariel's breasts, and she stroked down their soft slope, over the coral nipples, and under them, cupping their fullness, lightly squeezing to feel their softness. She moved the palms to cover the nipples, feeling them harden. Her mouth watered with wanting to taste them.

Quickly lowering her head, she eagerly sucked one of the peaks into her mouth and swirled her tongue around it. The areola puckered and pebbled, and she opened her mouth more fully to take in the entire nipple, groaning deep in her throat as the taste and sensations sent a current of desire to her groin. Tearing her mouth from the nipple, she returned to Ariel's lips, kissing them firmly and feeling the press of teeth. Ariel opened her mouth, allowing her once again to plunder the warm interior, the current of desire now intense, making her moisture flow warmly from her core.

Ariel was too passive though, holding her in a weak embrace. More, Kiernan needed more. She wanted to feel Ariel's hands caressing and stroking her as a lover. Drawing her mouth away from Ariel's, she whispered hoarsely, "Touch me, Ariel. Make love to me."

Ariel drew in a sharp breath, then growled angrily. She rolled them over and straddled Kiernan's waist, took hold of her hands, and pinned them above her head. Savagely Ariel descended on her mouth with a bruising kiss. Kiernan moaned as her arousal rapidly accelerated. Ariel jammed a knee up against Kiernan's wet core, and the effect was electrifying. Kiernan sucked in her breath.

Ariel tore her mouth away, hot air fanning Kiernan's face, and said in a voice both raw and menacing, "Make love to you? No, Kiernan, this is all you'll get from me." Once again, Ariel savagely descended on her mouth, ravishing her lips and demanding entrance with a forceful thrust of her tongue. A flash of rage struck Kiernan but the force and passion behind the kiss stoked her desire and overrode her anger. Her stomach and groin muscles spasmed and clenched. She tried to remove her hands from the grasp that held them, wanting to pull Ariel fully against her. She wanted to feel Ariel's heat and softness, the fullness of those luscious breasts pressed more firmly against her own. But the grip on her wrists was too strong.

Ariel broke the kiss and moved her head down, taking an aching nipple in her mouth to suck, tugging at it with her teeth. Kiernan loved the feeling in her nipple being a perfect balance between pain and pleasure that shot down to impact in her center. The beginnings of her orgasm erupted. She knew she soon wouldn't be able to hold back the impending tidal wave.

Ariel continued to nibble and lick the sensitive nipple, then moved to the other nipple, already hard and puckered, laving it with rough attention. Kiernan needed to free her hands to hold Ariel close to her as she orgasmed. She was so close now. With a gasp of effort, she pulled her hands free from the firm grasp, buried them in the blonde hair, and clutched Ariel tightly against her breast as the wave hit her.

Ariel slid from Kiernan's body and to her side while continuing roughly suckling and biting her nipple. Then a warm hand was on her stomach, trailing down to the tangle of coarse hair. A gliding touch to her engorged clitoris made her gasp. A finger penetrated her and Kiernan gasped again. A second finger worked into her wet opening. Ariel moved her fingers slowly but forcefully, in-and-out, in a steady rhythm. Kiernan threw her pelvis up against the hand and cried out in a voice strained with passion, "Faster."

The rhythm increased. Ariel's palm slapped against Kiernan's heated flesh. This drove Kiernan toward her release. Her orgasm was building fast, the first wave exploding forth, forcing her to cry out hoarsely. Ariel did not slow or soften her thrusts, and Kiernan was again pushed into the throes of orgasm. This one was even more intense, making her breathless. Still, Ariel continued until Kiernan said, "Enough." Ariel did not stop, and Kiernan peaked again. This time the release brought not only pleasure, but also pain. She tried to push Ariel away. "No more." Kiernan gasped slightly at the removal of fingers from her tender core and the release of her aching nipple from a hot mouth.

Ariel straddled her thigh, placed her hands on each side of Kiernan's body, and leaned into her arms. Kiernan felt the sensation of the rough brush of hair, and warm, wet flesh stroking along her upper thigh. Ariel increased the pressure and thrusting. Kiernan raised her thigh in rhythm and placed her hands upon the full breasts. She cupped them, rubbing her thumbs over the firm peaks. A feral expression shaded Ariel's features. Her hair was tousled carelessly around her face and shoulders, her mouth open, and breath harsh. With every thrust of her hips, she expelled a grunt.

Kiernan knew she needed help in her release. Sliding her hands down the slender waist, she placed them on each side of the hips and pulled the straining woman firmly against her thigh. Throatily she coaxed, "Come for me, angel, only for me." Ariel groaned loudly, her thrusting frantic. "Now, Ariel, come for me," Kiernan commanded in a husky voice.

This spurred Ariel over the edge. She threw back her head, gulping in a breath, holding it for a moment, and letting it out in a raw growl of release. Feeling a gush of hot wetness from Ariel's core flow down the sides of her thigh, Kiernan riveted her eyes on Ariel's face which was suffused with the intensity of her orgasm. Never had Kiernan seen anything so profound as this. Ariel's features were a sculpture of both rapture and vulnerability. Kiernan held her, feeling the shuddering aftershocks before she stilled, drawing in rasping breaths.

Ariel opened her eyes and gazed down and Kiernan was shocked by the level of bewilderment and hurt she saw. What had Kiernan done to cause that expression? Remorse assailed her that she allowed this to happen—that she wanted this to happen. Replacing the remorse was tenderness drawn forth by the bruised look in Ariel's eyes. She desired to hold Ariel close against her and feel her heart beat against her breasts and in rhythm with her own heart. She wanted Ariel to know she desired a connection with her beyond the physical. She stroked her hands soothingly down Ariel's back, seeing the eyes shut.

Ariel collapsed to the side of Kiernan, rolling onto her back, and flung an arm over her eyes.

"Let me hold you," Kiernan gently said. She put a hand on Ariel's shoulder, feeling it tense. She leaned over to place a tender kiss on Ariel's cheek, only to have her twist sharply away and hurl herself off the bed. "Ariel?"

Her back to the bed, Ariel pulled on her robe with agitated motion.

"Ariel, come back," Kiernan said softly. "I would like to talk to you."

Ariel tied the robe and spun to face Kiernan, her eyes hot, mouth twisted. "I don't ever want to hear what you have to say. The marriage is consummated. We are now legally married, and the contract is now in effect. I know the contract grants you conjugal rights. But know this, Kiernan—I will never make love to you...only fuck you." She swiveled and hurried from the room.

"Ariel, no, come back. Ariel—" Kiernan slid off the bed to follow, but faltered and flung herself back onto her pillow. "Damn, damn, damn!"

Her eyes watered and her throat closed on a sob that led to a further realization. She knew now that she should never have taken her anger and jealousy out on Ariel. She behaved like a bitch—worse than a bitch. Kiernan felt empty, sad, and very alone.

ARIEL ORDERED THE shower on full force. A pulsating stream of compact water, almost stinging, hit her skin. The temperature was on the hot side, as hot as she could tolerate. She wanted to wash away what she'd done, wash the scent of Kiernan's passion away—and her own. She soaped the washcloth and roughly scoured her skin. When she scrubbed between her legs, she jerked abruptly when the soapy washcloth rubbed her clitoris, still tender from her orgasm. She turned, and put out her arms stiffly, placing her palms on the back wall. Leaning, she felt the hot water thrum against her shoulders, back, and buttocks and sobbed aloud, "Why, why, why?" She knew the answer to why she did this, but couldn't explain the why of her response—why she lost control—why she fell.

"*I WILL NEVER make love to you...only fuck you.*" The words wouldn't leave, echoing over and over, as Kiernan lay in the dark agonizing over what had occurred.

The words pummeled her with guilt, regret, and shame, flaying her conscience into agonizing pieces. She left her bed, flung on a robe, and fled into the sitting room and over to the bar to pour a finger of whiskey into a snifter.

A wall lamp cast a muted golden glow, enough to see by, but didn't reach into the shadows. She shambled over to the fireplace and turned on the gas fire in an attempt to ward off the chill from her tumultuous emotions and sat in the old rocking chair that had been in her family for over two hundred years. Her mothers, Maureen and Nicole, rocked her in this chair when she was a baby. This chair also rocked Maureen, her grandmother Shanna, as well as generations of O'Shay babies before her. One day, she hoped to see Ariel in this chair rocking their daughter. Perhaps sitting in it would lend her solace. Rocking slowly back and forth, she stared forlornly into the fire, seeing nothing, yet seeing everything.

All of this was her fault. What in the hell did she think she was doing ordering Ariel to inform her who she saw and where she went? Ariel wasn't some wayward teenager who needed her permission. Then to make matters worse—Kiernan threatened to press charges against her mother. She had treated Ariel as some shady business negotiator trying to pull a fast one. But, wasn't this marriage business? She'd never been jealous over any business deal, or over any woman. She'd been attracted to Ariel ever since she first met her, but now this was more than attraction, much more. She couldn't consider this strictly a business deal at all, though Ariel must. Ariel hated her for sure and would probably always consider this relationship only business. Kiernan wasn't sure what to do. She would tell her she was sorry, and hope she'd forgive her.

"*I will never make love to you...*"
"*I know the contract grants you conjugal rights...*"
"Oh my God!" Kiernan said aloud.

Bolting from the chair, she hurried across the room to open the wall safe and withdrew the prenuptial agreement. She clicked on the desk lamp and flipped through the pages until she came to the spot she wanted and felt her blood go cold with rage. "I'm going to kill him."

THE SOUND OF soft sobbing woke her. Ariel opened her eyes, realizing they were full of tears, and her nose full of mucus, making her sniff forcefully. In her mind flashed an image of Mysha, her eyes dark obsidian, condemning and accusing. She had been dreaming of Mysha. Sorrow filled her, and she rolled onto her back, staring into the morning gloom. With sudden clarity, another image seared her thoughts: Kiernan, beneath her as she—"Oh, God."

The taste of bile flooded her mouth and an onslaught of dark emotions assailed her: anger, regret, and shame. But shame was uppermost. Shame that she'd allowed anger and lust to control her actions... and her reactions. She had succumbed to her attraction for Kiernan. Flinging the covers aside, she exited her bed, trying to leave behind the harpies who tormented her.

Gazing out her window, she saw the chill blue sky and the neighboring mountains still shrouded in clouds where the morning sun had not yet reached. A glance at the clock on her bedside table showed it was 9:30. Kiernan would be at Stellardyne, which was a relief, as Ariel was in no way ready to face her this morning.

The night before, she had disarmed Kiernan of her main weapon and now she couldn't threaten her family. But Kiernan still had other weapons to use against her—especially one she couldn't ignore. Kiernan could demand she have sex with her, and she had no choice but to comply. Her thoughts briefly touched on the pleasure she'd experienced, thinking that wouldn't be such a terrible thing. Shame once again pinned her, and she twisted on the needle point that often accompanied shame—guilt. How could she be such a traitor! She had to remember what Kiernan had done to her mother.

After all that had happened the night before, maybe Kiernan wouldn't want her now, didn't want to see the hate in her eyes and feel it in her touch. Ariel could only hope...for her own sake.

Chapter Twenty

"MS. O'SHAY. MR. O'Shay is here to see you," Kelly said over the desk-com.

"Send him in." Kiernan rose from her desk chair and crossed her arms over her chest.

Theodore opened the door and was a couple of strides in before he saw her expression. He stopped abruptly, consternation crossing his face.

Before he could open his mouth, Kiernan said, "You have some explaining to do."

"Kiernan, I don't understand...what's this about?" He approached the desk and stood across from her.

Gritting her teeth, she reached for the contract on her desk and tossed it to him. "Stipulation nineteen. I thought I told you to remove it."

"I thought I did." He searched over the contract. "Somehow, I inadvertently gave you and Ariel the first draft to sign. I have the corrected one and will get it to you —."

"Uncle, I think you need to retire. In fact, I'm going to insist on it."

"Kiernan...please. I'll drop by tonight and have you and Ariel sign the right document. I'll bring Franklin with me to notarize it. You will only need a couple of witnesses — Mrs. Belfort, and one of your staff."

"I'll expect you at seven tonight."

"Frankly, I don't see what the problem is."

This comment caused her to have the sensation that the top of her head would explode from rage. "No. Being male, you wouldn't. It's degrading, that's what it is."

"Degrading? Sex is sex. You're sounding like a prude. Why, it wasn't too long ago you —"

She put her hands up, palms out, to halt his words. "I don't want to talk to you. Go!"

"I'll never understand the female mind."

"GO!" Kiernan pointed at the door.

"Very well." Theodore ambled off, and Kiernan heard him mumble something about women, proof, and a different species.

As soon as he exited, Kiernan fell heavily into her seat. She let out a frustrated sigh. How could she ever make amends to Ariel? She had acted like a jealous fool, pushing Ariel into... She closed her eyes, trying to force images from her thoughts that made her feel shame, and arousal, which only compounded her shame.

The images were only replaced by the memory imprinted on her body of the feel of Ariel, and her touch. Never had anyone taken her so thoroughly. She was the one who always led the way in having sex — who took control. Never had she allowed a woman to dominate her in bed. Again and again, Ariel had brought her to orgasm. This was something she'd never experienced with any of her lovers. Once had always been enough. She couldn't help but wonder whether Ariel liked taking control if she wasn't angry or desperate. She couldn't help but wish she could find out.

Remembering bites on her nipples by neat white teeth, while that hot tongue flicked the swollen tips, caused them to harden. She moved her hand to her breast and felt the erect point push against the silk of her blouse. Grasping the hard tip between her thumb and forefinger, she pinched, imagining it was Ariel doing this. Raw lightning struck her hard in her core, and she moved her hands to the waist of her trousers, fumbling with the belt buckle. Suddenly, she froze, and removed her hands.

Enough! That wasn't going to happen with Ariel hating her. And what if someone walked in to her office?

She put her head in her hands.

Could she ever make things right? Where to begin? She'd apologize and work from there.

KIERNAN COULDN'T CONCENTRATE and left the office at three that day, wanting to go home and talk with Ariel. A heaviness of spirit and dread lay on her, dread of what she would see in Ariel's eyes.

As she climbed the steps to her suite, Mrs. Belfort called from the foot of the stairs, "Ma'am, you're home early. Is everything all right?"

"Everything's fine." She didn't owe her staff an explanation, and they knew not to expect one. "Is Ariel about?"

"Yes, ma'am. She's in the recreation room playing pool."

Kiernan went back down the stairs to the recreation room. She heard the clatter of pool balls before opening the door. Ariel peered up when the door opened and seeing Kiernan, her features tightened and posture straightened.

"I need to talk to you," Kiernan said in a soft voice.

"Yes?" Ariel asked cautiously.

"Can we go over to the sofa so I can sit?"

Ariel tossed the pool stick on the table and strode across the room to take a seat on one end of the couch, while Kiernan sat on the other end. They stared at one another, and Kiernan saw the wariness in Ariel's expression. She took a deep breath and let her words out evenly. "I want to apologize to you for treating you as a child yesterday. My behavior was unacceptable. Most of all, I want to apologize for my threats. I had no intention of annulling our marriage."

Ariel's eyes were steely, cutting right through Kiernan. "You want to apologize, do you? Why? Are you going to demand I have makeup sex with you?"

Ariel's words hit Kiernan hard, and she flinched. "No, Ariel, I would never demand sex from you—not even if it were one of the stipulations in our agreement."

Seeing Ariel's eyes widen with confusion, Kiernan said, "I have something else to tell you, something that...well...there has been a misunderstanding about a provision in the prenuptial contract. Stipulation nineteen, the conjugal stipulation, I never authorized it."

Confusion remained in Ariel's expression. "What do you mean?"

"Uncle Theodore—he was going by some sort of standard for these types of contracts and included it. When I saw it, I asked him to remove it, which he did, but somehow he managed to send us copies of the original contract and we signed the original one. He's coming by tonight with the corrected one for us to sign."

"I'll sign the contract, provided I can have time to review it."

"That won't be a problem. If you like, we can postpone the signing, and you can have Joyce—I mean your lawyer—go over it with you."

"That won't be necessary. Could you arrange for it to be signed in a few days?"

"I can do that." Kiernan hesitated, a tightness in her chest with what she wanted to say next. Meeting Ariel's eyes with her own, her words stumbled out. "Ariel...about what happened last night—"

"I don't want to discuss last night," Ariel said frostily, but her eyes were blazing. "Now, if you'll excuse me, I have something I need to do."

As Ariel stood to leave, Kiernan said, "I need to talk to you...about us. About—"

"There *is* no us, Kiernan! There's only you!" Ariel's face reddened. "No one else matters but you and what you want!" She pivoted and strode swiftly from the room.

Kiernan closed her eyes and leaned her head against the sofa, wondering where they could possibly go from here.

Chapter Twenty-One

FOR THE EIGHTH night in a row, Kiernan ate dinner alone. She would leave for work in the morning, come home, eat, work in her study, go to her suite to attempt to sleep, and never once see Ariel. Other than the few minutes when Theodore brought the corrected contract for them to sign, Ariel had been a ghost. Oh, Kiernan knew what she did during the day because Mrs. Belfort kept her informed. Ariel went to a Harley Owner's meeting. She visited her mother, or rode over to Cherokee National Forest with her Harley Group. She stayed in her room, or played pool in the recreation room, or went for a walk after lunch.

Kiernan knew things would need to change. They would need to come to an understanding, or this could be hell for the next five years. They needed to think about their future child. If they couldn't get along, their child might develop psychological problems.

This marriage, it had happened so fast. They didn't know each other. She should have waited and dated her, according Ariel the opportunity to get to know her better. Maybe that was what was needed. Tomorrow was Saturday, and she would see Ariel in the morning to present her case.

ARIEL WAS FINISHING downloading applications to a select few of the universities that offered courses in aerospace engineering. Embry-Riddle, Kiernan's alma mater, was one of those, as was her alma mater, MIT. Georgia Tech in Atlanta had a top-rated program. Atlanta was closer to Crestview Estate and would make it easier to go back and forth when required to attend campus. She heard a knock. "Come in."

Kiernan entered cautiously. "I hope I'm not disturbing you."

Ariel thought about making a snide remark, but kept her voice and features neutral. "You want to see me about something?"

"Yes. Can we sit on your sofa?" The nervousness was evident in Kiernan's voice and the slight wringing of her hands.

Ariel couldn't believe this was the fearless and intimidating business tycoon. Ariel tipped her head in agreement and took a seat at one end of the sofa, with Kiernan taking a seat in the middle to face her.

Ariel waited expectantly. Kiernan's features were somber, and her voice strained. "Ariel, I know things are not good between us. I would like to make things better. Not only for me, but for you, our future...and for our child."

Ariel knew Kiernan had a point. They couldn't continue to reside in the same house with things as they were. She would probably be pregnant in a few months. They had to come to some understanding, some resolution. She swallowed and asked evenly, "And, we will make things better...how?"

"What I'm asking is for you to give us a chance. I think...I know we could..." Kiernan ran her fingers through her hair and looked Ariel full in the eyes. "Ariel, will you go out on a date with me?"

Ariel stared at her, baffled for a moment, and not sure she heard right. "What?"

Kiernan repeated, "Will you go out on a date with me?"

"You mean, as in a date, date?"

"Yes, as in going out together," Kiernan said almost shyly.

Ariel drew back against the arm of the sofa and studied Kiernan closely, wondering whether this was a joke. "I'm not sure what you mean."

"We never really got to know each other, and that's my fault. I was thinking we should date."

Suspicion immediately entered Ariel's mind as to Kiernan's motives. She asked warily, "What does this dating include?"

"Going out together, finding out what each of us likes and dislikes—that sort of thing."

"Let me get this straight. When you say 'date,' you mean something along the lines of a friendship."

"Yes, and getting to know each other better. I still don't know what your favorite movies are besides *Star Wars*, and I don't think I ever told you what my favorites are. Who are your favorite authors, your favorite music, and musicians? We could learn more about each other...like you do when you're dating."

Ariel was still confused. "But we're married."

"Yes, but where is there a rule that says we can't date? We never had that. I know it won't be the same as if we're single, but we can get to know each other the same way."

Ariel rubbed her forehead, her mind going over what Kiernan said. Was this a good idea? Then again, she didn't have another idea. Kiernan would have to make concessions. Ones Ariel wasn't sure she would make. Sounding harsh, she said, "And who would call the shots, Kiernan. You? Like you've always done? 'Oh, Ariel, I grant you permission to pick out the restaurant we're going to tonight. I'll even grant you permission to wear what you want.' Is that the way it's going to be?"

Ariel rose, and Kiernan leaped up as well. "No, Ariel, I'll let you decide—"

"You'll let me decide? Let me?" Ariel challenged. There was a strained silence as each woman studied the other. Ariel waited to see what Kiernan's response would be.

"I grant I have a tendency to be...overbearing. It's in my nature to dominate, to control—"

"Who—you?" Ariel said sarcastically. "Dominate and control? I don't believe it." Staring at Kiernan, Ariel waited for an answer.

"I'm willing to work on my control issues. Will you be willing to give me a chance? Give us a chance to make this work, so we can get through the next five years...on friendlier terms?"

"I'll think about it and let you know. There are some issues we need to discuss, and I need to think about them."

"When?"

"When I'm ready," Ariel said in a surly tone.

Ariel saw Kiernan's lips tighten briefly as if angry, but Kiernan took a breath and said calmly, "Take your time."

"I think I'll go for a drive. I'm not sure when I'll get back."

"Be careful. It rained overnight, and there might be slick patches on the road. Might I suggest you bundle up warmly? It's chilly out today, and I don't think your jacket will keep out the cold."

"Yes, Mother."

Kiernan rolled her eyes, but said softly and with sincerity, "I don't want you to get sick again."

"I'm not taking the Harley. Today's forecast is for more rain, so I thought I would take my Ferrari and get used to the feel of it."

"Have fun and drive safe."

THE WATER CLOSEST to the riverbank gurgled and babbled like the belly of a hungry beast. Ariel tossed in another pebble, hearing the solid plunk as the current along the river's edge swallowed it up. She'd decided to drive her Ferrari along the road that skirted the Ocoee River before going to visit her family. The concentration on the road and the handling of her car took her mind off the earlier conversation with Kiernan until bits and pieces tumbled out, and she pulled over to a viewing area to review the proposal.

As much as Ariel hated to admit it, Kiernan was right. She couldn't spend the next five years avoiding her. Soon there'd be the baby to consider. She instinctively knew Kiernan would be a vital part of the child's life and would take an interest in raising her. Ariel intended to participate in her child's life and development as well. Her influence on the child would be as important as Kiernan's. Even more so, since she would be responsible for childcare while Kiernan ran Stellardyne. No way would she stand by and let Kiernan run roughshod over her concerning her child's upbringing. She needed to make her wishes known. She needed to stand up to Kiernan and make some demands of her own, and now was time to do that.

Kiernan needed her if she was to make her dreams come true, and with a sudden flash of insight, Ariel realized that if she stood up to her, there wasn't much Kiernan could do. She was trapped in this agreement and marriage for the next five years as was Ariel, and there was no way she could break the agreement, not if Ariel was willing to carry out her end of the bargain. She would see how serious Kiernan was about developing an amiable relationship. It would have to be one that was equal—where her input and thoughts were as important as Kiernan's.

Problems remained. Could she let go of her hatred for Kiernan? Maybe it wasn't the hate she first felt when her anger was raw and very consuming. Since then, her anger had changed to resentment, though she did hate what Kiernan had done to her mother. To be fair, Ariel didn't think she was a total bitch. When she was ill, Kiernan had shown a tender and caring side. She apologized for her behavior for the night that led to the consummation. She knew Kiernan was sincere in her apology and regretted her threats and words.

She decided she was willing to give Kiernan a fair chance. She might not hate her, but she didn't like a lot of things about her either, and she doubted she could ever trust her. Time would tell whether Kiernan was sincere and what her true nature actually was. Was Kiernan a selfish, manipulative, and conniving person? Or were the positive qualities she sometimes displayed actually her true personality?

And what about this attraction she had to Kiernan? Could she control it? Did she want to? She was sure Kiernan wouldn't object to including sex in this dating thing.

She remembered the feel of that firm body beneath her, evoking both a current of arousal and trepidation. That path might lead to falling into an emotional involvement she was unprepared for. She was still recovering from her relationship with Mysha. For the time being, she wouldn't go there. Ariel picked up one last pebble and tossed it in the river before turning to go.

JOANNA STOPPED BAGGING leaves when she spotted a sporty red car with a familiar blonde head on the driver's side. The car pulled in the driveway behind her Saturn, and the twins dropped their rakes and ran over, touching and admiring the car before Ariel could open the door and slide out of the driver's seat.

"Wow, Ariel, is this your car?" Seth said excitedly, his eyes wide with admiration.

"Yes, it is."

Leigh begged, "Take us for a ride in your car, please, please, please!"

"Yeah," Seth said, "with the top down."

"I don't even get a hug?" Ariel pouted while giving them puppy-dog eyes. They both hugged her with such enthusiasm they almost knocked her down.

"Now will you take us for a ride?" Seth asked.

"I will in a little while, but I don't know about having the top down. It's going to rain."

"I get the front seat!" shouted Leigh.

"I get the front," Seth said. "You're smaller and can squeeze into that place in the back."

"No, you—"

"All right you two, that's enough," Joanna ordered. "Finish raking and bagging these leaves, and let me talk to your sister."

They went to do as told, and Ariel asked, "Where's the yard bot?"

"The battery died, so I'm using my two standbys. You only need to charge them up with a pan of brownies."

"I know brownies sure would work for me."

"Stick around and I'll whip up a batch." Joanna gave the car an appreciative once over. "Nice wheels. Is this the car Kiernan gave you as a wedding gift?"

"This is the one. Drives like a dream. I'll let you drive it."

"No thanks, that's too much car for me to handle. I'll stick to the Saturn. Come on in and let me fix you a cup of hot tea."

Ariel followed her into the house, and Joanna put the antique kettle on the stove. Both she and Ariel preferred tea brewed the old-fashioned way. Joanna bent down and kissed the top of Ariel's head before taking a seat across from her. "How are you?"

"I'm okay. How are things here?" There was an edge to Ariel's voice, and Joanna knew things were not okay.

"No complaints." She saw pain and uncertainty in Ariel's expression and softly asked, "What is it, sweetheart? What's wrong?"

Ariel broke and wept. Joanna slid off her chair, knelt by Ariel, and took her daughter in her arms. Ariel hugged her close and sobbed on her shoulder while Joanna rubbed in comforting circles on her back, not saying anything, giving her the time she needed.

After a time, Ariel brought her head up from the comforting shoulder and rubbed her eyes with the heels of her palms.

Joanna stood and brought a towelette from the dispenser to Ariel, who wiped her eyes and face. Joanna lowered herself into the seat next to Ariel and took her hand, watching and waiting for her to speak when she was ready.

With a tremulous breath, Ariel said, "I'm all confused right now...about things...about Kiernan."

Joanna remained silent. She studied her daughter's pained face, brushed back a loose strand of hair, and stroked her cheek tenderly. The kettle shrieked. Joanna prepared their tea, handed Ariel a cup, took her own and once again sat across from Ariel.

Ariel spooned up some creamer. "Kiernan would like for us to work toward a better relationship."

"Oh?" Joanna knew there was a strain in the relationship, since Ariel hardly ever talked about Kiernan when she called and quickly changed the subject when Joanna brought up her name.

"She says she wants us to date so we can learn more about each other."

This surprised Joanna. "What does she mean...date?"

Ariel stirred her tea and explained what Kiernan had proposed. At the end, Joanna said, "It sounds as if she's willing to try for more than the current arrangement. How do you feel about this?"

"Part of me resents her for what she did. Another part—we will have a child together, and I think it's important we at least be on friendlier terms."

Joanna took a sip of tea before saying, "I agree. Both you and Kiernan will be the biggest part of this child's life. She'll pick up on any strain in your relationship—that can be hard on a child."

"I'm going to set some guidelines. Kiernan...she has a tendency to want to run things, and I'm not going to let her do that. If she's serious, she won't object to some things I want." There was a sureness of purpose in Ariel's voice, and her expression was one of certainty, leaving no doubt that she meant what she said.

Joanna brought the cup up to her mouth to take a sip of tea, but in actuality, she was attempting to hide her smile. The old Ariel, the stubborn, persistent one, was starting to re-emerge, and Joanna couldn't feel more delighted. She'd been so worried about her for so long, but Ariel was finally showing her true strength again. It appeared Kiernan O'Shay would need to learn how to bend. A lot.

KIERNAN HAD FINISHED dinner earlier and was now in her study checking her correspondence when the telecom beeped. She answered and perked up when she saw the silver-hair and gamine features of her cousin on the view-screen. "Beverly, how are you?"

Beverly's hazel eyes sparkled. "I'm doing great. So, cuz, I see you've been busy these past couple of months."

"My, my, news sure gets around, doesn't it?"

"I was shocked, until I remembered this is Kiernan Deirdre O'Shay, and nothing should shock me where you're concerned."

"Well, I do have a reputation to maintain. I can't let that slide."

Beverly Markos was Kiernan's second cousin on her grandfather Philip Markos' side of the family. He had been Shanna O'Shay's significant other. Beverly was a year older than Kiernan and had always been prematurely gray, making her a striking woman with her youthful appearance, olive complexion, and hazel eyes. She was a lawyer in Atlanta and headed the World Equity Foundation, the best known pro bono group in the solar system which did work for the poor guaranteeing their basic rights of fair and decent wages, housing, medical care, and property.

"Kiernan, your wedding has got to be the story of the year. Every time I go online to check the news, I see photos of you or your beautiful wife featured on every supposedly inside scoop."

Kiernan grimaced. "I hope the photos do me justice. I know there couldn't be a bad photo of Ariel in existence. Don't tell me the hogwash in that...fiction."

"I only look at the pictures. I don't read or listen to the gossip."

"Ha! Sure you don't. So, what can I do for you, cuz?"

"It's that time again, the dinner for the fundraiser. I have been sending you reminders for the past month and still haven't gotten your confirmation."

The fundraiser had become one of the biggest social events, not only in the South, but also in the world. Only the wealthiest could afford to attend the one-hundred-thousand-dollar-a-plate dinner. Kiernan also privately gave an additional generous donation every year.

"Uh...I've been busy."

"Yes. I imagine you have been...busy." Her laugh was throaty and Kiernan rolled her eyes. "It's being held at the Norwood Country Club in Marietta, and I've already reserved a place for you and the missus."

"Sure of yourself, aren't you?"

"Of course I am. You know I would never forgive you if you missed."

"We'll be there. When is it again?"

Beverly gave her an incredulous look and said with a slight admonishing tone, "God, Kiernan, come down from your honeymoon high. Since when have you ever not known well in advance when the fundraiser is? It's two weeks away. November 16th."

"I'll mark it on my calendar."

"Hey, that's great. I can't wait to meet Ariel. She must be special if she can make you forget an important date."

"Oh, that she is." Kiernan winked.

"I'll let you go. I don't want to keep you away from your wife. Give my best to the missus. The poor thing...being married to you."

Kiernan returned a Cheshire cat grin. "Give my best to Helen. Tell her I know a good divorce lawyer."

Dr. Helen Ortiz was Beverly's wife. She was a contagious disease specialist at the Center for Disease Control and Prevention in Atlanta.

Beverly stuck out her tongue and disconnected the call.

Kiernan tapped her fingers on the desktop. This would be their first social event together and Ariel's first introduction to a part of Kiernan's society. She had no doubt Ariel had the ability to carry it off. But there would be those present who might view her as an upstart and believe she married Kiernan for her money and status. She would need to be vigilant and be there for Ariel.

When Ariel came home, Kiernan would inform her about the event. She hoped Ariel remembered the part of the agreement where she would treat her with respect. She didn't expect Ariel to fawn all over her, but it would be nice if she were to show a modicum of liking.

"MISS ARIEL," MRS. Belfort said, "if you like, I can heat some leftovers from dinner for you to take up to your suite."

"No thanks, I've already eaten." She'd treated her mother and two siblings to dinner at Salty Dog's, and after dining, took the long route home, so they could enjoy riding in her car. The twins could barely squeeze into the seats in the back, but they hadn't complained except to say they wanted the top down.

Mrs. Belfort said, "Well then, I'm done for the night. Have a pleasant evening."

"Thanks, you too. Ah...Is Kiernan in her study?"

"No, she retired to her suite around an hour ago."

"Have a good night." Ariel climbed the stairs and paused at Kiernan's door, wondering whether she was still up or asleep. She didn't want to knock loudly and wake her, so she rapped lightly on the door.

"Enter."

Inside, she saw Kiernan relaxing in her recliner, dressed in a peach-colored robe and holding an e-reader which she placed on the chair arm. She pushed the chair down and stood.

"Sorry if I'm interrupting," Ariel said, "If it's okay, I would like to talk.".

"You didn't interrupt. Will you have a seat? Can I get you something to drink, a juice, or soda?"

"No, thank you." Ariel took a seat at the end of the sofa, and Kiernan settled in at the other end. "I thought about what you said—about dating—and I'm willing to do that under certain conditions."

"Yes, I'm listening."

Ariel set her features and voice to sternness. "There will be no more of you trying to control my life, or this marriage, and making all the decisions. We will make them together when it concerns our marriage...and that of the child we will raise together."

"I agree, we need to make decisions together that concern our future and that of our baby."

"I'm serious, Kiernan, there will be no more of you trying to order me around—or telling me who I can visit, where I can go, and what I can wear."

"If I do that—you let me know."

"Don't worry, I most certainly will." Ariel hesitated and her voice softened. "I'll concede you did have a point about the possibility of the paparazzi tailing me. I'll endeavor to be careful and try to behave in a way that doesn't result in scandal." Ariel couldn't help but be amused by the thought that what she did was now newsworthy.

Kiernan must have seen Ariel's amusement. "I'm not worried about that so much. I'm more concerned about your safety. You can do something completely innocent and the media will concoct some wild and outlandish story far removed from what happened. I would appreciate one thing though. When you get that tattoo could you have it in a discreet place to avoid it being splattered on every media outlet between Earth and Jupiter?"

Ariel mentally cringed when remembering telling that to Kiernan, and the circumstances. At the same time, she thought it amusing Kiernan had taken her threat seriously. "No need to worry. I'm not into body art—so no tattoo." Relief passed over Kiernan's features and Ariel couldn't help but add, "Yet."

Kiernan must have figured Ariel was pulling her leg and said, "Can I pick out the design?"

"Hmm, as long as it's not pink bunnies or bloody daggers stabbing a heart."

"Damn. There go my first two choices."

Ariel chuckled before changing the subject to something she

needed to say. "Kiernan, I know the one driving force in your life is to fulfill your dream. I know you believe you have no choice but to adhere to the stipulation in your grandmother's will if you want that dream to come true. Your grandmother was cruel to do that to you. That said, I do think you had, and now have, a choice in the methods you use in trying to achieve that goal. I feel resentment toward you—and you know why. But I'm willing to work on being friends."

Kiernan stayed silent, but Ariel saw the emotions race across her face: a swift flash of anger, of regret, and sadness.

Kiernan studied the floor as if debating what to reply. Finally, she lifted her eyes to Ariel's. "Thanks for your honesty. All I'm asking is for you to give us a chance to become friends."

Ariel saw the sincerity in the unwavering gaze and heard it in Kiernan's voice. She nodded. "Let's get back to the topic of dating. I was thinking we could take turns making suggestions about what to do."

"That sounds good, and I'll have no problems with that. Might I make a suggestion?"

"Yes, of course."

"When we're not actively engaged in dating, do you think you might have dinner during the week with me here at home? I would prefer your company at the dinner table, and we can talk about our day and what we did."

"I would be willing to do that." Ariel glanced away for a second, swallowing nervously before saying, "This dating thing—I don't wish it to include sex...at this time." Ariel realized she left the door open for the possibility of sex occurring in the future. A little devil part of her said, *"Well, you never know,"* while her angel of reason warned, *"Danger. Enter at your own risk."*

Kiernan said, "I don't expect that. I won't pressure you, and I'll take your lead in that matter."

If Kiernan was willing to include the physical, Ariel needed to stay on guard. She cleared her throat. "I guess that's all I have to say."

"May I go first and ask you out on a date?"

Suddenly feeling shy, Ariel blushed, "Yes."

"I know this little place over in South Cleveland called Jimmy Mac's where they make the best chicken and dumplings I ever had, and I thought I might take you there for dinner tomorrow."

Ariel wondered how someone of Kiernan's social station would ever hear of a place like Jimmy Mac's, let alone eat there. She grinned from ear to ear. "I've been to Jimmy Mac's with my Harley group, and they do have the best chicken and dumplings. And yes, I'll go out with you tomorrow."

Kiernan gave a wry smile as if picking up on Ariel's thoughts and the reasons for it. "I happen to know all the places in the vicinity for great home cooked vittles and barbecue. Hands down they all beat anything places like Le Pierre's have to offer. One other thing—the World Equity Foundation is hosting its annual fundraising dinner in Atlanta...well...Marietta...in a couple of weeks. It's a dress occasion, semi-formal to formal."

"Oh, I'm...umm, I've never been to anything that fancy before." *Especially with you,* was the rest of the thought that Ariel wisely kept to herself.

"Don't worry, you'll do fine, and I'll be there with you."

Ariel knew Kiernan would take care of her, if she needed it. She also knew she was capable of taking care of herself...in any social situation.

Chapter Twenty-Two

KIERNAN TOOK ANOTHER bite. "Mmm, these dumplings melt in your mouth," she enthused.

Ariel managed to agree around a mouthful of Jimmy Mac's World Famous Chicken and Dumplings.

Ariel had volunteered to drive them in her Ferrari, and Kiernan sat in the passenger seat enjoying the way the car hugged the curves at the faster than normal speeds. After a couple of Ariel's more daring maneuvers, Kiernan glanced over to see Ariel giving her a quick assessment as if to gauge her reaction. She gave Ariel a wide grin and received one in return. They'd arrived at Jimmy Mac's a few minutes before noon, beating the rush of Sunday churchgoers, and got a booth in a corner that would give them some anonymity.

After a few more bites of food, Ariel said, "I sent my application to Georgia Tech's Aerospace Engineering Department."

Kiernan swallowed her food. "Oh, Ariel, that's wonderful. When do you expect to hear back?"

"It should be in a couple of weeks. I want to start spring semester in early January. I already have the basic required courses — you know, English, humanities, math, others, and of course physics. I need fifty-two credit hours in the major to obtain an undergrad degree in Aerospace Engineering. I can do it in a year by taking three straight semesters."

"I'm sure you'll be accepted into the program. We can get you an apartment close to campus for those times when you have laboratory classes."

Ariel glanced furtively around and lowered her voice. "Er...Kiernan, we've never set a date for when the baby — you know — the implantation of an ovum."

Ariel bringing up the subject caught Kiernan by surprise. Since it had been upsetting to Ariel when mentioned in previous conversations, Kiernan hadn't planned to address it any time soon. Now she jumped to talk about it. "I'm thinking this coming July would be a good time. That's a year before I turn forty and will provide us plenty of leeway to plan."

"Then I should be able to obtain my degree three or four months before the baby is due."

Kiernan noticed Ariel always referred to their future child as *the baby* and not *our baby,* as she thought of her, evidence Ariel still hadn't reconciled with her role in this agreement. Or was it Kiernan's role as the child's other parent Ariel had a problem accepting? Now wasn't the time to go into that, so she put it out of her mind. "We need to plan a time to discuss an obstetrician and any birthing methods you want—things along those lines. We have time yet...to think about it...before we sit down and do that."

"We can ask Mom. After having me and the twins, I'm sure she'll have some advice on the subject."

"That sounds like a good idea. Now, how about I order us some of Jimmy Mac's peach cobbler, and when we finish that, you let me drive your Ferrari back home."

"Do you have the required license to drive vintage vehicles?"

"Of course I do. I'll have you know I've owned a 1965 Mustang convertible, 1972 Trans-Am, a 2009 Pontiac Solstice GXP, and various other vintage vehicles."

"Only if you promise to drive carefully and not drive it like a flitter racing around in the Asteroid Belt."

"Ha! And this coming from a woman who rides a—what is it called—a suicide machine?"

Ariel rolled her eyes. "Oh, okay. And remember, just because the Ferrari has a radar detector doesn't mean the highway patrol doesn't have other ways to catch you speeding. In fact, I heard from a member in my Harley group the Smokies cruise the roads in unmarked vehicles, clocking your speed by keeping behind you and using their odometers."

"Oh, goody. We can see how fast we can leave the Smoky behind." Kiernan smirked evilly and said, "Eat my dust, Smoky."

Ariel tried to deliver her an admonishing look, but failed and burst out laughing, Kiernan joining her.

Chapter Twenty-Three

"SORRY, MOM," ARIEL said. "I'm planning on taking Kiernan for a motorcycle ride on Saturday, but I'll come over Sunday and visit."

Joanna's surprise was obvious over the telecom screen. "Oh, is this part of the...dating...you two are doing?"

"Yeah, she took me out to eat Sunday, and I'm inviting her for a ride Saturday."

"Gee, Ariel," Joanna said dryly, "you sure know how to show a girl a good time."

Ariel stuck her tongue out, then said, "I think so—" A knock interrupted her. "Someone's at my door. I better let you go."

"Remember to ask Kiernan about Thanksgiving."

"I will. I'll talk to you later."

"I love you."

"Love you too, Mom, bye." Ariel watched as the image on the screen faded, before looking up from her desk toward the door. "Come in." She was surprised to see Kiernan enter.

"I hope I'm not interrupting."

Ariel pushed her chair back and stood. "Not at all. You're home early."

"My four o'clock conference call with the Baltic Federation cancelled at the last minute, so I called it a day. I thought instead of playing pool tonight after dinner we could watch the opening game of the Vols women's basketball team. They're playing Florida tonight at seven."

For the last three nights after dinner they had played pool in the recreation room. "I wouldn't miss it." Ariel said, "So, you're a women's basketball fan?"

"Not any women's basketball fan, I'm a Tennessee Volunteers women's basketball fan."

"Of course, watching any other teams play against each other is like watching a pickup game at the local park."

"You got that right."

"Why don't you take a seat? There's something—actually, two somethings—I want to discuss with you."

Kiernan hesitated, and Ariel saw uncertainty pass across her face before she said weakly, "Sure."

Kiernan took the chair, sitting alertly, and Ariel dropped across from her on the sofa. "Mom called and wants me to bring you over for Thanksgiving." A surprised, shocked expression appeared on Kiernan's face. Ariel said, "You know we're coming up on the holidays and haven't discussed any plans."

"I have Thanksgiving with Uncle Theodore and Jack. They usually have Jack's family over. It goes without saying you're invited. As for Christmas, I invite Theodore and Jack over on Christmas Day for dinner."

"I would really like for you to join me and my family for Thanksgiving," Ariel said with sincerity.

Kiernan looked away and pursed her lips as if considering her invitation.

Ariel knew Kiernan would need more persuading and probably felt uneasy accepting the invitation given the situation with her mom, not to mention the whole deal with the marriage. "Mom wouldn't have invited you if she didn't mean it." Ariel was surprised that the next words that popped out of her mouth were, "After all, you're family." But it was true. No matter the circumstances, Kiernan was her wife, and they would have a child, Joanna's grandchild, together. That made Kiernan family.

Kiernan's eyes widened slightly, before she said, "I'd be honored to go. But only on the condition that Joanna, Leigh, and Seth come here for Christmas Day."

"I'm sure they would accept."

"Good. Ah...there's something else you wanted to discuss?"

"I was wondering whether you would like to go out with me...er...go riding with me Saturday."

There was excitement in Kiernan's eyes and voice. "In your Ferrari?"

"On my motorcycle." Seeing Kiernan's face freeze, Ariel hurried on to say, "I thought we could take a leisurely ride through The Cherokee National Forest."

"I've never ridden on a motorcycle. It seems quite dangerous."

"No, it won't be. I'll give you some pointers before we go. All you have to do is hold on to me and enjoy the scenery. I've taken the twins for a ride, even Mom, and we've never had any issues."

"Er...but I don't have a helmet, or jacket."

"No problem, I can go over to Harley-Davidson in Chattanooga and get you those things." Ariel saw that Kiernan was still hesitant. She put on her most winning expression and persuasive voice. "Come on, Kiernan, I know you'll like it."

For a couple of seconds, Kiernan gnawed the bottom corner of her lip before a slow grin spread across her face. "All right—but I want a black helmet and a black jacket."

"That's a given... when you ride a Harley."

Chapter Twenty-Four

ROBERT PLACED TWO breakfast plates on the table in Kiernan's sitting room along with a pot of coffee and a carafe of orange juice. He asked, "Is there anything else I can get you, ma'am?"

"No. Thank you, Robert," Kiernan said and he exited the suite. She was waiting for Ariel to join her before she seated herself. The smell of the bacon, scrambled eggs, and big, flaky biscuits made her mouth water, and she glanced expectantly toward the door leading to Ariel's suite, debating whether she should knock. A light rap on the door, and she said, "Enter."

Ariel carried two boxes, both wrapped in black and orange Harley-Davidson gift paper. Ariel was dressed in riding boots, a pair of jeans, and a long-sleeved black shirt with the Harley Eagle clutching the logo emblazed on the front.

Kiernan was already dressed in a black wool pullover sweater, black jeans, and a pair of her old, black, above-the-ankle flitter racing boots that she'd dug out from behind her shoe rack.

Ariel placed the packages on the sofa and headed toward the table.

"What's in the packages—or need I ask?" Kiernan already guessed it was a helmet and jacket.

"The necessary equipment for the adventure we're about to embark on after breakfast."

Kiernan saw the eager look Ariel directed toward the plates of food, and said, "As you can see, breakfast is ready." Kiernan took her seat, and Ariel sat across from her.

Ariel chewed a piece of bacon. "Mmm, yummy."

Kiernan smiled at Ariel's enthusiasm and forked up some eggs. After a few minutes, Kiernan took a sip of her coffee and said, "You'll drive carefully, won't you? I don't want you whipping around the curves at ninety miles an hour and flinging me off the back of that thing."

Ariel swallowed her piece of biscuit. "This is coming from the woman who rode a rocket engine and won how many Asteroid Belt Runs—three?"

"It was four Asteroid Belt Runs and three Moon Races. You must not have been one of my fans if you don't know how many wins I had."

"To tell you the truth—I was a fan of Valerie Krantz."

"Fly-by-her-pants Krantz?" Kiernan placed both hands over her heart. "You wound me. She only won three events in the ten years she was racing. What was the big attraction?"

"She had—"

Kiernan hastily put her hands up, palms out. "Wait. Don't tell me. Let me guess—it was those skintight black cat suits she wore that left nothing to the imagination."

"Geez, Kiernan, I was only twelve years old when she started racing. I didn't think about those kinds of things."

"Ha! Sure you didn't. Perhaps not at twelve...though I doubt it...but later on at thirteen, fourteen...twenty?" She waggled her eyebrows.

Ariel's face tinged pink and she giggled. Kiernan had never heard Ariel giggle and thought it adorable.

Ariel said, "Well, yeah, maybe at fourteen. But that wasn't the main attraction. The main attraction was her flitter—*Darth Raider*. At the time I thought it was mega supreme."

"What's so mega supreme about black paint with some logo of a half-naked alien girlie holding a light saber painted on the nosecone? My flitter, *Solar Flair*, was prettier...and faster."

"It was pretty, I agree—"

"And faster."

"That too. And that little dancing female flame thingy logo was...cute...but...it wasn't kick ass."

"Well it sure kicked Krantz's ass—and other asses too. She only beat me once. And that by a millimeter after I had to detour around a damn media ship that strayed into the race lane. The only other wins she had came after I retired."

"That's true. And if you hadn't retired, you'd have probably continued to beat her." Ariel paused. "Do you mind me asking why you retired?"

"Grandmother died, and it was time for me to grow up and take charge of Stellardyne. Besides, I had too many narrow escapes out there. I'm sure I squandered eight of my nine lives and it was only a matter of time before my luck ran out and something bad happened. God, half of my competitors, some of them were friends, are only so much stardust now. So, I quit while I was ahead of the game."

"Do you miss it?"

"For a time I did, but not anymore." Kiernan paused, moving uneasily in her seat, wondering whether it was the right time to broach a subject that had been on her mind for the last few days. No time like the present. "Ariel, there is something I would like to discuss with you."

Ariel cautiously asked, "Yes?"

"I would really like for you to stop riding your motorcycle while you're pregnant, and for a while after our child is born." Holding her breath, Kiernan hoped it didn't sound like an order. If Ariel refused, would she make it an order? No. She needed to remember she agreed to refrain from telling Ariel what to do.

Ariel's expression became thoughtful, and she dropped her gaze down at the tabletop before looking back up at Kiernan. "To be honest, I hadn't considered doing that, but I think you're right, at least on the pregnancy part. I won't ride while pregnant. I'll have to think about how long I would give up riding after our baby is born."

Kiernan stilled for a second. Ariel had said 'our' baby and not 'the' baby as she had in the past. Was she seeing them together as a family? Dare she hope?

But it was too early for that. She thought about arguing the point of Ariel riding after the baby's birth, but since she looked forward to spending the day with Ariel, she didn't want to cause any friction that might put a damper on their time together. To tell the truth, she didn't want to do or say a thing that strained the amiable relationship they were developing.

Smiling softly, she reached her hand across the table, took Ariel's hand, and squeezed it lightly. "Thank you."

STANDING TO ONE side, Ariel watched as Kiernan put on the black Tefla-hide jacket in front of the mirror in her sitting room. "How do I look?" Kiernan asked as she spun from the mirror, giving Ariel a rakish grin.

"Great! It fits you really well." Ariel gave Kiernan the once over, thinking she looked better than great, much better. Her thoughts flashed to the memory of the well-toned and attractive body beneath the jacket—and beneath her. She blushed. "Er...you did put on some long underwear, didn't you?"

"Yes. And wool knee-high socks...extra thick. What about rain gear? There's a thirty percent chance of rain today and sixty percent this evening."

"We should be back before it starts to rain. Besides, I have only one rainsuit, and somehow the rain always manages to find a way to get in. Here—try on your helmet." Kiernan slipped on a black helmet that was identical to Ariel's, and Ariel helped her fasten it. "How does it fit?"

Kiernan moved her head from side-to-side and pushed the face shield down and back up. "Fits well." She took the helmet off and studied it closely. "What's this button on the chin area for?"

"That's for the com-unit built into the helmet. We'll be able to communicate with each other while riding. I had the Harley shop program it to the frequency in my helmet so no one can overhear our conversations. You can also use it to call anyone's telecom or IMP by saying 'activate telecom' and reciting their name or number."

"That's a good idea."

"You'll let me know if you have to stop or anything."

"Sure."

"Let me go and get my jacket and helmet, and we'll be ready to roll."

"I'm ready when you are...I think."

Squeezing Kiernan's forearm, Ariel said, "You'll be okay. I'll take care of you."

"Of that, I have no doubts."

THE HARLEY TOOK another sweeping curve, and Ariel felt Kiernan's hold tighten around her waist. After instructions from Ariel, Kiernan had caught on fast about leaning into the curves and not pulling against them. She had even informed Ariel that she found the scenery more enjoyable from her seat behind her than when she rode in a car.

They had spent the day touring the Cherokee National Forest and riding along the Ocoee River, stopping at scenic sites. At a picnic area they pulled their lunch from the Harley's saddlebags and enjoyed a Thermos of coffee and roast beef sandwiches Ricardo had made for them.

They had ridden farther than anticipated and were trying to make it home before the rain. A rolling rumble of thunder bowled through the mountains, and the sky was heavy pewter, threatening to spill its collected moisture.

A few drops of rain fell, dispersed far enough apart that the drops hitting them weren't of too much concern, but Ariel knew this could suddenly become a frog strangler. Ariel knew by the scenery that they were approaching the east side of the mountain where Crestview was located.

Over the earphones Kiernan said, "Ariel, slow down. I know a shortcut across the mountain." She slowed the bike, and Kiernan continued, "Around the next curve you'll see a post with reflectors on it that marks a road leading up the mountain."

"Okay. I'll be on the lookout."

"The road is gravel and narrow, but I keep it maintained, so I don't think you'll have any problems navigating it."

Ariel geared down to third, slowing the Harley for the curve, and entered the straightway. Seeing the turnoff ahead, she slowed to second gear, smoothly entering the narrow gravel road, which was barely wide enough for a sedan.

The darkened sky and the canopy of trees on each side of the road made it appear close to twilight. The light sprinkling of rain increased. Ariel figured they were in for a soaking before they could make it to Crestview.

The road continued upward with a few twists and curves. Ariel was careful not to drive close to the road's edge which overlooked the valley below.

Kiernan said, "Turn in ahead at that clearing on the left side. There's a cabin where we can stay until the rain passes over."

At the clearing ahead, Ariel put the bike into first, drove in, and carefully followed a rutted clay driveway. She stopped a few feet from the front porch of a rustic log cabin and turned off the bike. Once Kiernan jumped off the back, she put down the kickstand and slid off the seat.

Ariel surveyed the cabin's exterior, taking note of the aged, brown, square-hewed logs used in its construction. The porch extended across the front with a set of four wide wooden steps leading up to it. The front of the cabin had a plank door with an old-fashioned, paned glass window on each side.

"Wow. This looks to be pretty old," Ariel said in awe.

"It was built sometime right before the Civil War. The exact date isn't known, but we think it was in the late 1850's. Let's go on in. I'll build a fire so we can dry off."

The front of Ariel's jeans were soaking, but Ariel's body had protected Kiernan from a drenching, and hers were only wet at the bottom where her feet had been on the foot pegs.

Kiernan hurried up the steps and took her helmet off, setting it on the wood floor by the door. Ariel put her helmet and gloves beside Kiernan's helmet.

Kiernan lifted the wooden handle that opened the door latch and lightly pushed. A long squeak ensued as the door opened, and Kiernan allowed Ariel to go in before her. The interior was dark and Kiernan went to the windows, opening the heavy, blue plaid curtains to let in some light.

After Ariel's eyes adjusted to the gloom, she was able to see the generous fireplace at one end. An oval, braided rug done in browns, blues, and greens lay on the wooden floor in front of it. An old straight back chair with a wicker seat sat on one side of the hearth, and an ancient wooden rocking chair on the other. A stack of split wood leaned against the rock face of the hearth, and kindling strips peeked out of a tin bucket . Facing the fireplace was a well-worn sofa with upholstery decorated in brown and rust-colored autumn leaves. A folded forest green wool blanket hung over the back. An end table was located on the left side of the sofa.

At the fireplace Kiernan reached for a battery-operated LED lamp on the mantel. She clicked it on, and the bright white light pierced the gloom and spilled into the dark corners. "After you remove your clothes, you can hang them on back of the chair. That way the fire will dry them. Use the blanket on the sofa to cover yourself."

Ariel hung up their jackets and took a seat on the sofa to take off her boots. Kiernan opened the screen to the fireplace, arranged wood and kindling, and reached for a box of matches on the mantel. She knelt and took a thin sliver of wood, lit it, and held it under the grate until the flame caught the wood on fire from the bottom and spread.

Ariel set her boots aside, leaving on her dry socks. She unfastened her belt bag and placed it on the end table before pulling off her wet jeans and damp, black silk long underwear. She left her black panties on, and her jacket had kept her shirt protected from the rain. She rose and hung the jeans and underwear on the back of the chair. As she pivoted to go to the sofa, she caught Kiernan giving her legs a fast once over before the other woman turned back to the fireplace.

Kiernan rose, grabbed a poker, and stuck it in the fireplace to move the wood around a bit, then replaced the screen in front. After moving the chair with Ariel's wet clothes closer to the fire, she brushed her hands together.

Ariel watched discreetly as Kiernan sat in the rocking chair and removed her boots, belt bag, and damp jeans, leaving on her socks, sweater, and cream-colored flannel long-john bottoms. She hung her jeans on the rocker to dry, then swung the rocker around with the back facing the fire, and ambled over to the end table to place her belt bag by Ariel's.

"Brrrrr..." Kiernan said and hurriedly sat beside Ariel on the sofa. Ariel arranged the blanket to cover them both and drew her feet up on the sofa, as did Kiernan. Their shoulders and legs touched, and they both pulled the blanket up to their chins.

A clash of thunder heralded an increase in the rain, which made a thrumming sound on the roof.

Kiernan said, "I don't think this is going to let up anytime soon."

"I think you're right. Even if it does, it will be dark in an hour, and I wouldn't want to ride the bike on this road, not with a passenger. We might be stuck here overnight."

"That wouldn't be a problem. There's food in the kitchen, and there's more firewood on the back porch if we need it. This sofa lets out into a bed large enough so we won't crowd each other. There are sheets, pillows, and another blanket or two in the cedar chest under the window on the back wall. We can make up the bed later."

Ariel's first thought was she wouldn't mind Kiernan *crowding* her. "I get the right side of the bed. And no stealing covers."

"I promise, no cover theft will occur." Kiernan grinned.

The light of the lantern and the fire were enough for Ariel to make out some details of the cabin's main room. The cedar wall paneling's dark areas made interesting designs in the wood. Against the wall, to the left of a door was an old cedar armoire. Over the fireplace a framed needlepoint of flowers surrounded the words *Home, Sweet Home*. There were various knick-knacks on the mantel.

"This place is lovely, and cozy," Ariel said. "Do you stay here a lot?"

"Occasionally I spend a night out here when I'm in the mood for total peace and quiet and want to hear the breeze in the trees and have a real wood fire."

The atmosphere was cozy, but the cabin was too isolated for Ariel to want to stay in it by herself. She glanced at Kiernan. "You're not afraid of staying out here by yourself?"

"No. Security regularly patrols this road and I always keep my IMP with me. Which reminds me, I'll need to call Mrs. Belfort and let her know our plans. She can inform the guards we're using the cabin, so they won't burst in on us. We haven't had any problems with poachers or trespassers in years. It's a well-known fact around these parts that the grounds are patrolled. So it's pretty safe if you ever get in the mood to stay up here."

"It hardly seems dusty at all."

"I have someone come out here once a month to dust and check out the chimney for debris and bird nests."

"What type of wood was used in its construction?"

"Yellow poplar. The foundation is native rock. The interior was paneled with cedar in the early 1900's. The roof is cedar shingles and recently reroofed. There were McPhersons living in this cabin as late as the 1940's, until a bigger residence was built in the valley. The family moved to Knoxville in the late 1960's, but always kept the cabin maintained as a family vacation home up until Grandmother purchased the property in 2032."

"Interesting."

"The cabin is built on the old Scotch-Irish floor plan. It has this one room we're in, called a pen." She peered overhead, pointing to a loft covering a portion of the ceiling. Ariel saw a ladder leading up to it at one end. "That's the loft where all the McPherson children slept. The parents slept here in the main room."

"Not much privacy, was there?"

"No. But privacy was probably a luxury back in those days, only found in a secret hollow or a place down by the creek."

"I notice there's no electricity."

"It was never wired for that. And the only running water is from a hand pump to a well on what was the original back porch renovated in the 1920's to make a kitchen and a pantry." She gestured toward the door in the middle of the wall on the other side of the room. "That's the door to the kitchen which has a back door leading to another porch."

Kiernan left out one important room Ariel would need soon. She grew apprehensive thinking about the alternative. "Bathroom?" She held her breath waiting for the answer.

Kiernan hesitated, her lips suppressing a smirk. "Well—such as it is."

"Oh, no, Kiernan, don't tell me it's an outhouse."

Kiernan delayed her answer for a few seconds. Ariel squirmed while thinking the worst. Finally, Kiernan said, "No. It's right at the end of the back porch, one of those antique flush toilets from the turn of the century. You have to fill the tank to get it to flush. I keep four one-gallon containers of water in there for that purpose. It drains into a septic tank. I keep a supply of sani-wipes in there as well as sani-towelettes. When you're ready to go, I'll take you to it."

Ariel let her breath out in relief.

They sat silently for a few minutes, Ariel's attention on the fireplace where she watched the flames lick over the wood. The blaze made crackling and fizzing sounds, as the heat forced out air and moisture. This was the first time she'd seen a wood fire in a real fireplace. The closest she ever came before was the gas fire in the fireplaces at Crestview. The aroma from the burning wood was pleasant, and her imagination formed the uneven flames into interesting shapes of animals and fantastical beings, but she still felt a little on edge.

"I think I would feel uneasy staying out here by myself, Kiernan. Besides, I'd probably burn the place down trying to build a fire."

"You mean you were never a Girl Scout?"

"No. And I've never been camping, or roughed it."

"You mean to tell me you live next door to the Smoky Mountains and have never been camping? You were deprived."

"We do go skiing in winter for a day, and in the summer, white water rafting, and day hikes."

"You haven't lived until you eat canned beef stew warmed in a pot over a campfire—a real gourmet experience."

"Stew made with real beef?" Ariel had rarely eaten beef before marrying Kiernan. Now beef was on the menu at least once a week, and a few times Ricardo fixed her a real beef hamburger for lunch. She found the taste heartier and richer than the ersatz substitutes.

"Yep. I order the canned stuff from a cattle ranch in Texas along with the fresh beef. Dennard's Range-fed Steers. They have their own meat processing plant. The cans are the old-fashioned kind and not Pop-hots. You have to heat the contents up in an actual pan. Not as delicious as freshly-cooked beef, but still tasty on a cold, rainy night like this. I'm sure there's a stock in the kitchen, along with other types of food. Let me know when you get hungry."

"I'm feeling hungry." She paused before adding, "I have to go potty first."

"Let me call Mrs. Belfort, and then we'll go." Kiernan reached over to the end table to get her IMP from her belt bag while Ariel stood and walked over to retrieve her long underwear. She stroked a hand down the length of them, discovering they were dry and toasty warm as well.

She moved back to the sofa to put them on, once again seeing Kiernan gaping at her legs before quickly averting her attention to conclude her call. For some reason, knowing Kiernan had been checking her out didn't upset Ariel. She thought that if she were provided the opportunity, she would certainly check out Kiernan's bare legs. She remembered they were nice, as was the rest of her. A brief flush of arousal assailed her, which rapidly transformed into the heat of a blush.

Kiernan said, "Nature calls, let's go."

Ariel followed her through the door and into a kitchen dimly lit from windows on each end. An antique wooden table with lion claw feet sat in the center with four chairs around it. A woodburning cook stove was set against the wall next to a wood cabinet with a sink set into it and a hand pump over the sink. Shelves lined the other wall, filled with cans and cartons of food as well as cooking utensils.

Kiernan opened the back door to a screened porch. The rain pelted against the sides, and a little water drizzled in near the far end, but other than being cold, the porch was sheltered well. Firewood was neatly stacked at one corner. The other end was a closed off area with a door. Kiernan motioned with her head. "You go first."

Ariel opened the door into what was essentially a closed in toilet stall, around the size of one in a ladies room at any regular restaurant or store. A small window gave a view out into the gloomy twilight of the surrounding woods. A sudden thought hit her: Well, this is novel. A view while you poo. She laughed.

When she exited, Kiernan asked, "What was so funny in there?"

"Nothing."

"Come on. Tell me." Kiernan made the request sound like a command.

Ariel considered Kiernan's statement before saying, "What's the magic word?" Kiernan appeared puzzled, and Ariel said expectantly, "Come on. Tell me—?"

Kiernan rolled her eyes. "Please."

"A view while you poo."

Wrinkling her forehead in confusion, Kiernan said, "What?"

"You'll see what I mean."

"If you say so." Kiernan entered the bathroom, and a few seconds later Ariel heard a loud laugh.

IN THE KITCHEN Kiernan surveyed the pantry shelves. She found a flashlight on a shelf and clicked it on, shining the beam over the canned goods and cooking utensils. She picked up a gallon-sized iron pot with a wire handle and handed it to Ariel along with a wooden spoon and salt and pepper shakers. Next, she selected a good-sized can of beef stew. She skimmed her flashlight beam across the other canned goods. "Now for dessert. How about peaches, or do you prefer pears?"

"Peaches."

"Peaches it is. I'll grab a couple of cans of soda. We can take this out to the fireplace, and I'll come back for the plates and spoons."

After setting the items in front of the fireplace, Kiernan knelt in front of the fire, pulled off the lid for the stew, and poured the contents into the iron pot. Using the hooked end of the poker, she pulled out a two-foot long iron rod attached to a swivel from the left upper inside wall of the fireplace and placed the pot handle carefully over the rod. She pushed it with the poker until it hung over the fire. Retrieving the wooden spoon and handing it to Ariel, she instructed, "You watch the stew. Stir it a few times. I'm going to get the plates."

Kiernan took the lantern from the mantel, walked over to the front door and pushed in the dead bolt. Going over to the windows, she closed the curtains before heading to the kitchen. She locked the back door and retrieved two aluminum camp plates and spoons.

In the living room, Ariel sat in front of the fire, legs akimbo, stirring the stew.

Kiernan placed the lantern back on the mantel and plopped

down beside Ariel, laying the plates and utensils to one side. "Smells good. Do you think it needs salt and pepper?"

Ariel spooned up the stew and gingerly took a taste. "I think it does. Here, you taste and see what you think. Be careful, it's hot." She moved the spoon up to Kiernan's mouth.

Kiernan gingerly took a taste. "Definitely needs salt. Pepper wouldn't hurt either."

"I agree." Ariel added the necessary ingredients.

Kiernan watched Ariel stir the bubbling stew. She spooned up some, offering it once again to Kiernan. After taking a taste, she said, "I think it's ready."

Ariel took the poker and removed the pot from the hook, carefully placing it on the stone hearth. Kiernan held the plates and Ariel filled them with stew. Ariel settled back against the couch and crossed her legs, and Kiernan handed her the plate of stew. Kiernan took one of the soda cans and popped the top, feeling the instant chill of the self-frosting can. While they ate, they discussed the many sights they'd seen that day.

"I must say I thoroughly enjoyed riding on your motorcycle. Thanks for inviting me," Kiernan said.

Ariel beamed. "I enjoyed taking you. We'll have to do it again."

"You tell me when. I'm game."

"We might be able to get one more ride in before cold weather arrives. Soon, I'll have to store my bike for the winter."

"When do you start riding again—that is, when is the weather warm enough?"

"Late March, if it's an early spring. That's iffy though. April's hit or miss with some good days, and some rainy and chilly days. May is when you can expect the riding season to begin. Summer in the higher altitudes is nice, but there are a few days that are too hot and humid." Ariel discussed places they would enjoy taking rides to on her motorcycle or in her convertible.

They finished eating and stared at the fire for a few minutes in companionable silence. Kiernan heard Ariel yawn. She rose and took the cushions off the couch. "Scoot out of the way, and I'll pull out the bed." She went over to the chest and pulled out sheets, blankets, and pillows.

Ariel rose, and together they made up the bed.

Kiernan said, "Why don't you get into bed, and I'll turn off the lantern."

"What about the dishes?"

"We can wash them in the morning."

Ariel stood, pulled off her shirt, leaving on her black silk long-sleeve undershirt. Kiernan swiftly averted her eyes, but not before seeing how sexy Ariel appeared in the black, skintight underclothes. She knew it was going to be torture lying next to her and knowing what was beneath those garments.

She felt aroused thinking about Ariel's gorgeous breasts. She mentally shook herself, removed her sweater, and hung it on the back of the chair, leaving on her long-sleeve undershirt. She clicked off the lantern and slipped under the covers, keeping to her side. She rolled onto her back, very aware of Ariel a little more than a foot away.

For a few minutes, all she heard was the crackle of the fire, until Ariel said, "You ever sleep up in the loft?"

"Only a few times when I was a teenager when I had slumber parties here. It's dark up there because the ceiling is low. Mostly, we all camped out in sleeping bags around the fireplace."

"Yeah? I bet this was an ideal place for slumber parties. No parents to disturb you when you became rowdy."

"So right. It was out of the watchful eyes of Grandmother, and we always managed to get our hands on hard cider—not enough to get us rip-roaring drunk, but enough to get us high...and imagine we saw, or heard, the ghost of Molly McPherson pining away for her intended."

"This cabin is haunted?" Surprise was evident in Ariel's voice, and Kiernan glanced toward her. Ariel pulled the covers higher and jumped when a gust of rainy wind hit the windows.

Amused, Kiernan said in a teasing voice, "Why, Ariel, you mean to tell me your scientific and logical bent of mind believes in ghosties and thingies that go bump in the night?"

"Truthfully, I don't know what to believe. Throughout the centuries, there have been too many accounts of supposed encounters with what are termed spirits for the phenomena to be dismissed as overactive imaginations at work. I think there are scientific explanations, but who's to say those explanations aren't within the realm of what we term the supernatural?"

"I agree science doesn't have an explanation for everything."

"Tell me about this ghost that supposedly haunts this place."

"Over the past two centuries there have been reports of a ghostly apparition seen in the window." Kiernan riveted her eyes on the window to the left of the front door. Out of the corner of her eye, she saw Ariel glance nervously in that direction. Kiernan continued, "They say Molly's intended was Joshua Daniels, and he joined the Confederacy and left to fight. After the war was over, she waited for his return. She would place a lighted candle in the window. He never returned, but she continued to burn a candle for ten years after the war, until she died of a broken heart. Broken hearts were the leading cause of death among young people back in those days, if you believe all the tales that come out of these mountains."

"I thought it was 'Hatfield and McCoy' type feuds that killed you."

"A few feuds went on in these parts, and bloodshed was involved."

A distant flash of lightning drew a nervous glance from Ariel toward Molly's window. She focused her attention back to the fire, and then on Kiernan. "Have you ever seen this ghost?"

"No. I've never seen or heard anything out of the ordinary. Two of the guards patrolling this area reported seeing what appeared to be candle light and a shadowy form in the window a couple of times. When they went to investigate, nothing was there. Maybe it was the moon's reflection in the window, or a light from somewhere else." Kiernan rolled on her side and faced Ariel, continuing in an exaggerated whisper, "Or — maybe it was Molly's ghost waiting for her long lost lover. Woooooo, Joshua, oh Joshua, wherefore art thou, Joshua?"

Ariel giggled. She deepened her voice and accentuated her Southern accent. "My dear, Molly, I regret to tell you I done met me this here city gal over in Memphis, and I'm now plying my trade as a rumrunner on the Mississippi. You must forget about me."

Kiernan drawled, "Why you lowdown polecat, taking up with some Jezebel. I hold you in lower regard than I do a mangy, flea-bitten cur of a Yankee Carpetbagger."

"Frankly, my dear, I don't give a damn."

Kiernan laughed, and Ariel joined her. Just when Kiernan thought she'd finished, Ariel commenced to laughing again, triggering Kiernan once more.

A rumble of thunder rattled the windows, and Ariel jumped. "Geez!"

"Whoa, I guess Molly's not amused."

"Guess not."

"You know, you're close to the truth when you said Joshua was a rumrunner. The Daniels had a long history of moonshining — well up until the 1960's. I can show you the location where they kept one of their stills."

"I would like to see that. Anything left of the still?"

"No. In fact, there were a few 'Hatfield and McCoy' feuds between the Daniels and Bearfoots over still locations, and scandals between the two families of the Romeo and Juliet variety."

Ariel fluffed her pillow and regarded Kiernan. "This sounds like a great bedtime story. I'd like to hear more."

Kiernan told her tale of the Daniels and Bearfoots. When she reached the conclusion, she heard a puff of breath from Ariel and saw she was asleep, exhaling quietly. The golden glow of the fire played shadows over Ariel's face, drawing Kiernan's attention to the enticing dark dot at the corner of her mouth. She gently touched it with her right forefinger, feeling the slight bump. Ariel twitched her lip, and Kiernan jerked her finger away. She wistfully whispered, "And they lived happily ever after."

A JOSTLING MOVEMENT pulled Ariel from sleep. The warmth pressed against her back retreated, and there was more movement. She pulled herself partway up to see what was going on and heard Kiernan say, "Sorry to disturb you. The fire is going out. I need to put in more wood."

Ariel snuggled once more under the covers and listened to the sounds of Kiernan tending to the fire. The covers moved as Kiernan slipped into bed protesting, "Brrr, it's cold."

Ariel slid over to Kiernan, put an arm around her waist, and spooned against her back, feeling the solid warmth and inhaling a slightly smoky scent mixed with an earthier one that the primal part of her mind, now emerging as she descended into sleep, found alluring. Somewhere in the part of her that was still aware, she thought holding Kiernan felt so right, as if they belonged together.

KIERNAN NESTLED INTO the inviting warmth against her back, reveling in the protective arm thrown around her, right below her breasts. She had a new feeling, of security and safety, with Ariel holding her like this. She had always been secure and safe in the knowledge she was self-sufficient and capable, depending on no one but herself.

Suddenly, she sobered when she realized this new feeling was probably false. Ariel sought only warmth against the cold. But what was the harm in pretending, for tonight, that Ariel was indeed her protector? That her arms were the haven she needed when the haggling and dealing at the office left her drained and weary, and yes, feeling vulnerable.

She snuggled against Ariel, feeling the full press of breasts and the soft breathing tickling her ear. Ariel nuzzled her neck and moaned. Kiernan froze when Ariel moved her hand in comforting circles on her stomach. She sucked in her breath, and a current of arousal infused her body. She was about to turn into that enticing embrace when Ariel let out a snore. Kiernan realized her bedmate wasn't conscious of her actions. If Kiernan rolled over and kissed her, she would get a response, but it wouldn't be right to take advantage of Ariel when her defenses were weakened by sleep.

Instead, she put her hand over Ariel's to stop the seductive movement against her stomach. She willed her body to relax, gave a contented sigh, and fell into a deep and peaceful sleep, something she hadn't done in a long time.

Chapter Twenty-Five

"EIGHT BALL IN the corner pocket," Ariel said with satisfaction as she bent to take the shot that would clinch her first win against Kiernan since they'd started playing pool together. She gently hit the cue ball and tipped the black ball into the pocket.

She stood, raising her cue stick triumphantly in the air. "Yes! The new champion!"

"Ha! Just a fluke. I was off my game tonight. Tomorrow night will be a different story."

Ariel placed her cue stick back in the rack. "Face it O'Shay, I outplayed you tonight, and I'll do it tomorrow night, too."

Placing her cue stick in the rack beside Ariel's, Kiernan said sourly, "Famous last words."

"You'll see." Ariel headed out the door of the recreation room, Kiernan behind her.

When they came to the stairway, a strong tug on the back of Ariel's sweatshirt stopped her forward movement.

"Last one up is a rotten egg!" Kiernan sprinted past and up the stairs.

Ariel recovered, speedily taking the stairs two at a time, and almost pulling even with Kiernan who beat her by half a stride.

A winded Kiernan leaned over to catch her breath.

Ariel wasn't as winded as Kiernan and protested, "No fair. You had a head start."

Kiernan straightened and said, "Of course I did. It's called a handicap. Your legs are longer than mine, so I get a step before you do to even the odds of winning."

"More like six steps," Ariel said, as they headed down the hall toward their suites. She stopped in front of her door and said, "Good night. I'll see you tomorrow when you get home."

"Sweet dreams."

"You, too."

Ariel watched Kiernan head toward her suite before opening the door to her own and entering. She showered, slipped on a dark red velour robe, and went to her sitting room to find she had received no voice messages on the telecom, but the mailbox light blinked, indicating e-mail. She opened the mailbox and skimmed over the list of messages. When she saw a message from Georgia Tech's Aerospace department, she held her breath for an instant. With nervous anticipation she opened the correspondence. She would read it instead of having the computer do it for her. She scanned the contents and said a triumphant, "Yes!"

Rising from her chair, she hurried over to the door of Kiernan's suite, rapped sharply against the wood, and waited impatiently. She wondered if Kiernan was asleep. She barely got the thought out when the door opened.

"Ariel—"

"I'm a Ramblin' Wreck from Georgia Tech!" Ariel couldn't keep the excitement out of her voice.

Kiernan blinked as if confused. Then she grinned and said, "And a hell of an engineer."

"Yes, yes!" Ariel bounced on her toes a couple of times.

"I knew they would accept you. Was there any doubt?"

"You never know. They might have met their maximum enrollment in the program." Ariel then noticed Kiernan wore a blue terrycloth robe, and the end of her hair was damp. "I'm sorry. I didn't interrupt your bath...or anything?"

"Not at all. I just finished my shower when I heard you knock. Come on in."

"It's late and I better let you get your sleep."

"Nonsense. After news like that, we have to celebrate. And I know how to do it." Kiernan gave her a leer.

Ariel froze. "Er...how?"

"Ice cream."

"Huh?" She was a bit disappointed Kiernan wasn't suggesting her first thought.

"Yes, ice cream. I happen to know there's a freezer full because today was grocery shopping day, and I requested it added to the list. So, come on, let's go." Kiernan motioned with her head toward the front door of her suite.

"Shouldn't we get dressed first?"

"Why? No one will be up and about in the main part of the house this time of night."

"All right, then, lead the way."

She followed Kiernan into the dimly lit hallway and down the stairs to the kitchen. The night-lights were on throughout the house to prevent mishaps. When they entered the kitchen, Kiernan ordered the computer to turn the light above the table to medium. "Why don't you get the bowls and spoons, and I'll get the ice cream," Kiernan said. She headed toward the stainless steel refrigerator and opened the freezer side.

Ariel retrieved the bowls, dipper, and spoons, set them on the kitchen table, and then took a seat.

Kiernan called over her shoulder, "Vanilla, chocolate almond, butter pecan, orange sherbet, or lime sherbet?"

"Butter pecan."

At the table Kiernan removed the lid. "I'm having it too." She scooped a chunk into one of the bowls. "Say when."

Three scoops later, Ariel said, "When."

Kiernan slid the bowl over and scooped out some for herself, then took the chair across from Ariel.

Ariel placed a spoon full of the rich cream in her mouth, letting it melt and slide down her throat. "Mmm. This is good."

"Valley Shire uses all natural ingredients. That's why their ice cream is the best." Kiernan dipped her spoon in for more. As she was bringing the spoon up to her mouth, the dollop of ice cream slipped off and fell into her robe opening right below her neck. "Arghh!" She hastily put her hand up in an attempt to stop the ice cream from slipping down her front, but missed. Her robe opened and exposed her breasts.

Ariel stopped the spoon's path to her mouth. Kiernan closed her robe, stood, and hurried over to the counter to grab a towelette. Keeping her back to Ariel, she wet the towelette to clean herself, grumbling as she did so.

Ariel had managed to catch an eyeful of creamy breasts with stiffened nipples, the latter, no doubt, caused by the cold ice cream. A vivid flash of memory flooded her mind of the feel of those enticing peaks between her teeth as she flicked her tongue across them. She licked her lips. Her mouthed watered and there was a mild twinge of her vagina. She crossed her legs in an involuntary response, and shifted in her seat, hoping to stymie the surges in her nether region.

Despite the circumstances of *that night*, Ariel remained conflicted. A certain amount of embarrassment filled her when she recalled her motivations and her actions during their encounter. On the other hand, she took a guilty pleasure in remembering aspects of their sexual interaction. Kiernan now figured prominently in her more erotic dreams, as well as in her waking fantasies. She'd lost the mortification she had first experienced when pleasuring herself, and now she imagined it was Kiernan's fingers bringing her to orgasm.

She attributed this to a shift in her feelings for Kiernan. She liked her...a lot. The shift from hate to liking made her more aware of Kiernan's physical attributes. Of course, she tried to be discreet when checking her out. For instance, when they played pool, she was sometimes on the same side of the table as Kiernan and couldn't help but notice her nice posterior when she leaned over to make a shot. She was sure Kiernan caught her a few times, if she could judge by Kiernan's slight smile. One like she received when caught ogling Kiernan's legs on the way to the spaceport for Ariel's tour of *Celeste*.

It wasn't only Kiernan's physical appeal that attracted her. The more time Ariel spent around her, the more she discovered appealing things about Kiernan's personality. She wasn't only a flat surface of dark and shadow as Ariel had previously thought. She was multi-faceted and reflected both color and light, as well as shadow.

Ariel discovered Kiernan had a generous heart when she informed her she was adding her name as co-donor to her charity contribution list. Ariel had asked what charities these were, expecting only a handful. Kiernan provided her with a printout of over one hundred charities she supported, stunning Ariel. The dollar amount given to each charity stunned her even more.

Kiernan had a great sense of humor and Ariel liked the banter they traded. Ariel sensed Kiernan honestly cared about her plans for attending school and working for Stellardyne. They had yet to sit down and have a serious discussion concerning raising a child. Would Kiernan listen to wiser heads on child rearing: Ariel's mother for instance? She thought that was a good possibility considering Kiernan's history of directing Stellardyne to make it the most profitable business in the solar system. Kiernan didn't learn her business acumen overnight and probably listened to and took advice from those who were successful in running their own companies.

The Kiernan whom Ariel was getting to know didn't mesh with the Kiernan who had hurt her mother, leaving Ariel confused. She battled back and forth over that. Maybe Mysha was right. Maybe someone else set her mother up, perhaps due to jealousy. No, it was too much of a coincidence that Kiernan wanted to marry her on the heels of Ariel's refusal. She was convinced her mother was framed, and further, her mother believed Kiernan had done it to force Ariel into accepting the proposal. Had she not gone to Kiernan and made the deal to marry her, Kiernan surely would have approached her.

Kiernan's reputation was ruthless when it came to obtaining what she wanted in a business deal. As much as she liked her, Ariel wasn't ready to trust her. But it was becoming harder for her to hide her attraction. She dare not act on the attraction and succumb to a sexual relationship, knowing herself well enough to recognize that might lead to an emotional involvement where she was likely to end up seriously hurt.

Kiernan slipped back into her chair. "I guess I need to tie a napkin around my neck."

"Or a bib," Ariel said teasingly.

"You know, come to think of it, I think we have a few lobster bibs around somewhere. Grandmother passed them out on those occasions she served lobster to the important clients she entertained."

"Those plastic ones with the pictures of the lobsters on them, like they have at some of the seafood restaurants?"

"Certainly not. I've seen those tacky things, and I would die of embarrassment if I had to wear one. You never know whether the paparazzi are lurking around to take your picture. It would be my luck to wear one and end up plastered all over the media."

"Oh, no, you can't have that happen. Why, it would ruin your image, and Stellardyne would go out of business," Ariel said while trying to keep a serious face.

"How astute of you." Kiernan paused. "You know, I'll have to arrange a time for you to come to work with me, so I can give you the grand tour of Stellardyne."

"I'd like that." Ariel wondered why Kiernan hadn't invited her earlier. She would love to see the engineering end and the top-secret test lab located on the Stellardyne property.

"I think around Christmas would be a good time. Meetings slack off, and I'll have time to show you around."

"Do I get the VIP treatment?"

"No. You get the VSIP treatment."

"VSIP?"

"Very special important person. In fact, you'll be the first VSIP I'll ever have the privilege of escorting around Stellardyne. As an extra bonus, you also get to have lunch with the president."

"Will we have lobster for lunch?"

"If you wish. And you can wear a bib with a lobster pictured on it."

Ariel managed to keep a straight face and say, "Wow, I can't wait."

Chapter Twenty-Six

ARIEL PIVOTED IN different directions in front of the floor-length mirror in her dressing room, checking her appearance. The cherry-red dress softly molded to the shape of her body and fit her perfectly. The bodice was asymmetrical, leaving her left shoulder bare. The length was bias-cut, a tad above her right knee, and continued diagonally to mid-calf of her left leg. A pair of matching stiletto heels and matching evening bag completed the elegant ensemble. The jacket she chose was glacier white and designed from man-made and very expensive nature-fur material that was hard to tell from real fur in either texture or feel.

To complement the asymmetrical design of the dress, she had her hair swept back to one side, and held with a gold-tone clip. She wondered whether she should wear jewelry. She wasn't much on wearing jewelry, except for a pair of gold ear studs, and owned only a few pieces. None would go with the dress, nor were they quality pieces.

She heard a knock coming from her sitting room and hurried out. Before she reached the main door, the knock sounded again, and she realized it came from the door to Kiernan's suite. She opened the door to find Kiernan standing there, smiling.

Kiernan gave her an appreciative once over. "Oh, my. You look fantastic." This was one of the dresses Kiernan had specially made for Ariel before the wedding, and it was obvious by her expression she was pleased how it went with her hair and complexion.

Ariel gave Kiernan an equally appreciative once over. "So do you. Black looks very good on you. It shows your hair and coloring to advantage."

"Thank you." Kiernan beamed at the praise. She wore a black silk crepe dress, heavily beaded with a variety of tiny jet beads tapering off at the skirt. The slim skirt hung to a couple of inches below the knees. Tiny jet beads adorned the edging of the hem. The sleeveless fitted bodice showed off her trim figure.

Kiernan held an oblong black velvet box in her right hand. "May I come in?"

"Yes, of course." Ariel stepped aside and Kiernan entered.

"I have something for you—a gift to celebrate your acceptance into Georgia Tech. I think it will go well with your dress."

She held out the box and Ariel accepted and opened it. She drew in her breath when she saw the thin rope of sparkling diamonds and the matching solitaire ear studs. "I...oh, Kiernan, it's beautiful." She impulsively hugged her and whispered in her ear, "Thank you," before moving out of the embrace.

Kiernan's pleasure reached to her eyes, turning them bright emerald. "You're very welcome. Here, let me put the necklace on for you." Taking the box from Ariel's hand, she walked over to the mirror hung over the console table.

Ariel followed and Kiernan said, "Turn facing the mirror."

Ariel gave a slight shiver when Kiernan's hand brushed her bare shoulder. She lifted her hair and shivered again as Kiernan's warm fingers placed the necklace around her neck and touched the nape. The heat radiating from Kiernan's body, so close to hers, caused her heartbeat to quicken.

Kiernan moved back and Ariel fingered the necklace, admiring the beauty of its sixteen sparkling diamonds. Each was at least a carat and set in gold in one single strand. She caught Kiernan's reflection in the mirror and their eyes met. Ariel saw a melting, softness in the depths of Kiernan's eyes, and held her gaze, saying, "You're right...it goes perfectly with the dress."

"It does. Don't forget to put the ear studs in. I'll help you, if you wish."

"Thanks."

Kiernan sidled up close, almost against her, and removed the gold stud in her left ear. Ariel watched in the mirror, again feeling the heat of Kiernan's closeness. The brush of Kiernan's arm against her shoulder sent a delicious shiver down her spine. Kiernan carefully inserted the diamond stud into the earlobe and fastened it into place. "Turn toward me and I'll put the other one in."

Kiernan removed the gold stud. "This one isn't as easy to get in as the other. Hold very still." Kiernan's breasts brushed against Ariel's right arm. She inhaled deeply, holding her breath for a moment, and closed her eyes as she felt her arousal grow. Whether Kiernan noticed her intake of breath, she gave no indication. She successfully inserted the diamond earring, edged back, and said, "There. All done."

Ariel swiveled toward the mirror, admiring the ear studs. She took the moment to try to get control of her libido. "They're beautiful. I might not take them off after the fundraiser."

"Leave them in. Though I must say, I don't know how well they would go with your black motorcycle jacket and Harley. Might ruin your image as a tough biker babe."

"Biker babe?" She gave Kiernan a stare. "As I recall, that's your role. After all, you were the babe on the back."

Kiernan gave her a hard look, but Ariel knew she was trying to smother a smile. "I might have been on the back, but I'd hardly call myself a babe. Ready to go?"

"Let me get my coat—babe."

THE ORDERED CHAOS outside the limo's window held Ariel's riveted stare. A roped off area, complete with a red carpet, led up to the Norwood Country Club located on the northeast side of Marietta, Georgia. The media surged around the carpeted walkway behind the rope. Everyone jostled for the perfect spot to take videos and pictures, and each reporter was intent on getting interviews or reactions from the arriving dignitaries and celebrities. A line of uniformed security guards on the inside of the cordoned area worked to keep the throng out.

Kiernan slipped out of her seat by Ariel, and took the one across from her. "I'll go out first and wait for you to exit. Remember what I told you. Keep by me, and don't acknowledge they're there. Keep on smiling, even if you hear some outrageous questions thrown your way. Ignore them."

Ariel nodded her understanding as a valet in a black coat and tie opened the limo door. The valet offered her hand to Kiernan, and she gracefully exited the limo to stand a few feet away and wait for Ariel.

The sea of voices and shouts reached a crescendo as soon as the media realized it was Kiernan O'Shay. Ariel took the hand of the valet and exited the limo to stand beside Kiernan. She heard the voices rise to garbled shouts as questions were thrown her way.

Kiernan took her by the arm and led her up the carpet. The guards pushed back some individuals attempting to cross the barrier.

"Ariel O'Shay, look this way please."

"Ariel O'Shay, how long did you know Kiernan O'Shay before you married her?"

"Ms. O'Shay, is it true this marriage is a business arrangement?"

"Kiernan O'Shay, do you have any comments on your wife's involvement in a notorious motorcycle gang?"

Kiernan muttered under her breath to Ariel, "They have got to be kidding."

Ariel didn't know whether to be appalled or amused. She decided she would go with the latter and said out of the side of her mouth to Kiernan, "I should have worn my black jacket and black biker pants."

Kiernan laughed throatily. The sound caused pleasant goose bumps to tickle the back of Ariel's neck.

Finally, they came to the end of the gauntlet, and two door

attendants in black tailcoats opened the double doors of one of the South's most prestigious country clubs. They strolled into a grand lobby with marble flooring where a dozen people conversed. Conversation lulled as heads turned to see who entered. Within a matter of seconds, Ariel realized all eyes were focusing in their direction. She heard a few low whispers, then suddenly a voice close by said, "Well, well, if it's not my favorite cuz, fashionably late, as usual."

A gorgeous woman in a strapless sapphire dress with a pageboy cut of silver hair came up to Kiernan and hugged her.

Kiernan said, "As usual, I'm here. And you're as gorgeous as ever, cuz." She turned to Ariel. "I would like you to meet my cousin, Beverly. She's throwing this shindig tonight. Beverly, this is my wife, Ariel."

Ariel took Beverly's hand. "Hello. Kiernan has told me about you and the wonderful work your foundation is doing."

"Why, thank you. It's people like Kiernan who keep it afloat." She hugged her and said, "Welcome to the family, cuz." Ariel flushed when Beverly planted a brief peck on her lips.

Kiernan narrowed her eyes and said with a playful warning, "Hey, watch it there. That's a little too familiar."

"Kissing Cousin, Kiernan," Beverly said, and then added, "you better keep her close by. It's the full moon tonight, and there are some foxes—and a few skunks—here who will try and raid your henhouse."

Kiernan put a proprietary arm around Ariel's waist, wryly saying, "I can arrange for them to take a one way trip to that full moon if they try that."

Beverly and Ariel both laughed.

Beverly said, "Come on, I want Ariel to meet Helen."

Kiernan took Ariel's hand and followed Beverly. Many of Kiernan's friends and acquaintances stopped them on the way, and she made quick introductions, but didn't linger long enough to engage in conversation. Some of the names and faces Ariel recognized from the media. The people she met were very cordial, but several scrutinizing stares made her uncomfortable.

They sauntered through the lobby and into a cavernous ballroom with a high ceiling from which hung crystal chandeliers. Over a dozen round tables with snowy white tablecloths and place settings for eight were scattered about the room. Cards by each place setting designated who sat where. The front floor of the ballroom was clear for dancing, and the members of an orchestra were setting up their equipment on the stage.

A couple dozen guests socialized in groups of four or five on both sides of the ballroom. A few people were already seated.

Many of the guests directed their attention to the trio as Beverly led them to the corner of the room where the bar was located. The people procuring drinks from the bartender stared. A few friends and acquaintances of Kiernan's stopped her, and she introduced Ariel.

A voice behind them said with humor, "Why, I do declare, it's the one and only Kiernan O'Shay. I see you decided to come down from that mountain fortress of yours and grace us with your presence, Your Majesty." A petite, vivacious woman with caramel skin and raven hair done into a twist came up to Kiernan and hugged her.

Kiernan hugged back, and they separated. Kiernan appraised the black silk tuxedo with a red cummerbund. "Helen, I must say, you're very debonair tonight. I think I'll get me a tux."

"Debonair? I like that description. You're as lovely as ever, and that dress is so you." She appraised Kiernan with approval, before turning her attention to Ariel, her soulful ebony eyes seeming to drink her in. With a dazzling smile, she said, "Hello, I'm Helen. You must be Ariel."

Ariel shook the offered hand. "It's a pleasure to meet you, Dr. Ortiz."

"Please, it's Helen." She didn't let go of Ariel's hand and stoked her megawatt smile up a few kilowatts. "Your pictures don't do you justice. You're stunning." She gallantly kissed the back of Ariel's hand. Ariel blushed hotly.

Kiernan narrowed her eyes and placed her hands on her hips. "All right, Don Juanita, you want me to challenge you to a duel?" She removed Ariel's hand from Helen's and held it.

Beverly shot a slightly reproving look at her wife. "Helen, sugar, behave."

"I am behaving." Helen grinned wickedly. "Why, you can call me... Ms. Behaving."

Kiernan said, "Ha! That line is older than my Uncle Theodore. Speaking of whom, has he arrived yet?"

"Not yet," Beverly said. "He and Jack will be seated at my table along with you two and Joshua and Casey Chou." Beverly's expression changed to stony. She whispered out of the corner of her mouth, "Heads up, here comes trouble."

A skinny, blonde-haired woman approached the group. She was dressed in a strapless black dress that did nothing for her gaunt figure but emphasize her prominent collarbones and bony shoulders. She stopped in front of the couple, glanced dismissively at Kiernan, and focused her attention on Ariel with a haughty squint down her aquiline nose and sarcastically said, "I hear congratulations are in order."

Kiernan displayed a feral grin. "Thank you, Millicent. I want you to meet my wife, Ariel. Ariel, Millicent Tyler."

Ariel disengaged her hand from Kiernan's and extended it for a shake. Millicent ignored it and said disdainfully, "I believe I heard you were a school teacher before marrying Kiernan."

"I'm a—I was a physics professor at Missionary Ridge Junior College."

"And you met Kiernan through your mother, who was employed by her?"

"That is correct."

"How fortunate for your family to now be associated with the O'Shay name...and social station. How long did you know Kiernan before you married her?"

Ariel knew what Millicent was implying. She took Kiernan's hand and surreptitiously squeezed it. Kiernan drew in a breath as if she were going to reply.

Ariel said facetiously, "Long enough."

"Oh? Funny how I never heard your name mentioned when Kiernan and I were...together...a mere few months before you married her. In fact, no one, that is no one I know, has ever heard of you."

"And why should they? Given the media's interest in anything Kiernan does, we thought it best to keep our relationship private, and between us." She glanced to Kiernan. "Kiernan was clever enough to throw the media off track by..." she paused and grinned at Millicent "keeping up...*pretenses*. Very clever of her—don't you agree?"

Helen snickered, and Kiernan's grip tightened briefly in approval and support.

Millicent's face glowed red and she twisted her mouth. "Why—"

"Oops," Beverly said, "it's getting to be that time. I better get this event rolling." Beverly hastily jerked Kiernan's hand and she and Ariel chugged along behind Beverly like two little train cars.

The sound of Millicent's retort followed Ariel. "Why you little upstart—"

Ariel heard Helen say, "Hey, Millie, let me show you to your table."

Ariel glanced back to see Helen grab Millicent's elbow and try to steer her away. Millicent flung her arm out of Helen's grasp. "My name isn't Millie," she shouted before stalking off.

At their table Kiernan said, "Sorry about that. Good lord. Seems my past has come back to haunt me."

"Let's be glad it wasn't my past, or we'd be heading to the emergency room to fix your broken nose."

Ariel saw Kiernan's eyes widen and mouth drop open, but she recovered her composure at once. "I'll depend on you to protect me."

"Protect you? Something tells me you can take care of yourself. But just in case, I'll be there holding a towel with ice in it for your nose."

"You handled that very well."

"I can take care of myself." A part of Ariel enjoyed besting that snotty socialite. She wasn't going to let anyone put her or her family down because they perceived them as being lesser in that they weren't born wealthy and were from a different social strata. Another part hoped this wasn't the type of behavior she could expect in the future from very many of Kiernan's friends and associates.

"I can see that." Kiernan was surprised at Ariel's quick and clever retort. Every day she realized there was so much more to learn about her wife than she'd initially imagined. Now she knew that Ariel would amaze her and confound her, please her and aggravate her, make her laugh and make her cry. She was looking forward to it.

DINNER WAS A pleasant affair. Ariel discovered the Chous were both motorcycle enthusiasts. They owned a Honda Goldwing they used in touring various parts of the globe for four months each year. They'd recently returned from a motorcycle trip through the Balkans.

Ariel regaled the Chous with her most recent day tour with the H.O.G chapter to the Smoky Mountain National Park. She took delight in relating information about her trips down the infamous Tail of the Dragon, more than three hundred treacherous, twisting, and turning curves covering eleven miles of mountain road. Joshua had taken the ride down the Tail sans his wife, and he and Ariel discussed the thrills of maneuvering the tail and some of the spills they'd witnessed.

Kiernan wasn't at all thrilled to hear their accounts. She was glad Ariel planned to give up riding during her pregnancy and wished she would give it up permanently.

The caterers went table to table to remove the last of the dessert dishes, and the orchestra, which had played sedate classics throughout dinner, changed to up-tempo pieces meant for dancing, starting with a contemporary waltz. Helen pulled Beverly up from her chair and turned to Ariel and Kiernan. "Why don't you two hit the dance floor with us?"

"Shall we?" Kiernan held out her hand to Ariel, and they

followed the other couple out onto the dance floor. She placed her arm around Ariel's waist only to have Ariel shrug away and reposition herself. Kiernan said, "I see you're accustomed to leading."

Ariel smirked. "I see you are, too."

"How about we take turns. I'll lead this dance—you lead the next."

"Okay, I'm versatile."

"We'll see." Kiernan guided Ariel in the box step. Ariel had no problems following. "Where did you learn to dance?"

"At Mountain Airs Studio. A member of my Harley group owns the studio and she donated the lessons for the annual Christmas drawing last year. They drew my name."

"Let me see what you learned from those lessons." She led Ariel into some underhand turns and a promenade step across the floor. Ariel followed flawlessly. Soon Kiernan went back to the basic box step and pulled Ariel in closer, feeling the heat emanating from her. There was the slight brush of Ariel's breasts that heightened Kiernan's senses. She smiled up at Ariel. "You dance very well."

"So do you."

"Mandatory lessons from sixth grade to tenth grade, and years of attending events such as these," Kiernan said lightly, before leading Ariel in a series of complicated moves, impressed how her wife followed every one perfectly.

THE SONG ENDED and another began. Ariel took the lead and guided Kiernan in a slow foxtrot. As the dance progressed, Ariel spun Kiernan into a few turns and executed a dip. She pulled Kiernan close against her at its conclusion and felt the warmth of her body and the press of her soft breasts. Ariel caught her breath as a tremor of arousal coursed through her. At that instant, she stared into Kiernan's eyes, knowing they were both aware of what was occurring between them. She folded her left arm, bringing Kiernan's right hand against her bare shoulder, held the soft, warm palm against her skin, and melded against her. Taking a slow, deep breath, she drew in the scent of perfume and Kiernan's own intoxicating scent, and excitement flooded her senses. The softness of a smooth temple and the silky texture of hair rubbed lightly against her cheek.

Leaning her head slightly, she touched her lips to the warm forehead, right at the hairline, and heard a deep intake of breath. Kiernan peered up, met her eyes, and Ariel saw melting tenderness there as well as the desire. Letting her eyelids close, she brought her lips down to Kiernan's and lightly brushed against them, then placed her cheek once more against Kiernan's temple. The velvet touch of lips on the side of her neck made her shiver and inflamed her senses. A voice in the recesses of her thoughts told her she was in danger. Stop. But she had fallen in too deep now and couldn't pull herself free of the persuasive lure of Kiernan's sensuality.

The song ended, but the dance continued for a few more steps, neither woman able or willing to end it. Another song started, this one a slow American tango. They separated and stood apart, staring into each other's eyes. Ariel's breath caught as she saw the smoldering depths of Kiernan's passion. She knew it was Kiernan's turn to lead, but felt compelled to take her in the tango embrace. She wrapped her right arm around and rested it on Kiernan's upper back, then relaxed when Kiernan placed her left hand on Ariel's upper arm, tacitly accepting Ariel's dominance. They locked gazes, and the unspoken challenge that flowed between them electrified Ariel. She clasped Kiernan's right hand in her left, holding it out in the traditional dance position, and pulled her forward until they were only a few inches apart.

Ariel began the walk, slow, slow, quick, quick, and slow. The chase had begun and she pursued her quarry with the grace of a lioness.

KIERNAN HAD NEVER been so aroused when she danced with another partner, nor had she ever felt so in tune with another's body language. She sensed Ariel's every move before she made it. Slow, slow, a pause, quick, quick, closing with their bodies offset to the left and tight at the hip. Ariel executed a right lunge, and Kiernan stepped back with her right leg extended to the side, then shifted forward and sensually slid her left leg up Ariel's thigh. Ariel's eyes widened with surprise and passion before she led Kiernan into the next move.

Ariel changed sway, and Kiernan gave her the reproachful glance that was part of the dance, then met her eyes. In that moment, Kiernan knew after the song was over, and after the event was over, their dance would continue throughout the night. Ariel twirled Kiernan away and brought her back against her as the dance ended. They stood frozen in the moment, their bodies together, gazes riveted upon one another. They were unaware of the appreciative claps of their audience, who had stopped dancing to watch them.

Kiernan's heart raced. A wave of heat cascaded through her, causing her clothes to feel too binding and tight. Reading Ariel's eyes, she saw the unspoken request to leave. She took Ariel by the hand and led her to their table to retrieve purses and coats. Beverly came up to them with a big, silly grin. "Holy Moly that had to be the sexiest tango I've ever seen. It was just...just...Holy Moly."

"It was a great event, Beverly, and we're calling it a night." Kiernan leaned over and gave her a peck on the cheek.

Helen walked up, glancing from Ariel to Kiernan. "You two aren't leaving now, are you?"

Beverly elbowed her and said out of the side of her mouth, "They're still in the honeymoon stage." Kiernan rolled her eyes. Helen hugged Kiernan and Ariel, and they said their goodbyes.

Helen and Beverly watched them go. Beverly said, "Bet they continue that dance once they get home tonight."

"Bet they don't even wait to get home."

Chapter Twenty-Seven

DAVID HELD THE limo door open. Ariel glided into the back, taking the seat facing the front. Kiernan slipped in beside her to sit inches away. Kiernan ordered, "Computer, do not engage seatbelts. Raise privacy panel." Ariel watched as the solid panel between the passenger area and driver area closed, providing them with total privacy. Kiernan ordered, "Computer, open the roof window."

The window rolled open, revealing the full moon. Clear safety glass would protect them from the elements for the two-hour ride back to Crestview.

Kiernan shifted to her and stared openly and searchingly. Ariel met her gaze and saw Kiernan's eyes reflecting the diffuse light of the full moon and stars.

Ariel wasn't sure who moved first, but they were in each other's arms, pressed together, mouths hot and open. Teeth clashed and bruised tender flesh, and their tongues wrestled. The embraces of desperate arms tightened to nearly crush the breath out of the other. Throats tight with desire and want ground out guttural moans.

The connection of her mouth on Kiernan's sent a rushing wave crashing through Ariel's senses and broke with all its force in her groin. Strong contractions of desire clenched her center. Kiernan pushed Ariel's coat off and ran her hands over her shoulders. Ariel felt goose pimples down the flesh of her arms and eagerly returned the action. She removed Kiernan's coat and gathered her up to kiss her mouth with hunger.

Ariel was on fire. All reasoning burned away, leaving only this insane drive of sex and lust and a conflagration of the senses that would consume her if not extinguished. Kiernan's hand was at her knee, blazing a scorching path inside her thigh over the stockings and stays of her garter belt. She pushed up Ariel's dress and reached the destination where the inferno burned hottest. Kiernan deftly stroked between Ariel's legs, over the silken panties soaked with the evidence of her want.

Ariel tore her mouth from Kiernan's, removed the bold hand driving her to distraction, and pushed her against the back of the seat. She leaned on that hot body and said in a ragged voice, "This dance isn't over. I lead."

"You've had your turn, twice. My turn." Kiernan brought Ariel's mouth back to hers.

Ariel conceded for now, knowing she would lead again. She let Kiernan push her down on the seat and slide her body sensually over her, kissing and rubbing her mouth against Ariel's neck.

That hot and dexterous hand once again journeyed up her leg, reaching its goal. Fingers slipped stealthily inside one leg of her panties, slid against the wet crease, and lightly caressed the hardened knot.

Ariel sucked in her breath and placed her hand over Kiernan's, encouraging her to press harder.

Gruffly Kiernan said, "I'm leading this dance." She moved her hand from under the panties and with one rapid motion ripped them down enough to grant access to the source of wetness beneath.

A warm finger ran down her center, separating the hot folds of flesh. Ariel cried out. She pushed her hips up and ground herself into Kiernan's hand, silently begging her to keep fondling her clit.

Ariel had no thought of delaying, or of taking it slow. She was driven by an urgency to drown the blaze before it became an aching frustration. "Kiernan, oh, please, I'm on fire."

"Tell me what you want," Kiernan growled in a raw voice against her neck.

"I want you inside," Ariel said with a catch in her throat. She inhaled sharply as warmth and fullness pierced her hunger. A steady rhythm moved her higher and faster toward the summit. Her want was all that existed, and she surged and ground her center relentlessly against the heat and firmness penetrating her, urging a faster rhythm. The muscles within greedily contracted, pulling the source of pleasure deeper. She felt a gathering of forces within her, a pulsating energy compacted into one point that became her entire existence, until she thought the point could contain no more.

KIERNAN'S MOUTH FOUND that wildly beating vein on Ariel's neck, and she sucked, and licked, and scraped her teeth along it. She pushed her finger inside Ariel, and firmly and slowly withdrew, only to push forward again. The velvet walls pulled her in for a deeper touch. A throaty rasp from Ariel vibrated against Kiernan's lips as she continued to lave her neck with attention. Ariel's hands and arms were a vise around her back, and she surged in rhythm as Kiernan's fingers and hand fed her hunger.

Kiernan lifted her head from Ariel's neck and kissed her. She wanted to consume Ariel, to drink her in, to satiate her own hunger and fill the void in her center, and in her soul. She needed Ariel to know she belonged to Kiernan. And that she, Kiernan, belonged to

Ariel.

Feeling Ariel tense and arch her back, Kiernan knew she was reaching her peak. Her hips twisted and bucked, but Kiernan maintained the steady rhythm. Tightness around her finger let her know Ariel reached the summit. Quickly tearing her lips from Ariel's mouth, she moved her other hand to grasp Ariel's hair and pulled Ariel's head back more firmly against the seat, holding her in a firm grip. She needed to see her angel come, only for her...forsaking all others.

"Yes, darling angel, come for me."

The moonlight painted Ariel's face silver and ivory, and Kiernan saw the beautiful mouth held in an expression of ecstasy as Ariel gasped for breath. Her eyes were tightly shut, and her face darkened. Then a sighing cry, a sudden inhalation of breath and another cry, and another. An angel falls and Kiernan rejoiced.

THE BREATH ARIEL drew in burned, and her heartbeat thundered in her ears. She gasped to take in air to still the pounding and smother the fire in her chest. She blinked and saw Kiernan in the dark regarding her with eyes gone glistening jet black. Over Kiernan's shoulder, she saw the moon, a witness to her fall.

Kiernan descended, eclipsing the moon, as her mouth claimed Ariel's in a kiss. Warm breath fanned across Ariel's face, and Kiernan said, "The next dance is yours to lead."

Ariel licked her lips to moisten them to be able to speak, her voice hoarse. "Yes, I believe it is."

Kiernan slid off Ariel and onto the seat across from her. Ariel rolled into a sitting position and watched with avid attention as Kiernan quickly slipped out of her dress and removed her bra, panty hose, and panties. The moonlight luminesced over fair skin and reflected in the auburn hair changed to shadow with glints of dark fire. Kiernan was Fey...a Goddess.

"God, but you're breathtaking," Ariel said in awe, her eyes feasting on the beauty, and sexuality of Kiernan's womanly form. She reached out to Kiernan. "Come here—my dance."

ARIEL'S APPROVAL OF her body thrilled Kiernan. She slid onto Ariel's lap, feeling the silky dress slide against her sensitive skin. Warm arms closed around her. Ariel kissed her, running her tongue slowly over her lips, then lightly touched the tip between them. Kiernan opened to allow Ariel's tongue to savor the feel and taste of her mouth. Every plunge of Ariel's tongue caused the nerve endings throughout Kiernan's body to tingle.

Now Kiernan was the one on fire, burning, and she knew only one touch would bring her salvation. She separated her mouth from Ariel's and knelt with her knees on each side of Ariel's hips. The arms around her pulled her, and a wet, warm mouth closed around a nipple to suckle. She put her hands on Ariel's shoulders, and a soft hiss escaped her lips. The feelings were exquisite, but it wasn't the touch she needed to ease the throbbing between her legs. "Touch me, Ariel."

Ariel continued to suckle Kiernan's breast as she loosened her arm and brought her hand down to the junction of Kiernan's thighs. Moaning, Kiernan felt that hand slide through the patch of hair and cup her sex for a moment before Ariel slipped a finger between the wet folds. Kiernan gasped when Ariel entered her. She surged against her and drove the finger deeper, then felt the finger withdraw, only to push slowly but firmly into her aching need. Again, she moved her hips back and forth as Ariel glided in and out.

Ariel removed her mouth from Kiernan's nipple, and cool air replaced the wet warmth. She encircled her left arm around Kiernan's waist to hold her firmly. Kiernan quickened her undulations, and the way her breasts stroked and receded from Ariel's face made her all the hotter. Another finger smoothly entered her, and Kiernan couldn't help but gasp and then groan from deep within her throat. The strokes grew firmer and deeper. Ariel's palm stroked against the sensitive ridge, and drew out a trickle of wetness from Kiernan's core.

Kiernan cried out at every thrust and increased her tempo. Ariel returned to her nipple, lightly biting it, and Kiernan tightened her grip on Ariel's shoulder. She threw back her head and a quick cry tore from her throat. She paused and let out a deep-drawn breath, and her release swept over her. Her back arched and she rode Ariel's fingers and hand. With a final surge, she shattered. Her cry was raw and guttural, a roar, her body freezing in mid-movement. The feelings were etched in the moment. Shuddering, she collapsed into strong arms that held her as she sobbed, "Hold me."

THERE WAS A tug at Ariel's heart, almost sorrow, hearing that plaintive plea. Holding Kiernan like this, feeling her body warm against her, and hearing Kiernan's ragged breathing, made her long to discover whether this vulnerability was part of the real Kiernan. Who was the real Kiernan? Was it the Kiernan who cared for her when she was sick, read her *The Little Prince,* and shared her dream of reaching the stars? Was it the Kiernan who told ghost stories, the one who was kind and considerate? Was it the Kiernan who was vulnerable and needed to be held...after? She could love *that* Kiernan.

Everything was moving too fast, and she couldn't even begin to trust her own judgment. How could she manage to remember that Kiernan wasn't to be trusted, that she needed to back away from this liaison? How could she stop herself from this all-consuming rush of passion? But for tonight, Ariel still burned. She needed — she craved — Kiernan's touch. What little thought she could muster up whisked away like smoke in the wind.

KIERNAN'S BREATHING STEADIED. For some reason she was close to tears, so vulnerable and exposed. She moved off Ariel and onto the other seat, gathered her clothes, and dressed. Kiernan regarded Ariel closely, trying to read her expression in the moonlight. Glittering, silver eyes returned her scrutiny. She wanted more of Ariel. She wanted Ariel to hold her afterward...forever. She wanted Ariel to love her. Make love to her. Ariel love her? She was kidding herself. Ariel had sex with her...had fucked her.

But if that's all she could get from Ariel, she would take it, as long as she could have her. "Stay with me — tonight."

"Yes."

Chapter Twenty-Eight

"ONLY SHE HAS graced my bed."
"She has taken me to her bed."
"Her hair spills light across my pillow."
"Her hair sparks embers in the moonlight."
"Her eyes are silver pools in the starlight."
"Her eyes are deep wells in the darkness."
"I pour my want into her mouth."
"Her mouth pulls from me my need."
"I drink in her warm breath."
"She has taken my breath away."
"Her voice is the soft patter of rain."
"Her voice is the night breeze in the hollow."
"Her caress is so gentle, as if she cares."
"Her touch is so tender, as if she feels."
"She is the storm that breaks the bough."
"She is the ocean wave that conquers the shore."
"My need for her is an ache in my heart."
"My need for her is bitter-sweet surrender."
"Her angel wings flutter against my tongue."
"Her passion rises and ebbs against my mouth."
"I drink the sweet spring water."
"I taste the briny ocean."
"Her cry is the sigh of an angel."
"Her cry is the keening of a hawk."
"She flies."
"She soars."
"An angel falls into my arms."
"Her talons have struck the earth."
"She has placed her seal upon my heart."
"She is a thief and is stealing my heart."
"Oh, God. I have fallen..."
"Oh, God. I am falling..."
"...in love with her."
"...in love with her."
"If she cannot give me tomorrow, I will take..."
"Tomorrow does not exist. There is only..."
"...the now."
"...the now."

Warmth cradled Kiernan's shoulders, and heat beneath her

cheek moved in a steady rhythm, up and down. *Breathing.* Realization struck. She wasn't alone. Ariel was with her, in her bed. *The first.* Even though Ariel had come to her bed once before, it wasn't like this. Kiernan had brought her here this time. Never had she taken another to her bed, it was always some other bed. But this was Ariel, and she wished to keep her here for always, as she now kept her in her heart.

She was afraid to move, lest she be Psyche to Ariel's Cupid and the divinity take wing and flee. She was content to savor this time and listen to the heartbeat beneath her ear measure out time as a metronome, to the song's final note to wakefulness. Breath wafted warmly across the top of her head, stirring her hair. Her arm rested across Ariel's torso, right beneath the breasts, and her leg draped over a soft, warm thigh.

Her head rested upon a soft pillow of breast. She wondered how close the nipple was to her lips and whether she dare move enough to discover it. Feeling her mouth water at the thought, she pushed it out of her mind, afraid her angel would awaken and flee if she acted.

She let her thoughts unravel and gave her mind free range over images, impressions, and sensations. Ariel was the hunter, demanding and taking, yet tender and giving. And she was the hunted, surrendering to and accepting Kiernan's passion.

Kiernan wanted to believe Ariel was seeing her in a different way, beyond only friendship. But she feared it was only the dance and the moonlight that stirred that ancient madness and released it from the primal darkness. The madness would return to the dark place in the light of day, and truth would emerge. And the truth was she loved Ariel, but Ariel did not love her.

WARMTH ACROSS HER torso and upper thigh and arm held her so she couldn't move. Solid softness rested on her breast, pressing against her chin and the side of her cheek and mouth. She inhaled the scent of rich loam and briny estuaries. The taste of the ocean still lingered on her tongue. Sleep clouded her reasoning and the images flickering and flashing behind her eyelids existed in an ephemeral dreamscape. Kiernan in the moonlight. The dream Kiernan, giving and gentle as a lover and as ardent as a champion on the field of battle, conquering all. And in the dream, Ariel was falling in love.

Reason emerged, sleep retreated, and the puzzle pieces of dreams scattered, leaving only reality. Her eyes shot open in startled realization. No, no, no! The cold morning light slapped her hard in the face, and she tensed her muscles, ready for flight.

She tried to sit up, but Kiernan tightened her grip and held tight.

"Let me up." The pressing warmth receded, and she tried to rise, only to have two strong hands press her shoulders hard against the mattress.

"Ariel, don't go. Stay. Please."

The soft beseeching voice lulled her for a moment. She lifted her eyes to the face looking down at her, seeing a melting tenderness she could easily mistake for a stronger feeling she wasn't willing to name. Was this the truth or only the remnants of the night?

"I only want to talk to you. Please?"

Ariel stilled but did not relax. She licked her lips, dry from sleep and nervousness. Her voice was husky from apprehension. "I...what about?"

"I—I—last night, I want..." She stopped for a moment and bit her lip. "Will you have breakfast with me?" Kiernan asked in a shy voice. A soft smile appeared and squeezed around Ariel's heart for a moment, invoking memories of soft caresses and gentleness in the night. "I'll have Ricardo make whatever you want. We'll take it in my sitting room. Or yours if you prefer."

Ariel needed time alone though. She needed to analyze and process what had occurred. She needed to sort through the tumultuous emotions and examine them—break them down to simple equations she could understand. Any other contact with Kiernan, at least for the day, would distract her. No. She couldn't deal with Kiernan until she dealt with her chaotic emotions and with the way Kiernan reversed the polarities of her feelings. If only it were as simple as a physics problem. She said gently, "I need to be alone...for a little while."

She rolled hurriedly from Kiernan's hands and off the bed, not bothering to pick up her clothes, and retreated to her own suite.

Kiernan watched as Ariel took her heart and fled, leaving a hollow place not even her tears were able to fill.

Chapter Twenty-Nine

THE BLACK ARTERIES that led to all four quadrants took Ariel on that Zen toward the perfect Nirvana. She journeyed into that mysterious realm of woman in metamorphosis. One with the metal beast she rode, she was no longer flesh and blood, but also steel and rubber. She's the modern embodiment of the ancient centaur: part woman, part machine.

Lean, lean, throttle, up shift, down shift, lean, throttle, up shift — the motions were as natural to her as breathing. Her engine heart was as real to her as the living muscle in her chest. Its roar was now her voice and sang oracles from the road gods that only she can decipher.

The wheels spun in an eternity of three hundred and sixty degrees, moved through time and space and dissolved the past, present, and future, as they took her to her destination. She arrived at that perfect nirvana. She was no longer Ariel, but all things and all knowing. She was nihility.

The cold seeped underneath her helmet and sifted in through the micro-fiber of her gloves pulling her back into time. Feet and hands numb and stinging, she pulled her bike into an overlook and along the side of a railing that hugged the edge of a drop. She dismounted, removed her helmet, and placed it on the seat.

She took in the vista of the mountains in mid November. The brilliance of autumn's splendor was fast fading, leaving the mountainsides a patched worn coat of gold, rust, and muted reds with only the occasional smear of evergreen. The sky was a crystal blue eternity with no clouds to mar it.

She opened one of her black saddlebags, pulled out a Thermos of coffee, and walked over to a nearby picnic table. After brushing the dry leaves from the seat, she sat. The coffee she poured into the deep lid roiled with steam. She brought the lid to her mouth, feeling the steam condense warmly on her cold nose. She sipped slowly, feeling the warmth go down her throat and thaw the chill.

Once again she turned her eyes to the autumn vista, but her brain had disconnected from that sense and what she saw didn't register. Instead, her memory came into focus, sharp and clear. Kiernan.

Her synapses zipped at light-speed to images in the moonlight, in Kiernan's bed, in her arms, the sound of her voice.

"Tell me what you like."

"Is this touch too much?"
"Yes, like that."
"Touch me."
"My angel."
"Come for me."

Could it be Kiernan was considering her as more than a means to something else? Could it be possible that Kiernan had feelings for her beyond friendship? Or was last night a trick of the moonlight? The moon had waxed full and would soon wane. Would this Kiernan wane with it?

She wanted to believe that this Kiernan — the one she was falling in love with — was the real Kiernan. But she wasn't ready to trust her. Kiernan had the power to hurt her. Falling in love? No. She must put it aside — hide it away with her desire and hunger from the light so it wouldn't grow — for how long, she didn't know.

THE SKY WAS one of the deepest blues Kiernan had ever seen. There wasn't a cloud or vapor trail to distract the eye. She gazed toward the nearby mountains, wondering whether Ariel was up there on one and looking toward the mountain Kiernan was on. She scampered up on a flat gray boulder and sat, feeling the cold seep through her dark brown corduroy trousers. This was the highest place on her mountain. From this spot she could see the Ocoee River below and the mountains of east Tennessee and North Carolina. She brought her knees up to her chest and wrapped her arms around them. A nip in the air heralded the arrival of winter. She lifted up the collar of her heavy green wool shirt and a slight stirring of air, not even a breeze really, touched her face.

She closed her eyes, remembering the moonlight, and Ariel. Images of Ariel beneath her, over her, and beside her. Ariel in command, wringing orgasm after orgasm from her until she thought she would die from pleasure. Ariel surrendering, hearing her soft moans and almost breathless cries. She could still taste her, feel her softness and the muscles flex beneath her hands.

For the first time in her life, Kiernan was in love. For the first time in her life, she made love. Before, with others, it was all about sex and physical gratification, emotions played no part in it.

For Ariel she sensed it was all about making love and not sex. For her sex was tied in with emotions of love and caring. Was that why she ran away this morning? She acted on the physical and not the emotional, perhaps feeling guilt, shame, and confusion.

Kiernan knew Ariel liked her and desired her. In time, she might even come to love her. Ariel needed to come to terms with what happened in her own way.

With Ariel probably feeling confused and vulnerable, now wasn't the time for Kiernan to tell her she loved her. Ariel would think she was lying to get her way. But she could show Ariel she loved her. She could be patient, supportive of her goals, listen when she needed it, and be a friend. Kiernan also felt a niggling of fear. Fear that the progress they were making, the friendship they were forging, might be hurt by what occurred the night before. All she could do was wait — and hope.

ALMOST AN HOUR later, Kiernan walked down the road from the mountaintop and turned the curve. She paused, startled for a brief moment. Ariel sat on the low stone fence of the orchard eating an apple. Ariel took an apple out of her jacket pocket and held it up. This gesture gave Kiernan hope things would be all right. She picked up her pace, almost running, and stopped breathlessly in front of Ariel "For me?"

Ariel handed her the apple. "For you. Have a seat."

Kiernan clambered on top of the stone fence next to her and bit into the apple. Its crunch was loud, and she tore off a chunk with her teeth causing a fine mist of apple juice to spray. Around the mouthful Kiernan said, "Good."

Ariel took a bite of her apple.

"How did you know I was up here?"

"I asked Mrs. Belfort. She said you headed up the road a little over an hour ago."

"I never told her where I was going."

"I have a feeling all of your staff knows where you are at all times — and where I am as well."

"Yes, I suppose you're right. Did you go up to the falls to search for me?"

"No. I wasn't sure where you were, so I figured if I sat right here you would eventually pass by."

They ate their apples in silence, glancing occasionally at each other and smiling shyly.

Kiernan watched as Ariel's expression became serious. "Kiernan, about last night. I have to be honest. I wasn't ready for that. I'm sorry."

"There's nothing to be sorry for. I understand, more than you know. Let's chalk it up to the tango and the full moon."

Ariel smiled shyly at first, but in a blink, her expression became dazzling. "Would you like to watch a *Star Wars* movie with me tomorrow night?"

Kiernan couldn't keep the silly grin off her face, feeling things between them would indeed be fine. "Sure. What time?"

"How about my place at eight? I'll provide the movie, and you arrange for the popcorn and sodas."

"That I can do."

Ariel threw her apple core across the road, stood up, and brushed her hands on her jeans. "I guess we should head on back. It'll get dark soon." She held out her hand and Kiernan took it. Ariel pulled her up, but didn't let go of her hand as they walked back down the road toward home.

Chapter Thirty

1:30 P.M. DISPLAYED on the LED clock on Kiernan's desk. She glanced at it frequently, not only because she was anticipating her date with Ariel, but also because the clock was the bottom portion of a Plexiglas frame that held a picture of Ariel in her red dress. Helen had taken it at the fundraiser and e-mailed it to her the night before. Kiernan had printed it to photo paper and brought it into work this morning, replacing the picture of *Celeste* with it.

Reluctantly, she went back to the various reports for the day, slogging through them until she came to the report from Dwayne Campbell about the recent completion of updates and engine overhaul for *Celeste*. She buzzed through that one with keen interest, delighted to learn that the ship was now ready for whenever Kiernan wanted to use her.

She remembered when Ariel first boarded her, the excitement in her eyes, and the smile she couldn't keep off her face. Those memories brought a wistful expression, followed by a brief laugh. "Why the hell not?"

KIERNAN KICKED THE door to Ariel's suite while trying to keep steady the tray full of soda cans and a big bowl of popcorn.

"Come in."

"Ariel, open the door please."

A few seconds later Ariel opened the door, and Kiernan handed her the tray.

Ariel sniffed loudly. "Yummy, hot butter on the popcorn. I'm impressed."

"You should be. I popped it myself."

"What else can you cook?" Ariel placed the tray on the coffee table and took her seat on the sofa.

"A lot of things I'll have you know."

"Oh? Name me three things you can cook—besides popping popcorn."

"Fried eggs, scrambled eggs, and boiled eggs."

"I bet you bust the yokes on the fried eggs."

"Do not. Before you start the movie, I have to make a trip to your bathroom. I'll be right back. Don't eat all the popcorn."

"I can't guarantee that. Better hurry."

On the way out of the bathroom, Kiernan saw Ariel's

motorcycle helmet on the dresser and picked it up. She put it on, closed the tinted shield, and walked back into the sitting room. She stopped in front of Ariel, and gave her best Darth Vader harsh breath sounds.

Ariel laughed. "What do you think you're doing?"

"Luke, Luke, I'm your daddy, Luke." Kiernan's voice was low and muffled by the helmet.

Ariel snorted in amusement. "I'm your *father*."

Kiernan lifted the helmet's face shield. "Funny, I never knew I had a father. And you certainly don't favor either of my mothers."

Ariel threw a piece of popcorn at her. Kiernan took off the helmet, set it on the end table, and plopped down on the sofa. She reached into the bowl of popcorn between them and took a handful. Ariel ordered the EM to play the movie and they settled back to watch.

A quarter of the way through the movie there was a knock at the door, and Ariel called loudly, "Come in."

Mrs. Belfort entered carrying six gold and six silver metallic balloons attached to a doll. Her expression was one of fleeting surprise when seeing Kiernan, which she soon replaced with satisfaction. "I have a special delivery for Ariel."

Ariel wore a puzzled expression as she went to retrieve the delivery.

"EM, pause movie," Kiernan said, watching Ariel with a glow in her eyes.

Mrs. Belfort exited after handing Ariel a stuffed gold C-3PO doll with the balloons attached by foot long strings to his waist. Ariel examined the doll, searching for a card. Kiernan leaned back against the sofa cushions, trying to appear casual.

Ariel squinted at her suspiciously. "What's this?"

Kiernan shrugged innocently. "Why don't you ask C-3PO? If you press the little red dot on his right hand, he'll tell you why he's here."

Ariel did so, and a recording of C-3PO's voice said, "Greetings, Ariel. I am C-3PO, and I am acting in my function as an official Protocol Droid, and as an Ambassador for Kiernan O'Shay. Be it known, your presence is required aboard *Celeste*, on December Second, to embark on a journey to the red planet, Mars. Kiernan guarantees you will have a good time."

Ariel's mouth dropped open in surprise. She gazed in wonder at Kiernan, who said, "Cat got your tongue?"

Ariel plunked down on the sofa, and delivered a squeezing hug. "This is—wow!" They disengaged, and Ariel said, "That's only two weeks away."

"I guarantee *Celeste* will be fully crewed and ready to go."

"Er...what about Christmas and my family coming over? Won't we miss it? Not that I would miss a trip to Mars for the world."

"We should be back a few days before Christmas." She said in her best command voice, "Ready to report for duty, crewman?"

Ariel straightened up, with chest out and shoulders back, and saluted. "Reporting for duty, Captain O'Shay, ma'am."

Kiernan made an effort to keep her eyes on Ariel's face and not on her prominently displayed chest. She gave a rakish grin. "At ease, crewman, before you slip a disc."

Ariel dropped her salute. "Permission to speak freely?"

"Granted."

Ariel leaned over and kissed her on the cheek. "Thank you."

"You're welcome."

Ariel moved the popcorn bowl to the coffee table, scooted over beside Kiernan, and put an arm around her shoulders. "Now, back to the movie. EM on."

Kiernan settled contently against Ariel's side.

Chapter Thirty-One

"I SWEAR IT, it goes in one ear at the speed of sound and comes out the other ear at light speed," Joanna said to the twins who sat on the sofa by Ariel and Kiernan. Joanna sat across from them in a chair. "I'm sorry, Kiernan. I told these two not to pester you about going with you and Ariel on the Mars trip."

Kiernan leaned forward slightly to say to the twins, "I'll tell you what. How about I arrange for you two and your mom to take a tour of *Celeste* and stay aboard a couple of days when you have your spring break?"

Leigh said, "Can we, Mom, please, please?"

"Please, Mom," Seth begged.

"That depends on how well you two behave," Joanna said, looking from one to the other. "So far, it doesn't look good."

"We'll behave. Won't we, Seth?" Leigh promised.

"Yeah. We'll behave."

Joanna rolled her eyes. "For around five minutes." She said to Kiernan, "Thank you. That's a few months away, and I'm not sure what I'll be doing at that time. But you have my permission for these two to go. I warn you though, they're a handful."

Kiernan glanced at Ariel, a sly smile on her face. "Ariel can keep them in line, I'm sure."

"Just show me where the airlock is located," Ariel said as she made faces at her brother and sister.

"Mega supreme!" Seth said. "Wait 'til I tell Larry and the gang."

"Thanks, Mom." Leigh said.

"Don't thank me—thank Kiernan."

Leigh grinned. "Thank you, Kiernan."

"Yeah, thanks," Seth said.

"You're welcome."

Kiernan and Ariel had arrived at the Thorsen residence some fifteen minutes earlier for Thanksgiving. She was nervous on the ride over, not knowing what kind of reception she would get, but the warm welcome she received from Joanna and the twins put her at ease. So far, they'd managed to avoid any uncomfortable topics, and Joanna had not brought up the new computer processing job she started a week ago at a credit union.

A few minutes after arriving, Kiernan had surveyed the living room with interest to see whether there was any new furniture or anything else to indicate Joanna had spent any of the money Kiernan paid out as part of the prenuptial agreement. Granted, she had been in the house only one time and hadn't taken a tour, but it appeared the furniture was the same older pieces showing wear from daily use. She also noticed the older model Saturn in the driveway when they drove up to the house.

She was puzzled by Joanna's returning to work when she didn't have to and by the lack of material goods. Joanna could well afford to move into one of the upscale gated communities. The more Kiernan thought about it, the more she felt suspicious that something didn't ring true with the notion that greed had been the motivating factor in Joanna's theft of the new engine specifications. She decided that she would have the matter more thoroughly investigated when they returned from the Mars trip.

A buzzer sounded from the kitchen and Joanna said, "I need to check on the turkey and a few other things."

"Are you sure I can't help?" Ariel asked.

"I have it covered. Why don't you show Kiernan your picture album? I'm sure she wants to see your baby pictures."

"Oh, Mom, no," Ariel whined.

Kiernan glanced at her, seeing a flush of pink on her cheeks. "I'd really like to see them."

Seth and Leigh jumped up, jostling each other as they ran over to a bookshelf. They grabbed a digital album at the same time and tried to pull it out of the other's hands.

"I had it first," Leigh said.

"I did. Let go." Seth tugged it away.

"Alright you two. Hand me the album." Joanna held out her hand to a pouting Seth who relinquished it with ill humor. She gave it to Ariel, and Seth and Leigh hastily took seats by their sister. Joanna admonished the twins. "You two behave," and left for the kitchen.

Ariel sighed. "Here goes." She clicked on the album. The first picture displayed the typical newborn shot that hospitals provide to parents. Ariel was wrapped in a pink blanket, lying in a hospital baby bed. Underneath the picture were her name, Ariel Lynn Thorsen, and date of birth, April 21, 2073, 10:20 PM, weight 8 lbs. 1 oz. Length 22 inches.

Kiernan couldn't help but wonder whether their baby would favor Ariel. "Aww, you were a beautiful baby."

This comment set the twins to giggling. Kiernan looked across the album, seeing them rolling their eyes. Apparently, they didn't share her sentiments.

The next was newborn Ariel in the arms of a proud, handsome, and tall man with light blond hair.

Ariel said, "This is my dad holding me right after I was born"

"I can see where you got your height and blonde hair. He was a very handsome man,"

"Ariel's a red raisin," Leigh said.

"No, a sun-dried tomato," Seth said.

"Will you two put a lid on the comments, or leave?" Ariel said in an irritated voice.

"Nope," Seth said.

"Mom!" Ariel called out.

Reluctantly, Leigh said, "All right, I'll behave."

Seth said, "Me too."

"Yeah, well, see that you do." Ariel clicked to the next picture which showed a young Joanna holding a wide-eyed Ariel who wore a yellow knit cap on her head. There were more pictures of her being held by parents and sleeping in her crib.

Ariel came to one of her dressed in a light blue jumper and sitting, or rather propped, against the back cushion of a sofa. She appeared to be around three months old and wore a light blue ribbon with a bow around her head.

Kiernan examined the picture closely, thinking Ariel's hair was so pale and fine she appeared bald. On closer inspection, Kiernan saw, in fact, that she was bald, and teased, "My, what big beautiful blue eyes you have...and beautiful locks of golden hair."

Seth snickered. "Ariel's a buzzard head."

"Bald as a buzzard and stinky diapers I'll bet," Leigh teased.

"Yeah," Seth said, "so stinky a momma buzzard would tote Ariel away to her nest thinking she was her baby."

Kiernan was losing the battle to keep a straight face. A sharp elbow poked her in the ribs. In a low voice out of the side of her mouth, Ariel muttered, "Et tu Brute? Now see what you started?"

Both twins giggled, and Kiernan bit the inside of her mouth to keep from laughing, but an undignified choking sound escaped.

Ariel scrunched up her nose. "Ha, ha, look who's talking. You two weren't even around when I was born, but I sure was around to see both of you—and smell you, too. You two had heads shaped like buzzard eggs. We couldn't put you two in the sandbox to play without every cat within a six block radius getting a whiff of your stinky diapers and coming over to cover you up."

Kiernan burst out laughing, and Ariel joined her.

The twins were not amused. They crossed their arms, their faces sullen. Leigh stuck out her tongue.

Kiernan focused once again on Ariel's picture, wondering whether their child would be that precious...and bald. "I think you look sweet and adorable."

"Sweet! Adorable! Yuck!" Seth blurted. He stuck his tongue

out and jabbed his right forefinger toward his open mouth while making retching noises.

Leigh giggled and said, "Ariel sure was one u-glee bay-be!"

"Mom! Make them leave!" Ariel called out toward the kitchen. She clicked off her album.

"All right you two," Joanna said as she walked into the living room, "get in the kitchen now. I need some help,"

"But, Mom, I want to see the pictures," Leigh protested.

"Yeah, me too," Seth said.

"You two have seen those pictures a hundred times. Now," Joanna said sternly, "I need some help in the kitchen."

"We never get to have fun." Seth got up from the sofa, and headed toward the kitchen, Leigh following.

Joanna said, "I'll keep the kids occupied and out of your hair."

"Thanks, Mom," Ariel said.

"Dinner should be ready in thirty minutes." Joanna headed back to the kitchen.

Kiernan reached for the album on Ariel's lap, but Ariel clutched the album tightly and said, "Oh, no you don't."

"But I want to see more pictures."

"Only if you promise to show me pictures of you growing up."

"Sure. I have an album with nothing but baby pictures, and another one full of childhood pictures."

"I bet you had a bald head."

"Did not. I was born with hair, and kept it."

"Red hair?"

"Let's say, redder hair. It darkened when I grew older."

"You know what they say about redheaded babies," Ariel said in a matter-of-fact voice.

"No. What do they say?"

"I'll think up something and tell you later." Ariel poked Kiernan lightly in the ribs with her elbow, then clicked the album back on to go to the next picture.

For the next half hour, Kiernan was engrossed in viewing the pictures of Ariel at various ages. She discovered her wife was quite a tomboy when viewing a picture of her at nine holding a bullfrog she had caught. There was one of her and a friend swinging their legs out of a tree house they had built. And of course, several pictures of her wearing a blue cape, a bicycle helmet painted silver, a pair of goggles, and swinging a toy light saber while standing in front of the cardboard boxes she'd made into a spaceship to save the universe from evil in her role as Major Marvel.

The last few pictures were of Ariel's graduation from Beaumont Accelerated School. There was one of her in a blue graduation gown with her mortarboard set at a cocky angle and her arm around her mother's shoulders. Another was of her at the graduation podium delivering the class speech as class valedictorian. And the last was of her and a group of friends throwing their mortarboards in the air.

Ariel placed the picture album on the coffee table and leaned back against the sofa. "Umm, I can smell the food. I hope we eat soon."

"Smells good and I'm hungry. I need to make a trip to the bathroom."

"Come on, I'll take you to it."

Following Ariel down the hall, Kiernan passed by two rooms containing neatly made beds. At the end of the hall was another bedroom, and on one side of the hall was a room with a closed door across from the bathroom.

"Here we are," Ariel said. "I'll wait out here for you."

"This won't take long," Kiernan said as she entered and closed the door.

A short time later, she exited the bathroom to find Ariel leaning against the wall, and said, "There, all done."

Ariel headed back to the living room.

"Ariel, would you mind showing me your bedroom?" Kiernan asked.

"Sure, right this way." She walked the few steps to the closed door across from the bathroom, opened it, and allowed Kiernan to enter before her.

Kiernan looked around, curious to see Ariel's private space while growing up. Where she slept, and dreamed, planned her future, talked to friends on the IMP, and shared secrets with school chums she would invite over for slumber parties.

Festooning the walls were MIT school pennants and a few posters. Kiernan smiled to see a *Star Wars* poster. But there were also posters of various astronomical phenomena.

A bookcase displaying model spaceships on one of the shelves caught her attention. She stopped to get a better look, impressed by what she saw. "Oh, Ariel. These must be the model spaceships you told me about constructing. They're wonderful."

Ariel flushed slightly. "Thank you."

A beautifully crafted and painted model drew Kiernan's interest. The colors were silver, with black and turquoise designs, and fashioned after the old comic book rockets, complete with tail fins, but with the addition of two slim rockets on each side. "This is beautiful, and the detail is astounding."

"That's one I kit bashed. Go on and pick it up."

After carefully picking it up, Kiernan held it at different angles to see the details. "Is this modeled after a particular craft from a movie or show?"

"No, it's strictly from my imagination. That's the one I always imagined I would fly around in saving the universe. I named it Dragonfly."

"I'm jealous. *Celeste* isn't nearly as pretty, or I bet, as fast as this one."

"She could travel one hundred times the speed of light to reach the far ends of the galaxy in a few minutes and outrun the bad guys." Sheepishly Ariel said, "Of course, going that fast would defy a lot of the laws of physics and is probably impossible."

Kiernan said, "Anything is possible in the imagination." While turning to put the ship on the shelf, one of the side rockets fell off to the floor. Letting out a gasp, she hastily set the ship in place. She bent to retrieve the piece but the top of her head bumped against Ariel's, who was also bending for it. She staggered back, but Ariel grabbed her shoulders, steadied her, and pulled her forward into an embrace.

"Are you all right?" Ariel asked with concern.

Kiernan reached up and felt the top of her head. "Yes, I'm pretty hardheaded." She looked up into Ariel's eyes. "How about you?"

"I'm okay." Ariel still held her close against her breasts while gazing into Kiernan's eyes. Her pupils were slightly dilated, and Kiernan stilled, almost in shock, as Ariel's eyelids fell. She lowered her head, her lips parting, and only a hair's breadth away from Kiernan's own.

Kiernan closed her eyes in anticipation, relaxing her mouth to receive the kiss she knew Ariel was about to give her.

Hurried footsteps sounded right outside the door, and Ariel abruptly let go of Kiernan. She stepped back as Leigh came in and said, "Hey, dinner's ready."

"We're on our way," Ariel replied calmly. Glancing at Kiernan, her face red, she said, "Let's go. They're waiting for us." She didn't wait for a reply before she whirled and headed for the door.

It took a moment for Kiernan to gather her wits and follow.

"LEIGH, DON'T PLAY with your food," Joanna said, imparting a chastising look to her youngest daughter, who had a string bean perched under her nose, pretending it was a mustache. She looked down to the end of the table where Ariel was seated, busily eating. "Ariel, would you like more dressing or anything else?"

"No thanks, I have plenty."

Joanna examined Kiernan, seated to Ariel's left side. "How

about you, Kiernan?"

Kiernan glanced up from her plate and said, "Nothing for me, thanks."

"Mom," Seth said, "I want another crescent roll."

"No. You've already had five and you need to leave some for others."

"Man can't live by bread alone," Ariel wryly said.

"I'm not a man. I'm a boy, and I'm still growing, so I need plenty of food." Seth glowered at Ariel.

"Then finish what's on your plate," Joanna said. She glanced at Ariel, seeing her and Kiernan trading brief smiles.

When Ariel had first seated herself at the table, she had seemed subdued and not as inclined to talk as usual. Kiernan was also quiet. But Joanna didn't know Kiernan well enough to know whether this was normal for her, though she had been quite talkative during dinner at Le Pierre's. A few times, she did catch Ariel and Kiernan glancing at one another with slightly dazed expressions.

They were talkative enough while going through Ariel's photo album. Whatever occurred happened when they disappeared into the back of the house right before dinner. Joanna had a suspicion something of a personal nature, maybe romantic, occurred. Both were slightly flushed when seating themselves and it didn't appear they had fought or were upset.

Right after they arrived at the house she had noticed they both seemed at ease with each other, sitting close together, their arms brushing, and exchanging glances with softening expressions.

Joanna would almost bet their relationship had advanced to the newly in love...or falling in love stage. But this was only conjecture on her part. Ariel was always reluctant to discuss Kiernan, except for telling her some of where they went and what they did on their dates.

She hoped Ariel wouldn't get hurt. She was willing to accept Kiernan into the family, if Ariel so desired—with reservations of course. Those reservations were hinged on how she treated Ariel and the child they were going to have—her grandchild. She would be willing to let bygones be bygones, if Kiernan did right by them.

ARIEL GAZED OUT her bedroom window at the black mountains silhouetted against the indigo night sky. The night was clear, and cold, perfect for viewing the constellations and planets. Her sight took in the distant pinpoints of shimmering lights, and some portion of her brain registered what she was seeing as her thoughts turned inward, to memory, and emotion.

She'd almost kissed Kiernan and would have if Leigh hadn't

interrupted. That brief moment illuminated the budding emotion she tried to keep hidden in the shadows. Somehow, light managed to slip into the darkness, feeding this emotion until it grew and bloomed into love.

Ariel was of two minds about her love for Kiernan. On one hand, Kiernan was considerate, funny, caring, giving, and warm. This Kiernan was the one she had fallen in love with, who brought the light. But, there was the other side of Kiernan, the one she wasn't ready to trust. The ruthless side that let no one and nothing stand in her way to get what she wanted. Though, the more Ariel interacted with Kiernan, the more she had her doubts that Kiernan had framed her mother. But she wasn't quite ready to believe otherwise.

Now, her reasoning and desire warred. She desired Kiernan and knew Kiernan desired her. Every day that desire broke down her resolve not to involve herself in a sexual relationship, knowing that once she surrendered, there was no turning back. She would belong to Kiernan in every way.

For the time being Ariel would do nothing, could do nothing but control her desire and, most of all, guard her heart.

KIERNAN SAT IN the old rocker in front of the fireplace, her attention not on the flickering flames, but turned inward, remembering the day's events, especially what had happened in Ariel's bedroom, or, she should say, what almost happened.

After their almost kiss, they joined the others in the dining room. Ariel was a bit subdued, but soon was back in good spirits teasing her siblings and even Kiernan herself.

On the way home, they discussed the visit and laughed over things the twins did or said. Neither one brought up the almost kiss. Kiernan was tempted, but refrained, thinking the ball was in Ariel's court, and it was up to her to broach that subject.

She sensed Ariel was battling back and forth with succumbing once again to having sex. Kiernan must tread carefully, knowing she could easily lead Ariel back to her bed. Ariel had made it clear she wasn't ready for that to happen again. But it was so hard to mask her desire. She was sure Ariel was aware of it.

And it wasn't 'just sex' that was involved. Kiernan loved Ariel. It was so hard for her not to tell Ariel she loved her. She needed to be patient and not declare her own love first. Ariel didn't trust her and would think she was lying. She would wait and see whether Ariel fell in love with her before she revealed her own heart. And if Ariel didn't fall in love with her? It would hurt, but she was willing to be whatever Ariel wanted her to be.

Chapter Thirty-Two

KIERNAN HELD ARIEL'S hand as they strolled through the shuttle door into the umbilical and walked down its length into *Celeste*'s corridor. A thin, gray-haired man who appeared in his early fifties greeted them. Two silver bars gleamed from the left chest of his blue jumpsuit.

"Welcome aboard, Ms. O'Shay," he said. To Ariel, he gave an acknowledging nod. "And Mrs. O'Shay."

Kiernan surreptitiously examined him, noticing his loss of weight and haggard appearance since she'd last seen him a year earlier. "Welcome back, Fred, it's good to have you here in command of *Celeste*."

"It's good to be back, Ma'am," he said in a flat voice, his demeanor unanimated.

Kiernan said with pride, "Let me introduce you to my wife. Ariel, this is Captain Fred Pearson, commander of *Celeste*."

"It's nice to meet you, Captain Pearson."

With a wan smile, he took Ariel's hand in a gentle shake. "I'm glad to meet you, and congratulations on your recent marriage. I wish both of you much happiness."

After returning their thanks, Kiernan took Ariel's hand back in hers, and said, "Let's go to our quarters and get settled in."

As they left, she gave a final nod to Captain Pearson whose eyes were dull and lifeless. Kiernan briefly wondered if he had recovered enough from his grief to return as *Celeste*'s captain. But his psychologist reported he was fully capable to function in that capacity. She had provided him a year's paid leave after the death of his wife, Jennifer, who had worked as a copilot for Stellardyne. She was on a typical delivery flight from Earth to the O'Shay Orbiting Docks and was performing a routine check of the shuttle's cargo bay when the cargo of engine parts shifted, crushing her against the bay wall. The containment belts had loosened for no known reason. Stellardyne hired professionals to investigate and conduct tests. The report concluded it was human error and not an equipment malfunction. Kiernan had fired the personnel who had the job of securing the cargo properly.

Once in their quarters, Kiernan turned to Ariel and said, "I'm giving you the master bedroom."

"Kiernan, no, I'll be perfectly satisfied with the other bedroom."

Kiernan held up her hand to stop any further protest. "No. You're taking it, and that's final."

"Thank you."

"You're welcome. We have two hours until launch, and as is custom, the crew will gather in the mess to drink a toast to a successful trip. Of course they will insist on drinking a toast to our marriage, and then another one to my beautiful bride."

"They won't be so intoxicated they'll hit Earth will they?"

"No, but they may shave off a few mountaintops on the moon."

THE BRIGHT BLUE and green marble called Earth slowly grew smaller as Ariel stood beside Kiernan in front of the window in their quarters. To her it was one of the most awe-inspiring sights she had ever seen. For the next nine days she would see sights she had never witnessed before as *Celeste* made its way to Mars. Granted, Kiernan informed her much of the trip was boring with only the blackness of space in the windows for most of the way. Ariel didn't care though. She planned to spend time in *Celeste's* observatory taking pictures of the various astronomical sights. She couldn't wait to e-mail the photos to her family using Kiernan's computer connected to the ship's light-speed communications center. There was also a gym and a racquetball court to occupy their time. Ariel didn't know how to play racquetball, but Kiernan said she would teach her.

She looked forward to spending time with Kiernan but was also apprehensive, fearing she would no longer be able to control her desire. Would their close proximity lead her into something she would regret? Why not surrender now? She knew it would be impossible to hide her love and desire for long. There had to be a resolution, and soon. The battle with herself was making her crazy. She had never been so indecisive and torn. But did she trust her? Yes. No. She didn't know. If only it could be proven Kiernan didn't hurt her mother. It might never be proved she did or didn't. Ariel needed to go with what her heart told her. Should she tell Kiernan she loved her? What if Kiernan didn't feel the same? Would Ariel love her less? No. She knew Kiernan cared for her and liked her. In time, Kiernan might come to love her.

Why was this so damn hard? she wondered. Because, what's worth having never comes easy.

"MR. SPIVIK, DO you know this woman?" FBI Agent Connie Braswell handed a picture across the desk to Jack Spivik.

He studied it carefully before handing the picture back to Agent Braswell. "Sherry Woodard. She worked for me for a short while and resigned a few weeks back."

"Do you know her location at present?"

"No. I can have our personnel office provide you with her last known address."

"What was her function here?"

"She monitored our computer system to make sure no activity occurred that went against company policy or would jeopardize our secure research. Can you tell me what this is about?"

"Her real name is Sharon Cohen. Sherry Woodard is one of the many aliases she uses. She and her father, Brady Cohen, often work as private investigators and operate a detective agency. Both are currently of interest to us for illegally accessing electronic files and networks and in some instances entering bogus information into files and networks. As to Sharon Cohen, our agency would need to have access to any computer she used so we can see whether or not she visited any restricted sites and downloaded information."

Jack had the sensation of being pushed out of an airlock. Could this Sherry Woodard, or Sharon Cohen, have stolen confidential information from Stellardyne and compromised their research in sensitive areas?

"You know," he said, "we here at Stellardyne keep a lot of sensitive information."

"Our Agency is willing to work closely with you in determining what has been compromised. It will remain confidential."

"I'll cooperate and personally work on this with you."

"I'll arrange to have one of our experts begin right away. I require you to secure the computer or computers assigned to Cohen as soon as possible."

"She was assigned one computer. I don't know whether she used any others."

"Thank you for your cooperation, Mr. Spivik. We'll be back in touch with you, possibly as early as tomorrow morning, to make arrangements to have our agent present on the premises to work on this case."

After Agent Braswell left, Jack reviewed the records from Sherry Woodard's tenure at Stellardyne. Her work was excellent, especially in uncovering Joanna Thorsen's...

"Oh, no."

He remembered Theodore recommending Sherry Woodard, saying she was the niece of John Woodard. And how did Joanna Thorsen fit into all of this?

He would tell Theodore none of this until he found out more.

Kiernan had departed on vacation the day before and wasn't due back for three weeks. He would contact her if the investigation uncovered something of importance. He had a bad feeling about this, though, a very bad feeling.

Chapter Thirty-Three

STUDYING THE CHESSBOARD, Kiernan calculated her next move. This was the second time she and Ariel played chess in the six days they had been on *Celeste*. Ariel had beaten her the night before in a quick-paced game, despite the fact that Kiernan had managed to spring a few unexpected and brilliant moves. Tonight she paced herself and was more deliberate. She could tell by Ariel's slower pace that this game's outcome wasn't certain.

The intercom in Kiernan's quarters chimed, followed by the voice of Second Mate Paula Gooding announcing, "Ms. O'Shay, you have a call from Jack Spivik at Stellardyne headquarters."

Jack wouldn't be calling unless it was important. She hoped nothing had happened to her uncle. "Put it through to my office." She rose from her seat. "I'll be right back." She entered her office and accessed her shipboard communications system. Jack's image appeared on the screen, and she asked, "What's up?"

"Are you somewhere private?"

"Yes."

"Joanna Thorsen...she's innocent."

Kiernan wasn't sure she was hearing correctly. "Repeat that."

"Joanna Thorsen. She's innocent. She never downloaded information. It was a set-up."

"What?"

"Yes, and she passed the polygraph test, too."

"How...why...why would anyone set her up?"

"I'm sorry to tell you this, but Theodore's behind it. He tricked me into hiring an expert hacker for the Security Department. This hacker performed the download to Joanna Thorsen's computer as well as replacing Ms. Thorsen's results with an old polygraph of someone who failed."

A passing wave of nausea gorged her throat. Kiernan swallowed, forcing it down. "Why?"

"He was banking on Ariel being the dutiful daughter and offering to marry you if you didn't press charges against her mother."

"Oh, God."

"He's resigned. He said he did it because he loved you and wanted you to be happy."

"That's a warped way of showing his love—by ruining an innocent woman's reputation and..." Ruining Ariel's life. She gritted her teeth. "E-mail the report to me here on *Celeste* so I can go over it myself."

"I'll do that now. I'm sorry, Kiernan. I was going to wait until you got back—"

"No. Thanks for telling me."

"I should have done the background checks on this hire and handled things myself. I'll have my resignation on your desk—"

"You most certainly will not! This isn't your fault. We both trusted Theodore. Who would believe he would do something like this."

"Thank you. If you need me..."

"I know how to get in touch with you."

She terminated the call and sat for a moment stunned. She should have trusted her instincts about Joanna Thorsen. Instantly the full impact of it hit. Ariel would leave her now, because the real motive for her marrying Kiernan was to protect her mother from prosecution. Kiernan ached inside, but she knew she would let Ariel go because she loved her and would do anything she wished. She might lose Stellardyne and her dream...but her dream paled if she couldn't share it with Ariel.

Feeling sick to her stomach, she knew she had to tell her about Jack's call. But they were having such a good time together and she was afraid this news would somehow drive a wedge in their friendship. Was it wrong that she wanted a little more time with Ariel before she walked out of her life? She decided that, right or wrong, she would wait until they returned home to tell her.

She composed herself and returned to the recreation room, forcing a smile. "You didn't move any of the pieces, did you?"

"Of course not. I don't need to cheat to beat you."

"Beat me? We'll see." She sat back down and tried to study the board, but her mind kept going over what Jack's call could mean to her.

Kiernan made a few amateurish moves that apparently caught Ariel's attention. "Is everything alright? You seem preoccupied. Jack didn't have bad news, did he?"

"No, just routine business. I'm starting to get a headache."

"Maybe you should retire. It's getting late."

"I think you're right. Let's finish this game tomorrow night."

"Okay. A day won't make a difference. You'll still lose."

"We'll see." Kiernan turned away to hide the pain she knew she wouldn't be able to conceal. She was certain she would lose more than a chess game.

HE MOVED RAPIDLY through the umbilical to *Celeste's* corridor. No one would question his movements as he had every right to be anywhere on the ship. He opened a door and entered the room containing the umbilical controls, reached the control panel, and pressed a button, then watched out the window as the umbilical disengaged from the shuttle and retracted back into the corridor. He pried open the front faceplate of the control panel, exposed the circuit board, removed two energy router micro crystals, and placed them in his pocket. He replaced the faceplate, closed the door behind him, and hurried down the corridor to finish the next stage in his plan. "O'Shay, you'll pay for what you did to her—for taking her away from me. Vengeance is mine, sayeth the Lord."

"KIERNAN, YOU'VE HARDLY touched your breakfast," Ariel said, her concern apparent.

Kiernan finished taking a sip of her coffee which she hoped would help bring her out of her lethargy. "I didn't get much sleep last night."

"Do you still have a headache?"

"No. Just one of those nights." She pasted on a smile. "Got anything exciting planned this morning?"

"I'd like to go to the observatory. You want to come with me?"

"I think I'll pass this time and listen to some music."

"Okay." Ariel lifted her eyebrows, and said with a bit of excitement, "Think I'll see some UFOs?"

"There have been some reports of unidentified flying objects sighted by other ships, but no one has gotten any pictures of them."

"I'll be the first then." Ariel rose and said, "Later."

Kiernan watched her go. Sighing, she left the table and went to the recreation room to listen to some music, try to relax, and take her mind off the future.

THE DOOR SLID open silently as Ariel entered Kiernan's quarters and headed to the office to use the computer. She paused at the door to the recreation room. Classical music played in the background, and Kiernan was asleep in one of the easy chairs, her head lolled to the side. She found the sight endearing. Feeling breathless from her emotions, she knelt by the chair and studied Kiernan's face. She appeared so young and vulnerable when asleep. Ariel desired to kiss her. But if Kiernan woke, Ariel would surely take her to the bedroom. She thought, Why not? It was inevitable. Tonight, after dinner, she'd tell Kiernan her feelings—and take it from there.

She slowly rose, and silently entered the bedroom. Going to

the office and over to the computer, she downloaded the pictures she had taken of various astronomical sights she wanted to e-mail her family.

The download complete, she accessed the mail, which put her on the inbox page. She was about to enter in a new letter when an e-mail titled 'Joanna Thorsen Investigation' caught her attention. From the time and date stamp, she saw that Jack Spivik had sent the mail from Stellardyne the previous night. Ariel suspected that this matter was what had provoked the call Kiernan had taken during their chess game. She hesitated briefly before opening it.

A JARRING SHAKE of the chair woke Kiernan from sleep. She quickly opened her eyes to see Ariel staring down at her with anger. After adjusting her chair to an upright position, she sat at alert attention. "EM, stop music. What is it?"

"When were you going to tell me?" Ariel said angrily.

"Tell you?"

"My mother. You've known since last night."

Kiernan got to her feet in a hurry and faced Ariel. "I planned on telling you – later."

"Why didn't you tell me immediately?"

"I wanted you to enjoy this trip and not worry about anything."

Ariel stared contemptuously at her, nostrils flaring, and her voice strained with outrage. "You didn't think this would make me happy? My mother cleared!"

Kiernan shriveled under the laser blue stare riveted on her.

Ariel's features contorted into an angry mask. "Answer me!"

A sudden jolt almost sent them to the deck. The lights flickered off and on for a brief moment.

"Warning. All hands abandon ship. All hands abandon ship. Engine overload imminent in thirty minutes."

There was a frozen moment of silence as they looked at each other in disbelief.

Kiernan said, "What the...?" She couldn't detect the minute vibration of the deck or the faint hum of the engines. "The ship has stopped. Follow me. We have to go to the shuttle."

They hurried through the quarters to the door, expecting it to open automatically only to have Kiernan stop before she ran into it. "Crap!"

"Why isn't the door working?" Ariel asked.

"I don't know." Kiernan opened a side panel, and pulled the handle down to manually unlock the door. "Damn, this thing is stuck."

"Here, let me try." Ariel pushed with the force of her weight behind her. "It won't budge. Now what?"

"This doesn't make sense. All emergency systems are checked before each voyage," Kiernan said.

"You don't think someone tampered with the door, do you? Or the engines?"

"Sabotage?" Kiernan said unbelievingly. "Sure, I have enemies, but I don't see them doing something so drastic. Computer, activate com-unit to any available station." After a moment of nothing happening, she ordered, "Computer, acknowledge." Nothing but silence. "What the hell is going on?" It puzzled Kiernan as to why the computer permitted the warning, but wouldn't permit outside contact.

"Maybe someone will come by and check on us. Ricardo or one of the crew."

"Yes, the ship has an emergency coordinator whose duty is to make sure everyone is accounted for."

"That's good to know. Can we get far enough away in the shuttle before the engines overload and explode?"

"Yes, even though they're nuclear fusion, they're not going to explode like a bomb with a big mushroom cloud and incinerate everything in the vicinity."

"I know that, but engine overload certainly can cause an explosion." Ariel sounded insulted that Kiernan would explain the obvious.

"Sorry...Dr. Thorsen," Kiernan both teased and apologized.

Ariel stuck out her tongue.

Kiernan snickered. "The only danger that would cause is whether you left the ship with less than three minutes to spare. You have the risk of getting caught in the force of the explosion."

"Warning. Engine overload imminent in twenty-five minutes."

"SIR, THE UMBILICAL won't engage," an excited crewmember said as she punched the activate button.

The handful of crew present in the room murmured uneasily.

"Move and let me try," First Mate Dwayne Campbell said. He punched the button with no results, turned, and ordered loudly so those in the corridor heard him, "Hey folks. Listen up. We're going to have to use the escape pods. Let's go at an orderly clip. Line up in front of the pod you're assigned to so we can see who's here, and who's not."

The crew made their way to the pod bay and took their places in front of assigned pods. The Emergency Coordinator, Second Mate Paula Gooding, called the roll, and coming to the end said to

Campbell, "Captain Pearson, Ms. O'Shay, and her wife are not present."

Campbell asked, "Has anyone seen the Captain or the O'Shays?"

Ricardo answered, "Yes, I last saw the O'Shays at breakfast this morning."

Abigail Morotore, one of the pilots, said, "I was on the bridge when the Captain handed it over to me and said he would be back. That was well over three hours ago."

"I want everyone assigned to pod six reassigned to spaces in other pods, and we need to start launching now." He said to his Emergency Coordinator, "You too, Paula. The Captain's quarters are on the same floor as the O'Shay quarters—I'll check them both."

"I'll go with you."

"You're next in command. You'll be needed in case I don't make it out in time."

"But, sir—"

"Go. There's not much time." Campbell watched as she entered her pod. He waited until all the pods were safely away before sprinting out the bay and to the stairs.

"COME ON, SOMEBODY." Kiernan paced impatiently in front of the door.

"Do you think everyone is alright?" Ariel asked in a concerned voice.

"I don't know. It worries me that the computer is down and the locking mechanism on the door failed. I wonder whether the controls on all of them malfunctioned."

"You don't think—" The pneumatic hiss of the door opening interrupted her.

Kiernan said, "Thank God. Dwayne—"

Campbell pointed an antique automatic pistol at Kiernan. "Back away from the door."

"Kiernan!" Ariel said in alarm.

"What's going on here?" Kiernan demanded, jutting her chin out defiantly. She glared at Dwayne.

"You'll find out soon enough. Move it." He motioned with his gun toward the living room. "Over there, by the sofa."

Ariel glanced at Kiernan who looked at her and nodded once. They moved to where Campbell indicated and stopped.

Kiernan's eyes bored into his. "What the hell are you doing, Dwayne?"

"Doing what I should have done a long time ago. Getting rid of a pervert."

"What the hell are you talking about?"

"You're an abomination, O'Shay. You're an affront to God and everything decent. You deserve to die," he screamed. "Die for spreading your perversion and filth, for corrupting the innocent!"

"I've never corrupted anyone—"

"You lie! You corrupted Barbara. You took her away from me. Now she's a damn pervert!"

"Barbara? I don't know who..." The past rushed up to catch her and she remembered. She'd accompanied Dwayne Campbell to a few victory parties right before Kiernan quit racing. One night after a party at Kiernan's apartment, Barbara came back about an hour later, saying she'd lost a necklace. Kiernan had lifted up the sofa cushions, thinking it might have slipped between them. She had sensed Barbara close behind her and turned to find herself in the woman's arms. The affair lasted around three weeks. Campbell never said anything or acted as if anything happened. Two months after the affair, Barbara and Dwayne married. Kiernan recalled receiving an invitation to the wedding, but her grandmother had recently died, and she was wrapped up in dealing with the estate. She sent the couple a nice gift and went about the business of running Stellardyne. Later, she heard they'd divorced but didn't know the details.

"Yeah, O'Shay, I see you remember now. I've been waiting for this day to come."

"That happened a long time ago. It's time to move on, don't you think?"

"I'm moving on. But you, O'Shay, you'll watch as I take that little whore of yours away from you. Then you'll join her—in hell where all you perverts belong!"

"This is between me and you, Dwayne. Leave Ariel out of this. She has nothing to do with what happened. Let her go."

"No. I'm staying." Ariel placed her hand on Kiernan's shoulder.

"Oh, how touching. The loyal little wife. She's a pervert like you, O'Shay. She deserves to die."

"Tell me how do you think you'll get away with this?"

"Oh, tsk, tsk, the computer's control matrix failed and shut down most of the ship, including communications, and locked your door from the inside. Too bad the engines were off line and the cooling rods didn't shut down. We couldn't extend the umbilical to get to the shuttle. The crew had to use the escape pods. Somehow, you, your whore, and Captain Pearson never made it to the last remaining escape pod. I searched and searched for you three. There was barely enough time left for me to escape until—Boom!" He sneered.

"What happened to Captain Pearson?" Kiernan demanded.

"Why, he had an accident when he went to investigate a report he received concerning a fuel leak onboard the shuttle."

"You murdered him so you would be in command." His eyes held madness, and her fears were confirmed when he smirked. "That's why you disabled the umbilical, so no one would find him on the shuttle and notify me. You knew I would alert Planetary Security on Mars and they would rendezvous with us in less than two days. A full investigation and polygraph test would catch you. You're a sick bastard, Dwayne. You're the one going to hell."

"Shut up! You're the one who's sick. You and those like you. Now, get away from your whore. She goes first, while you watch."

"It's about time you got here," Kiernan said in relief, her eyes focusing past him toward the door.

Campbell swiveled his head, and Kiernan rushed forward. She slammed her body hard against his. He fell and Kiernan fell with him, both rolling on the floor. Dwayne managed to roll on top of her and drew his arm up to aim his gun at her head. As fast as lightning, Ariel kicked his hand. The gun went flying and skidded along the carpet to slide under the sofa. Ariel kicked him hard in the ribs. Kiernan jabbed him sharply under his chin with the palm of her hand, snapping his head back.

Ariel twisted her body to the side and used a sidekick to his torso, sending him off Kiernan and allowing her to get to her feet. "Run Ariel, to the escape pod!"

"Warning. Engine overload imminent in five minutes."

Kiernan followed Ariel out the open door and ran down the corridor on her heels. They swerved down another corridor and stopped at the elevator. Ariel slapped the button. "Ariel, no. The elevators are offline. Take the stairs." It was standard procedure during an emergency to stop the operation of the elevators to prevent anyone from becoming stuck if the power went offline.

They ran hard down the corridor for another sixty feet to the stairwell. As Ariel hit the button to open the door, there was a loud bang and something whizzed close by.

"Shit, he's shooting!" The door slid open. Kiernan crowded close behind Ariel, breathless. "Go down two flights." They stampeded down and exited into the corridor.

There was another loud bang, and the bullet struck the deck by Kiernan's right foot.

"Left!" Kiernan shouted. They headed toward the far end of the corridor where the pod bay was located. The door was already open. Ariel sprinted into the bay and slowed, searching for the remaining pod.

Kiernan noticed that many of the airlock indicator lights were red, which meant the pods had launched. Ariel ran down the bay to the one remaining green light. She hit the airlock release button and the door to slide open. She hurled herself into the pod, Kiernan hard on her heels.

Ariel hit the button to close and seal the door. Before the door fully shut, a bullet whizzed by and smacked into the pod deck. Kiernan flung herself into the pilot's seat. The safety harness closed around her as more loud pings hit the outside of the pod.

Chapter Thirty-Four

"YOU HAVE TO buckle in," Kiernan shouted. "Hurry!" Her finger hovered over the launch button set into the control panel on her seat's right armrest. As soon as she saw Ariel securely seated, she pushed the button. "Hold on."

There was a forceful jerk, and the g-forces of the sudden acceleration slammed them back against their seats. The pressure continued for ten seconds before fading. Kiernan knew the forward momentum of the pod was carrying them rapidly away from *Celeste* and they would be out of range of the explosion. The pod's one porthole was facing away from the ship so they wouldn't see her demise, for which, in a way, Kiernan was thankful.

She eyed Ariel, searching for any injuries. "Are you all right?"

"I'm okay. How about you?"

"I'm fine."

Kiernan lifted slightly off her chair and against the safety harness. "We're at zero gravity." Suddenly, there was an irritating beep on the control panel. Kiernan read the display. "Damn! The bastard must have shot the battery and damaged it."

"What does that mean?"

"Readings show the battery is malfunctioning. We have only seven hours of power left instead of seventy-two."

"Mars is almost three days away," Ariel said, the alarm evident in her voice.

"I know, but there's a good chance we'll run into a supply ship or survey crew in the area." She pressed a button for the homing device and read the display. "Our homing device is functional. At light-speed radio bursts I'm sure the whole solar system has picked up the distress signal by now. Help is on the way."

"Can we somehow conserve energy, maybe turn down the heat, turn off the interior lighting? Would that save some power?"

"That might work. The lights operate off their own battery cells, but the heat and air filtration operates from the main power battery. There are no controls to adjust or turn off those functions, so we'll have to go into the battery box." She motioned with her head to the carpeted deck. "It should be right there where that square section of carpet is located."

Ariel focused on the area. "You mean where the bullet hole is?"

"Yes. There's a tether right below the armrest that pulls out so you can attach it around your waist to keep from floating."

They disengaged their harnesses, pulled out the tethers, and hooked them around their waists. Kiernan floated out of the chair and used the tether to pull herself down. Ariel somehow managed to aim herself to the place on the deck where the battery box was located. She grabbed hold of a cloth handle on the section of carpet to steady herself and pulled on it to dislodge the carpet piece and expose a panel set into the floor.

"How do you open this thing?" Ariel asked. She took an elastic band out of her pants pocket and pulled her wildly floating hair into a ponytail, securing it.

Kiernan managed to float over and stop four feet above the panel. "Push the rectangular area in the center of the panel and a handle will pop up."

Ariel grabbed the handle, pulling the panel loose, pushing it away to glide to the other side of the pod. There was an exposed three-foot-by-three-foot area consisting of a square box-shaped object which Ariel knew was the battery. One side of the battery had a puncture in it where a bullet entered. "I'm glad the battery stopped the bullet, and it didn't penetrate the outer shell," Ariel said in a relieved voice.

"No chance of that. The pod's outer skin is made from the toughest alloys known and is able to withstand anything as obsolete as an antique projectile made from lead."

"So, I did hear bullets bounce off the pod. I thought I imagined it."

"If they had penetrated, we'd be dead by now." Kiernan pointed to a square area in the corner of the opening. "That's the circuit board."

Ariel checked it and said with relief, "This pretty much tells us what circuits control what function. Everything is labeled."

"We have to consider one thing—if we shut off the heat we'll freeze to death pretty fast."

"Hmm, well, let's not shut off the heat then." Ariel studied the board. "It appears there are four energy router micro crystals controlling each function. If one is pulled will the heat continue, but at a reduced level?"

"That might very well be. I know *Celeste* uses several dozen crystals for the same function, so if one is blown the others will still work. I'm not sure about a temperature drop. We can always try it and see."

"I'll pull one crystal and if there is a drastic drop in temperature I'll quickly reinsert it."

Kiernan took a second to think it over. "Let's do it."

Ariel pulled the crystal and placed it in one of her pants

pockets. After a few seconds, she said, "I don't notice a change in temperature. Do you?"

"Let's wait a few minutes and see." Kiernan held out her hand to Ariel. "Here, pull me down."

At deck level, Kiernan pushed away a hank of hair floating in her face. "You have another band I can use to pull my hair out of the way?"

Ariel searched her pants pockets and drew out a broken band. "Here, turn your head, and I'll tie this around your hair. I can't guarantee it'll hold — but it's all I have."

Ariel gathered her hair tightly in a ponytail and tied the band securely.

Goose bumps popped up on Kiernan's arms, making her slightly shiver, and she said, "It has cooled in here."

"Do you think the temperature will continue to drop?"

"I'm not sure. It dropped slowly, so perhaps that's a sign the heating system is still functioning to some degree. We'll see. I don't think there will be a sudden drop, and that'll give you plenty of time to put the crystal back in, if the temperature gets too low." She pushed up from the floor and pulled her tether, floating over to the control chair where she maneuvered herself until she could easily read the display panel. "We've managed to add three hours to the battery life."

"Every little bit counts."

"That it does."

Kiernan maneuvered herself until she was hanging upside down. She opened the enclosed space under one of the seats to check for an emergency blanket. The space contained four sixteen-ounce water bottles and sixteen high-protein ration bars.

Ariel checked for supplies under the other seats. She called out, "I found food and water, and an emergency blanket in the first aid kit."

"I found plenty of ration bars and water." Kiernan paused. "Damn, I'm cold. Break out the blanket."

Ariel managed to sit close to the floor and lean against a chair. She opened a packet and unfolded the thin, silver insulated blanket. "Come here and let me hold you so we can share the blanket and body heat."

Kiernan pushed over to Ariel, but used too much force and crashed into her, slamming her back against the chair.

"Ouch," Ariel exclaimed. Her hand flew up to her nose, and she gingerly touched the bridge.

Kiernan muttered, "Sorry," and caught the edge of the seat to steady herself.

Ariel pulled Kiernan down beside her. "I'll undo my tether and attach it to yours."

"Good idea."

Ariel unclipped her tether and pulled enough out to loop it around her waist and attach the end to Kiernan's tether at her waist. She wrapped the blanket around their shoulders and settled back with a sigh. They were silent for a couple of minutes until Ariel said, "I don't think the temperature will drop any further."

"I think you're right." Kiernan keenly searched Ariel's face. "How's the nose?"

Ariel lightly pinched the bridge, wiggling it. "It doesn't feel like it's broken and it doesn't hurt much."

Kiernan took Ariel's chin in her hand, and leaned her head to one side and then the other to study the nose more closely. "It's not bleeding or swollen." She let go of Ariel's chin. "I'm sorry about that. I'm clumsy in zero gravity."

"That's not what I heard," Ariel said suggestively with an impish smirk. "Rumor has it you have plenty of practice in zero gravity."

"I don't know where you heard...ohhh. So, you heard about my secret *room*, did you?"

"You mean it's true? I didn't find it on *Celeste*."

Kiernan shot Ariel a wicked grin. "Don't tell me you actually searched for it."

"Well..." Ariel flushed, her eyes darting guiltily.

"You did." Kiernan laughed.

"Oh, all right, I did sort of search a couple of days ago," Ariel admitted sheepishly.

"You won't find it. It doesn't exist...except in the prurient imagination of the media."

"Oh."

"You sound disappointed. You're not interested in doing that, are you?"

"Of course not," Ariel replied with mock indignity. "Well...I have wondered what it would be like. You ever *do it* in zero gravity?"

"I have. It's not all it's cracked up to be...and dangerous. You can snap a wrist if your fingers happen to be in a...certain place...and the motion is too enthusiastic. You're *coming* apart instead of *coming* together, *if* you know what I mean."

Ariel's cheeks tinged red. "I'll take your word for it." She pulled Kiernan more closely against her side, and after a pause, she let out an amused chortle.

"What is it?" Kiernan asked.

"Dwayne fell for the oldest trick in the book."

"It was all I could come up with."

"It worked. He must have been crazy. No one believes homosexuality is a perversion, except those outlandish cults of Christian fundamentalists and a couple of backward Islamic sheikdoms."

Kiernan sighed. "Dwayne, of all people. I would never in a million years think he would—" Kiernan swallowed the lump in her throat.

Ariel squeezed Kiernan's shoulders, her voice sad. "I'm sorry, Kiernan. About Captain Pearson and *Celeste*, too."

"I'll have Jack do an investigation of Dwayne. As for *Celeste*—I can build another one like her in a year—even better. I'll dedicate her to the memory of Captain Fred Pearson." They fell into silence. Kiernan looked at Ariel with sorrowful eyes and said with a tremor in her voice, "I'm sorry—for everything."

Ariel dropped her gaze to the deck and was silent. Kiernan saw her expression was one of contemplation. She waited in nervous anticipation for Ariel to say something—say anything.

Finally, Ariel quirked up one corner of her mouth. She lifted her eyes to Kiernan. "Are you asking for my forgiveness?"

"No. I don't deserve it."

Ariel replied wryly, "Good then. Because if you were, I would think you were asking it because you knew we were going to die and wanted a clear conscience."

"Ha! I would have to ask a lot of people's forgiveness to have a clear conscience. And I don't think it's my time to die."

"That's reassuring. That means it's not my time either." Ariel's face sobered and her eyes grew pensive. "I forgive you. I should be the one apologizing. I accused you unjustly of hurting my mother."

"You had every reason to believe I did. However, rest assured when we return home there will be a reckoning. Theodore has resigned, but I'm going to demand he apologize to Joanna, and to you, both in person and by letter. If Joanna wants to sue him, I'll support her in that. I hope I can make amends to her. I need people like her working for me."

"Once she sees the truth, I think she'll be willing to sit down with you and talk...about a lot of things. As for the reckoning—I have a few things I want to say to Theodore. You know, he read me so well. He was the one who suggested I take you up on your proposition on the condition you didn't press charges against my mother. At first, I thought he was trying to help you without your knowledge. Later, I thought you sent him to manipulate me into marrying you."

"Why didn't you say anything?"

"I gave him my word I wouldn't. Later, when I believed you sent him, what was there to say?"

Kiernan smiled with tender sadness. "You are without a doubt the most trustworthy and honest person I have ever met."

"I'm not perfect. There's times I stretch the truth or tell only a part of it."

"But I bet it's when you have to keep from breaking your word, or to spare others."

Ariel didn't comment.

Both anger and sadness descended on Kiernan. Theodore had manipulated them both. He had presented Ariel as a possible wife for her. He didn't have any other candidates. He'd used subterfuge to gain information on Ariel. That right there should have made Kiernan follow her instincts—should have made her suspicious concerning the guilt of Joanna Thorsen. She felt like such a fool.

Both Ariel and Joanna had suffered from Theodore's treachery. Ariel, perhaps, suffered the most. She was manipulated into marrying Kiernan and was made to be afraid for her mother.

Guilt joined her anger and sadness. It wasn't only Theodore who'd manipulated Ariel. She'd also manipulated Ariel by leading her to believe she would prosecute her mother if she didn't stay married to her and have her baby. And to make matters worse, Kiernan had once again proved she was untrustworthy by not being upfront about Jack's phone call.

She watched Ariel's eyes and felt sad and serious. "Ariel, I'm not proud of what I did to keep you in this marriage—the threats, and all. At the time, I believed I had no choice. The thing is…I failed to realize there's always a choice, but it might not be the one I'll like. What I'm about to tell you is the truth. I didn't tell you about Jack's call because I was being selfish. I didn't want this time together with you to end, and I figured that the minute you found out the truth, you'd be history. None of this is your fault, and you shouldn't have to suffer any longer. When we return home, I'll initiate the divorce procedures right away and void the agreement. You'll be free and clear of any obligations to me. I'll arrange for you to have a generous settlement, as well—"

"So, you want to give up on us?" Ariel stiffened and drew away from Kiernan. "Is that what you're telling me?"

"Ariel?" Kiernan said with surprise.

"You said you'd like for us to get to know each other better. I thought we were doing that, I thought we were making progress, I thought…" Ariel swallowed, her eyes tearing.

Kiernan searched Ariel's face, almost afraid to hope. "Are you saying what I think you're saying? You truly want to give this—us…a try?"

"Yes, I do!"

"After being bullied into this marriage and bullied by my

threats?"

"Bullied? You offered me a business proposition and I accepted," Ariel said with shining eyes.

Kiernan almost couldn't believe what she was hearing. She gently stroked Ariel's soft cheek, feeling overcome with emotion. "I love you, Ariel. Oh, I love you so very much."

ARIEL STARED AT Kiernan, trying to make sense of what she'd said. Had she heard correctly? Yes! She saw it in Kiernan's eyes. Kiernan loved her. In a voice made unsteady by emotion, she declared, "I love you, Kiernan." She pulled Kiernan close into a fierce hug and cried.

Kiernan brought Ariel's head down on her shoulder. Tearfully she said, "Oh my beautiful angel." Ariel felt the soft kisses placed in her hair before Kiernan buried her face in it.

Finally, the tears ceased for both, but they still held each other close.

After a couple of minutes, they separated and searched one another's faces. They chuckled nervously upon seeing each other's red faces and puffy eyes.

Ariel reached for Kiernan to pull her in for a kiss. She noticed a few watery droplets floating between them and reached out to touch one, causing it to shimmer and float away.

"Tears," Kiernan said. "Those, I believe, are mine. Yours should be right behind me from crying on my shoulder."

"I guess I better not blow my nose."

Kiernan rumbled out a low laugh, a sound that always sent a delightful shiver down Ariel's spine. Her smile slowly disappeared, her lips parting, soft and inviting.

They surged toward each other and traded devouring kisses. A warm hand slid under Ariel's shirt and under her bra. As she pulled Kiernan closer, the blanket dislodged and floated above them.

Reluctantly Ariel pulled away from soft lips. Kiernan's hand slid away as Ariel made a lunge for the blanket. Her body shot upward pulling out more tether length from her chair. The end of Ariel's tether remained wrapped around Kiernan's waist and twisted Kiernan until she was under Ariel. Then the tether snapped back hard, ramming Ariel into Kiernan and forcing her against the floor.

"Oof," Kiernan said as Ariel landed on top of her. She pushed Ariel up, and off, causing the tether to once again loosen, sending both spiraling upward. Ariel grabbed Kiernan and twisted their bodies upright so when the tether snapped back, they landed on the deck in a sitting position. Ariel hastily freed a hand to reach out, and snagged the edge of the seat to stabilize them. Once steadied, she was able to reach the corner of the blanket to bring it down and wrap it around their shoulders.

"Are you okay?" Ariel asked.

"Yes." Kiernan gave Ariel a leer. "Thanks for the ride, darling."

"You should see what I can do when gravity comes into play."

"I intend to." She stroked Ariel's face tenderly. "I love you."

Ariel cradled the hand stroking her cheek and kissed the palm. "I'll never grow tired of hearing it."

"Good. Because I intend to say it every day — for the rest of my life."

They melded into another kiss, this one done slowly and sensuously in view of the lack of gravity.

After a blissful kiss, they once again separated to search each other's eyes. Kiernan's sparkled with tears, but they did not fall.

Kiernan said, "Angel, I want you to know...I have never said the words *I love you* to anyone. I've never loved another. You are my first, my only, and my last."

Feeling her throat closing from the tears forming, Ariel said while still able, "You are my first, my only...and my last. I love you, Kiernan Deirdre O'Shay, with everything that I am."

Once again, they held each other tight, sharing tears of joy and passionate kisses.

ARIEL SAID, "SHE could have either blue or green eyes."

"I want her to have your blue eyes and your blonde hair," Kiernan insisted.

"Chances are she'll have hair a lighter shade than yours — more of a true red."

"Grandmother's hair was red. Oh God, I can see it now — we'll be raising a brood of red-headed hellions."

Ariel stared at her with eyes gone wide in surprise. "Brood? You want more than one?"

"That's one thing I missed while growing up, having siblings to play with."

"They can be fun — at times. I'll have our first child, and you'll have our second. Any more are negotiable."

Kiernan reared back and said, "No way am I doing the pregnancy thing."

"Why not?"

"It's not me."

"I don't know whether it's me either. But I think I would like more than one child." Ariel gave a devilish grin and slyly said, "I'll have the second one and you'll have the first."

"You'll have the first and I'll have the sec... Wait a minute, what am I saying? You tricked me."

"I'll hold you to that."

Snuggling up close to Ariel, Kiernan smiled when feeling a kiss placed on top of her head. For the last few hours, they passed the time discussing their future together, including offspring, and plans and possibilities for their first light-speed starship.

There was no chatter on the radio to indicate another ship was anywhere in the vicinity, and both agreed not to check the remaining time on the battery power.

Kiernan lifted her face up to Ariel and kissed her gently on the lips. "Mmm. You have the sweetest lips I've ever kissed."

Ariel asked teasingly, "Sweet as in candy sweet?"

"No, as in *you* sweet."

They kissed again, and this time the kiss was more passionate with mouths open and hungry tastes of sweetness as their tongues parried, sliding against each other, igniting the senses.

Kiernan buried her hands into the golden mane to grind her lips more firmly against Ariel's, making the kisses bruising in their intensity. She felt Ariel's kisses as intensely as they sought to drink in the very essence of the other. She ended the kiss and said breathlessly, "Oh, my angel, I'm so glad you have come into my life. I—"

"*Celeste. This is Sydney, do you copy?*"

Chapter Thirty-Five

SYDNEY'S BRIEFING ROOM thronged with *Celeste* crew who had all been safely retrieved before Kiernan and Ariel arrived aboard. The faces of the crewmembers were somber as Ariel watched Kiernan inform them of Captain Pearson's death, without going into too much detail as to motive. Kiernan had already used *Sydney's* communications center to call in a report to Planetary Security, informing them of the incident. Of course, when they reached Mars in two days they both would have to appear before an investigative board to relay their stories.

Kiernan also contacted Jack and informed him of what occurred and ordered him to commence an investigation of Dwayne Campbell. Jack had relayed some interesting news concerning the framing of Joanna for espionage. The FBI had apprehended Sharon Cohen, and she'd admitted her part in Theodore's scheme.

Somehow the media had gotten hold of the story about the scuttling of the *Celeste* and its subsequent explosion. Ariel contacted a very upset Joanna, assuring her they were safe and well. She also informed her mother about Theodore and Sharon Cohen's role in framing her. When she ended her conversation with her mother, Ariel found Kiernan finishing up with Captain Sloan. Ariel joined them, putting an arm around Kiernan's shoulders.

Captain Sloan said, "Let me show you to your quarters. I'm assigning you the cabin I reserve for guests. It's not very spacious, but does have a private head and will afford you privacy." This last part was said by the good captain with a smile and twinkling of eyes.

"That's much appreciated," Kiernan said sincerely.

"Yes. Thank you, Captain Sloan," Ariel said. She was delighted she would be alone with Kiernan. There were some things she needed to do that one couldn't do in front of an audience, unless you were an exhibitionist. This reminded her of the showers.

When they'd first come onboard, they were provided with something warm to eat and taken to the head where they could freshen up, shower, and don a clean pair of gray crew coveralls. She was appalled to find out the showers, a set of six stalls with curtains across them, were communal. She had envisioned taking a leisurely shower with Kiernan and getting to know her body better. But their guide informed them second shift was starting in thirty minutes, and soon a flood of crewmen would be hurrying to get ready and go to breakfast before their shift began.

Sure enough, the warning was no sooner out of the guide's mouth when the door opened and three of the crew came in wearing robes and carrying towels and toiletry items. Ariel and Kiernan exchanged disappointed glances. Kiernan whispered that were this a Stellardyne ship and not a Lunaway one, all crewmembers would have their own cabins with a head. Then they promptly took separate shower stalls while they were still available.

They followed Captain Sloan to their assigned quarters. Once the door closed, Kiernan surveyed the cabin and said, "Damn, this is small — not much bigger than my closet at Crestview."

Ariel said dryly, "If your closet is the same size as mine, we could sleep all of *Celeste's* crew in it." She gazed up and saw a three-foot square porthole over the bed. "At least we have a great view."

"Sleeping under the stars." Kiernan bent to press against the double bed mattress. "Not bad. It can be as hard as a slab of moon granite, and I'll still be able to sleep like a baby."

Ariel slipped her arms around Kiernan's waist from behind and pulled her against her body, saying in a seductive purr in her ear, "I know something else we can do under the stars besides sleep."

Chapter Thirty-Six

KIERNAN SHIVERED AS the words, and resonance, of Ariel's voice tickled her ear. Then a warm nose nuzzled her hair, before soft lips descended to the side of her neck and sent tingles racing down her spine. A smooth cheek and nose nuzzled under her chin, forcing her head back against a firm right shoulder draped with soft, golden hair. This exposed her throat to a warm, wet open mouth. She moaned. Teeth lightly grazed her pulsing vein, soon to be replaced by Ariel suckling her skin and painting it with rapid tongue strokes as if lapping her lifeblood to drink.

She tried to turn into the embrace, wanting to hold Ariel against her, and thirsting to drink her fill from that passionate mouth. But the arms tightened around her waist and pulled her tighter against the warmth and softness. A voice vibrated against her neck. "Don't move. Not until I'm ready for you to move. Don't speak. Just feel."

Kiernan groaned. Her nipples hardened and she felt a strong pulsing in her groin. She quivered with anticipation. Ariel was in command.

Warm hands receded from her stomach and slowly traced up her ribcage, over her breasts, brushing against peaked and tender nipples hidden beneath gray cloth, until they were at the Velcro fastening at the front of her coveralls. She felt a tugging between her breasts and heard the scratchy sound of Velcro separating to free her bare breasts and stomach, stopping at the white panties covering the juncture between her legs. Her areola pebbled from the sudden contact to air.

Then Ariel's warm hands cupped her breasts, lifting them slightly as if weighing them. A prolonged hiss sounded close to her left ear, and Ariel's thumbs circled around the stiffened peaks, making the areola pebble even more.

Kiernan couldn't help but whimper. It was as if her nipples were direct conduits to her vaginal walls and the muscles there contracted in the most delicious and glorious way.

Ariel's hands moved to lovingly massage her breasts. She pressed a kiss on Kiernan's left temple. The sound of ragged breathing caressed her ear, and a voice rough with emotion, holding an ache, said, "I want to sear you — and the moments to come — into my memory forever. From this moment on, when I touch you like this, I'll be making love to you."

"Oh, Ariel," Kiernan cried.

"Shhh, quiet," Ariel ordered. She moved her hands languidly from the breasts and up to Kiernan's shoulders, peeling the coveralls off them and part way down her arms. When Ariel's hands moved back to her breasts, this time the fingers tightened around the nipples. Ariel's mouth was suddenly on Kiernan's left shoulder, teeth biting down hard, and fingers squeezing her nipples. Kiernan gasped in pain, as well as pleasure, with a strong echo resounding down to impact her core.

The bite gentled, replaced by the soothing stroke of tongue while a thumb gently stroked each nipple. Then lips traced up the slope of Kiernan's shoulder to her neck and ear. Ariel's hand came under Kiernan's chin, arching her head farther back against the shoulder, and turning it slightly so her mouth could descend upon Kiernan's mouth, hot and demanding.

Kiernan opened to her, greedily sucking that demanding tongue. Ariel's hand descended over her breast, along her side, and down to the top of her panties, where it quickly slid between skin and the fabric, scratching through the course hair to her core, which was wet with the evidence of her want.

Kiernan whimpered deeply, feeling Ariel's own whimper enter her mouth, where she caught it and returned it. Hot fingers circled her clit and teased. Pressing against those fingers, she hoped to push them deep inside her.

Ariel tore her mouth away and whispered, "Yes, so wet — all for me." There was a gentle push, and the tips of Ariel's fingers found the source of the wetness. Kiernan drew a harsh intake of breath. The fingers slowly retreated, and Kiernan cried out at the loss. Ariel tightened her hold under Kiernan's chin, forcing her head back even more against her shoulder and upper arm.

Ariel swiveled Kiernan's head to delve into her eyes with eyes seeming to burn a blazing blue, the color of the heart of the flame that burned hottest. "Do you want me Kiernan? Do you want my fingers buried deep within you?" The breath from her words fanned hotly over Kiernan's mouth.

Kiernan swallowed. "God, yes, you know I do."

"Do you want me to taste you? To drink you?"

Kiernan wet her dry lips with the tip of her tongue. "Yes."

Kiernan was pinned by Ariel's eyes, and then Ariel drew back slightly and her hand came up, wet with the proof of Kiernan's want. Ariel closed her eyes and inhaled deeply. "Mmm." She opened her eyes, and her mouth parted slightly as the tip of her tongue touched her top lip. She caressed her wet fingers across Kiernan's lips. Kiernan felt and smelled her own essence, heady and intoxicating. Ariel hungrily descended to mesh her mouth against Kiernan's and taste what she'd painted there.

Kiernan wanted to lift her arms to hold Ariel, but the coveralls were pushed halfway down her arms and prevented her from doing it. She responded only with her mouth. Suddenly Ariel's ardent mouth left hers, and the hand on her throat moved away. Kiernan was spun around in the firm arms and brought up hard against the front of Ariel's body. Her bare breasts rubbed against the fabric of Ariel's coveralls, and she felt soft breasts right above her own.

Their kisses were bruising, and they drank deep from each other's mouths as if to slake a long thirst. Ariel pushed the coveralls down farther, past Kiernan's arms, and they slid into a puddle at Kiernan's feet. She hurriedly kicked off her shoes and stepped out of the coveralls, leaving on only her panties.

Ariel's eyes seemed to scorch as they caressed her breasts and moved down her torso and legs.

Ariel pulled Kiernan once more into a fervent embrace. Kiernan wrapped her arms around Ariel, crushing herself against the welcoming warmth. Ariel removed the arms that embraced her and held them against Kiernan's side as she kissed Kiernan, ravaging her mouth, and leaving her light headed.

Ariel slowly separated from the kiss, and said, in a growl, "I want to taste you, to draw from you all you have to give and drink my fill." She angled Kiernan toward the bed, still holding her arms to her sides, until the back of her legs were against the edge of the bed, and forced her to sit. Ariel let go of her arms and pressed against her until Kiernan lay flat against the mattress, her legs hanging over the side of the bed.

Ariel moved between her legs and knelt. She pushed her legs farther apart with her shoulders and stroked Kiernan's inner thighs up to the tops of her panties. In a smooth motion, she pulled them down and off. Kiernan tried to rise up on her elbows to witness what was about to happen, but Ariel said, "Don't move. You know what I'm going to do — take you, and take from you."

Kiernan mewled in intense anticipation, and hoped Ariel wouldn't prolong this sweet torture. She shivered as those hands stroked above her vagina, lightly brushing against her clit. She drew in a sharp breath, then cried out in frustration as the hands retreated back to her thighs. Suddenly the silky cool sweep of hair was on her legs, and sultry breath wafted across her entrance. Her legs trembled, and she bit her lip to keep from begging Ariel to take her. There was the soft press of lips against her mound, a gentle kiss ending far too soon. No longer was she able to hold back her plea. "Don't tease, please, angel."

A sharp nip on her inner thigh brought forth a gasp, but a tender kiss on the hurt spot begged forgiveness. She heard a strangled sound and felt Ariel rubbing her face back and forth in the wetness. Kiernan surged against Ariel, her restraint shattered. She reached down with both hands to grab a handful of hair, forcing Ariel hard against her throbbing ache.

Ariel slipped her hands under Kiernan's hips to bring her even closer and thrust her tongue rapidly into her.

Kiernan ascended swiftly towards release, clenching her teeth and pulling the handfuls of hair without mercy. She ground her center against Ariel in relentless abandon. Her shout was guttural when she came. "Ariel! Ariel! Ariel!" was her mantra and the only name she knew. Nothing and no one else existed.

ARIEL'S FACE WAS bathed in warm wetness, her mouth flooded with the elixir of passion so reminiscent of the ocean. The warm flow of moisture from her own small orgasm soaked through her panties and her coveralls. She was still ablaze, on fire. She wanted to consume more of Kiernan, to grind herself with all the need and passion she possessed into her solidness and softness, branding her with the invisible mark of conquest, and leaving her no doubts she was Ariel's, that her love was Ariel's, as well as her passion.

The hold on her hair lessened as the thrusts subsided into the slow waves of the sleepy ocean. She softly lapped the warm trickle of passion, knowing Kiernan had more yet to give her. She would take it, but wanted at the same time to pour herself into Kiernan.

Arial wiped the wetness from her face against Kiernan's thigh, stood, and ripped open the Velcro closure of her coveralls. She peeled the coveralls off, taking the panties and shoes with them, and she kicked them out of the way. She removed her sports bra, tossing it carelessly to one side. The tightness between her legs was a throbbing ache.

Kiernan had recovered enough to slide up fully onto the bed. She held out her arms, and coaxed, "Angel, come here. I want to love you."

But Ariel wasn't ready to capitulate—she wanted to continue to lead the dance.

She crawled onto the bed, resting on her knees, and drew Kiernan up against her. She kissed her savagely before pushing her hard against the mattress and falling upon her. Placing lips close to Kiernan's, sharing her breath, she said, "I want to feel you beneath me when I make you come again. I want to meld you to me, flesh into flesh, feel your blood pulsating, and your heart beat in rhythm with mine."

Kiernan gasped with surprise and pleasure. Ariel took her

mouth in a searing kiss, then separated enough to nibble Kiernan's lower lip and to run her tongue over it, tracing the shape. She straddled Kiernan's right thigh, pressing her center against it, feeling the warm firmness. She had come full circle. This is how she had taken her pleasure from Kiernan that first time. But that time had been with anger and hate. Now she was closing the circle with joy and love.

Kiernan's arms twined around her back, drawing her down so she rested on her forearms and could search deep into desire-laden eyes. Kiernan whispered roughly, "Oh love, what you do to me." The timbre of her voice drove Ariel's movements faster and stronger. She reared up off her arms, still rocking against the firm thigh that was now lifting in rhythm with her. Supporting her weight with her one hand against the mattress, she reached down with the other hand and found the rigid knot, right above the apex, damp with Kiernan's passion and the feasting from her own mouth. She caressed her wife's crease, keeping her rhythm steady and in tandem with her own movements on Kiernan's thigh. When she slid a finger into the source, Kiernan surged against her, eyes still open and pouring out all her passion and love.

Still maintaining her gaze into Kiernan's eyes, she panted out the words, "I love you. Say it, Kiernan."

Kiernan answered in strained passion, "I love you."

"Again."

"I love you, I love you." They began a tempo, a balance of point and counterpoint. Ariel was aflame, pulsating like a great sun gathering the last of its strength to nova. She slid in another finger, heard a gasp and a catch in Kiernan's throat. Hot hands caressed her breasts, and she fell into the depths of passion-laden eyes, their brilliance a well of heat and fire, love and desire. The eyes became unfocused and glazed, the mouth falling open, and the breath ragged and arduous. The sounds Kiernan made were now guttural and deep, and her own were a matching echo. Control slipped from Ariel, and she hurled herself into a sun gone nova, the intensity forcing her eyes shut. Somewhere in that maelstrom of losing herself to sensation and ecstasy, she sensed Kiernan follow.

ARIEL'S HEART WAS near bursting. Surely she was dying. No one could live through an orgasm that intense. The labored movement of a breathing chest beneath her brought her back to her senses, and she slowly withdrew her fingers, feeling the caress of Kiernan's warm velvet and then the coolness of the surrounding air.

Kiernan grunted, and Ariel rolled off to nestle by her side.

After a few moments she rose onto her elbow and saw Kiernan regarding her with bright eyes and a radiant face.

Kiernan whispered, "Hi." Ariel thought it was such a simple word of greeting, but when said by Kiernan, it held a universe of meaning.

"Hi," Ariel echoed. She positioned Kiernan so her head rested on her shoulder.

Ariel heard what sounded like a contented sigh and Kiernan snuggled up against her, lightly stroking Ariel's breast. Kiernan said, "I need a few minutes to regain my strength, darling, then I'll do unto you what you've done unto me." She let out a yawn.

Ariel tried unsuccessfully to smother her answering yawn. She stroked Kiernan's hair. "Why don't you sleep while I hold you?"

"I don't want to sleep," Kiernan said with a pout in her voice. "I want to make love to you."

Kiernan was stubborn, but Ariel knew she would coax her to sleep. After all, she had an ally—not even the mighty Kiernan O'Shay could withstand the call of Morpheus. "We've been awake for close to twenty hours, and I need to sleep also. I'll be here when you wake, and you can love me then for as long as you want, and how you want."

Kiernan lifted her head and gazed at Ariel with eyes full of hope. "Promise?"

"Promise."

"For always?"

"For always," Ariel pledged. She bent her head and lovingly kissed Kiernan in confirmation of the promise.

Stroking Kiernan's back soothingly and nuzzling her hair, she soon heard her breathing smooth into sleep. She gazed overhead at the viewport and beyond to the darkness of space, which stretched like a black, velvet canvas covered with a sprinkling of diamonds, and into a vision of the future.

One day their children would travel to those distant planets on light-speed spaceships built by Kiernan. Somehow, she knew it was the destiny of future generations of O'Shays to walk upon distant planets under night skies with constellations they would name. She kissed the top of her wife's head and knew she would soon join her in sleep, and in dreams, dreams of the future. And she knew whatever moment of time they were in, they would be together, and it would always be the now.

Epilogue

KIERNAN SLIPPED ON her robe, exited the bathroom, and walked into the sitting room. She smiled when she saw her wife nursing their three-month-old daughter, Celeste, in the rocking chair that had rocked generations of O'Shay babies.

She bent and kissed Ariel tenderly on the lips and knelt by the rocking chair to stroke her daughter's head, feeling her soft, downy, red hair. She leaned over and bestowed a kiss on top of the hair, letting her lips rest there for a moment.

Celeste was apparently enjoying her breakfast since she frequently made smacking and loud sucking sounds. Kiernan said, "My, enthusiastic little leprechaun, isn't she?"

A spark of devilment was in Ariel's eyes as she said, "She inherited that trait from her mother."

"I agree...but she has my nose."

Ariel laughed, causing her nipple to disengage from Celeste's mouth. The unhappy baby protested with a fussy cry until Ariel once again placed the nipple in her daughter's eager little mouth. This time Celeste clamped down tightly, and Ariel winced and exclaimed, "Ouch."

Kiernan winced in sympathy. "Are you sure you want to nurse her for another three months? Just wait until the teeth start coming in. Though I have to say I do enjoy sharing this time with you."

"I enjoy it, too." Ariel smiled at their daughter and stroked her head before regarding Kiernan with bright eyes. "One day I envision you in this chair with our second daughter and watching *you* nurse her."

Kiernan's face froze. She was at a loss for words for a moment. "Er...you know, we don't have another ship to name any more children after."

Celeste Dawn, Kiernan's replacement for the *Celeste,* had been completed six months earlier, and Kiernan had insisted on naming their daughter Celeste Dawn, after the new ship.

"Kiernan, that's the silliest and lamest excuse I've ever heard. In another three years our prototype light-speed ship will be complete, and we'll have another name."

Now that complete control of Stellardyne was Kiernan's, she had created a special department devoted to designing the light-speed ship. Joanna had returned to Stellardyne and recently received a promotion to the position of senior executive in charge of data processing. Ariel finished her degree three months before Celeste was born and soon would be working as a design engineer for Stellardyne's new light-speed ship department. She would work primarily from home, connected by computer to the engineering department.

As for Theodore, Kiernan and Ariel duly chastised him. Whether he was truly sorry, who could tell?

Jack's investigation into Dwayne Campbell's background revealed he spent his childhood in an isolated Christian Fundamentalist enclave in Idaho. The State removed him at fifteen, along with the sect's other children, when discovering they'd been physically and sexually abused. He lived in foster homes until he was eighteen, joined the military for four years, and trained as a fighter spacecraft mechanic. After his stint in the military, Kiernan hired him as part of her race crew.

Jack located Barbara in New Zealand. She and Dwayne had been married for three years. She told Jack that Dwayne was kind and considerate — until he found her diary and read the account of her affair with Kiernan. For Barbara it was an experiment. She said Dwayne was never religious, but suddenly had commenced quoting biblical scripture that condemned homosexuality. He accused her of being a lesbian, blaming Kiernan for changing her into one. He soon became more rabid in his views against homosexuality and seemed obsessed with the topic. She left him a few months later and filed for divorce. That he had severe psychological problems associated with years of brainwashing, and abuse, wasn't in doubt.

"Ah, do you really want to name our next daughter... Elmer?" Kiernan teased.

"You're incorrigible. Why not name the ship after our daughter? That's the way it's usually done."

"I like the idea of naming our daughters after the ships we build. Call it a new O'Shay family tradition." She gazed tenderly up into Ariel's eyes. "Or we could name the ship after my beautiful wife."

Returning the tender regard, Ariel said, "That's sweet, my love, but you promised me the honor of naming our light-speed ship."

Kiernan recalled that she had made that promise, and that she'd said she would bear their next daughter.

Ariel said smugly, "In fact, I already have a perfect name in mind for this ship, and for our next child."

Kiernan asked suspiciously, "What name have you picked?"

"Shenandoah," Ariel said with a smile that lit up her face.

"Shenandoah, daughter of the stars. I think that's a wonderful name." It was the perfect name for a starship that would travel to the distant stars, and the perfect name for a daughter who might one day reach the stars in that ship.

That was for future generations. With Ariel, Kiernan had already reached the stars.

The End

Other Yellow Rose Titles You Might Enjoy:

The Other Mrs. Champion
by Brenda Adcock

Sarah Champion, 55, of Massachusetts, was leading the perfect life with Kelley, her partner and wife of twenty-five years. That is, until Kelley was struck down by an unexpected stroke away from home. But Sarah discovers she hadn't known her partner and lover as well as she thought.

Accompanied by Kelley's long-time friend and attorney, Sarah and her children rush to Vancouver, British Columbia to say their goodbyes, only to discover another woman, Pauline, keeping a vigil over Kelley in the hospital. Confronted by the fact that her wife also has a Canadian wife, Sarah struggles to find answers to resolve her emotional and personal turmoil.

Alone and lonely, Sarah turns to the only other person who knew Kelley as well as she did-Pauline Champion. Will the two women be able to forge a friendship despite their simmering animosity? Will their growing attraction eventually become Kelley's final gift to the women she loved?

ISBN 978-1-935053-46-0

Love Another Day
by Regina A. Hanel

Plagued by nightmares and sleepless nights after a tragic loss, Park Ranger Samantha Takoda Tyler longs for a calm day at Grand Teton National Park in Wyoming. But when she's summoned to the chief ranger's office and introduced to Halie Walker, a photojournalist working for The Wild International, her day is anything but calm. When she's assigned to look after Halie, their meeting transforms into a quarrelsome exchange. Over time, the initial chill between the women warms. They grow closer as they spend time together and gain appreciation for each other's work.

But Sam's fear of loss coupled with rising jealousy over an old lover's interest in Halie grinds their budding relationship to a halt. Halie finds that anywhere near Sam is too painful a place to be, and Sam is unable to find the key to open the door to a past that she's purposely kept locked away.

With fires raging out West and in the Targhee National Forest, Sam works overtime, helping fill the staffing shortage. She misses Halie and wants to take a chance with her. Before she gets the opportunity to explain herself, Sam learns the helicopter Halie is on has crashed. Ahead of an oncoming storm, Sam races to the rescue. Can she save the woman she loves? Or will the past replay, closing Sam off from love forever?

ISBN 978-1-935053-44-6

OTHER YELLOW ROSE PUBLICATIONS

Brenda Adcock	Soiled Dove	978-1-935053-35-4
Brenda Adcock	The Sea Hawk	978-1-935053-10-1
Brenda Adcock	The Other Mrs. Champion	978-1-935053-46-0
Janet Albert	Twenty-four Days	978-1-935053-16-3
Janet Albert	A Table for Two	978-1-935053-27-9
Georgia Beers	Thy Neighbor's Wife	1-932300-15-5
Georgia Beers	Turning the Page	978-1-932300-71-0
Carrie Brennan	Curve	978-1-932300-41-3
Carrie Carr	Destiny's Bridge	1-932300-11-2
Carrie Carr	Faith's Crossing	1-932300-12-0
Carrie Carr	Hope's Path	1-932300-40-6
Carrie Carr	Love's Journey	978-1-932300-65-9
Carrie Carr	Strength of the Heart	978-1-932300-81-9
Carrie Carr	The Way Things Should Be	978-1-932300-39-0
Carrie Carr	To Hold Forever	978-1-932300-21-5
Carrie Carr	Piperton	978-1-935053-20-0
Carrie Carr	Something to Be Thankful For	1-932300-04-X
Carrie Carr	Diving Into the Turn	978-1-932300-54-3
Cronin and Foster	Blue Collar Lesbian Erotica	978-1-935053-01-9
Cronin and Foster	Women in Uniform	978-1-935053-31-6
Pat Cronin	Souls' Rescue	978-1-935053-30-9
Anna Furtado	The Heart's Desire	1-932300-32-5
Anna Furtado	The Heart's Strength	978-1-932300-93-2
Anna Furtado	The Heart's Longing	978-1-935053-26-2
Melissa Good	Eye of the Storm	1-932300-13-9
Melissa Good	Hurricane Watch	978-1-935053-00-2
Melissa Good	Red Sky At Morning	978-1-932300-80-2
Melissa Good	Thicker Than Water	1-932300-24-4
Melissa Good	Terrors of the High Seas	1-932300-45-7
Melissa Good	Tropical Storm	978-1-932300-60-4
Melissa Good	Tropical Convergence	978-1-935053-18-7
Regina A. Hanel	Love Another Day	978-1-935053-44-6
Maya Indigal	Until Soon	978-1-932300-31-4
Lori L. Lake	Different Dress	1-932300-08-2
Lori L. Lake	Ricochet In Time	1-932300-17-1
K. E. Lane	And, Playing the Role of Herself	978-1-932300-72-7
Helen Macpherson	Love's Redemption	978-1-935053-04-0
J. Y Morgan	Learning To Trust	978-1-932300-59-8
J. Y. Morgan	Download	978-1-932300-88-8
A. K. Naten	Turning Tides	978-1-932300-47-5
Lynne Norris	One Promise	978-1-932300-92-5
Linda S. North	The Dreamer, Her Angel, and the Stars	978-1-935053-45-3
Paula Offutt	Butch Girls Can Fix Anything	978-1-932300-74-1
Surtees and Dunne	True Colours	978-1-932300-529
Surtees and Dunne	Many Roads to Travel	978-1-932300-55-0
Vicki Stevenson	Family Affairs	978-1-932300-97-0
Vicki Stevenson	Family Values	978-1-932300-89-5
Vicki Stevenson	Family Ties	978-1-935053-03-3
Vicki Stevenson	Certain Personal Matters	978-1-935053-06-4

| Cate Swannell | Heart's Passage | 978-1-932300-09-3 |
| Cate Swannell | No Ocean Deep | 978-1-932300-36-9 |

About the Author

Linda is a fifth generation Floridian who lives in North Florida with her partner of twenty-nine years, five cats, and a dog. She got her start as an author by writing Star Trek Voyager Fan Fiction under the name of cygirl1. She is an unabashed romantic who believes in happy endings. Her hobbies are writing, Harley Davidson motorcycles, toy steam engines, toy wooden boats, and collecting Star Trek action figures.

VISIT US ONLINE AT
www.regalcrest.biz

At the Regal Crest Website You'll Find

- The latest news about forthcoming titles and new releases

- Our complete backlist of romance, mystery, thriller and adventure titles

- Information about your favorite authors

- Current bestsellers

- Media tearsheets to print and take with you when you shop

Regal Crest titles are available from all progressive booksellers including numerous sources online. Our distributors are Bella Distribution and Ingram.